CW00847647

Impossible Depths

Coral McCallum

Copyright © 2015 Coral McCallum

All rights reserved.

ISBN-13: 978-1519794345

ISBN-10: 1519794347

The characters, names, places, brands, media and events are either the product of the author's imagination or are used fictitiously. Any similarity to real persons, living or deceased, is coincidental and not intended by the author.

The author acknowledges the trademarked status and trademark owners of the various products referenced within this work of fiction, which have been used without permission. The publication/use of these trademarks is not authorised, associated with or sponsored by these trademark owners.

Thank you for respecting the hard work of this author.

Cover Design by Coral McCallum

Cover image – © Artemfurman | Dreamstime.com - Sexy Man Photo

Celtic Dragon Knot- created by Fiona Knox

Impossible Depths

So, here I am, on the eve of the publication of "Book Baby 2" aka Impossible Depths...can't quite believe it.

The last year has been a roller coaster ride.

To those of you returning to the Silver Lake fold, welcome back and huge thanks for all the love and support that you've shown me over the past few months. The response to Stronger Within, Book 1 in the Silver Lake series, has been incredible and I'm completely overwhelmed by how well it has been received.

To those of you being introduced to Jake and Lori and all things Silver Lake for the first time, a warm welcome and I sincerely hope that you enjoy the journey through life with them.

As before, Impossible Depths is largely set in the USA but has been written in UK English so I'll offer my humble apologies now to the language purists among you. If the S's instead of Z's and the British terminology offends then I'm sorry.

None of this would have been possible without the continuing love, support and words of encouragement from my "infamous five". Seriously, I couldn't have done this without you. Huge hugs and much love to each of you.

And to "the cavalry", my beta readers, who rocked up at the end. Thank you!

To my writer "fairy godmother", huge thanks for your technical assistance once again and for teaching me how to wave my "magic wand".

The birth of Impossible Depths has been another lengthy labour of love and I'd like to thank my long-suffering family for their patience and support.

And, finally, a huge thank you to YOU for picking up this copy of "Book Baby 2".

Love and hugs to you all and happy reading!

Coral McCallum   13 February 2016

Gently the breeze blew in off the ocean as a family of dolphins made their leisurely way through the waves. Cresting and diving, they played in the ocean swell, oblivious to Lori watching them from the shore. Spring sunshine had warmed the day, but, as the afternoon drew to a close, a breeze from the ocean brought a chill with it, reminding her that it wasn't summer for a while yet. Drawing her hoodie tight around her, Lori adjusted her grip on her cane and turned towards home. Being out on the beach in the sun had blown away the last remnants of the gloom of winter. The last three months had been more lows than highs and life had closely mirrored the ocean swell she adored. For Jake and the band, things had gone from strength to strength. The antipodean tour with Bodimead had been a sell-out success. A deluxe edition of their album had been released with an accompanying DVD - the footage shot by Scott during their UK tour- and was riding high in the rock chart. For Lori, her lows had again been health related, causing her to miss out on travelling to the southern hemisphere to support Jake and the rest of Silver Lake.

When she had returned to visit her doctor, John Brent, during the first week in January the news hadn't been good. As he had advised her when she saw him before Christmas, he had referred her x-rays to her original orthopaedic surgeon from New York, Ben Hartson, who had responded that he wanted to remove the broken screw from her surgically repaired femur. The second blow was that he had an opening in his schedule for later that week and was happy to operate on Lori in Delaware to save her the trip to New York. It had barely given her time to get her head round things before he had arrived in town and performed the surgery on 11th January. The surgery had gone smoothly- a small high – but had been more extensive than she had expected – another low. Apart from removing the broken screw, the surgeon had inserted two more small plates to strengthen the section of bone that had shown signs of stress. Following the surgery, when Dr Hartson had explained to her exactly what he had done and why, Lori had understood and reluctantly accepted that it had been her best option. After ten long days in the medical centre, she had returned home to start her recovery all over again. Jake had left for New Zealand less than two weeks later.

During the four long weeks that Silver Lake were away, Lori had pushed herself to the limits. She had engaged the daily services of one of the physical therapists from the medical centre, Billy, and had worked with single-minded determination. It had taken every ounce of her physical and mental strength, but, by the time Jake strode back in the door, suntanned after the tour, the crutches were gone and she was back to walking with the aid of one cane around the house. Now, a further six weeks down the road, or the beach in this case, she was back where she had been the previous November, with high hopes for more improvement.

Checking her phone for missed calls or messages, Lori took note of the time and realised she had been away from the house longer than she had intended. She had promised Paul, the band's drummer, that she would take care of Maddy while Silver Lake were in New York for a few days. It had been such a beautiful afternoon though that Maddy had insisted she go for a walk, promising to call if she felt any labour pains. At almost thirty-seven weeks pregnant with twins, Maddy was not moving anywhere far from the house, but Lori had managed to convince her to sit outside on the lounger on the sun deck while she took a stroll along the sand. Jake had called over three hours before to say that was them leaving the city so Lori guessed she still had time to get back to her friend before the boys arrived home

As she came up the path towards the house, she could hear Maddy talking on the phone. From her tone of voice, it was obviously a business call and Lori guessed, correctly, that it was from Jason from the band's management company. Stamping the sand off her feet, Lori signalled to Maddy that she was going indoors to fetch them a drink. When she came back out onto the sun deck with two mugs of coffee, Maddy was finishing up her call.

"Everything ok?" asked Lori, as she watched her friend lever herself into a sitting position.

"Just Jason being Jason," she muttered, gratefully accepting the mug of coffee.

"I meant with you and the meatballs," commented Lori, sitting at the table. Ever since Grey's daughter, Becky, had joked about Maddy looking like she had swallowed a big meatball, the nickname for the unborn twins had stuck.

"I'm fine," retorted Maddy, her tone sharper than she intended. "As long as I don't want to move or breathe."

"Only a few more days," sympathised Lori, smiling at her friend.

"Thank Christ for that!" Maddy sighed, rubbing her hugely pregnant belly.

"Any word from the boys?" asked Lori, checking the time.

"Yes," replied her friend. "Paul called about half an hour ago to say they were passing Dover Downs. Grey's mom called to say she would drop Becky off here at five. All of them should be here anytime."

"You'd better drink that coffee quick then," giggled Lori. "I don't want Paul giving me into trouble for feeding your caffeine habit."

Lori had just placed the two empty mugs in the dishwasher when she heard Jake's truck pull into the driveway. Before she could call to Maddy that the boys were back, her friend came into the kitchen. The pale, strained look on her face concerned Lori but she said nothing. A few seconds later, the back door opened and Silver Lake came charging into the kitchen, all talking at once, continuing loudly with a debate that had been raging in the truck.

"Hi, li'l lady," said Jake, hugging Lori tight and kissing the nape of her neck. "Missed you."

"Missed you too, rock star," she whispered almost shyly.

Behind her, she could hear Paul fussing over Maddy, suggesting she should be sitting down.

"You fucking well try sitting down comfortably with a belly like this," she snapped as she waddled out of the kitchen towards the bathroom.

"Go easy on her, Paul," suggested Lori quietly. "She's really struggling. She rested all afternoon. I promise."

"Hmph," he muttered, wandering out of the kitchen towards the door down to the basement.

"He's struggling too," commented Grey, watching the door close behind the drummer. "I'll be glad when these babies arrive."

"Won't we all," sighed Jake as he filled the water reservoir for the coffee maker.

Car tyres crunched outside announcing the arrival of Grey's mother, Annie, and Becky. Excusing himself, the bass player darted back outside to collect his daughter. The band had only been away for three days, but it was clear from the speed that he shot out the door at that he had missed his little girl.

"Is everyone staying for dinner?" asked Lori, silently praying that the answer was going to be no.

"Paul said they were going straight home," replied Rich, accepting a mug of coffee from Jake. "I'm meeting Linsey at her place so I'll be out of here once I've drunk this."

"Grey's staying," added Jake. "We've a bit of work to finish off. Are you alright to watch Becky for an hour or so after dinner?"

"Sure," agreed Lori without hesitation. "So, that's four for dinner?"

"Not exactly," said Jake. "Six."

"Six?"

"Yeah. Gary detoured to collect Scott at the airport. They'll be here in an hour or so."

"Why's Scott back so soon?" she asked curiously.

"Lord Jason wants him to film some of our recording sessions. Thinks he can use the footage as internet promo stuff," explained Rich shaking his head. "More camera dodging for all of us."

"He's a sweet kid," laughed Lori, feeling the band's pain at the thought of the over-enthusiastic film maker's return.

The back door flew open and a small blonde tornado of a little girl bowled in yelling, "Uncle Jake! Uncle Jake!"

"Hi, princess," said Jake as he scooped Becky up into his arms. "How's my favourite girl?"

"The tooth fairy came!" squealed Becky, pulling her bottom lip down. "Look!"

"Wow, your first visit from the tooth fairy," he laughed. "I hope she left you some cash for it."

"Five dollars," said Becky proudly. "But I had to write her a letter to say sorry that I swallowed the tooth."

Her innocence made them all laugh.

"What's so funny?" asked Maddy as she re-entered the kitchen.

"I lost a tooth, but I swallowed it," announced Becky, showing the band's manager the tiny gap in her mouth.

"Oh, honey, have you been kissing boys?" teased Maddy, rubbing her aching back.

Becky looked at her seriously, then shook her head.

"Can I feel the meatballs kicking?" she asked hopefully.

Jumping down from Jake's arms, Becky scampered over towards the pregnant Goth.

"Put your hand here," instructed Maddy. She placed the little girl's hand to one side of her enormous bump and, after a few seconds, one of the twins obligingly kicked hard. Becky giggled as Maddy screwed up her face in obvious discomfort.

"You'll get to meet them soon, Becky," Maddy promised, as another sharp kick caught her breath. "I go to the hospital to have them on Monday."

"Three more sleeps!" counted the excited little girl jumping up and down.

"What's sleep?" muttered the worn out mother-to-be. "I've not slept properly for weeks."

Jake reached over to give her a hug. "It'll be worth it in the end, Maddison."

"Hmmph," she sighed. "I'm going out to the car. Tell Paul to move his ass. Thanks for everything, Lori."

"Do you need a hand, boss?" offered Jake, flashing her one of his special smiles.

"You could be a sweetheart and grab my bag for me."

"No problem."

Gently Lori hugged her friend. "Let me know if you feel up to lunch on Sunday. If not, I'll see you Monday or Tuesday."

"I'll call," promised Maddy. "The way I feel right now, though I don't see me lasting till Sunday."

"Do you think you might be in labour?" whispered Lori, suddenly concerned.

"I think it might be starting. I'm not sure. I've had a few runs of contractions for the last few hours but nothing regular. If these two arrive before Monday, I'll not be complaining," she replied, forcing a smile.

"Call if you need me."

Sitting round the dinner table an hour or two later all thoughts of babies were long gone as Grey and Jake were deep in conversation with Gary about the upcoming recording sessions. There was loose agreement around the content of the next album, but the band had agreed to take their time and not to rush headlong into pre-production or recording sessions. From a management and a record company angle, Gary was pushing for sooner rather than later. At the far end of the table, Scott, the young British filmmaker, was falling asleep, jet lag catching up with him.

"Does anyone want a coffee before I take Becky through to the sun room to watch a DVD?" asked Lori as she began to clear the dinner plates away.

"I'm fine, li'l lady," replied Jake, rising to help clear the table. "You go on through and we'll tidy up here."

"I'll not argue about that," she declared with a smile. "Come on, Becky. Let's leave the boys to work for a while."

"We'll be done by eight thirty," promised Grey. "Becky, behave for Lori."

"Yes. Daddy," she replied, jumping down from her seat.

"I'll go with the girls," yawned Scott. "Lori, can I sleep on your couch for a while?"

"Of course," she agreed. "Or the spare room is made up if you'd rather stay over?"

"Couch is fine," he said, stumbling up from his seat. "I was filming a show last night in London and only grabbed a couple of hours sleep before I left for the airport. I'm knackered."

With Scott stretched out on the larger couch, the two girls cuddled up together on the smaller one. Choosing a DVD had been easy. Becky wanted to watch Beauty and the Beast, her current all-time favourite. Within a few minutes of the film starting, Scott was sound asleep and snoring softly. Before the film was halfway through, Becky too had dozed off, with her head in Lori's lap. Gently she ran her fingers through the little girl's sunshine blonde hair. Since their first meeting, almost a year before, Becky had stolen part of Lori's heart. It was impossible not to be captivated by her.

Down in the basement, Gary was making himself useful by recording the new song that the two guitarists had been working on. Both of them had stayed up till the early hours of the morning working first on the riff and then on the melody. It was the first song that they had collaborated on and Jake, ever the teacher at heart, was keen to encourage Grey's creative side. They played through a few variations of it until they were both happy with one. After a few more practice runs, they were ready to record the bare bones of the song so each of them could go away and work on the rest of it. Jake's assignment for the weekend was to come up with some lyrics. As they had driven back from New York, they had discussed several potential themes but they were still to reach a consensus.

"I'm out of here," declared Grey, realising it was almost nine. "I need to get Becky home."

"No rush," said Jake, putting his guitar back on the stand. "It's Friday night after all."

"I need to go, Jake," said the bass player calmly. "Anyway, you and Lori need some space too."

"I'd better get Scott to the hotel," added Gary. "Kid's been up for like thirty hours plus."

"How long's he here for?" asked Jake.

"At least ten weeks," answered the band's tour manager. "Don't panic. He's got a couple of projects to pick up other than filming you guys."

"Thank Christ for that," muttered Grey. He picked up his guitar case, then added, "Where are you staying this trip?"

"At the hotel for now. I've finally got all the work permit paperwork in order so I'm here indefinitely."

The three of them headed up the narrow staircase that opened out into the house, between the dining room and lounge room. When they reached the top step, Jake turned round and said, "You could use my apartment, if you want. It's empty. Rent and services are all paid up."

"Where is it?" asked Gary, instantly liking the idea of his own space.

"Just off the boardwalk, near the centre of town. It's not much, but it's better than the hotel," replied Jake. "Paul and I lived there for a while before he moved out. In fact, Rich was there too for a few months. You could share with Scott, if he's ok to sleep on the couch."

Glancing into the sun room and spotting the film maker curled up sound asleep, Gary commented, "Looks like he might be ok with that."

"Have a think. If you want to see the place, give me a call and I'll take you over there."

"Thanks," said Gary, clapping Jake on the shoulder. "Appreciate it."

"Shh," cautioned Lori, as the guys clattered noisily into the sun room. "The kids are asleep."

Scooping his sleeping daughter into his arms, Grey apologised, "I hope she didn't hurt you lying on you like that, Lori."

"She's fine," assured Lori then, winking at him, added, "Wrong leg."

"Right, I'm off," he said quietly. "I'll catch up over the weekend or early next week."

With the bass player and his daughter gone, Gary debated over wakening Scott.

"Just leave him," whispered Jake, passing him a blanket to cover the sleeping photographer. "He'll be fine there."

"Are you sure?"

"Let him sleep," replied Lori as she switched off the DVD. "We'll drop him off tomorrow or he can stay on here."

"If you're sure."

"We're sure," added Jake. "Better leave his luggage though."

Nodding, Gary headed back through the house towards the front door. Carefully Lori pulled the French doors to the sun room over and turned off the lights. She left a small table lamp lit, just in case their unscheduled guest wakened during the night. While Jake went out to get the bags from Gary, she fetched them a glass of wine. There was an open bottle of Pinot Grigio in the refrigerator with enough left in it for two glasses. Lori had just set the glasses down on the coffee table in the lounge when Jake came back in. Having deposited Scott's bags outside the sunroom, he wandered through to join her on the couch.

"God, I've missed you," he sighed, putting his arm around her and hugging her tight. "It's good to be home."

"It's nice to have you back for a while," she purred, snuggling in closer to him. "You are home to stay for a while, aren't you?"

"Yup," replied Jake. "No shows until July. Just writing, writing, rehearsal and recording until then. At least that's the current plan."

"No overseas trips?"

"Not until the end of the year. We may go to Canada in August for a few days, but nothing's confirmed."

"Best news I've heard for a while," sighed Lori with a contented smile.

Still cuddled up together on the couch, sipping their wine, Jake asked Lori about her own work commitments for the coming months. While she had been confined to the house in the early part of the year, she had completed all the projects she had committed to. For the last couple of weeks, she had turned her focus to a new set of jewellery designs for her LH range. The first two limited edition collections had sold out, largely due to the clever marketing strategy adopted by Lin, her designer friend from college.

"So what's next?" asked Jake curiously.

"I've to talk to Jason next week," she replied, finishing the last mouthful of her wine. "He mentioned that he had two, maybe three, commissions that he wanted to discuss. He's also approached me about keeping my calendar free to do the artwork for the next Silver Lake album."

"Do you think you can schedule a couple of weeks for a vacation?" Jake asked hopefully. "It would be good to go somewhere hot and sunny to just chill."

"Vacation? Not honeymoon?" she asked with a mischievous twinkle in her eyes.

"That's up to you, li'l lady. Have you given much thought to our wedding?"

Looking sheepish, Lori whispered, "Not much."

"No rush," assured Jake, kissing her gently. "I don't know about you, but I'm ready for bed. It's been a long day."

Before Lori could reply, Jake scooped her up into his arms and carried her down the hall to their bedroom. Gently he laid her down in the centre of the large, soft, white bed. Straddling her swiftly, he bent to kiss her, his hair falling around her face. Playfully he bit her lower lip, then kissed her hard, almost forcefully. Still exploring her mouth teasingly with his tongue, Jake balanced himself on his knees and one hand while he unfastened her jeans. He slid his warm hand down inside her lace panties, tenderly exploring her feminine moistness with his long slender fingers. Under his caress, Lori moaned softly, arching her back to meet his touch.

"Hungry are we?" whispered Jake.

Slowly he withdrew his hand, then roughly pulled her jeans and underwear off, tossing them onto the floor. Lifting her like a doll, Jake slipped her T-shirt over her head, then expertly removed her white lacy bra. The sight of her naked before him was almost too much for him as his erection strained against the confines of his own jeans.

"Two can play at this game," taunted Lori, reaching up to unfasten his shirt buttons.

With her fiancé's shirt discarded on the bed, she reached to unbuckle his belt. Her fingers fumbled slightly and Jake brushed her aside, unfastening the buckle himself before sliding his jeans and boxers off in one well-practiced manoeuvre.

"Not the only one who's hungry," purred Lori as she ran her finger lightly down the length of his erect manhood.

"Ravenous," he declared as he entered her with one firm thrust.

With a low, throaty growl, Lori succumbed to the urgency, feeling her own orgasm build as Jake moved rhythmically inside her. Each stroke teased her to a higher level of ecstasy. Unable to hold back his own climax, Jake brought her to their mutual point of orgasm in two hard deep strokes. Lori gasped as she spiralled into a sexual paradise for those few wonderful moments. With a final gentle stroke, Jake withdrew from her and rolled off to lie beside her.

"Naughty Mz Hyde," he commented with a mischievous grin.

"Likewise, rock star," she countered, rolling onto her right side to face him. "Told you I'd missed you."

"Maybe I should go away more often if this is the welcome home I get," suggested Jake, running his finger down the long, fresh scar on her thigh.

"Don't," she whispered. "Please."

"Sh. That's your artwork. Your story, li'l lady," soothed Jake, his voice husky with emotion. "Your recovery roadmap."

"I know, but…"

"No buts, Lori," Jake interrupted as he sat up and bent over her. Slowly he kissed her naked hip bone, then delicately ran his tongue along the length of the older silvery scar. When he reached the knotted puckered end of it, he delivered feathery kisses to the various other smaller, ragged scars that surrounded it before licking the fresher surgical scars. "I love every bit of you. Every last mark, every freckle and every scar no matter the size. Remember that."

"I'll try," she promised, her voice barely more than a whisper.

"Come here. Time to get some sleep," said Jake, lying back down and pulling her into his embrace.

♫

Aromas of fresh coffee stirred Lori from slumber early the next morning. Lying curled up beside Jake, she listened carefully and could hear their house guest moving around in the kitchen. A glance at the clock told her it only six fifteen. Knowing that Scott was awake and in unfamiliar surroundings, Lori decided that she couldn't leave him alone in her kitchen. As quietly as she could, she slipped out of bed and pulled on her pyjamas. Tip-toeing, she left Jake snoring soundly.

When she opened the kitchen door, she startled the young filmmaker.

"Morning," greeted Lori with a sleepy smile. "Did you sleep well?"

"Oh, Lori, I am SO sorry," apologised Scott. He was standing beside the sink in his T-shirt and boxer shorts, his usually neat dark hair sticking out like a scarecrow's. "Gary should've wakened me."

"Nonsense," she stated as she opened the refrigerator to fetch some orange juice. "You were dead to the world."

Nodding, Scott admitted, "That's one comfy couch. I slept like a baby. Thanks."

"You were snoring when we turned out the lights," she teased.

He blushed bright red, the scarlet flush disappearing down beyond the neckline of his crumpled T-shirt.

"Sorry."

"Stop apologising," she giggled. "And pour me a coffee."

Laughter and the smell of bacon roused Jake a couple of hours later. Remembering their house guest, he jumped in the shower, then pulled on some jeans before going through to the kitchen. Scott and Lori were sitting at the kitchen table with a map of the area spread out in front of them.

"Geography class?" enquired Jake, glancing down at the map.

"Morning," said Lori, smiling at her fiancé. "Scott was asking about places to use for a video shoot. He's looking for a deserted beach location with an access road."

"No shortage of sand around here," agreed Jake. "What are you filming?"

20

"Jason wants me to take one of his new acts, Time March, out. Their first release is called "Sands of Time". Low budget affair so the beach seemed like an easy location choice," Scott explained. "It was only a thought."

"Hold that thought," said Lori, folding away the map. "Let me show you something."

She excused herself from the table and went to fetch her laptop from the study. While it was powering up, she explained that she had worked on the artwork for the band and that beach theme might not link in with the existing approved visuals. It took her a minute or two to find the folder she was searching for but, when Scott finally saw the proofs for the band's album and single "Sands of Time", he realised that Lori was right. The artwork was themed around ancient Egypt and the band's logo incorporated a broken hour glass running with blood red sand.

"Beach is definitely out," he declared with a sigh of defeat. "Shit!"

"Sorry, Scott," apologised Lori, closing over her laptop. "What about trying to find somewhere with pillars at the entrance that you could perhaps mock up as an Egyptian temple?"

"Perhaps," he muttered, then changing the subject asked, "Would you mind if I took a shower before I call a taxi to take me out to the hotel?"

"Not at all," answered Lori. "You know where the bathroom is. You'll get clean towels in the cupboard behind the door. When you're ready, I'll run you out to the hotel."

"Thanks."

While Lori drove Scott out to the hotel to meet up with Gary, Jake wandered down into the basement studio to start work. He had the beginnings of a new song running through his head, a melody line that had haunted him ever since he stepped into the shower that morning. He had been keen to get it recorded before he forgot it and was silently relieved when Lori offered to drive Scott out to the hotel and equally relieved when she said she was going to the outlets on her way home.

As he plugged his guitar into his favoured practice amp and set up his laptop to record the melody, Jake switched off all thoughts of the rest of the world, solely focussed on his music.

Once he had recorded the melody line and checked the file had saved properly, he replayed the track he had recorded the night before with Grey. Listening to it again, he could hear another dimension to it and he began to work out another variation of it – a darker more tortured soundscape. As Jake played it over, the lyrics began to unfold in his mind. His notebook lay on the floor beside his guitar case. He reached for it and began to scribble down the words. The song's theme had shown itself at last. He just hoped that Grey agreed with his ideas. Words tumbled out onto the page telling a tortured tale of drowning that fitted in with the dark heavy piece of music.

Time lost all meaning to Jake as he played and wrote, played then re-wrote. Totally immersed in his music, the morning moved on to afternoon. Undisturbed, he barely moved from the chair he had seated himself on.

Weekend shoppers crowded the outlet stores by the time Lori pulled into the Seaside parking lot. Seeing so many people milling about almost made her turn back, but there were a few things she wanted to pick up, including some more baby items for Maddy. Once she had made her first purchase, Lori began to feel more in the mood to shop. The Osh Kosh children's wear store was having a big sale in their babywear department, but she was unsure what else Maddy needed. Still in the store, Lori took out her phone and dialled her friend's number.

"Hi, Lori," came her friend's voice on the second ring.

"Morning. You ok today?" asked Lori brightly.

"Same as yesterday," replied Maddy sounding tired. "Still having runs of contractions then they just stop. I called the hospital but they said that was normal. No need to go in yet."

"Is that good or bad?"

"I don't know," admitted Maddy with a sigh. "I just want this over and done with now. I can't breathe properly. I can't get comfortable in any position. I ache all over. The skin on my stomach is so tight it feels like it could burst. It hurts to do everything."

"Just another day or two to go," assured Lori softly, empathising with her friend's discomfort. "I was calling to check what else you needed for the meatballs. I'm at the outlets just now."

"Honey, I've no idea," sighed Maddy. "I've vests and all-in-one suits for newborns and small babies. I've got a couple of blankets and things. Till they are here, I've no idea about colours."

"Ok," sighed Lori, casually browsing through the sale rail in front of her. "I'll see what jumps out at me."

"Don't spend too much, please," said her friend. "You've bought us a lot already."

"I'll behave," promised Lori. "I'd better go. I'll call you tomorrow about lunch."

"Let's skip lunch," replied Maddy wearily. "I just can't be bothered with anything this weekend. I'm sorry. Do you mind?"

"It's ok. I understand. If you change your mind, you know where I am."

"Thanks, Lori. I'll talk to you later."

"Bye for now."

Something about the tone of her friend's voice worried her. Lori just hoped it was only tiredness and pre-birth nerves. Slipping her phone back into her bag, she turned her attention to the rack in front of her. It only took her a few minutes to select an armful of tiny clothes in various sizes all gender neutral colours. On her way to the cash desk, she picked up a couple of packets of tiny socks as an afterthought. As she was paying for the items, the cashier asked if she had seen the baby blankets that were on special. When Lori commented that she hadn't, the cashier called to one of the other assistants to bring over a couple of white ones to let her see them. They were soft Microfleece with a rainbow embroidered on one corner.

"I'll take two," said Lori smiling as she felt how soft they were. "My friend's having twins."

"Lord, that'll be hard work," declared the cashier, ringing up the sale. "When's she due?"

"She's going into hospital on Monday."

"Wish her good luck from me."

"Thanks," said Lori, signing the credit card receipt.

With her baby purchases made, Lori only had two more stores to visit on her way back to the car. She picked up some new jeans for Jake in the Levi's outlet as an afterthought. By the time she reached the car, she was laden with bags. The traffic on the way back into town was light and it only took her fifteen minutes to reach the house. When she turned off the engine, she could hear Jake's guitar echoing out from the basement. The sound of his music made her smile. She never tired of listening to him play.

Dumping the bags in the hallway, Lori went straight into the kitchen to make a sandwich. For a moment she thought about preparing one for Jake, but decided he might not thank her for interrupting him. Over the months they had devised a simple system. If the door to the basement was open, then he could be interrupted; if it was closed then he wanted to be left undisturbed. The door was tightly shut.

Sandwich in hand, Lori wandered through to the study to check her emails. It was still early afternoon and, satisfied that none of the mails needed her immediate attention, she decided to take her sketchpad outside and sit in the sun for a while. Pad and pencils in hand, Lori headed out onto the sun deck. It was warm for April and, as she took a seat at the large wooden picnic table, she relaxed in the spring warmth. While she stared at the blank page, she caught sight of her butterfly tattoo. Gently running her fingers over it, Lori began to wonder if she should design another one for herself or perhaps one for Jake. Over the months she had thought about getting a second design done, but had never really made her mind up. Part of her wanted to disguise the scarring on her thigh, but she was reluctant to draw attention to that part of her body. It told her story just as it was she supposed.

Allowing her mind to wander, she casually began to draw a treble clef design with a Celtic/tribal twist to it. Soon she was lost in adding shading and detail to the detail. When it was completed to her satisfaction, she turned the page and began to draw an impish fairy with delicate wings. As the design emerged from the page, Lori shaded the fairy's dress in purples then added pink and silvery hues to her wings. Totally absorbed in the drawing, she never noticed that the music had stopped until Jake appeared behind her.

"Having fun, li'l lady?" he whispered in her ear, making her jump.

"Jeez," she squealed. "You gave me a fright!"

Jake laughed as he admired the design she was working on. "That's cute," he commented. "Nice lines."

"Just a bit of fun," said Lori, turning the page back to the treble clef. "As was this?"

"Nice," he said. "Are you planning a second visit to Danny?"

"Maybe," she replied with a smile.

Danny was the tattoo artist who had inked her butterfly design and all of Jake's artwork.

"What's the plan for the rest of the day?" asked Jake, still admiring the treble clef.

"No plans. You?"

"Gary called. I was going to show him my apartment," said Jake, stretching his arms above his head and yawning. "Feel up to a walk into town? We could go to dinner too?"

"Is Gary going to rent your old place?"

"Maybe. He's here indefinitely this time and staying at the hotel's no fun. I offered him the apartment so he wants to take a look," Jake explained. "I said I'd meet him outside The Turtle at five."

"A walk sounds good, if we take it slowly," said Lori. "When do you want to leave?"

"As soon as you're ready, li'l lady."

So early in the season, the beach was almost deserted, as they walked hand in hand along the sand. In front of them, small sea birds were pecking furiously in the damp sand, then scurrying away as the next wave came flooding towards them. Watching them made Lori smile. As they walked, she asked Jake how he'd got on with his practice session. Shrugging his shoulders, he was non-committal about the progress, but declared he was happy to be home and to have time on his hands to write. He confessed to struggling a bit for inspiration. Squeezing his hand, Lori said she knew how he felt and that it would pass. Halfway into town she asked if they could detour up onto the boardwalk, confessing that she was struggling a bit on the sand.

"Do you want to rest for a minute?" asked Jake, once they were safely off the beach. "There's a bench right here."

"Just for a minute," Lori agreed, grateful for the seat. "I guess I took more out of myself when I was shopping than I realised."

"Don't push too hard, li'l lady," cautioned Jake, placing his hand gently on her thigh. "I don't want to be visiting you in the hospital again."

He shuddered at the memory of the day she had undergone surgery in January. It had been one of the longest, scariest days of his life as he had paced the corridors of the medical centre waiting for news. Watching her fight her way out of the anaesthetic fog had been painful as she had reacted badly to it. Seeing her in so much pain and distress had torn him apart.

"I don't want to go back either, Jake," she whispered. "I've had enough surgeries to last me a lifetime."

She glanced down the boardwalk, blinking away the tears that were threatening to form and spotted a young couple coming towards them. The boy had his arm draped over the girl's shoulder and a guitar case in his other hand. They looked vaguely familiar and, as they drew closer, she recognised that it was two of Jake's former students.

"Hi, Mr Power," called Todd as he spotted his former teacher.

"Hi, Todd," said Jake with a smile. "And its Jake now, remember?"

"Yes, sir," replied the boy, blushing slightly.

Jake recognised the girl as Kate, another talented former student with a fantastic singing voice.

"Where are you guys off to?" he asked.

"Rehearsal at Kate's dad's," answered Todd. "Can't rehearse at home. My mom can't stand the noise."

Before he had left his teaching post at the school, Jake had spoken to Todd's mother to explain that he wanted to buy him a guitar as a gift. The woman hadn't impressed him and her total lack of interest in her son's talent had really angered Jake. When he had presented Todd with an acoustic guitar, as an eighteenth birthday gift, the boy had wept openly. His reaction had touched Jake's heart and he had promised himself he would keep in touch with the boy, mentoring him as best he could. They had met up a few times to play together but hadn't seen each other for almost a month.

"I'm about for the next few weeks," began Jake. "Come by the house sometime."

"I'd like that," said Todd shyly, then feeling more confident asked, "Are you going to do any workshops at school this semester?"

"Maybe. I've not given it much thought," admitted Jake. "I'll call the principal and see what I can set up. You leave this summer don't you?"

Todd nodded. "Mom wants me to find a job. I want to go to college. It's a bit of a touchy subject at home."

"What do you want to do at college?" asked Lori, her own anger rising at the thought of the boy's education being stopped.

"Music," Todd replied. "There's a course that teaches you all the technical stuff and management. I don't know if I can do it part-time though. It's in Baltimore. I'll work something out."

"So you want to go into band management?" pressed Lori.

"To be honest, Mz Hyde," confessed Todd. "I'd like to be part of the stage crew on a big tour and see the world."

Jake laughed. "You'd make a great guitar tech, Todd. Give me a call during the week about coming over. I'll put you to work on my gear."

"Thanks, sir," said the boy. "I'll call."

As the young couple walked out of earshot, Jake watched them closely, an idea beginning to form in his mind. Getting to her feet, Lori said, "I can hear that thought forming, rock star."

"What?" he asked innocently with a small smile.

"You want to get Todd on your stage crew."

"More or less," he confessed. "I'll need a guitar tech if we're doing the summer festival circuit. It might be the break the kid needs. I'll talk to Gary about it."

"You're a big, soft hearted lump," laughed Lori, giving him a hug. "But I think it's a great idea. He's a nice kid."

The closer to the heart of town they got, the busier the boardwalk became. By summer standards, it was still quiet. There were families out enjoying the spring sunshine and teenagers congregating around the amusement arcade. As they approached The Greene Turtle, they saw Gary sitting on a nearby bench, chatting on his phone. On his right, Scott was sitting texting on his.

"Hi, guys," said Lori brightly.

"Afternoon," greeted Gary, slipping his phone back into his jeans' pocket.

"Sorry, we're a minute or two late," apologised Jake.

"We only just got here," said Gary. "So, where's this

apartment?"

"A couple of blocks back on Laurel Street," Jake replied. "Not too far."

"Ok, let's go," said the band's manager, getting to his feet.

"Jake," began Lori. "I'll wait here. I can't face those stairs up to your apartment."

"You sure?"

Lori nodded. "I'll take a wander along the boardwalk."

"I could buy you a beer," offered Scott shyly. "To say thanks for letting me sleep on your couch."

"Sounds good," agreed Lori, smiling at the young filmmaker. "We'll go and grab a table in the Turtle. You boys take your time."

The restaurant/bar was quiet for a Saturday when they entered a few minutes later. While Scott went up to the bar to order two beers, Lori took a seat at one of the tables, grateful to be able to rest for a while. Every time she visited the bar, the stairs up from the boardwalk seemed to get steeper. The muscles in her weaker thigh were aching from the climb. She was still massaging away the tightness in her leg when Scott came over to join her.

"They're bringing the drinks over," he explained as he sat opposite her. "Isn't this where we came after the school dance show?"

"Yes," giggled Lori. "Although I'm amazed you remember!"

"I remember arriving," confessed Scott blushing. "But not much else."

"The last I saw of you, you were passed out across the table," she sniggered. "That was a fun night."

"Wasn't much fun the next day," he admitted, remembering the hangover.

The waiter came over with their drinks and asked if they wanted to see the menu. Both of them shook their heads and Lori added that they were waiting on friends joining them. As they sipped their drinks, Scott quizzed her about life in the seaside town, comparing it to British coastal resorts he had visited as a child. It struck Lori that he sounded almost homesick as he reminisced about family holidays.

Fishing in his jacket pocket for the keys, Jake explained to Gary that he hadn't checked on the apartment for a few weeks.

Opening the door, they were welcomed by a musty, stale odour. One of the neighbours had put Jake's mail through the letter-box and there was a small paper mountain jamming the door. It took a minute or two, but he cleared the pile of trash mail away, then welcomed the band's manager in. Having seen round the compact abode, Gary agreed it was an improvement on the hotel.

"Did you say three of you lived here?"

"Yeah," said Jake grinning at the memory. "Rich, Paul and I shared this place for a few months. Long time ago!"

"Tight squeeze more like," laughed Gary. "I guess if I'm moving in, I'd better ask Scott if he wants to camp out on the couch."

"Up to you, boss," said Jake. "He's a good kid."

"And you're sure you don't mind me using this place?"

"It's all yours for as long as you need it," said Jake, handing him the keys. "I've kept a spare set of keys for emergencies. Rent is all paid up for the next six months."

"How much do I owe you a month for it?" asked Gary, accepting the keys.

"Don't worry about it just now," answered Jake. "Let's go and grab a beer to celebrate."

When they entered the Turtle a few minutes later, Lori and Scott were deep in conversation about Scott's video shoot, trying between them to work out a new theme and location. The table was strewn with napkins covered in scribbled drawings and ideas. Gathering them up into a neat pile, Jake joked about them being "priceless Mz Hyde originals." He signalled to the waiter to bring over four beers then asked if they had solved Scott's dilemma.

"We're working on it," replied Lori. "But it's quite a challenge."

"I'll call Jason on Monday," said Scott with a resigned sigh. "See if there's more budget. Might be easier to relocate it to Vegas."

"Worth asking, I guess," agreed Jake.

"So what's the verdict on Casa Power?" Lori asked, glancing between Jake and Gary.

"It beats the hotel. I'll move in during the week," Gary replied.

"It'll be nice to have somewhere in town and not have to drive everywhere."

"Well, if you need a hand, let me know," offered Jake, as the waiter brought over their drinks.

Taking a deep mouthful from his beer, Gary looked over at Scott then asked, "Do you fancy swapping a comfy hotel bed for Jake's pull-out couch?"

"Are you serious?" asked the younger man.

"Always. Can't leave you out at the hotel on your own," said the band's manager with a smile.

"Thanks. Couch sounds perfect."

It was still early when Jake and Lori finished dinner and left the Turtle, having promised to catch up with the two Englishmen later in the week. The boardwalk was quiet and most of the shops were closing up for the night as they walked past hand in hand. As ever, the amusement arcade was busy with teenagers, some of them spilling out onto the boardwalk. Once they were passed them, Lori could hear one group debating about whether it had been "that rock star guy" or not. It made her smile, but she could feel Jake cringe beside her. He still struggled with being recognised when he was out and about. Reaching the end of the boardwalk, the beach suddenly seemed very dark. Both of them stepped carefully down onto the soft sand. This time it was Jake who felt Lori tense up beside him. Before she could say anything he scooped her up into his arms to carry her the last few yards home.

"Reminds me of the day I met you, li'l lady," he said, before kissing her lightly on the forehead.

"Seems a lifetime ago," mused Lori softly.

"In some ways," agreed Jake. "We've both come a long way since then."

"It's been quite a year," she said with a wistful smile up at him. "I wonder what this one will bring?"

"Babies. Music. Dramas. Tears and laughter," surmised Jake, as he set her down on the sun deck. "And maybe a wedding?"

"We will need to give that some thought," she giggled, as she fished in her bag for the house keys. Tossing them to Jake, she said, "You open up, then let me in through the sunroom. I don't want to risk that path in the dark."

As Jake loped off into the darkness towards the back door, she heard an almighty clatter followed by a loud stream of expletives. Eventually, she heard him unlock the back door and saw the kitchen light, then the sunroom lights come on. Jake was rubbing his knee as he slid open the patio door.

"You ok?" she asked, stepping inside.

"Fucking trash can attacked me," he growled, closing the door over behind her.

Giggling, Lori flopped down onto the couch.

"Glad you think it's funny," retorted Jake, trying hard to sound angry.

"Would another beer make it better?" suggested Lori, reaching out to rub his tender knee.

"It might. You stay there and I'll fetch them," he said. "There's a price though."

"What?"

"Can you listen to the tracks I was working on earlier?"

"Of course."

Mixed emotions flowed through Lori as she listened to the Grey and Jake collaboration for a second time. It was a move towards a heavier style and she liked it, but, as Jake sang the lyrics, it lost something. He had played her the other new melody and she nodded approvingly. It was more like the band's usual style.

"Spit it out," said Jake bluntly. "I can see you're trying not to say something."

"Switch the drowning theme to the second song," she suggested quietly. "It's more haunting and tortured. I love the heavy one. Really love the riff, but the lyrics don't go with it. They felt all wrong."

"Come downstairs. I want to try something," he said, the creative wheels in his head already gathering speed. "You might be onto something here."

Down in the basement studio, Jake cleared space for Lori to sit on the couch that sat in the back corner of the room. Piling leads and pedals and other paraphernalia on the floor, he began switching things on and hooking his laptop up. His guitar, the one that the management company had presented to him for his birthday, was still set up from earlier. With a few minor adjustments to the tuning, Jake began to play the second, more tormented track. He played it slower than previously, before adding in additional sections and altering some of the original chord progressions. In the corner, Lori nodded her approval. After a few runs through, Jake set up the microphone and prepared to record a rough version of the song. When he began to sing, Lori could feel herself begin to tingle. His vocals this time were still haunting but more rasping. There was a new desperate edge to it that captured the panic and fear of the drowning themed lyrics. As she listened, Lori was suddenly aware that she was listening to something special- a song destined to become one of the main tracks on the next Silver Lake album. When the song was finished, Jake stopped the recording before he spoke. His reaction wasn't what Lori had anticipated. He threw back his head and laughed.

"That was intense."

"It sure was," she agreed with a smile. "I love that one already."

"I'll mail the file to the guys and see what they think," said Jake, turning his attention to his laptop. "Still need to come up with lyrics for the first one."

"They'll come to you in good time."

With the music file forwarded on to his fellow band members, Jake reached for his acoustic guitar. Instead of playing the full heavy version of the first song, he began to play it acoustically in the hope that he might feel something different in it. Halfway through, he stopped playing. It wasn't translating well and he could feel himself growing frustrated.

"Move on to something else for a while," Lori suggested, sensing his growing exasperation.

"Time to call it a night," stated Jake, setting the guitar back on its stand. "Need to sleep on this one."

"How many tracks do you have for the new record?" asked Lori, as she got slowly to her feet.

"Not enough," admitted Jake with a yawn. "We've got about seven, maybe six, depending on how this works out. Ideally, we want at least fourteen. Plenty time yet though."

"I sense a few late nights on your horizon, rock star," predicted Lori with a knowing smile. "And long days."

♫

Instead of being a day of rest, Sunday turned into a day of work for both the creative souls living at the beach house. Jake's song-writing muse hit him early in the morning while he was out for a run along the beach. His mind had wandered over a few ideas as he had pounded his way along the sand. When he returned to the house, he had charged straight down to the basement to record a new riff and a new melody line quickly before he forgot them. He then came back upstairs to grab a shower before disappearing back down to the studio. The door was tightly closed, a clear "do not disturb" sign to Lori.

There must have been something in the air because she too had had a flash of inspiration for a new project that she had received an email about. Since resurrecting Mz Hyde almost a year before, Lori had thrown herself back into her design work. When she had checked her business emails, there had been one from the lead singer of one of the first band's she had designed for back at the end of her student days. Attached to the email had been a music file with four short excerpts from tracks for the singer's solo album. At the first time of listening, Lori hadn't connected with them, but she had played them through a couple of times and looked back over previous designs she had completed for the artist. Inspiration had struck her as she had done a load of laundry. With a smile, she thought it must have been the soapy swirls of water visible through the door of the machine. Whatever it was, it was enough to light the spark and to get an idea flowing.

As she listened to Jake's music taking shape below her, Lori sat at her drawing board, teasing her design to life. Unlike her fiancé, she stopped for a break around lunchtime and enjoyed a quiet hour out on the sun deck with a salad, a juice and the Sunday newspaper. Before she returned to work, she made herself a coffee and sent a quick message to Maddy to check if she was alright. Upon returning to her drawing board, Lori was soon so engrossed in her work that it slipped her mind that her friend hadn't replied. Several hours later, as the light began to reflect the hues of dusk, Lori heard her phone chirp. The sudden sharp noise reminded her that she hadn't heard from Maddy all day. Quickly she opened the message.

"At the hospital. In labour. All ok for now. No need to panic. Maddy x"

Lori's hands were trembling as she replied, "Are you ok? Thinking about you. Tell Paul to call as soon as there is any news. Hugs. L x"

A few minutes later, the basement door opened and a weary looking Jake emerged, his phone clutched in his hand.

"Paul called. Maddy's in labour," he announced with a grin. "This is it!"

"I know. Maddy messaged me," replied Lori smiling. "Scary exciting, isn't it?"

"A bit," he admitted, as he came over to give her a hug. "Hey, that's quite something!"

"It's a bit creepy, but it fits with the remit," said Lori, gazing down at her drawing. "Not my usual kind of thing."

The drawing was a sink drain hole with tortured, skeletal faces peering up and long thin bony arms reaching through.

"It's kind of weird," agreed Jake. "Who's it for?"

"You know better than to ask that," she chastised. "How did your day go? It sounded good."

"I've made some progress. I've been emailing files to Grey and Rich on and off all day. We'll see how it all comes together," he replied. "My train of thought derailed when Paul called."

"Same here," Lori confessed with a giggle. "Waiting's going to be the hard bit now."

"How long do these things take?" asked Jake, not too sure that he really wanted to hear the answer.

"As long as they take. I'm not actually sure," Lori answered. "I just hope they're all ok."

"They'll be fine," assured Jake confidently. "Now, how about we make some dinner? I'm starving!"

Each hour dragged by endlessly. Neither of them could settle. After dinner they sat down to watch a movie, but Lori couldn't concentrate and abandoned the film after less than an hour in favour of finishing off the laundry. Jake too was struggling to focus on the screen, but he persevered until the end. Without saying anything to Lori, he sent Paul a message to see if he could find out how things were progressing. He got no reply.

When it got to midnight and there was still no news, they both conceded it was time for bed. Side by side, they lay awake in the dark, both of them listening anxiously for their phones. At some point during the night, they finally drifted off to sleep.

Early morning sunlight was filtering through the voile curtains, when Lori's phone finally rang. Instantly she was awake and reaching for the handset.

"Morning, Lori," said Paul sounding cheerful.

"Is everything ok?" she asked without pausing to say hello.

"Everything's wonderful!" declared the Silver Lake drummer. "I'm a dad! I have a son and a daughter."

"Fabulous! Congratulations, daddy. How's Maddy?"

"Exhausted. She's sleeping just now. So are the babies. She was incredible, Lori. The whole thing was amazing. Scary but amazing."

"And the babies?"

"Perfect," he sighed. "I'll send photos in a few minutes. No names yet."

"I'm just relieved everyone is ok. Did she need a C-section?"

"No," answered Paul. "That wonderful woman delivered them both naturally."

"Are they a good weight?"

"What is this? Twenty questions?" teased the new father. "Baby boy was six pounds and four ounces. Baby girl was five pounds and twelve ounces. Both beautifully healthy. They arrived at two fifteen this morning. I didn't want to call you guys in the middle of the night though."

"We've been awake most of the night listening for the phone so you could've called," giggled Lori. "This is the best news to start the day."

"Isn't it just," agreed Paul with a yawn.

"When can we see everyone?"

"There's visiting this afternoon at two," replied Paul.

"We'll be there," promised Lori. "Let me know if you need me to bring anything."

"Will do," said Paul. "I'd better go. Calls to make and I need some sleep. See you guys later."

"Take care, daddy," said Lori as she ended the call.

Just after two, Jake pulled into the parking lot beside the maternity wing at the medical centre. Hand in hand, he and Lori walked towards the hospital. Over her shoulder, Lori had a canvas bag with two teddy bears poking their heads over the edge. Jake had called Paul to say they were on their way in and, as they reached the door, he came rushing out to meet them.

"What kept you guys?" he said hugging Lori. "The boss has been driving me insane asking when you were arriving."

"Sorry, my fault," apologised Jake, hugging his friend. "I went for a run and was longer than I meant to be."

"Let's go in," suggested Paul.

He led them along the corridor and round a few corners before finally opening the door of a small, private room. Over by the window, Maddy was sitting in a rocking chair with her newborn twins asleep in her arms. As Lori and Jake entered, she smiled at them and whispered, "Hello."

Gone was the business-like Goth that Jake was accustomed to. In her place was a slightly pale and tired version of Maddy, who looked happier and more content than he had ever seen her. Putting her bag down on the end of the bed, Lori walked over to her friend, tears welling up in her eyes.

"Oh, Maddy, they're beautiful," she said, gently touching the soft, downy hair of one of the twins. "So tiny!"

"Thanks. They didn't feel so tiny last night I can tell you," laughed Maddy. "Want to cuddle them, Aunt Lori?"

"Let me sit down first," said Lori, taking a seat opposite her friend. "I've never held a newborn baby before."

"You'll be fine," assured Maddy with a smile. "Who do you want to cuddle first?"

"Oh, have you chosen names?"

"We wanted you two to be the first to know," said Paul coming over to lift his sleeping son from Maddy's arms. "Meet Hayden Paul Edwards."

Instead of handing the baby to Lori, he turned and handed him to Jake. Expertly Jake settled the baby in the crook of his arm.

"Our newest drummer?"

"Maybe," agreed Paul smiling proudly.

Carefully Maddy shuffled forward in her seat, then stood up rather gingerly to hand her sleeping baby daughter to Lori. "And this is Wren Maddison Edwards."

Nervously Lori cuddled the sleeping baby girl in her arms, marvelling at the perfection of her - the tiny ears, the perfect fingernails, tiny rosebud mouth. "Oh, Maddy, she's beautiful. So perfect."

"Congratulations, both of you. These two are precious," said Jake coming over to admire little Wren. "I think they both look like you, Maddison."

"Wren does a bit, but Hayden's like Paul," replied the proud mother. "I just can't believe they're here and I'm watching you guys holding them. It just blows my mind."

"So how bad was it?" asked Lori, anxious to know what her friend had endured.

"That's our cue to talk band talk," joked Jake, nudging Paul.

"We could go and fetch these girls a juice while they chat about the messy stuff," conceded Paul.

"You two stay right where you are," said Maddy sharply. "There's juice over there if you're thirsty."

"Yes, mom!" laughed Jake, sitting down on the edge of the bed. "Hayden, your mom's a scary lady."

Visiting was only scheduled to last for an hour, but, when the hour was up, the four friends were still chatting and laughing together. The new parents had loved the two teddy bears and placed them in the babies' plastic crib. Hearing the story of Maddy's labour and the twins' arrival into the world wasn't as traumatic as either Lori or Jake had expected and, seeing how fit and well Maddy looked, reassured Lori that she really was telling them the truth and not watering the tale down. Photos were taken of each of them holding the babies; photos were taken of the girls with the twins; photos were taken of the boys with the twins. The whole scene couldn't have been further removed from the "rock world" if they had tried.

Eventually little Wren began to fret and grizzle and Maddy commented that they were due to be fed.

"We'd better go," said Lori softly. "When do you expect to get home?"

"Tomorrow hopefully," replied Maddy putting her little finger in her baby daughter's mouth to soothe her. "Maybe Wednesday."

"If you need anything, just call me," said Lori, hugging her friend.

"We'll need to go out for a few beers to celebrate," stated Paul, clapping Jake on the shoulder.

"Just tell me where and when," agreed Jake with a wink.

With a final wave, they left the new family in peace to get to know one another.

♪

Despite the disruption and celebration of the twins' arrival, life had to return to normality for the rest of Silver Lake. For the remainder of the week, Jake locked himself down in the basement during the day, working tirelessly to come up with songs for the new record. Each evening Grey or Rich or both of them would come over and they would work together until late. While the band were writing and rehearsing, Lori refocused on her own work commitments. By the following Wednesday, she had three more offers of work from Jason, including a formal offer to complete the Silver Lake cover and another to do the latest Weigh Station album. It was to be a greatest hits compilation, due to be released ahead of their US summer festival tour. The third offer was for an all-girl pop band and, when she heard the accompanying music files, Lori turned it down flat. Her refusal prompted an immediate irate call from Jason himself and, after she had listened to his tirade of abuse about her declining the project, her answer, much to his annoyance, remained a definite no. When she checked her emails over breakfast on Thursday there was a fresh project offer from him to complete the artwork for an up-and-coming UK rock band called Nothing To Prove. She listened to the music samples a couple of times as she finished off her coffee, then emailed back accepting the commission. With the deadlines indicated, Lori now had enough work to keep her occupied over the summer and well into the fall.

Just as she closed the dishwasher up and pressed start, there was a knock at the back door. Lori opened it to find Todd, Jake's former student, standing there.

"Todd! Good morning!" she exclaimed in surprise. "Is Jake expecting you?"

"Not exactly," replied the teenager awkwardly. "Is he home?"

"He's in the shower. Come on in and wait," said Lori, stepping aside and showing the boy into the kitchen. "Do you not have school today?"

Todd nodded. "I'll go in after I speak to Mr Power."

"Take a seat. I'll let him know you're here," invited Lori warmly. "Help yourself to coffee. The mugs are in the cupboard over the stove."

When Jake came through to the kitchen a few minutes later, Todd was sitting at the table, a half drunk mug of coffee in front of him. In his rush to discover what the boy wanted, Jake had thrown on his jeans, but hadn't bothered with a shirt or socks. The sight of the rock star, hair still wet from the shower, stripped to the waist caught the boy off guard.

"Sorry. Is this a bad time?" asked Todd, trying not to stare at his former teacher's tattoos.

"Not at all, Todd, What's up?"

"I need your help," began the boy, dropping his eyes to the floor. "My mom's kicked me out. I'm staying at Kate's house. I've got a job on the weekends and one night a week at the skate shop in town."

"So where can I help?" asked Jake, concerned to learn that his young friend was in this predicament.

"I don't have enough money to pay my guitar tuition. I need to cancel my tutor," Todd replied. "And I was kind of wondering if you'd teach me? I thought I could do some work for you to pay for the lessons. Yard work or something."

"Is that all you need my help with?" laughed Jake, relief echoing in his laughter. "I thought you were here to tell me you were in real trouble! Of course I'll help you when I can but remember, I don't work regular hours and I'm away from home a fair bit."

"Thanks, sir," said the boy, lifting his eyes from the floor and smiling.

"Less of the sir," chastised Jake warmly. "It's Jake. Now, shouldn't you be in class?"

Todd nodded, then said, "I wanted to see you before I went in. The school have been great, but I don't get on too well with the new music teacher. I wanted to talk to you first before I had to talk to him."

"Let me grab a shirt and some shoes and I'll drive you out to school," offered Jake. "We can work out a loose schedule in the truck."

"Thank you," said Todd. "You've no idea how much this means to me."

When Jake returned to the house, Lori was sitting out on the sun deck sketching, her ear phones in and iPod lying on the table. Oblivious to her fiancé's presence, she squealed as he bent down to kiss the nape of her neck.

"Christ, you scared the hell out of me!"

"Sorry, li'l lady," he apologised as he sat down beside her. "I need you to draw up a list of chores that you need done about the place."

"Don't you have enough to do with writing for the new record?"

"I didn't say I was going to be the one doing the chores," countered Jake. "I've made a deal with Todd. He needs tuition, but can't pay hard cash. He wants to work to pay for his lessons."

"Ah, it's a male pride thing," observed Lori, understanding the situation. "Well, the fence needs painting for a start and the front yard could use some attention."

"That'll do for a start. He'll be over tomorrow after school."

"For a lesson or to work?" enquired Lori, conscious that Jake had been secreted in the basement studio all day every day recently.

"We'll play that by ear. It depends how my day goes," Jake replied. "Now, I'd better get some work done. I've lost enough time today."

"Makes two of us," agreed Lori, closing over her sketch pad. "My drawing board awaits me."

It was late afternoon before either of them stopped for a break. Down in the basement, Jake was finally making headway and the song count was up to eleven possible tracks. Via text and email plus a few phone calls, the band had agreed to meet and run through what they had stockpiled on Saturday before going into town to celebrate the twins' safe arrival. Both Rich and Grey had been exchanging music files with him throughout the week and, as well as the eleven songs, he had the bare bones of two more taking shape. Each of them had a different musical style and preference. The challenge came in harnessing the best of their individual ideas and finding common ground without anyone's ego getting in the way.

Upstairs Lori was finalising her "zombie drain" as she now affectionately thought of the piece. Several times she had paused to listen to Jake playing, part of her looking for any emerging theme that may help when it came to tackling the Silver Lake commission. After a couple of hours, she began to realise how big a distraction the band rehearsing and recording was going to be. When the basement had been converted, it had been soundproofed but she could still hear Jake's guitar quite clearly. While he was practicing a particularly loud and heavy riff, she walked through to the bedroom to see if it was any quieter at that end of the house. It wasn't. Still deep in thought, Lori walked back down the hallway. When she drew level with the door to the attic, she paused. Maybe it would be quieter upstairs? Carefully, she climbed the steep, narrow stairs up into the attic. Since her return to the house over a year before she had only ventured up there once. It was a huge space, but there were no windows and therefore no natural light to work in. On the plus side, she could barely hear Jake playing.

An idea forming in her head, Lori slowly made her way back down the stairs. When she sat back down at her desk, she fired off an email to David, her financial advisor and mentor, asking him to find her an architect and a builder, briefly outlining her plan. Once her email was sent, she returned her attention to the drawing on the board in front of her.

The ringing of her phone a while later shattered her concentration. It was Maddy's number on the screen.

"Hi," greeted Lori brightly as she answered the call. "How're things?"

"Chaotic!" snapped Maddy sharply before adding, "Sorry. I didn't mean to bite."

"It's alright," answered Lori softly. "But are you ok?"

"Tired. Sore. Emotional."

"That's to be expected, Maddy. How're the babies?"

"Hungry little monsters. They need fed every couple of hours. We're both exhausted."

"It's early days. Do you want me to come over tomorrow?" offered Lori, suddenly anxious to see her friend and the twins.

"Could you?" replied Maddy, her tone almost pleading.

"Of course. When?"

"Come over for lunch," suggested Maddy. One of the babies began to cry in the background.

"Why don't I bring some food in for us all?" Lori proposed,

keen to keep her visit simple for her friend's sake. "Will Paul be home?"

"I guess," sighed Maddy. "He's smothering me in kindness."

"We can always send him over here to see Jake."

"Sounds like a plan. I'd better go. Hayden's fretting. I'll see you tomorrow, honey."

When Jake finally emerged from the basement, he found Lori in the kitchen preparing dinner. An open bottle of red wine sat on the counter with two glasses beside it, one empty and one part full. A pot of Bolognese was bubbling away on the stove and the tantalising smell reminded him just how hungry he was.

"Productive day?" asked Lori as Jake wrapped his arms around her slender waist.

"I think so," he replied, inhaling the subtle floral notes of her perfume. "You?"

"Not too bad actually. The zombie drain is more or less finished. I'll scan and email it off tomorrow before I drive out to see Maddy. She called a while ago," explained Lori. "I also had an idea for some home improvements?"

"Oh?" said Jake raising one eyebrow. "Should I be worried?"

"No," she giggled, before explaining about the distraction of him playing and her plan to convert the attic into a studio for herself.

"It's worth checking out," agreed Jake, pouring them both some wine. "I'm no construction expert, but I guess it could be done."

"I've emailed David and asked him to find an architect to design it. We'll see what he comes up with and if it's possible. The structure of the roof might be an issue."

With a couple of hours work completed and her zombie drain design sent off for approval, Lori headed out to visit Maddy and the twins. The new family were renting a former farmhouse on the outskirts of town, out beyond the outlets. En route, Lori stopped and picked up some steak sandwiches for lunch, then drove out to Wolfe Neck Road. It wasn't an area she was overly familiar with but she had been out to visit a few times since they had moved in, usually with Jake driving. When she spotted the driveway and Maddy's Mustang outside, she breathed a sigh of relief. Grabbing the insulated bag with lunch in it, her canvas tote and her cane, Lori climbed out of the car. Paul was standing in the doorway waiting for her with one of the twins nestled in the crook of his arm.

"Glad you made it!" he called out cheerfully. "Did you bring lunch?"

"Of course," declared Lori as she carefully climbed the front steps. "Steak sandwiches all round."

"Perfect!" stated the band's drummer, stepping aside. "The boss is in the kitchen. Go on through."

The large kitchen at the back of the house was bright and airy with a huge bleached pine kitchen table being the focal point of the room. Over at the sink, Maddy was busy preparing bottles of formula for the twins. At the sound of Lori's cane on the tile floor, she turned to welcome her friend.

"You're looking fabulous!" said Lori, hugging Maddy tight.

"Thanks," replied the new mother with a worn-out smile. "I feel like a zombie."

"It's early days," sympathised Lori, noting the dark circles under her friend's eyes. "I brought hot sandwiches. We'd better eat them before they get cold."

"Oh, you're an angel, Lori!" sighed Maddy. "Let me grab some juice to go with them."

With the twins sleeping peacefully in their stroller in the adjoining family room, they were afforded the luxury of time to relax and chat over their meal. Neither of the new parents had really been out of the house for over a week, apart from Paul's occasional trip to the food store, so they were keen to hear what had been happening in the world beyond the farmhouse. Lori got the feeling they were disappointed when she said that all she had really done was work. She told them about her completed "zombie drain" project and about Todd turning up looking for help but that was all the news she had. Pouring them a coffee at the end of their meal, Paul said he would take a run out to see Jake for an hour or so. Exchanging glances, the girls laughed and Maddy suggested he take his time.

Just as Paul was preparing to leave, the babies began to cry. He stopped in his tracks, but Lori said, "You go on. I'll help Maddy out here."

"Thanks, Lori," he replied, looking relieved at being able to escape for a couple of hours. "I'll be back by four, Maddy."

"No rush," she called back as she went to warm up the bottles of formula milk. "Lori, are you sure you're ready for this?"

"As I'll ever be," giggled Lori a little nervously. "This is a whole new experience for me."

Under Maddy's guidance, Lori went through a steep learning curve over the next hour. Amid a lot of giggles, she managed to change her first diaper, despite a rather wriggly Wren trying to make the task nigh on impossible. With the diaper secured and her body suit fastened up, Lori lifted the restless baby girl into her arms and sat on the couch to give her a bottle - another first. As the little girl suckled on the teat, she marvelled at the perfection of her mouth, her long dark eyelashes and big bright brown eyes. The baby stared up at her intently with a look that seemed to say, "You're not my mommy or daddy, but you're feeding me so that's ok." Soon the bottle was empty and Maddy explained to her that she would need to "burp" the baby. Obligingly, Wren let out an almighty burp for such a tiny person then uttered a soft whimper of a cry.

"I think she gave herself a fright," laughed Lori, settling the little one in her arms.

"She's done that a few times," admitted Maddy as she laid Hayden on her shoulder, rubbing his back gently. "It's as though she knows it's not ladylike whereas this young man would release gas all day and not flinch!"

"Typical guy!"

With Paul out of the house, the two friends spent the afternoon enjoying a good "Girl's Club" chat. Understandably, it was initially centred round the babies and the trials and challenges of getting through the day with them. Both babies fell asleep as the girls talked and eventually conversation moved on to music and art and Silver Lake.

"Jason called yesterday," commented Maddy as she put Hayden down in the stroller to continue his nap.

"Not about work, surely?" asked Lori, reluctantly putting Wren in beside her brother.

"Yup," replied Maddy. "He wanted to know if I was planning on going on the festival circuit over the summer with the band."

"He's something else that guy! What did you tell him?"

"That I'd think about it," confessed Maddy quietly.

"You wouldn't take the twins out on tour so soon surely?"

"I don't know," said Maddy with a sigh. "It's not like a regular tour. I told him to ask me again at the end of June. Paul's already said he wants the three of us with him if it's practical."

"I guess you've got plenty of time to work out the logistics. I know Grey's keen to take Becky with him. Maybe between you, you could hire a nanny to watch all the kids," suggested Lori, silently thinking that it sounded a nightmare of an idea.

As promised, Paul returned shortly after four looking more relaxed. Excusing himself, he went through to the study with his laptop, explaining that Jake had given him some tracks to work on before the band got together next day.

"Oh, Lori," he exclaimed as he left the room. "Jake asked me to tell you to pick up some paint for the fence on the way home. That kid arrived as I was leaving."

"Thanks, Paul," said Lori. "I'd better make a move if I've to go to the hardware store on the way back."

"Do you have to go so soon?" Maddy asked.

"I'd better," said Lori with a smile. "I don't want to get caught in traffic. Why don't you all come over on Sunday?"

"Oh our first family outing!" proclaimed the new mother. "I'd love to! After lunch?"

"Whenever you are ready," said Lori, lifting her bag. "If it's nice, we can BBQ."

"Sounds wonderful!" Maddy declared with a smile.

It was over an hour later before Lori pulled into the driveway at the beach house. She had stopped off to buy some white paint for the fence and some paint brushes, but had then got stuck in the late afternoon traffic on the highway. Leaving the paint in the car, she entered the house via the back door. There were voices and acoustic guitar music coming from the sun room. Quickly she poured herself a glass of water, then wandered through to see how the lesson was progressing.

"Hi, Miss Hyde," called Todd cheerfully when he spotted her in the doorway.

"Hi. And its Lori, Todd," she corrected.

"We won't be long, li'l lady," said Jake with a grin. "Fifteen more minutes."

"Ok," replied Lori turning to leave. "Oh, I got the paint. It's still in the car."

"We'll fetch it when we are through here," promised Jake then he returned his focus to his student. "Once more from the top, Todd."

Leaving them to finish the lesson, Lori headed through to the study to check her emails. The gentle strains of guitar music were almost soothing as she read her way through the messages. It didn't take long to deal with the handful of mails and to delete the usual barrage of junk mail. There was a response to her "zombie drain" design. The artiste had approved it and requested that she expand on it and add four T-shirt designs to the commission. She referred them to David to re-negotiate the costs involved, relieved that the design had been approved so quickly. For a few moments she sat studying the design, trying to work out which bits to extract for the T-shirt designs. Lifting her sketch pad and a pencil, she began to roughly draw one of the faces, trying to visualise it tearing through the cloth of a T-shirt. Engrossed in the gross drawing, Lori didn't notice that Jake's fifteen minutes stretched to almost an hour. It was the squeal of the patio door sliding over that brought her back to the present.

"School's out," declared Jake a few moments later as he walked past her work space. "How was Maddy?"

"She's doing great," said Lori, closing over her sketchpad. "The twins are gorgeous. I invited them all over on Sunday."

"You are remembering that the boys and I are going out tomorrow to celebrate the twins' arrival?"

Lori nodded. "I just felt that Maddy could do with a change of scenery. She's not been out of the house in over a week."

"It's fine with me. Paul might not be so keen. He was planning to party tomorrow night,"

"So there's a reasonable chance he'll be here?"

"If I was a gambling man," began Jake, "I'd say yes."

"I see tomorrow night getting messy," prophesied Lori. "Now, what's the plan for dinner, rock star?"

Neither of them could be bothered cooking so Jake suggested

they go into town for some sushi. It had been a while since they had been to their favourite sushi restaurant and Lori didn't take much persuading. As they left the house a few minutes later, she handed the car keys to Jake and asked him to drive. With the rock radio station playing loudly, they headed into town. Cars lined the street outside the restaurant and Jake had to circle a couple of times before finally securing a space two blocks away. Putting a protective arm around Lori's shoulder, they walked back down the street. He noticed that Lori was walking better than she had been for a while. Her cane and her limp never bothered him, but he worried about her if she seemed to be limping more than usual. Today, despite her trip out to Maddy's, was obviously a good day.

The restaurant was busy when they finally arrived, but the hostess said they had a table ready. Soon they were seated at the corner table in the window, browsing the familiar menu. When the server returned with their drinks, she asked if they were ready to order. Without a second glance at the menu, Lori ordered for both of them.

"You'd think we'd been here before," teased Jake as the girl headed back towards the kitchen.

Giggling, Lori confessed, "I just ordered all my favourites."

"I noticed," commented Jake, smiling at her. He sat staring at her for a few moments, then reached over to take her hand. "Have I told you how beautiful you look tonight, li'l lady?"

Blushing, Lori lowered her eyes, fixing her gaze on the edge of the table.

"It's easy to forget how lucky I am," he continued softly, still holding her hand. Fingering her engagement ring, he added, "I don't know what I'd have done if you'd said no."

"Someone's in a romantic mood," observed Lori with a smile. "What's brought this on?"

Shrugging his shoulders, Jake said, "I'm not sure. A song I was working on earlier. A few things Paul was talking about. Got me thinking."

"Happy thoughts?"

"Some of them," he admitted. "Song was quite deep and emotional. Stirred up a few memories."

"The dangers of looking inside yourself," she observed, before taking a sip of her white wine spritzer.

"I guess," he conceded, then raised his beer. "Here's to us. To long life, good health and happy thoughts."

"Amen to that."

By the time they had paid the check and were leaving the sushi bar, it was growing late. Most of their fellow diners were long gone. Only two other tables were still occupied. Their hostess wished them a safe journey home as she held the door open for them. Outside a small group of their fellow diners were standing chatting. Spotting Jake and Lori, one of the women approached them.

"Excuse me," she began politely. "Can you help settle an argument please?"

"If we can," said Jake, taking Lori's hand.

"Are you the singer with Silver Lake?"

"Perhaps," replied Jake with a smile. "Depends on why you are asking?"

"My friend here recognised you from the Surfside festival last year, but the guys say we're wrong," she explained, looking a little awkward. "They say you're a teacher at one of the local high schools."

"What if you're both right?" teased Jake.

"Jake, stop it!" laughed Lori, unable to control the fit of the giggles that was welling up inside her.

"Sorry," he apologised sincerely. "Yes, I sing with Silver Lake and yes, I taught at the high school."

"I knew it!" exclaimed the young woman. She turned to her friends and declared, "We were all right. Kind of."

"Is there anything else I can help you with?" asked Jake.

"An autograph would be nice," she said, rummaging in her bag for a pen. She produced a fine tipped marker pen and handed it to him.

"Do you have a piece of paper?" he asked, tugging the lid off the pen.

"Sign here please," she said, sliding down the waistband of her jeans. "Across my hip."

"Are you serious? This is a permanent marker."

"Deadly serious. I'll get it inked in tomorrow. I'm going anyway."

"Tattooed!" exclaimed Jake in disbelief. "You want my

signature tattooed on your hip?"

"Is that a problem?"

"Not at all, but that's a hell of a commitment," responded Jake, glancing over at Lori. "It's your body though. Just my signature?"

"Yes, unless you want to add a design."

"I'll leave designs to Lori," commented Jake as he carefully autographed the girl's skin. "There you go, angel."

"Mz Hyde?" asked the girl. "Can I tempt you to add something? And your signature too?"

As Lori was about to decline, Jake gently nudged her, "Go on, li'l lady. Dress up that name."

"If you say so, rock star," said Lori taking the pen. "Hold still, honey."

Quickly she drew a few musical notes below Jake's signature, then signed her own name.

"Will that do?"

"Perfect," declared the young woman. "Thank you so much. Sorry for interrupting your evening."

"I have to ask," began Jake, curiosity getting the better of him. "Why?"

"Why ink anything?" countered the girl. "I've collected a few over the years. Rock stars. Actors."

"So who else has signed your body?"

"Here. See for yourself," she replied, bending over and lifting up her T-shirt. Much to Jake's amazement, her entire back was covered in signatures and doodles. He recognised Dan Crow from Weigh Station's autograph, Slash's, complete with drawing and the date, Lemmy's from Motorhead, plus at least half a dozen award winning actors.

"Wow!" he exclaimed. "That's some collection. And you've met them all?"

"Every last one for a few precious moments," she replied proudly.

"I'm honoured to be asked to join the collection. It's a motley crew," said Jake, still amazed by the array of names in front of him.

"They've signed up too," she joked. "Thank you for being so sweet about this."

"Who's going to ink it in for you?"

"Danny," she replied. "Who else?"

"Touché!" laughed Jake. "Tell him I said hello."

"You know him?"

"He's done all of my own ink," explained Jake. "Now we really need to get going. Good luck with the tattoo."

"Night," she called. "And thanks again."

Jake was still marvelling at the eccentric young woman's request when they reached the car. Her tattoo collection prompted a discussion about why people choose to have certain images added to their skin. The debate continued until they reached the house. Both of them agreed that tattoos were very personal things; both of them agreed that celebrity autographs were a unique form of self-expression and not one that either of them intended to copy.

"So what's your next addition to the art gallery going to be, rock star?" asked Lori as they entered the house.

"Still trying to decide on that one," he replied. "I know where. I just don't know what. What about you?"

"I'm undecided," she admitted. "But I suspect there may be a second one at some point."

"I told you so," teased Jake. "One's never enough."

Sun shone down on Rehoboth next day, sending the mercury levels soaring up into the low eighties. As the morning wound towards noon, the various members of Silver Lake arrived at the beach house to rehearse. Gary, with Scott in tow, was the last to arrive. The basement studio felt crowded with all six of them crammed in. After a while, Gary called them all to attention and asked what they expected to achieve from the band meeting.

"A time frame for getting the record done for a start," stated Rich bluntly.

"Some loose agreement on the new songs we've been working on," added Jake.

"Ok, that's a start," agreed Gary glancing round at the band. "Here's where I'm at with Jason and the record company. They want the album recorded by the end of July with a provisional release date of October 7th. I called Dr Marrs yesterday and confirmed the dates that he's available. I've provisionally booked out his time from June 10th through until around the end of July. We have a few days there to play with. That's assuming that you want to work with him again?"

"So that gives us about six weeks to finish writing and agree on arrangements?" quizzed Grey.

"More or less."

"That's achievable," said Jake confidently. "It's more time than we've had before."

"I also don't think you can record here," Gary added as he looked round at the lack of space. "I've been looking into available studios in the area that are suitable but there's not much."

"What if we got premises and set up our own studio?" asked Paul hopefully, silently dreading the thought of being away from home to record the album.

"It's an idea, but an expensive one."

"Ok," butted in Jake. "See what you can find that ties in with the dates. Are we agreed that we are staying with Dr Marrs on this record?"

Everyone quickly agreed to retain the producer's services.

"On that basis," Rich began, "Let's book out his services from mid-June until the end of July."

"Agreed," added Grey, happy to have some concrete dates to work to. "Does he know of any studios around here?"

"I'll check," said Gary. "Now, Jason has emailed me some summer outdoor festival dates he's booked you guys in for. I'll send on what I've got from him so far so check your emails later and get back to me with any questions. That includes you, Jake."

"Right, so the plan is to rehearse and write from now until mid-June. Record June and July. Potentially tour August into September assuming that's when the festival dates fall. Aim to put the new record out in October," summarised Jake. "Then what?"

"Tour," Gary stated plainly. "Europe first, then USA then the rest of the world. Depends on promoters. Costs. Album sales. You know the score."

"Yeah?" said Rich. "I guess that's this year and most of next mapped out!"

"Pretty much."

"Rock and fucking roll," muttered Paul. "Are we going to rehearse today?"

"I'll leave you boys to it for now," said Paul, shutting over his laptop. "What's the plan for tonight?"

"A meal in town, then some drinking," answered Grey. "We've booked a table at the Turtle for six thirty."

"See you guys there then," agreed their manager. "Come on, Scott, let's leave these guys in peace to work."

Rehearsal time went slowly after the band's manager left. All of them were more than a bit stunned by how direct the young Englishman had been. He hadn't been the usual relaxed Gary they knew and loved. Out of all of them, Paul was the most frustrated. It was no secret that he loathed flying and the prospect of so much travelling scared him. He took his frustrations out on his drum kit. The calibre of his angry solo raised a round of applause from his fellow band members.

"We need to use that!" declared Grey with a grin. "Best I've ever heard you beat them skins!"

It broke the ice and the tension gradually dissipated as they worked on the new material. Jake played back the recordings he had made of the songs he had been working on. It was a relief to him to see his fellow band members nodding appreciatively to the tracks. The recording was stopped and started numerous times as Grey worked out a bass line, then Rich joined in with an alternative to part of the guitar track. Some of their ideas worked well immediately, while others felt clumsy and inept. By late afternoon all of them were growing tired and claustrophobia was setting in.

"Beer o'clock?" suggested Jake, laying his guitar down. "Let's wrap this up and get the party started."

"Music to my ears," declared Grey loudly.

"I'll call Maddy to check everything is ok at home, then I'll be up," said Paul reaching for his phone.

"Your beer will be waiting for you," Jake replied as he led the way up the stairs to the house.

Out on the sun deck, Lori had spent the afternoon lying in the sun listening to music and reading her book. When she heard the boys coming through the house, she reached for her sarong and tied it round her waist so that the soft material covered her scarred thigh. Stepping out onto the deck, Jake let out a long sigh and handed her a cold beer.

"Mind if we join you, li'l lady?" he asked, sitting on the edge of the lounger.

"Not at all," replied Lori sipping her beer. The ice cold beer tasted good. "How'd it go down there?"

"So, so," replied Rich, stretching out on the other lounger. "It's coming together."

"Gary looked angry when he left," she observed. "Is there an issue?"

"He was just laying a few things on the line," defended Jake. "He was a bit direct. I'd guess Lord Jason has been putting pressure on him."

As he stepped out to join them, Paul added, "Got it in one, Jake. I just spoke to Maddy. She's had Jason on the phone. He's wanting her back on board by the end of July. Doesn't think Gary is working hard enough for us."

"That's a bit rough on the guy," Lori commented quietly.

"It's all politics," Rich commented. "It'll settle down once we've started pre-production and recording."

"Christ, I hope so," growled Grey into his beer. "I hate ill feeling in the air. Life's so much easier when we're one big happy Silver Lake family."

"I'll drink to that!" declared Rich raising his beer bottle. "And to Hayden and Wren."

An early morning mist had rolled in off the ocean creating an eerie atmosphere along the beach. It had been early when Lori had crept out of the house to go for a walk. She did some of her best thinking alone down on the sand. Over the months her confidence and her physical strength had grown allowing her to walk along the shoreline without a constant nagging fear of falling. With the broad base plate attached, she still used her cane for support, psychological as much as physical. She had left Jake snoring loudly in bed, his long limbs spread out over more than his fair share of the mattress. When she had come down the hall, she had found Rich asleep on the lounge floor, his leather jacket serving as a blanket. As she wandered through the sun room, Lori wasn't surprised to find both Paul and Grey asleep on the couches. The last two revellers hadn't even made it indoors. Gary and Scott were dead to the world on the sun loungers outside. Someone had had the good sense to cover them with the fleecy blankets from the sun room. Images of the sleeping rock stars made her smile as she strolled along the sand. This early the beach was deserted and the pockets of morning mist created her own small private thought bubbles.

After two phone calls the previous evening she had plenty to think about. Shortly after the band had left to go into town, Jason had called her with a business proposition. Calmly she listened to what he had to say and freely admitted that she was interested, but that she would need a few days to chew it all over. In his usual domineering manner, he had tried to force her to commit to the proposal there and then, but, unfazed by him, Lori stated that either she was given three days or there was no deal to be done. Accepting that this was as much as she was prepared to commit to, he had promised to call her on Tuesday night. The phone was barely back in its base unit when it rang again. It was Maddy, who wanted to know if she had spoken to Jason and committed to his project. The two friends discussed the idea, the practicalities of it and the costs. Both of them knew that it wasn't about the money, but Lori was not one to invest in anything without checking it out fully. There were pros and cons to the proposal. After her chat with Maddy, she had emailed David and asked him to look into the feasibility of Jason's suggestion.

Now, as she walked along the shore, alone with her thoughts, Lori was torn about the project. She desperately wanted to discuss it with Jake, but, with the rest of the band camped out in the house, they were unlikely to get time to talk until much later. The mist was beginning to lift and the sun was burning its way through, promising another warm sunny day. Deciding she had walked far enough, Lori turned and began to retrace her steps. Before she was halfway back, she saw a shadow coming towards her through the mist. It was Jake.

"Hey, li'l lady," he said hoarsely. "You're a long way from the house."

"I'm fine," she assured him. "I just needed some fresh air and space to think. I didn't mean to worry you."

"I wasn't worried until I realised how far along the beach you'd walked," said Jake, hugging her tight. "You're almost out as far as the bath house."

"Sorry," she apologised quietly. "How was last night? I saw you brought the boys home."

"We had a good night. Suffice to say we toasted the twins enough to last a while," laughed Jake. "I stopped drinking about midnight, but the rest kept going till about two in the morning. Scott kept throwing up. That's why he ended up outside for the night. They'll all be suffering today."

"And you're not?"

"Maybe a bit," he conceded with a grin. "Now what brought you out here so early?"

"Your snoring," teased Lori playfully, dodging the issue.

"Li'l lady," began Jake seriously. "What's eating at you?"

"Let's sit down for a minute," suggested Lori. "Jason called last night with a business proposal."

"Sounds ominous," commented Jake as he helped her to sit down on the soft sand. "Shoot."

"He wants me to invest in a joint venture with him personally and Jim Marrs. There's a property for sale near here. A house with multiple large outbuildings. I believe it has its own private airstrip too," explained Lori, drawing patterns in the sand with her finger. "The plan is…"

"To turn the outbuildings into a recording studio," finished Jake. "Why did he approach you?"

"Hyde Properties," she replied with a smile. "I've emailed the details to David and agreed to give Jason an answer on Tuesday. The property in question is vacant and, if he can pull the deal together, he wants to exchange contracts on it by the end of next week. He wants it fitted out in time for Silver Lake to record there in June."

"That's a big ask of you."

"But not an impossible one," she answered. "Would you have a problem with Hyde Properties co-owning the studio?"

"Why should I?" Jake asked. "If David thinks it's a sound investment, then that's all it is. It's an investment like any other you make. A business deal."

"I guess," she sighed wistfully. "And you wouldn't feel as if I was stepping on your toes? Interfering with your business?"

"No. Why would I? We'll be in a studio for a month. Maybe six weeks. It'll be hired out to other bands for the rest of the year. There could be money to be made on this deal, Lori."

"That's what Jason is forecasting," she admitted. "He seems to think the secluded location plus on-site accommodation would be its unique selling point."

"If David advises against it, what will you do?"

"I trust his judgement," stated Lori. "If he says no, then there's no deal to be done."

"What's the split? Is it an equal three-way thing?"

"No," replied Lori. "Jason's looking for a forty percent contribution from me. The rest is split equally between him and Jim."

"Does he realise the risk he's taking by putting you in control?" teased Jake, trying to lighten her mood.

"And what's that meant to imply?" she exclaimed, giving him a playful shove.

"Nothing at all, li'l lady," laughed Jake, pulling her closer to him. "Don't stress over this. It's too beautiful a morning to fret about Jason and money."

"You're right," she agreed with a sigh of relief. "We'd better head home and see if our party animals have surfaced yet."

The two sleeping beauties on the deck were still snoring in the morning sunshine when Jake and Lori returned, hand-in-hand. As they entered the house through the sunroom, Paul was beginning to stir on the settee. Fresh coffee aroma was filtering through and they found Rich and Grey sitting at the kitchen table, both of them with their heads resting on their hands.

"You look like the zombies from my last commission," giggled Lori as she poured coffee for herself and Jake.

"I feel like one," groaned Rich, his voice hoarse. "Remind me again why we started doing shots?"

"No idea," muttered Grey. "It was a bad move. A really bad fucking move."

"You're getting no sympathy from me," chastised Lori, tossing a packet of Advil onto the table. "Take two of these then go and walk off your hangovers along the beach."

"Can I lie down and die in the sand?" asked Rich, pressing two of the pills out of the strip.

"If you feel you must," said Lori, trying not to laugh.

Draining the last of his coffee, Grey said, "A walk's probably not a bad idea. Do you mind if I ask my mom to drop Becky off here?"

"Not at all," replied Lori. "Maddy's bringing the twins over later. I'm sure Becky would love to see them again."

"Christ, babies and the hangover from hell," mumbled Rich getting to his feet. "I'm out of here. I'll walk back later for the truck. I'm going to Linsey's to die quietly on her couch."

As Rich closed the back door behind him, Paul came staggering in from the sun room. Pale as a ghost, he started to speak, then dashed towards the bathroom.

"Another casualty?" Lori asked Jake. "What kind of lightweight rock stars did you bring home?"

"They're no lightweights, li'l lady," he laughed as they tried to ignore the retching noises coming from down the hallway. "Celebrating the arrival of twins involves a shit load of tequila."

"You'd better go check on the other two," suggested Lori, with a laugh. "I'm going to get showered and dressed before Maddy gets here."

Midday sun had burnt off the last remnants of the morning's mist and the temperature was starting to climb. Out on the sun deck, Jake had put up the parasol umbrella to create a shady spot for the twins. The BBQ coals were lit and a cooler full of juice and beers had been brought out. Feeling somewhat healthier, Grey had gone down onto the beach with Becky and, from the deck, Lori could hear the little girl laughing as she played Frisbee with her father. In the sunroom, Paul was asleep again on the couch, still suffering from the shots consumed the night before. Both Gary and Scott had left while Lori was in the shower, promising to wander back later on once they had freshened up.

The crunch of car tyres on the gravel out front announced Maddy's arrival just after one. Pausing to rouse Paul on the way through the house, Jake went out to help her in with the twins.

"Lord, what a morning!" declared Maddy as she stepped out onto the deck.

"I'll second that," agreed Lori, hugging her friend.

"Just when I thought we were ready to leave, Hayden threw up everywhere. I had to strip him and start again."

"Like father, like son," quipped Jake as he came out carrying the two car seats with their sleeping occupants.

"Where is father of the year?" asked Maddy looking round.

"Bathroom," replied Jake as he set the babies down gently in the shade.

"Suffering?" Maddy enquired, raising one well plucked eyebrow.

"Most definitely," answered Lori, remembering the sound effects from earlier.

"Hell mend him!" laughed Maddy. "Where's everyone else? I heard they all crashed here."

"Grey's on the beach with Becky," began Jake. "Rich crawled off to die at Linsey's. Our two English friends went home a couple of hours ago, but promised they'd be back later."

"You seem very fresh, Mr Power," observed the band's manager. "No hangover?"

"I skipped the shots competition."

"Ah," nodded Maddy. "Explains it all. Paul and cactus juice

don't go well together."

"Don't let him fool you," interrupted Lori with a mischievous smile. "He was rough this morning too."

The idle banter and friendly, relaxed mood lasted for the rest of the day. Soon Jake had food grilling over the coals and had fetched the girls a drink. Smelling the BBQ, Grey and Becky came back up from the beach. When she saw the babies, Becky squealed in delight, then went to sit in the shade beside them, announcing that she would look after them all day. Eventually Paul ventured out of the house to join them.

"Beer?" offered Jake with a cheeky grin.

"Fuck off," muttered the drummer as he sat on the lounger beside Maddy. "I'm never drinking again."

"Heard it before," laughed Jake, passing his friend a sugar laden soda. "Drink this."

Typically, the twins wakened for a feed just as Maddy had taken the first bite out of her hamburger. As she was about to put her plate down, Jake stopped her. "Where are their bottles? Grey and I'll sort them out. You relax for a while, boss."

"In the black diaper bag. End pockets," replied Maddy, somewhat overwhelmed by the offer. "Thank you."

Taking one baby each, the two musicians disappeared indoors to tend to their feeds. With her eyes wide in wonder, Maddy stared after them.

"They'll be ok," assured Lori softly.

"That just blew me away," breathed Maddy with a smile. "If their fans could see them now."

"It's a good job their fans never saw them first thing this morning," giggled Lori. "Trust me, it wasn't a pretty sight!"

Late afternoon Gary and Scott arrived back at the house, bringing some BBQ supplies with them and a large bunch of flowers for Lori to say thanks for letting them stay the night before. She was touched by the gesture, immediately taking the blooms indoors to find a vase. Much to everyone's relief, Scott had left his video camera at home, but he had brought his stills photography equipment, explaining that he thought Maddy might like some shots of the twins and some family shots. Having been reassured that these were private photographs, Maddy agreed to let him photograph the twins. Both babies were awake and content after being fed by their "Silver Lake uncles" so Scott seized the opportunity to capture the moment. Wren had spat up on Jake's shirt after her feed and he had stripped it off, unable to stomach the sour smell. The first few images that Scott captured were of him with the little girl nuzzled into his bare shoulder. For almost an hour the twins tolerated being passed from person to person to be photographed. At Lori's suggestion, Jake brought out a pile of cushions from the sun room and one of the blankets to create a "nest" for Becky to sit in with both babies. The little girl was thrilled to pose for Scott. Eventually Hayden's patience ran out and he began to holler loudly. Upon hearing her brother cry, Wren joined in.

"Too noisy!" stated Becky with a frown. "Uncle Jake, will you play Frisbee with me?"

"Come on, princess," agreed Jake. "Let's hit the beach."

Hand in hand, Jake and the little girl headed down the path towards the sand. Lifting her screaming son, Maddy nodded to Paul to pick their daughter up. Despite their parents' best endeavours neither baby would settle.

"We'd better head home," began Maddy anxiously. "Before these little monsters out stay their welcome."

"You don't have to rush off," replied Lori. "We've all heard babies cry before."

"Thanks, honey, but I'm getting tired too," confessed Maddy. "It's been fabulous to get out of the house for a while."

"You know you're welcome here anytime."

"I know," said Maddy with a smile as she fastened Hayden into his car seat. "Paul, have you got Wren sorted over there?"

"Almost," he replied as he clicked the harness into place. "Got it!"

While Maddy lifted the diaper bag, Paul lifted both car seats and gently swung them in a final attempt to soothe the twins.

"Lori, can I leave the truck here until tomorrow?" he asked. "I'll be back first thing for rehearsal."

"Leave it as long as you want," declared Lori. "As long as you're not blocking me in."

"No, you're good," he assured her. "Thanks for today."

"See everyone later," called Maddy as she headed off round the side of the house.

As the sun set and more coals were added to the BBQ, conversation inevitably turned to writing, rehearsing and recording. Worn out after playing on the beach, Becky had curled up in the sun room watching cartoons, leaving the adults to talk in peace. Both Jake and Grey were in agreement that the band needed a few sessions together to work on the material they had written so far. It helped that they could email music files to each other, but they really needed to get some quality rehearsal time under their belts.

"How's the schedule looking for the week?" asked Gary as he sipped on a beer.

"I've committed to a two-day workshop at the high school Wednesday and Thursday," replied Jake casually. "I can do evenings those days though. I'm fine for Monday and Tuesday."

"Monday and Tuesday work for me. I'm heading out of town on Friday afternoon," added Grey. "Becky and I are going to my cousin's wedding in Chicago. We'll be back Sunday night."

"Any idea of Rich's plans?"

"He's at the school with me both days," explained Jake. "And if I can talk him into it, I'd like Paul there on Thursday. You too, Grey, if you can spare a few hours."

As he put more burgers on the grill, Jake added, "Two full days should give us a good start here, Gary. There's no need to panic yet."

"I know," replied the band's manager. "Do you need me out here this week?"

"Well, "suggested Grey. "Why don't we all meet on Friday morning for a couple of hours to review where we're at?"

"Fine by me," acknowledged Jake, flipping the burgers over. "Lori, are you ok with all of this?"

"Sure," she answered with a smile. "I'm not cooking for you all though. I've work to get on with too. Deadlines to meet."

"We'll take care of ourselves, li'l lady," promised her fiancé.

"Just keep the coffee pot filled, Lori," teased Grey. "We're all going to need it!"

"Not a problem."

♫

An immense creative cloud covered the house for the next forty-eight hours as Silver Lake ensconced themselves in the basement studio, while Lori worked in her own small studio space. Both projects progressed rapidly. Silver Lake pulled together seven definite tracks to put towards the new album from the stockpile of ideas they had gathered. Lori worked on her additional skeletal zombie pieces, occasionally drawing her inspiration from the snatches of powerful, heavy rock music blasting up from the basement. On the whole, she kept out of the band's way while they were working, but there were points during the day when she would meet one or other of them in the kitchen or they would pop by her workspace to ask her a question. Late on Tuesday afternoon, Todd, Jake's protégé, arrived at the house. When Lori explained that the band were rehearsing, he said that Jake had called him to come over. Without a backwards glance, he too disappeared down into the basement.

Eventually, well after dark, the band plus Todd came stomping up from the basement, all debating whether one band was better than another. They drifted into the kitchen and, from her drawing board, Lori could hear them cracking open the beers and debating what to do about dinner.

"Lori!" called Jake loudly. "Have you eaten dinner yet?"

"No," she called back, as she slid her chair back and got stiffly to her feet. "Are you sending out for food?"

"I was going to run into town for it," shouted Paul. "What do you feel like?"

"Anything," stated Lori as she joined them in the kitchen. "A beer would be a good start."

Passing her a cold bottle of beer, Jake said, "What about Chinese?"

Everyone agreed and, as Paul scribbled down a note of what they all wanted, Lori noticed Todd standing quietly in the background. He hadn't stated a preference yet. After another moment or two, Lori said quietly, "Todd, what about you?"

"I'd better head back to Kate's," he began awkwardly.

"Stay for dinner, kid," instructed Grey sternly. "You've earned a free meal and a beer today."

"Ok, but I don't want to intrude," he replied, still looking out of place in the midst of the older musicians.

"What do you want, Todd?" asked Jake warmly.

"Some Hong Kong style shrimp and noodles would be great," answered the younger man shyly. "I can't stay long though. I've an assignment to finish for the morning."

"We'll have you home for ten," promised Jake. "What subject?"

"American History."

"Is that all the orders?" asked Paul as he wrestled the truck keys out of his pocket.

"Don't forget the fortune cookies," called Lori.

"Won't be long, folks."

While the Silver Lake drummer was fetching dinner, the others spilled through into the sunroom, continuing the music band debate from earlier. Leaving them to it, Lori went through to set the table in the dining room.

"Need a hand, Miss Hyde?"

The voice behind her startled her.

"Thanks, Todd," she replied. "And it's Lori. Can you fetch some napkins from the kitchen? They're on the countertop near the coffee pot."

"Sure. Anything else?"

"No, that's all, I think," she answered. "I've already put some plates in the oven to heat."

A few seconds later he was back with the napkins. The teenager still seemed a little awkward and nervous.

"How are things, Todd?" asked Lori softly. "You ok? You seem a bit out of sorts."

"Things are ok, I guess," replied the boy. "Kate's folks are great. It's just not home. I tried to talk to my mom at the weekend, but she blew me out."

"That's not so good," said Lori taking a seat at the table. "Is school still ok?"

"School's great. Work's fine. Mr Power, I mean, Jake's been really cool," he began taking a seat beside her.

"But something's missing?"

The boy nodded.

"I'm not sure Jake or I can help. Would it help if he tried to talk to your mom? Tried to mediate?" suggested Lori, out of her depth with the subject of teenager versus parent.

"I doubt it," he said sadly. "She's given notice on the apartment and moves to Atlanta next month."

"Without you?"

"Yup," stated Todd, forcing a smile. "Sucks, doesn't it?"

"How long can you stay at Kate's for?"

"I don't know. Things are a bit tense between me and her. If we break up, I don't know what will happen."

"Have you applied for the college course we were talking about?"

"Yes," he replied instantly. "And I don't know how that's going to work out either. I need to talk to the school about it. I'm not sure I'll be able to afford the tuition if I get in."

Their heart to heart was interrupted by Paul as he arrived back with a large box of food.

The interrupted conversation with Todd was still preying on Lori's mind when she went to bed that night. Beside her, Jake was lying propped up on the pillows reading a magazine. Hard as she tried to concentrate on her book, Lori couldn't shake the image of Todd's anxious face as he'd explained his predicament.

"Hey, li'l lady," began Jake quietly, putting the magazine on the night stand. "What's eating at you?"

"Todd," she replied flatly. "I was talking to him earlier, while Paul was away for the food. The kid's worried. Did you know his mom's moving away?"

"Without him?" asked Jake sharply.

Lori nodded. "She's going to Atlanta."

"He never said. I put him to work as soon as he arrived. I never really spoke to him today."

"Are the band going to hire him as part of the crew?" Lori asked, closing her book and laying it aside.

"I spoke to Gary about it, but he couldn't promise much," admitted Jake. "I was thinking about paying him myself. He's a good kid."

"I was having a similar thought," confessed Lori. "I'd like to sponsor him through college if he gets accepted for the course. But, if you guys employ him, he might not go to school."

"I hear what you're saying," said Jake seriously. "What if we made getting into school a condition of summer employment with the band?"

"That might work," she agreed. "Can you talk to him? Find out how much his tuition fees will be, living expenses and things like that. Get me a ball park figure and I'll set something up with David."

"I'll see what I can do, but, if he feels this is charity, he might refuse it."

"Fair point. It's up to you to sell it to him in the right manner. Lay down some ground rules if need be," said Lori. "I just want to help him out. He deserves a break."

Reaching out to hug her, Jake said, "You are too soft hearted sometimes."

"Maybe."

"Don't ever change, li'l lady," he said, kissing her gently. "I love you. Soft heart and all."

"Oh, while I remember," she began. "I spoke to David earlier. He's sending an architect out next week to look into converting the attic. He also said the studio idea looked to be a potential gold mine."

"He did?"

"Yes. I called Jason to say to count me in."

"Why didn't you say earlier?"

"I wanted to tell you before the others heard," she explained, kissing him softly. "You're sure you're ok with it?"

"I told you I was. It's just a business deal, Lori," he said, pulling her close to him. "Just don't let Jason and Dr Marrs railroad you."

"I won't," she promised. "I'm not putting this in Hyde Properties name though. It'll be in my own name."

"Whatever David has advised is good for me," assured Jake. "Will it be ready for us to record in?"

"Jason seems pretty confident it will," she said. "Time will tell."

Time seemed to fly by, as April moved swiftly into May. Silver

Lake, or various parts of the group, spent several hours most days down in the basement working on material for the new record. Like the late spring weather, sometimes temperatures and tempers ran high and at other points things were quite cool. Two or three times a week, Todd would come over after school and, on Jake's instruction, split his time between chores round the property and time down in the studio with the band. In preparation for the boy's intended college course, the band were trying to involve him in the more technical aspects of their job. The teenager was a magician at tuning guitars and setting them up. It was a natural talent that never ceased to amaze all the members of Silver Lake. Having bided his time and chosen his moment carefully, Jake had finally spoken to him about sponsoring him through college. Tears of relief and gratitude flowed freely down the boy's cheeks as he gratefully accepted the generous offer. Together with Lori, they spent time working out the costs of the sponsorship. With an educational trust fund set up, Todd promised faithfully to give his total commitment to the course and to Silver Lake over the summer.

While the band were pulling everything together, Lori was kept fully occupied. The architect that David had sourced visited the beach house in early May, listened to what she hoped to achieve and said he would go and see what designs he could come up with. In theory, he hoped it would be possible, but he was concerned about the amount of glass Lori was hoping to put in, commenting that there may be structural issues with the weight. He left, promising to get back in touch by the end of the month. Plans for the studio were moving at a far faster pace. All the paperwork and contracts were completed by the 10th May and the contractors started work on the 13th. Their deadline for completing the main recording studio was the 7th of June, with the band scheduled to start work with Dr Marrs three days later. A second, smaller rehearsal studio was planned and the house required a degree of upgrading too. The target completion date for the whole project was mid-September. Leaving Jason and Jim Marrs to decide on the structural and technical aspects of the project, Lori was tasked with selecting interior décor and artwork for both studios and the house, plus the design of the logo. After a lengthy debate on the name, they had finally agreed to keep it simple – JJL Studios.

Aside from these projects, Lori spent her time between her Mz Hyde commissions and in visiting Maddy. The friends met up twice a week for lunch and the occasional shopping trip. Despite adoring motherhood, as the weeks wore on and work with the band gathered speed, Lori could sense her friend's growing frustration at being on the periphery of the business end of things. On one of Gary's regular trips out to the beach house, Lori cornered him and asked if he could catch up with Maddy to keep her in the loop. At first he had been very defensive, but quickly warmed to the idea when Lori reminded him of the extensive network of contacts Maddy had, especially in relation to the summer rock festivals.

Mid-May, Jake and Rich had run another two-day workshop out at the high school. The first one the previous month had been deemed a huge success and had seen them put together two rock bands, comprising of various junior and senior students. Not surprisingly, Todd was playing lead guitar with one, while Kate was nominated as lead singer. The second workshop was a follow up with the same group of students, this time with the aim being to get them prepared for a charity fundraiser event at the school. As the two former teachers were packing up on the Friday evening, the school principal, Dr Jones, came into the music department looking for them. After exchanging pleasantries, he cut to the chase.

"We need something to get people engaged with this fundraiser. I was wondering if you could both perhaps perform for us?"

"Not the whole group?" asked Rich curiously.

"My thinking was to keep it linked with the workshops you've done," began Dr Jones a little awkwardly. "Perhaps a more acoustic performance on this occasion?"

With a smile, Jake said, "I get it. More melody, less noise?"

Laughing to cover his embarrassment, the principal confessed that he had hit the nail on the head.

"We'd need to clear it with the others," said Rich, not wanting to offend their fellow band members. "But we should be able to do something."

"Even if you could perform half a dozen songs it would help sell tickets."

"Are you auctioning anything on the evening to raise more funds for the charity?" asked Jake as he fastened his guitar case.

"We're starting to gather a few items together. If you can donate any items that would be fantastic."

"Sure," agreed Rich. "That's not a problem at all. We can even throw in a couple of one hour guitar lessons."

"Perfect," declared Dr Jones, relieved that they were supportive of the event. "And if Miss Hyde wants to contribute anything…"

"I'll ask her," promised Jake. "Now we'd better make a move. What date is the fundraiser?"

"June 7th."

"Ok," nodded Rich. "We'll get back to you next week to firm up the arrangements."

"Thanks, boys."

"Pleasure as always, sir," added Jake as they prepared to leave.

When the rest of the band heard the proposal for the charity fundraiser, Paul and Grey were more than happy to let Jake and Rich take to the stage without them. All four of them agreed to donate an hour's music tuition as an auction item and to throw in a Silver Lake goody bag, including a signed guitar as a further item. When Jake told Lori about the event, she too agreed to donate a piece of artwork to the cause.

The day of the school fundraiser dawned warm and clear. With their album rehearsals more or less complete, the band had agreed to take a few days off before relocating to the newly completed JJL Studio. Not wanting to waste a minute of the beautiful morning, Jake set out on a long run along the beach before breakfast. The fresh, sea air was good for his soul and, as he pounded his way along the shore, his mind thought on ahead to the set list for the evening. It had been almost four months since they had last played live and far longer since either he or Rich had done an acoustic set. Originally they had agreed to perform half a dozen numbers, but, after a bit of persuading, Dr Jones had talked them up to ten songs that should take them about an hour to perform. The two student bands that they had helped to form would each play for half an hour, with an auction slot between them, then there would be a second slot before Jake and Rich played, with a final silent auction for the major items at the end of the evening. If the update Rich had had from Linsey was accurate, tickets had sold out and the fund raising target was ten thousand dollars. A steep ask for the school, but one that would benefit local charity groups.

As he jogged back to the house, Jake spotted Lori walking along the sand towards him. The ocean breeze was catching her hair and it was flying in the wind like golden silk threads.

"Morning, li'l lady," he called, flashing her a smile. "You ok?"

"Fine. Just felt like some fresh air before I sit down to finish off the piece I'm working on," replied Lori, taking his sweaty hand. "Are you ready for tonight?"

"More or less," he answered. "I've to meet Rich at the school for a run through at two."

"I'm looking forward to it," she confessed. "It's been a while since I saw you on stage."

"It'll be good to get up there again," commented Jake. "I miss playing live."

"How many are going to this tonight?"

"I'm not sure. Around one fifty I'd guess."

"A small, select audience," she teased, squeezing his hand.

"There better not be any heckling from your table, Mz Hyde."

"Never," she promised with a giggle.

"And no bidding for auction items you don't need," he cautioned.

"We'll see about that."

By seven o'clock, the school hall was beginning to fill with guests. Jake and Lori had arrived shortly after six thirty to give Jake time to warm up before he was due out on stage. When they arrived, Rich was already sitting at their table beside Linsey. After delivering a swift kiss to her cheek, Jake had left Lori with the couple and disappeared off towards the music department. Both Grey and Paul were coming along, as was Maddy. Grey's mother had offered to watch Becky and the twins to allow the new parents to attend the event. Gary and Scott had also bought tickets, then, as a last minute addition, Dr Marrs had been invited along. He had arrived in town a couple of days before to supervise the finishing touches being put to the JJL Studio and had donated ten hours of studio time along with his services as an extra auction item when he heard about the fundraiser.

A few minutes after Lori had settled herself at the table, Grey arrived with Scott, Gary and Dr Marrs. He apologised that Maddy and Paul were running a little late but were on their way.

"I think this is their first night out since the meatballs arrived," Lori observed. "Maddy'll be a wreck about leaving them."

"Paul sounded a wreck when he called to say they'd be late," laughed Grey. "He's worse than the boss is."

While Grey and Gary went to fetch them some drinks, Dr Marr's asked Lori if she had been out to see the studio.

"I was out last week when they put the signage up," she replied. "It's looking great. Are you staying at the house?"

"Not till the end of next week. No water," replied the producer. "I'm at the hotel on the highway. The one where the last record's launch party was."

"Oh, I know it well!" giggled Lori. "Maddy practically lived there for months!"

"It's fine for a week or so."

"I guess," she agreed before adding, "I've still got the artwork for the studio lounge out at the beach house. Do you want Jake to bring it in on Monday? Or you can come over to pick it up over the weekend, if you'd prefer?"

"I could pick it up tomorrow afternoon," he replied. "I've no plans for the weekend."

"Come over for lunch," invited Lori warmly.

As the boys returned with their drinks, Paul and Maddy arrived. They had all just taken their seats when the lights dimmed and the school principal stepped out on stage.

"Welcome, ladies and gentlemen, to our annual charity auction," he began, the microphone crackling loudly. "This year we've set things up a little differently. There will be three musical interludes and three auction slots. There will also be two short intermissions to allow you to refill your glasses. Without further ado, let me introduce you to the first act of the evening. Please welcome on stage Candy Apple!"

The audience clapped politely, as the first of the two student groups came nervously out onto the stage. As she scanned their pale, anxious faces, Lori didn't recognise any of them. When they started to play, their nerves slowly vanished and they performed a solid set of five well known pop and rock songs. Dr Marrs was soon tapping his foot in time to the music, but, in stark contrast, Maddy had her unimpressed face on.

"They're only kids," whispered Lori to her friend between songs. "You're not here scouting for talent."

"I'm always keeping an eye out for talent," confessed Maddy quietly. "Old habits die hard."

When Candy Apple finished their last song, the audience cheered and clapped loudly. One table were on their feet, whistling, much to the young band's acute embarrassment.

As they left the stage, Dr Jones returned to the centre spot and began the evening's first auction segment. The first five lots included vouchers for some of the stores in town and culminated in a voucher for a dinner for two at the local steakhouse. As the bids for this item topped one hundred dollars, Maddy placed a high bid of two fifty.

"Sold to the lady on my right," declared Dr Jones proudly. "And thank you for your generosity."

There was a polite round of applause from the audience.

"Now for our second musical performance. I'd like to welcome out on stage Hunt 'Em Down!" announced the principal with a theatrical flourish.

Again the lights dimmed and, under cover of darkness, the band took their places. When the lights went up, Lori instantly recognised Todd and Kate and the song. It was Silver Lake's Dragon Song. The Silver Lake party gave them a huge cheer as Kate stepped up to the mic.

"Now, there's potential there," commented Maddy as Hunt 'Em Down began their second song. "The girl's great, but that boy on lead guitar has real talent."

"Jake's protégé," explained Lori with a wink. "We saw him first. I'm sponsoring him through college."

"And," added Grey leaning into their conversation. "He's Jake's guitar tech for the summer."

"Oh!" gasped Maddy somewhat taken aback. "Guess I missed the memo on that one."

Hunt 'Em Down played three more hard rock classics before finishing with a more gentle version of Bon Jovi's Wanted Dead Or Alive. As Todd played the guitar intro flawlessly, Maddy nodded her approval to Lori. The boy was good, very good. Kate's voice had a husky warmth to it that lent itself perfectly to the song. Everyone in the hall was on their feet, cheering, as their short set ended. Before the band had a chance to leave the stage, Dr Jones stepped out and asked, "Who wants to hear these guys play one more?"

The crowd's reaction left the young band in no doubt. With a few quickly whispered thoughts and nods, they reached agreement about what to play and Kate stepped back up to the microphone.

"Thank you," she said humbly. "This is something we've been practicing. This is Patti Smith's Because The Night."

Again, when the song was over, the small crowd were on their feet applauding loudly. In a theatrical gesture, Kate made a deep curtsey with imaginary skirts and called out, "Thank you, one and all, and good night."

There was a few moments delay while they set up the second auction slot. Dr Marrs nudged Lori and asked, "Can you send them to see me?"

"I'll speak to Jake about it. Impressed?"

"Very," he nodded. "I'm tempted to buy back my own auction lot just to get them into the studio with me."

Lori laughed before adding," Let's see what happens on that one."

The second auction slot included slightly more diverse items for sale. Gary put in the winning bid on a day's fishing trip while Lori was the winner of a two-hour slot at Danny's tattoo parlour. When the others quizzed her about it, she just giggled before confessing to having a design in mind. The last item was a limited edition skateboard and Scott put in the winning bid at the last moment for it. This prompted a round of teasing from Grey and Paul, followed by a caution from Gary to be careful.

After a short interval, the principal took to the stage to introduce the final musical segment of the evening.

"I mean this from the bottom of my heart," he began warmly. "I really am delighted to welcome back two former colleagues and friends. These guys have given up their precious free time to coach the two groups you heard earlier and have also worked tirelessly behind the scenes tonight. Calming nerves. Tuning guitars. Re-stringing one, I believe, at very short notice. Now it's their turn to perform for you. From local and international rock sensation Silver Like, I'm delighted to welcome Jake Power and Rich Santiago out on stage."

As the small crowd applauded enthusiastically, Jake and Rich stepped out from either side of the stage. Two stools had been set up, with their guitars on stands at the side of their respective seats. Settling himself on the stool and adjusting the microphone to the correct height, Jake said, "It's nice to be back on stage and to be invited along tonight. It's been a while so bear with us, folks."

The crowd cheered again.

"We're going to play a mix of our own music and some other stuff. Some old, some newer songs. We'll even throw in a few personal favourites. We'd like to start with one of Rich's favourites. This is a Guns 'n' Roses' song. Patience."

Rich began the intro and the small audience cheered approvingly. The duo followed their opening number with two more well-known rock cover versions. Everyone in the hall was hanging on their every note.

"You still with us?" asked Jake as he changed guitar.

"We sure are!" yelled someone from the back of the hall.

"Ok," laughed Jake, settling himself back into position. "Now, can you guys keep a secret?"

There was a loud chorus of "yeah"

"Well, this next song is brand new," continued Jake. "We're working on a new album and this looks likely to be on there. This is Same Day New Life."

At the Silver Lake table, Maddy and Lori exchanged glances, while Grey and Paul smiled conspiratorially. A soft, delicate melody drifted out across the hall, then Rich came in and the new song took a different turn. Jake's vocal was slightly lower in his range than normal, but was crystal clear. As they listened to the words, Lori saw Maddy reach for a tissue. Tears were flowing freely down her cheeks as she listened to the boys singing about the twins' arrival into this cold, harsh, tortured world. It was the first time Lori could remember seeing her friend so overcome with the emotion of a song.

"Maddison," said Jake warmly when the song was over. "That one's for you."

From the stage, he could just make her out and was as surprised as Lori to see her crying. Part of him felt guilty, but another part was flattered to see that she had felt the emotion that had gone into their new acoustic, rock lullaby.

"Another favourite," continued Jake. "One of the first songs I ever learned how to play. This is Maggie May."

They followed the Rod Stewart classic with two more of their own, then declared that their final song for the night would be Simple Man, a Lynyrd Skynyrd classic. This was one of Lori's personal favourites and she usually only heard Jake sing it in the car. Seeing him on stage, lost in the song, was a beautiful sight. Beside her, Maddy had regained her composure and she leaned over to whisper, "I'd almost forgotten just how good Jake was. They've been fantastic tonight."

"Long way from Surfside," mused Lori quietly, smiling proudly at her fiancé's performance.

Before the song was fully over, the whole hall was on its feet, clapping and cheering wildly, crying for more. On stage, Rich and Jake exchanged a few words, then Jake leaned forward.

"Thank you," he said, gazing round the hall. "If it's ok with Dr Jones, we'll play two more."

The principal, who was seated at the table in front of the stage, shouted up, "It's fine by me."

"Ok, two more it is," agreed Jake. "Last time we played here was a special night for Rich and I and the rest of the band. It was also a special night for me on a personal level. This song is what made it. Lori, this is for you. Wonderful Tonight."

Now it was Lori's turn to feel her emotions begin to get the better of her. Tears welled up in her eyes as she subconsciously fingered her engagement ring. Throughout the song, Jake barely took his eyes off her, both of them lost in memories of their dance at the school's Christmas social and Jake's proposal.

"Now this really is our final number," called out Jake. "A Silver Lake show always ends with Flyin' High!"

Despite cries for more, Rich and Jake took a final bow at the end of Flyin' High and, leaving their guitars on stage, both jumped down and went to join the Silver Lake table. As they made their way across the hall, several members of the audience stopped them to congratulate them or to shake their hands. Still smiling and on an adrenalin high, Jake hugged Lori tight as he sat beside her.

"Love you, rock star," she whispered, kissing him on the cheek.

"That was a blast," declared Rich, still grinning like a big kid.

"You guys were fabulous," conceded Paul as Grey nodded in agreement. "We hate you for it."

Laughter erupted around the table, causing most of the audience to turn round to see what the joke was.

Up on stage, Dr Jones was standing ready to commence the final auction segment of the evening. Several members of staff were circulating the hall, placing bundles of envelopes, sheets of paper and pens on each table.

"Now, ladies and gentlemen, how do I follow that?" declared the principal. "Let's have another round of applause for Rich and Jake."

He didn't have to ask them twice. Cheers echoed round the hall and, in their seats, both musicians blushed in embarrassment, feeling humbled by the reception they had received. As the applause died away, Dr Jones continued, "The last section of the evening will take the form of a silent auction for our more valuable and prized lots. Some of the items are on display at the back of the room and there's a full list on each table. Please place your bids by writing the amount you wish to bid and your name on a piece of paper, sealing it in an envelope. On the envelope, please write the lot number. Bidding will be open for the next fifteen minutes."

There followed a flurry of activity for the next few minutes as people moved around the hall, either to view the items on display or to replenish their glasses. A couple of members of staff came over to talk to Jake and Rich. Having been seated all evening, Lori took the opportunity to stretch her legs and wandered to the back of the hall to browse the display of lots. Her own two small drawings were on display and appeared to be attracting a lot of attention. Some of the senior pupils were eyeing up the signed Silver Lake guitar.

"Are you going to bid on anything?" a voice asked from behind her. It was Jim Marrs.

"I think so," she replied. "Are you?"

"Maybe," he answered with a shy smile. "I love your pieces. Different."

"Thank you," she blushed. "I didn't think they were ready for some of my "rock" pieces."

"Seriously. Those are stunning."

From the stage, Dr Jones called out a five-minute warning and asked for all bids to be placed in the red, plastic crate sitting on the stage. When bidding closed, and the box had been taken away to be sorted, the principal announced a special musical extra from a newly formed super group. Excusing themselves, the four members of Silver Lake headed off towards the stage. A few minutes later, the lights dimmed in the hall and the stage lit up to reveal the two student bands plus Silver Lake lined up and ready to play.

"Folks, this is genuinely unrehearsed," called out Jake. "Tonight wouldn't have been possible without "A Little Help from My Friends". Feel free to join in."

It was the perfect song choice for the impromptu musical finale and the audience lapped it up, singing along from the start to the finish. The professional musicians were happy to take a back seat and let the students finish the song off.

While the applause from the crowd was still echoing round the hall, Dr Jones came back in, clutching two sheets of paper.

"Ladies and gentlemen, our very own super group!" he yelled. "Fantastic!"

The cheering continued, along with some rowdy whistling from Gary and Scott.

"Now, we've the winners of the silent auction to announce then I'll reveal the grand total raised this evening."

Quickly he rattled through the list of winning bidders. Lori listened out to see who were the new owners of her two drawings but she didn't recognise the names. The autographed guitar went to the head of the music department, while Kate's dad won the one-hour lesson with Rich. The singer/guitarist with Candy

Apple was awarded the lesson with Jake, thanks to a generous bid by their parents. One of the maths teachers won the lesson with Paul, while the school secretary won the lesson with Grey for her son. When Dr Jones saw the winner of the studio slot, he raised an eyebrow towards the Silver Lake table and nodded approvingly. Lori had submitted the winning bid in the name of Hunt 'Em Down. At the side of the hall, the young band looked stunned by the generosity.

"Thank you, ladies and gentlemen," said Dr Jones, folding the sheets of paper. "We set our target for the evening at ten thousand dollars. Our final total is an incredible twenty-one thousand four hundred and thirty-three."

More applause drowned out his final words of thanks and all the audience were able to hear was "Good night and a safe trip home."

Darkness blanketed the beach house. Lori entered the sun room, carefully setting the open bottle of wine and the glasses down on the floor, before switching on the lamp. While Jake brought his guitars in from the car, she poured them both a glass of Chardonnay then curled up on the couch to wait for him. A few moments later, Jake wandered in, carrying his acoustic guitar, his baby. Setting it down against the couch, he sat on the floor in front of Lori and lifted his glass.

"To you, li'l lady. For tonight," he toasted. "You made those kids very happy."

Taking a sip of her wine first, Lori replied, "It wasn't much. They deserve a chance."

"How much did you bid for that studio time?"

"Enough," she responded with a giggle. "More than I bid for the tattoo appointment with Danny."

"Yes, Mz Hyde," teased her fiancé. "I heard a rumour about that. Pray tell?"

"My lips are sealed," she giggled.

"Now, where are you planning to ink this time?" asked Jake, kneeling round to face her. Slowly, he reached out and took the glass out of her hand. Placing it to one side, he reached up and lifted her down onto the floor beside him. His long, warm, slender hands raised her top up, then he delivered feathery kisses to the base of her spine.

"Here, perhaps?" he murmured, as he slipped the silky top over her head. "Or here?" as he kissed the nape of her neck.

"Not even close, rock star," whispered Lori, running her fingers through his long, blonde, tousled hair.

With one swift move, Jake had lifted her again and laid her down on her back on the Oriental rug. The button fly of her jeans was no challenge to his nimble fingers and, within seconds, her jeans lay up on the couch. Gently, he ran his fingers over her hip bones.

"Am I getting warm yet?"

"No," purred Lori, small electric shocks of pleasure shooting through her as he touched her bare skin. His left hand lingered a few moments on the silvery scar on her soft, pale skin.

Sitting back on his heels, Jake smiled down at her as she lay on the rug, wearing only her pale pink bra and lace panties. Her long, blonde hair was fanned out behind her, spread out like a golden halo. No matter how many times he saw her naked, her beauty took his breath away. Feeling his erection straining against his jeans, Jake bent and tenderly kissed her knees then her ankles. Beneath his caresses, Lori let out a low moan of anticipation.

"Warm yet?" he enquired, as he kissed the tips of her painted toes.

Lori nodded, purring in contentment.

"Left foot?" Jake guessed as he ran a finger over her small, slender foot.

"Yes," whispered Lori, before adding, "But I'm not saying what just yet."

"Now, can I collect my reward?"

"Yes, you may, rock star."

Jake needed no second invitation. He slipped his T-shirt off over his head then stood up to remove his jeans and boxer shorts. Naked, he towered over Lori as she lay perfectly still on the rug. Kneeling down, then straddling her, Jake pulled her up into a sitting position, kissed her shoulder, then unhooked her bra, tossing it up onto the couch. Running his hands teasingly down her sides, he paused when he reached the thin waistband of her panties then slide them down, discarding them on the floor. He gently feathered her breasts with kisses, pausing to suck hard on her nipples. Feeling her body shudder with pleasure, he ran his tongue slowly across her flat stomach. Beneath him, Lori moaned softly, arching herself up to meet him. Painstakingly slowly, he fingered the nub of her clitoris before thrusting his erect manhood deep into her moist feminine depths. Lori sighed as he began to move in long, slow rhythmic strokes. In an attempt to prolong their mutual pleasure, Jake made love to her slowly, teasing her body to the point of orgasm. Eventually he couldn't hold back any longer and thrust hard and fast inside her. Entwined together, they spiralled into previously hidden depths of sexual ecstasy.

Wrapped in a soft fleecy blanket, both still naked underneath, they sat sipping their wine and began to talk over the plans for the coming weeks. First thing on Monday, the band were due in the studio to start recording. Six long weeks out at JJL lay before them; six short weeks at home before they started the rock festival season.

"Any chance of getting Todd's group on stage this summer?" asked Lori sleepily.

"Maybe. There's a couple of radio station beach parties they may be able to play at. It's very early days for them. I don't want to push them too far, too fast plus I need Todd to be free to come out with us."

"True," yawned Lori, resting her head on her fiancé's shoulder.

"Come on, li'l lady," he whispered as she dozed off. "Time for bed."

♫

Stepping into the newly completed JJL Studio One brought out the inner children in Silver Lake. Everything was brand new state of the art and they all wanted to touch everything. A surprise awaited them as Dr Marrs gave them the tour of the facilities. In the lounge, reclined on one of the soft, leather chairs, was a young woman with the longest dark brown hair any of them had seen.

"Let me introduce you to your sound engineer," said Dr Marrs with a grin. "This is Kola. She's been working with me for the past few months."

Standing up to greet the band, Kola smiled before saying a rather shy, "Hello."

"No need to be shy, sweetheart," said Rich shaking her hand. "We don't bite."

The girl blushed scarlet, glancing across at Jim Marrs for reassurance.

"The boys will be gentle with you," he promised warmly. "Why don't you all get to know each other over a coffee, then we can plan out the day?"

Over coffee, the young engineer relaxed a little and, after a barrage of gentle teasing from Paul, she began to chat with the members of Silver Lake without blushing. When they finally moved from the lounge into the studio, Jake asked her how long she'd been working for Dr Marrs.

"Six months. I was in LA for two years after college," she replied, her voice husky and warm, suggesting perhaps that she was a regular smoker.

"It's a bit quieter round here than in LA," laughed Jake.

"I'm based in Philly, so I can get my city fix," she replied. "I'm sharing an apartment with my brother while I'm here."

"That's a fair commute," he mused.

"It's not so bad. I like the solitude of the road on my bike," she answered.

"Bike?"

"I ride a Harley," revealed Kola smiling up at him. "It's parked out back."

"Guess, this is going to be a day of surprises," laughed Jake, lifting his black Gibson Les Paul out if its case. Turning to the others, he declared, "Let's get this party started!"

Silver Lake's week in the studio was relaxed- the calm before the storm. Teething problems blighted them for a day or two, but they worked their way patiently through them. By the end of the first week, they had played all of their new material through for Dr Marrs. He had listened to it all and recorded demos of each track before calling them back to the start. Song by song, he took each one back to its bare skeleton, then began to rebuild them, suggesting improvements to their arrangements, tweaks to the tempo, alterations to the timing. At times, it was hard for the band not to get too defensive, too protective of their new material. Past experience told them all that the producer knew his stuff and, having worked with them all before, he knew what they were capable of.

It was late on Friday night before they had the recording schedule mapped out on the board. Some of the tracks were in doubt but, for now, Dr Marrs had included them in the plans. In the corner of the studio there was a white board that had been gridded out by Kola while they had debated and now it listed all the songs and tracking to be completed. Seeing it sitting there, blank apart from the working titles of the fifteen songs, served as a stark reminder to the band of the amount of work to be done.

"Right, guys," declared Dr Marrs as they packed up for the night. "Let's take a breather for the weekend. Paul, I want you and Grey here early on Monday. We start with you guys. Rich, can you re-work the solos on tracks four, eight and eleven. I'm still not convinced about those. Jake, lyrics for twelve and fifteen. Park what you have. We need something dark. Something evil. Haunted."

"Yes, boss," muttered Rich under his breath.

"Do you need Rich and I out here at the start of the week?" asked Jake with a yawn. "If not, we can work together back at the house."

"Up to yourselves. Plenty space here for you to work. If I don't see you before it, I want you here on Wednesday," said the producer. "Jason's dropping by for a "royal visit." We need to look good."

"Ok," agreed Jake, lifting his book bag and two of his guitars. "I'm out of here."

Bright sunlight flooded the bedroom when Lori finally roused herself from sleep on Sunday morning. Instantly she knew she had slept late, but, if a girl couldn't have a long lie on her birthday, when could she? A single red rose lay on the night stand beside the bed with a small white card underneath it. On the card there were written a series of musical notes and the words "Happy Birthday, li'l lady. J x" The night before, both of them had worked on until after midnight, hence the lie in. One of Lori's deadlines had been pulled forward, causing her to work flat out for three days solid, trying to cram two weeks of work into the tight timeframe

Pulling on one of Jake's discarded T-shirts, Lori lifted the rose and wandered through to the kitchen to put it in some water. A bud vase, already filled with water, was sitting on the counter and under it was another card. This time, the card had the same musical notes drawn on it but there was also a picture of the sun. Curious, Lori placed the flower in the vase, then limped through to the sun room. Silence was filling the house and she felt confident that she was alone. In the sun room, one of the small occasional tables had been moved to the centre of the room and, in the centre of the table, was a vase with eleven red roses and another card – more musical notes and a champagne glass plus a small pile of sand drizzled on top. With a smile, Lori headed bare foot across the deck to the edge of the path then down to the beach.

She spotted Jake immediately. Without pausing to dress or to fetch her cane, Lori very carefully made her way across the hot, soft sand towards her fiancé. As she drew closer, she saw he had a champagne picnic brunch all laid out on a rug for them. He was sitting with his back to her, facing the ocean and was quietly playing his favourite acoustic guitar.

"Hi," said Lori softly as she reached the edge of the picnic blanket.

"Good morning, li'l lady," said Jake turning to face her. Carefully, he laid the guitar in its case and got gracefully to his feet. In two strides, he was beside her and had wrapped his arms around her waist. "Happy birthday, beautiful."

"Thank you," she said with a bright smile. "I never expected this."

"That was the general idea," replied Jake, taking her by the hand and helping her to sit down on the soft blanket. While Lori settled herself, Jake popped the cork on the bottle of champagne, firing it off towards the ocean. Bubbles flowed over the rim of the bottle as he poured them each a glass.

Passing her a half full glass, he said, "Here's to many more birthdays, li'l lady."

"To us," she toasted, raising her glass to meet his.

Spread out on the rug was an array of pastries, croissants, fruit, yoghurt and cheese. Nibbling on a croissant, Lori asked, "When did you find time to organise all of this?"

"I had a little help," confessed Jake, looking a little sheepish. "I got Todd to collect the food for me. He dropped it off on his way to work this morning. I had the roses delivered yesterday and just prayed you didn't come down into the basement."

"Thank you," she whispered again with a shy smile. "This is wonderful."

"Nice to see you dressed for the occasion," teased Jake, noticing she was wearing only his Led Zeppelin T-shirt.

Blushing, Lori admitted, "Curiosity got the better of decency." Sub-consciously her hand moved to cover the exposed scars on her thigh.

"Good job it wasn't a surprise party with fifty guests."

Laughing her wonderful musical laugh, Lori had to agree with him.

After they had both eaten their fill and drunk most of the champagne, Jake lifted his guitar out of its case, adjusted the tuning then turned to face her. "This is part of your present. I hope you like it."

Lying reclined on her side with her head propped up on her hand, Lori listened as he began to play a delicate, almost country style, introduction. Softly, his voice barely more than a whisper at times, Jake sang to her of love and determination, of inner strength and outer beauty. Tears welled up in her eyes as the words touched her heart. The song perfectly reflected the battles she had faced over the previous eighteen months. By the time he finished the song, a large tear had escaped and was gliding down her cheek.

Reaching to brush it away with his thumb, Jake said, "I didn't mean to make you cry, li'l lady."

"That was beautiful," she said with a sigh. "Perfect."

"And it was just for you and I," he said kissing her gently. "It's too personal to share with the band."

"Thank you."

"Now I hate to break up a party, but," began Jake, checking the time. "You might want to go and get dressed. We're expecting company."

"We are?" Lori asked, looking surprised.

"Yes," said Jake. "In less than an hour. Now go and get your glad rags on, birthday girl."

"Help me up, please," she said, moving to get up from the rug. "Who's coming?"

"It's a surprise," stated Jake, helping her to her feet. Realising she was stiff after sitting on the sand for so long, he subtly offered to come back up to the house with her. He slipped his guitar back into its velvet lined case, snapped the clasps shut, and picked it up then took her hand. "I'll come back for the rest in a minute."

As she fastened her necklace, Lori heard a car arrive outside. She glanced out of the side window and was surprised to see the driveway was full of cars. The latest arrivals were Maddy and Paul with the twins. Pausing to brush out her hair, Lori hurried through the house to greet them.

"Happy birthday, honey," said Maddy as she hugged her friend at the front door. "You're looking stunning. I love that colour on you."

"Thanks," replied Lori, glancing down at the pale blue sundress she had slipped on. "One of my sale bargains from the outlets."

"It's gorgeous."

"Come on through," said Lori suddenly realising they were all still on the doorstep.

As he entered the hallway carrying the sleeping twins in their car seats, Paul paused to kiss her. "Happy birthday, beautiful."

When they stepped out onto the sun deck, Lori was stunned to find David and his wife there, plus her friend Lin from New York. Then she spotted Jake's sister, Lucy, and her husband sitting in the corner. Amid squeals of delight at seeing each other and a chorus of "Happy Birthdays" Lori was totally overwhelmed by it all. While she was hugging Lucy, she asked where the boys were.

"Down on the beach with Jake. Grey and his little girl are down there too," she replied. "Oh, Simon's dropping by later on. He's at Dover for a few days."

"This is incredible," sighed Lori, gazing round at all the familiar faces. "I knew nothing about this."

"I think Jake just wanted to make it special for you," said Lucy, giving her another hug. "He's been planning this for a while."

A few minutes later, Jake came running up the path from the beach, his long sun-bleached hair tousled and windswept. When he reached Lori, he lifted her up into his arms and held her tight.

"Surprise, birthday girl," he said with a grin. Kissing her gently, he set her back down on her feet. "I'd better get the BBQ going."

"Have we enough food?" whispered Lori, gazing round.

"Plenty," assured Jake. "I have this under control, li'l lady."

"You sure?"

"Relax and enjoy your party. Rich and Todd are assistant chefs for the day. Todd's just gone to get more ice and to pick up Kate."

Lifting a glass of champagne from the table, Lori wandered across the sun deck to mingle with her guests. There was a spare seat beside David and his wife, Olivia, so she went to sit with them first. It had been several months since she had seen him and he complimented her on how well she looked. Eventually he apologised to have to talk business, but confessed to having brought some urgent paperwork for her to sign. Excusing themselves, they slipped indoors to get the business matters out of the way.

When Lori returned to the party a few minutes later, she discovered the picnic table had been set with salads and rolls and dressing. At the BBQ, Jake was grilling burgers, chicken and shrimp. His protégé, Todd, was standing beside him chatting, his arm draped protectively round Kate's shoulders. The young girl looked nervous and out of place.

"Come on, Kate," said Lori, taking her hand. "Have you met the girls properly yet?"

"No," replied the teenager awkwardly,

Lori led her across to where Lucy, Linsey, Lin and Maddy were all sitting chatting about the twins.

"Ladies, have you been introduced to Kate?" asked Lori, interrupting their conversation.

"Ah the girl with the best rock voice I've heard in a long while," declared Maddy, moving aside to make room on the bench for the young songstress. "Come here, angel."

Nervously, Kate sat down between Maddy and Lin.

"When are you guys going to use your studio time? I'm really keen to hear what you come up with?" asked Maddy with a smile.

"We've not set a date," replied Kate shyly. "I think Silver Lake need to record their record first before there's a slot for us."

Satisfied that the young girl was in safe hands, Lori wandered back over to the BBQ to see her fiancé. Without her cane to steady her, she was extra careful as she made her way towards him.

"Having fun, li'l lady?" asked Jake as she reached him.

"I still can't believe you organised all this," she replied, hugging him tight. "I love you, rock star."

"Love you too."

Their intimate moment was interrupted by the arrival of Jake's brother, Simon. He appeared from the path beside the house, carrying a huge bouquet of flowers and a bottle of champagne. Setting his gifts on the table, he swept Lori up into a warm hug, wishing her a very happy birthday. He kissed her on both cheeks, then turned to greet his young brother. Spying her brothers together, Lucy came rushing over and threw her arms round both of them.

"I've brought a guest," said Simon calmly. "I hope that's alright."

"Of course. The more the merrier," declared Lori brightly. "Where have you left them?"

"Sitting in the car," he replied, looking a little anxious.

"It's not another new woman is it?" teased his young sister.

"Not at all," he answered. "It's Peter."

Both Lucy and Lori exchanged worried glances, then both turned to look at Jake, trying to gauge his reaction. His face was a mask of calm as he focussed on turning over the shrimp on the grill. Silence hung in the air among them. Laying the tongs aside, he finally spoke. "Grab yourself a drink, Simon, I'll go and fetch him."

"Are you sure this is ok, Jake?" asked his brother.

"I'll go and fetch him," repeated Jake, his voice void of all emotion.

They watched him stride round the side of the house without a backwards glance.

Out in front of the house, the driveway was crammed with cars. It was easy to identify Simon's rental car with the company logo emblazoned down the length of it. The passenger door was open and Jake could see his eldest brother sitting in the seat with his head bowed. Even from this distance, he looked pale and drawn. The two brothers hadn't seen each other for the better part of six years. Their last conversation, at their mother's wake, had been decidedly hostile, when Peter had confronted Jake directly about his drug abuse. His words still rang loud and clear in Jake's memory. Taking a deep breath, he walked over to the car.

"Peter," he said calmly.

His brother looked up. "Jacob."

"It's Jake," he corrected, his voice level and quiet.

"My apology," said Peter with a sigh, "One of many I owe you."

"Many?"

"I was a complete bastard towards you at mom's memorial. I'm sorry," apologised Peter, his tone sincere. Avoiding looking Jake in the eye, he added, "I should've tried to reach out to you then. Tried to help you. I didn't. I let her down."

"That was a long time ago," began Jake, hearing his brother's scornful words echo from the past in his mind. "Let's leave that shit back there. Fresh start?"

"More than I deserve," replied Peter, with a rueful smile. "But a fresh start sounds good to me."

"Come and get a beer," suggested Jake with a warm smile. "And I'll introduce you to the birthday girl herself."

"Best idea I've heard all day," agreed his brother as he swung his long legs out of the car. The movement seemed to make him flinch and he let out a low groan.

"You ok?" asked Jake, getting a sudden sense that all was not well.

"Didn't Simon say?"

"Say what?"

"The reason he got sent overseas and then back here to Dover was to escort me home," admitted Peter, his voice quiet and self-conscious. "I was wounded in action. He flew in with me and my boys. I lost four good men out there, Jake."

"Sorry to hear that," replied Jake, fully understanding what it meant to his brother to lose his crew. He'd heard his father talk about it long enough and often enough over the years. "And you?"

Standing up a little unsteadily, Peter drew himself up to his full height of six feet five and shrugged his shoulders. The action caused a grimace of pain to wash over his pale face. The short sleeve of his checked shirt hung empty on the left.

"Shit," muttered Jake, feeling the blood drain from his face as he spotted the bandaged stump below the hem of the sleeve. "I'm sorry. I.... "

"Don't, Jake," said Peter swallowing hard. "I'm alive. I'll get over this. My men won't."

Without another word, Jake reached out and hugged his brother. Neither of them said anything; the silent exchange healing years of ill feeling.

"Let's get you that beer," said Jake warmly.

"Thanks. I think I need it."

Together they walked back round to the sun deck. From the tear-stained look on Lucy's face, it was clear that Simon had explained what had happened to their brother. When she saw him, she rushed towards him, flinging her arms round his waist and sobbing quietly into his broad chest.

"Sh. I'm ok, Lucy," he said, smoothing her hair gently. "Don't cry."

"Oh, Pete, I'm so sorry," she sobbed.

"I'm alive. I'm here," said her eldest brother calmly. "Now I thought this was a party?"

"It is," confirmed Jake, who was standing close by with his arm around Lori. "And let me introduce you to the birthday girl, my fiancée, Lori Hyde."

"Nice to finally meet you," said Lori with a smile.

"The pleasure's all mine," said Peter, taking her hand and kissing it theatrically. "Happy Birthday, Mz Hyde."

"Thank you," she replied, blushing at another demonstration of the Power charm. "Come and get a drink."

As afternoon wound its way towards evening, the party spread out throughout the house. Early on, Todd and Kate had made their excuses and left, hand in hand. After hours of playing on the beach with Becky, Lucy's two sons were exhausted. The three weary children were contentedly sprawled on the couches in the sunroom watching cartoons. In the lounge, David, his wife and Linsey were all chatting with Grey about education in the area. Everyone else was still out in the sun, including the twins who were contentedly lying in their mother's arms. From her seat on the sun lounger, Lori subtly watched the three Power brothers chatting together over at the grill. They appeared relaxed in each other's company, the past well and truly left behind them. Peter eventually stepped away and wandered off down towards the beach on his own. Without making a fuss, Lori picked up her cane and casually followed him down onto the sand. The air force captain hadn't gone far. He was standing at the shoreline gazing out across the vast ocean.

"Any dolphins?" asked Lori as she approached him.

"Pardon?"

"Dolphins," she repeated with a smile. "They usually come by here around this time of day. I love watching them."

"I haven't seen any," replied Peter quietly. "I was lost in my own world."

"I've stood here often enough lost in mine too," commented Lori, casually leaning on her cane for support. "The ocean's good for healing the soul."

He turned to face her and nodded, noticing her cane for the first time.

"Simon said you would understand. You've made quite an impression on him."

Reaching out to touch his hand, Lori said, "I understand about pain. About injury. About loss. The healing has to come from

Impossible Depths

within, Peter. I came here after my accident to recover physically and mentally. It takes time."

"It's been a few weeks though...."

"Peter," interrupted Lori softly. "Don't rush it. You need to go through all the emotions. The anger. The grief. The "why me?" You have to allow yourself to go through it before you can pick up the pieces. You'll get there. We all do in our own time."

"Jake's a lucky man," commented Peter taking her hand. "I'm not too proud to admit I was scared about coming here today. I said a lot of things to him the last time that we met that I've regretted. I wasn't sure I'd be welcome."

"I can understand that, but surely Simon reassured you?"

"He tried."

"Come on back up to the house," Lori suggested warmly. "We're missing the party."

As they turned to walk back across the sand, Peter said, "Do you think Jake would play his guitar for me? It's a long time since I've heard him play."

"You can ask," said Lori. "He doesn't usually take much persuading."

Like all good parties, it had found its way into the kitchen by late on in the evening. Most of the guests had said good night but Grey, Rob and the three Power brothers were congregated in the kitchen talking NASCAR. In the sun room, the three children were sound asleep on the couch. After some persuading, Lucy had agreed to stay overnight instead of leaving to find a motel. Leaving the sleeping children, the two girls fetched some wine and retired to the lounge to chat. Eventually the boys wandered through, beers in hand, to join them. As Jake settled himself on the floor, leaning back against Lori's chair, she leaned forward and whispered in his ear. Nodding, he got up and disappeared down to the basement. When he came back into the lounge, he was carrying two acoustic guitars. With a wink, he passed one to Grey.

"The birthday girl has requested some music," he teased as he sat down again. "Grey, you ok to help out with that?"

"For a while, then I need to get Becky home," replied the bass player. "Plus Dr Marrs is expecting me in the morning."

"Message received," said Jake as he adjusted the tuning.

91

"Track six, if you please. I want to try something."

Grey nodded. "I'll do my best. Not my usual weapon of choice. Too many strings."

The new, unfinished song was unfamiliar to Lori and she wasn't prepared for the powerful intro to it. Music filled the room as Grey played a simple bass line, then Jake began the lyric. His voice was warm and rich, the song teasing out a fresh depth and warmth. In the rocking chair by the fireplace, Peter sat mesmerised, totally entranced by his brother's impromptu performance. With the new track out of the road, Jake began the intro to Simple Man knowing it was one of Lori's favourites.

"Encore!" declared Peter when the song ended.

"Not from me," said Grey, resting the guitar against the wall. "I need to get Becky home and I need my beauty sleep."

After Grey had departed, Peter asked Jake to play some more. As Lori had said, he didn't take much persuading and contentedly played a variety of rock classics and Silver Lake songs until after midnight.

"I'm done," he stated after playing Maggie May at Lucy's request.

"That was incredible!" enthused his young sister. "When do we get to see you on stage next?"

"End of July," replied Jake with a yawn. "We're playing a rock festival near Bethlehem."

"I'll be in the front row!" promised his sister proudly.

"And we'll be right beside you to make sure you behave," added Peter, with a wink to Simon.

"Well, let's see what I can sort out," said Jake. "I'll talk to Gary about VIP passes, if you guys are serious."

"I'm serious!" Lucy stated emphatically.

"We'd never have guessed," teased Simon glancing at his watch. "Peter, we'd better get going. The search party will be out for us."

"I suppose," said Peter getting reluctantly to his feet. "Thank you for a fantastic day."

"Come back any time," said Lori, genuinely meaning it. "How long are you in Dover for?"

"I'm not sure," replied Peter. "Maybe a few weeks. Maybe long term."

"I'm leaving tomorrow night," added Simon, searching in his pocket for his car key.

"Well, we're around for the next few weeks," said Lori. "If you want to come over just pick up the phone and one of us will drive up and get you."

"I'd like that," said Peter giving her a hug.

Listening to the sound of his brother-in-law snoring in the guest bedroom, Jake lay awake, sleep evading him. He cast his mind back over the day. It felt like he was the one who got the biggest surprise at Lori's surprise party. Seeing his elder brother again after all those years had been a shock. In the dark, he reflected on his relationship with Peter as they had grown up. He was five years Jake's senior and was always right – something he never let Jake forget as a kid. Seeing a vulnerable, softer side to Peter at the party had been alien to Jake. Both his air force focussed brothers had always appeared so upright, strong and invincible. To see Peter, wounded as he had been, had been tough. Tough to handle; tough to accept.

Under the duvet beside him, Lori wriggled into a more comfortable position. When they had come to bed, she had declared it had been the best birthday she had ever had. Now, as she lay asleep beside him Jake realised he had forgotten to give her his gift.

His mind wandered away from family towards the band's new album and to the songs he had been asked to re-work. In his heart, he knew Dr Marrs was right about the lyrics from the two tracks. A theme had been gradually emerging for the new record so it felt right to re-work those songs in a sense. In another, Jake felt it would destroy them, turn them into something other than the vision he had had for them. The only alternative was to come up with two new songs. Staring up at the ceiling as if it was a computer screen, showing the inventory of material that he had to draw from, Jake began to recall an entirely different melody- one from a long time ago; one from his own dark days. Hearing the melody playing in his head, he silently tried to compose a chorus for it and a strong riff.

Creativity drove any thought of sleep from his mind. Soundlessly, Jake slipped out of bed, hauled on a T-shirt and a pair of jeans, then crept out of the room and down the hallway towards the door to the basement. Despite his best efforts, the door creaked loudly as he eased it open and squealed again in protest as he closed it behind him. Once downstairs, he switched on the lights and his laptop, then trawled through his music files until he found what he was looking for. He listened to the melody a few times, then picked up his guitar. Conscious that he didn't want to wake the entire household, Jake tried to work the song out softly. It was one of those rare, precious nights when everything fell into place. The old scrap of music became the foundation stone for a new Silver Lake anthem. Lyrics flowed effortlessly from his pen onto the pages of his journal. Jake wrote from his brother's perspective about the loss of his men, loss of his limb and of a dark night engulfing him. Focussing on creating the guitar solo for the midpoint of the song vanquished any lingering thoughts of sleep.

In the kitchen next morning, Lucy and Lori were relaxing over their coffee when Rich knocked at the back door, before striding in. Without waiting to be asked, he poured himself a coffee and joined them at the table.

"You hungry?" asked Lori. "There's bacon in the refrigerator or there's bagels over in the drawer."

"Coffee's good, thanks," he replied. "I need to be away by three. I've to pick Linsey up. Where's Jake?"

"I'm not sure," confessed Lori. "He might have gone for a run. I haven't seen him this morning."

"He'll turn up," said Rich with a smile. "He always does eventually. So what's your plans for the day?"

"We're heading home," said Lucy sadly. "Rob needs to get back for work."

"You know that you and the boys are welcome to stay," offered Lori warmly.

"It's tempting," sighed Lucy. "Very tempting."

"Why not stay on for a few days?" quizzed Rich. "Could your husband drive back down on Friday night?"

"He could. And the boys would love to be at the beach for a few days."

"It's up to you," said Lori, getting up to fetch the coffee pot to refill their mugs. "I've some work to finish off this week, but you can walk into town from here. Jake'll be coming and going too."

"Let me go and talk to Rob," Lucy stated. "If he's ok with coming back down next weekend, we'll stay."

Excusing herself, she went off to find her husband, leaving Rich and Lori at the table. Draining his mug, Rich said, "I'm going to head downstairs and make a start."

"I'll send Jake down when he shows up."

Nodding, Rich poured himself another coffee, then headed down to the basement studio. A few moments later he was back in the kitchen, trying hard not to laugh.

"What's up?" asked Lori curiously.

"Come and see your rock star," laughed Rich, taking her hand and leading her towards the door.

When they reached the bottom step, Lori tried hard to stifle a giggle. The band had spread a few old rugs around the basement and Jake was curled up sound asleep in the centre of one, using a soft guitar bag as a pillow.

"Will you waken him or will I?" asked Rich quietly.

"Oh, I think you should," whispered Lori with a mischievous grin. "Musically."

"I hear you, Mz Hyde."

Without disturbing the sleeping musician, Rich crept over to the far side of the room, picked up a guitar, plugged it in and began to play the intro to "Smoke On The Water" at full volume.

"What the...." screeched Jake as he sat bolt upright.

Instantly the music stopped, only to be replaced by the helpless laughter of Rich and Lori. Lying back down on the carpet, with his heart pounding, Jake began to see the funny side of it.

"Thanks, guys," he muttered as he got awkwardly to his feet. "What time is it?"

"Almost nine," giggled Lori. "Have you been down here all night?"

Jake nodded as he ran his hands through his hair. "I couldn't sleep so I came down here to write. It was after five before I lay down there."

"Why didn't you come back to bed?" asked Lori, giving him a hug.

"The intention was to close my eyes for a few minutes, then to get back to work. Guess I fell asleep."

Still laughing, Rich said, "Go and get cleaned up, then show me what you came up with."

"Give me half an hour. I think you'll like this one."

♬

Life at the beach was far from quiet over the next few days. Having persuaded Rob to drive back down on Friday night, Lucy and the boys decided to stay on. It was the boys' first real experience of being at the shore and their excited screams and yells filled the house from morning until night. The luxury of being able to run straight off the sand and back indoors for a snack or a juice wasn't lost on them and it wasn't too long before you could follow them by their trails of damp sand through the house. Despite having deadlines looming, Lori allowed herself the luxury of afternoons off to spend with Lucy and the boys. The first afternoon had been taken up with a run out to the outlets to buy them all some clothes for the week. On the way home, Lori stopped and treated them all to ice cream before promising that they could make smores on the BBQ after dinner.

For two days Rich and Jake were locked away in the basement, the strains of their creativity serving to drown out the noise of the boys. It was almost a relief to both Lucy and Lori when Jake left for JJL early on Wednesday morning. Having packed a picnic lunch, Lucy headed out not long after her brother with her two sons. She had promised them a full day on the beach further south of the house, leaving Lori in peace to get a few hours work done. With the house suddenly silent, Lori found it difficult to concentrate but, with the help of her iPod, was soon engrossed in the task at hand.

Coffee and cakes from an Italian bakery were the order of the day out at JJL. A routine had been established from the start of the week – Kola brought the pastries down from Philadelphia; Grey brought the coffees. Life in the studio was remarkably calm and laid back. When Jake had driven in on Wednesday, he had played the new song to his fellow band members and Dr Marrs. It needed work. It needed a bass line and a drum track, but there was unanimous agreement that it should replace track twelve on the board. Paul had pulled two late night sessions to record most of the drum tracks. When he heard the new song he nodded approvingly, declared he needed a few hours sleep before working on the drum track then headed out into the lounge.

While the drummer napped on the leather couch in the lounge, Grey began work on the bass line. The three of them worked and tweaked the song for several hours before Kola stopped them for a break. She had taken a run out to the nearest deli, returning with a variety of sandwiches and juice. Both Jake and Rich noted that the sound engineer was subtly a little more attentive to Grey and that he, in turn, kept his eyes on her as she sat quietly in the corner with her sandwich and a rock magazine. Watching them surreptitiously watching each other gave Jake a flash of inspiration for the lyrics that were needed for track fifteen. Excusing himself, he took his sandwich and iced tea outside along with his acoustic guitar and his lyrics journal. He settled himself in the shade round the back of the building, leaning against the back wall of the studio.

"Jake!"
The voice derailed his train of thought.
"Jake!"
"Round the back," he called back.
A few seconds later Grey came striding round. Standing towering over his friend, the bass player declared, "Your presence is requested inside. Now."
"On my way," he replied, getting to his feet. "Has Paul surfaced yet?"
The bass player nodded. "And he's come up with something sweet."
"That was quick," commented Jake, impressed that his friend had supplied the drum track without any drama.
"Jason's arrived," stated Grey bluntly as they reached the front door of the studio.

The Englishman was standing in the middle of the studio chatting with Rich when they walked in. After exchanging pleasantries with the band, he asked where Gary was.
"On his way," replied Kola, before any of the members of Silver Lake could answer. "He'll be back in a few minutes."
"Why isn't he here?" demanded Jason sharply.
"Coffee run," explained Dr Marrs. "It was his turn."

"Convenient," muttered the Englishman under his breath. "I've not got long. I need to be back in Philly for six thirty. I'll cut to the chase. We've firmed up the festival dates. There's six of them for now and I'm waiting word on two more in Canada. I've emailed the details to Gary. The record company also wants you to play at an event in Philadelphia on 6th July. It's a lunchtime slot. Three songs. Two old and one new. I need the single recorded by then if possible."

Behind them the door creaked open and Gary slipped in carrying a cardboard tray of coffees. It was his first trip to the studio that week, but the band said nothing.

"Sorry, there was a queue," he apologised. "Jason, I got you a latte."

"Thank you, but you're late, Mr York," he stated bluntly as he accepted the tall waxed- paper cup. "Now where was I?"

"July 6th," prompted Jake calmly. "We'll be ready by then. When's the first festival gig? Is it the Bethlehem one?"

"Yes. July 27th. You've got an hour on stage around six o'clock," replied Jason. "So, how's recording going?"

"We're only into the second week," began Dr Marrs. "But we're on schedule. Drum tracks are nearly there. We've made a start on the bass tracking this morning. There was a bit of re-writing required and Jake's substituted a new song in the track twelve slot."

Jason nodded approvingly as he sipped his latte. "Is Mz Hyde around?"

"No," said Jake. "She's working at home."

"Pity. I've some music files for her next project with me."

"I can pass them on to her."

He tossed Jake a USB flash drive. "Tell her I'll call tomorrow morning to discuss it."

"Sure," promised Jake as he slipped the flash drive into his jeans pocket. "Want to hear what we've been working on so far?"

Silver Lake performed three of their new tracks for Jason, who nodded in approval. While he sat talking animatedly with Gary in the corner of the live room, Jake played and sang the re-worked lyrics for track fifteen. Sitting out in the shade, he had come up with a lyric around moving out of the shadows of grief into the daylight warmth of love. He sang it with a straight forward no frills honest, warm tone to his voice.

"I like that," approved Rich when his friend was finished. "Could that be our single?"

"Perhaps," agreed Dr Marrs. "Run through it again."

On the third run through, Jason interrupted them. "Radio stations will love it. That's your single, gentlemen."

"Looks like we're all agreed," observed the producer, glancing over at Kola. The sound engineer nodded.

"Glad that's sorted. Progress. I like that," Jason stated. "I'm out of here. Gary, call me on Friday with a detailed update. Guys, I'll see you on 6th July."

With a slam of the door, he was gone.

Gary slumped back on the couch and sighed.

"Thanks, Kola. I owe you one."

The sound engineer drew him a look and, on her way out of the live room, hissed, "You need to be on hand more often. You're slacking."

The door slammed behind her.

"Are you going to let her speak to me like that?" protested Gary, sounding all too much like a simpering child.

"Yes," stated Grey, seeking nods of agreement from the others. "You have been slacking. Maddy wouldn't have let us on such a long leash. Good job we're professionals with a strong work ethic."

"Don't play the Maddy card with me!" snapped their manager angrily.

"And why not?" came a sharp, familiar voice from the doorway.

All of them turned to see Maddison standing there, her face a mask of fury.

"Gary, outside please," she said coldly, holding the door open to allow him to exit past her. "Paul, I'll get you outside shortly."

Despite the studio's sound proofing, the band all heard Gary's dressing down from an irate Maddy. Embarrassed for the guy, Jake tried to block out the raised voices by practicing his solo from one of the heavier tracks. Picking up on his lead, Grey began the bass line, but even when Paul came in on drums Maddy's shrill New York fury could be heard.

"Let's call it a day," suggested Jim Marrs, admitting defeat. "Early start tomorrow. Be here for seven."

"Fine by me," said Jake setting his guitar down.

"I'll be here for nine," added Grey. "I can't drop Becky off until day care opens at eight thirty."

"Bring her over to us tonight," suggested Jake. "My sister's still here with the boys. She can sleep over and spend tomorrow at the beach with them."

"If you're sure," Grey replied. "Then I'll be here for seven, boss."

"See you all in the morning," said the producer. "It'll be a long day tomorrow. We need to catch up after today, so I'm warning you now, boys."

"We hear you," acknowledged Rich.

"Hmm and Maddison," muttered Jake as he lifted his book bag and his jacket before heading for the door.

When Jake walked round to his truck a few moments later, Gary was sitting on an upturned crate at the side of the building. His head was in his hands and he was staring down at his feet. Seeing him looking so dejected bothered Jake.

"You ok, buddy?" he asked, laying a hand on Gary's shoulder.

"I'll survive," muttered the band's manager without looking up.

"Do you want to talk?" offered Jake hesitantly. "Looks like you need a friend."

"I've been offered another tour," Gary stated plainly. "An eight-week gig through Europe. I've tried to work out a way I can still manage you guys until Maddy's back on board and do the tour. I had hoped to spend time in Europe and catch up with my family. I miss them. Guess I've just spread myself too thin."

"And Maddy found out?"

"She sure did. I grossly underestimated the reach of her circle of friends," sighed Gary. "I need to choose. She says she's not coming back on board full time anytime soon."

"Is she going to say anything to Jason?"

"She already has," confessed Gary sounding completely defeated. "Now I need to make a decision before tomorrow."

"Well, it's your choice at the end of the day. You need to go with what feels right for you," began Jake sincerely. "Personally, I'd hate to see you leave us. You bring a sense of balance to proceedings. We need that. Don't rush the decision, my friend."

"Thanks, Jake. Appreciate the support."

"If you need to talk, you know where I am. I'll see you back out here tomorrow."

"Bright and early," promised Gary forcing a smile. "I'll bring breakfast."

When he pulled into the driveway almost an hour later, Jake could hear his nephews laughing and squealing round the back of the house. The two boys were wrestling with each other on the sun deck as he came round from the side of the house.

"Hey, guys!" shouted Jake startling them. "Save that for down on the beach, please."

"Sorry, Uncle Jake," said Sam scrambling to his feet.

"Give me a few minutes to get changed and I'll take you both down to the beach before dinner," suggested Jake. "I feel like a swim."

Jake found Lori and his sister in the kitchen preparing marinated chicken to be grilled on the BBQ and a large bowl of pasta salad.

"I said I'd take the boys down to the beach for a while," said Jake as he kissed Lori at the nape of her neck. "I need a swim."

"Long day, rock star?" Lori asked, noting the strained look on his face.

"Something like that," he replied, then fishing the flash drive out of his pocket added, "Gift from Lord Jason. He'll call you tomorrow morning about it."

"Thanks," said Lori. "Leave it on my desk, will you? Don't be too long. Grey called and said he'd be here with Becky within the hour."

"Ah, I meant to tell you about that."

"It's fine," she assured him warmly. "They are joining us for dinner."

"You're an amazing woman, Mz Hyde."

As he loped off down the hall to get changed, Lucy commented "You two are fabulous together. My mom would've loved to see him this happy."

"Mine too," admitted Lori, a hint of sadness in her voice. "She always worried about me."

"Part of the job description," said Lucy with a wistful smile. "I still miss her."

"I still miss my mom too," confessed Lori quietly. "I was eighteen when she died."

"Oh, that's young," exclaimed Lucy with sympathy. "I was just glad my mom got to hold Sam before she passed away. That was an important moment for me. Precious memory."

"I wonder what she would have had to say about Jake's success?" mused Lori in an attempt to lighten the mood.

"Oh, that's easy!" laughed Lucy. "She was his biggest fan. She always believed he would succeed. She would want to be front row for every show!"

A gentle breeze blew in from the ocean, causing the flames of the citronella candles to flicker, casting dancing shadows around the deck and across the table. The glow from the dying embers of the charcoal was just visible. Beside the grill lay the discarded skewers, marshmallows and Graham crackers. The kids had finished the chocolate. At the table, Jake was finishing off his last mouthful of smores while his sister herded the three youngsters indoors to get cleaned up for bed. Pouring them all some wine, Grey commented, "That was quite some beating Gary took today?"

"Sure was," agreed Jake, licking his fingers. "He's got a lot on his mind."

"Did you try to talk to him?" asked the bass player.

"Briefly," replied Jake before adding, "He's thinking about leaving us."

"Who's leaving?" asked Lori as she came back out onto the deck carrying a bowl of tortilla chips.

"Gary, possibly," said Jake. "He's been offered a tour with another band and he's tempted."

"Who?"

"Doesn't matter, Grey," continued Jake. "I never asked and he never said. Someone told Maddy and she's told Jason. He's to make a decision by tomorrow. What a mess."

"What did you say to him?" asked Grey, taking a handful of

chips.

"Told him it was his decision, but that I'd be sorry to see him go. He's good for us. Brings a bit of balance to the party. Personally, I'd miss him."

"Likewise," agreed Grey getting to his feet. "I'll maybe give him a call when I get home. Anyway, thanks again for dinner, Lori. And for watching Becky. I'm going to say good night to her then head home."

"Pleasure, Grey," replied Lori smiling.

"See you out at JJL in the morning, Jake."

"Night," called back Jake, sounding distracted.

After they'd heard the roar of Grey's truck heading off along East Lake Drive, Lori asked Jake if he thought their young manager would leave.

"I've honestly no idea," he sighed, then added, "Come here, li'l lady and sit on my knee."

"Am I in trouble, rock star?" she giggled as she sat on his denim clad legs.

"I got a message from Danny. Asked if I wanted to book the appointment slot after yours."

"Oh!" exclaimed Lori blushing. "Do you?"

"Not this time," he teased. "So tell me more, li'l lady?"

"Friday morning," replied Lori. "And that's all I'm telling you."

"Still your foot?"

"I'm not saying," she stated with a giggle. "You'll have to wait and see."

All week Lucy had promised her sons that she would take them for a trip on the Lewes ferry. First thing on Friday morning, Lori drove them to the ferry terminal, promising to collect them late afternoon. Traffic was light and she made good time back to Rehoboth, arriving at Danny's tattoo parlour half an hour early. Having parked at the rear of the building, Lori went across to the deli to buy two coffees as instructed by the diminutive ink artist. Cardboard tray in hand, she returned to the tattoo parlour. Carefully she opened the door, smiling as the wind chimes tinkled musically.

"Good morning, princess," called Danny brightly.

The small tattoo artist was working on a client, inking an angel onto the woman's shoulder.

"Sorry I'm early," apologised Lori, setting the tray down on the bench.

"Skinny latte there for me?" enquired Danny.

"Of course," she replied with a smile. "As you ordered, sir."

"I'll be with you in ten minutes. Maybe fifteen," he replied, pausing his work to collect his coffee cup.

Fifteen minutes became an hour and, when his client finally closed the door behind her, Danny apologised profusely for keeping Lori waiting for so long.

"Its fine," she assured him. "I was intrigued watching you work. It's an amazing skill you have there."

"Why thank you, princess," he said with a theatrical bow. "Now pick your throne."

As before, Lori opted for the middle chair, sitting down somewhat nervously. Pulling over a stool, Danny sat down beside her.

"Now, you sent me two designs. Are we doing both?" he asked hopefully. "I've prepared the transfers for both."

"Just the one," replied Lori. "I'm still undecided about the other one."

"They're both beautiful. So feminine. So delicate," commented Danny, subtly trying to coax her into both.

"Let's do the ankle one and I'll see how I feel after that," compromised Lori.

"Sounds fair. The ankle design is intricate. It may take longer than I'd originally allowed for. Fine work can't be rushed."

"I've got all day, Danny. I don't need to be in Lewes until four thirty."

The design that Lori had eventually decided upon was a fine chain draped round her ankle with a small selection of music notes on varying lengths of chain cascading down the outside of her foot. When he had seen the design for the chain links, Danny knew these would be tricky, but he loved the overall delicacy and simplicity of the design. Once the template was drawn on and Lori was satisfied with it, he suggested they take a break. His assistant had arrived at the shop while he had been drawing on the template and Danny promptly despatched him to fetch some coffees and, realising the time, some sandwiches for lunch.

It was almost three o'clock before Danny was finished the musical anklet tattoo. Gazing down at the finished design, Lori smiled contentedly. He had done an incredible job. She just hoped Jake would agree. Deliberately, it had been inked using silvery grey colours and that added to the detail and delicacy of the finished tattoo.

"Decision time, princess," said Danny as he put a dressing over the fresh ink. "I can do the other one in an hour if you want to go ahead with it."

"Go for it," stated Lori confidently.

"Sure?"

She nodded as she stood up from the chair.

"Ok, follow me, Mz Hyde," said the tattoo meister. "The cubicle is ready and waiting."

Lori had designed a trellis of small flowers that she had originally intended for her foot. Instead, though, she had re-designed the perspective of it and asked Danny to tattoo it over the surgical scar on her hip. Lying on her side on the table in the small clinical cubicle she suddenly felt very self-conscious. Despite the number of medical staff who had treated her over the previous eighteen months, she was embarrassed to bare her derriere for Danny.

"That's been a neat job," he mused as he swabbed her skin before applying the template.

"I guess," muttered Lori quietly.

"We'll soon have it disguised, princess," he said warmly, placing a reassuring hand on her shoulder. "I sense you won't be sorry to cover it up."

"I won't be," sighed Lori. "It's the easy one to hide."

"Lie still and relax," he suggested softly. "Leave this to Daniel."

As good as his word, Danny had the trellis design completed within the hour. His delicate touch had amazed her again as she surveyed the completed tattoo in the mirror. At least that was one reminder of her accident gone forever, hidden beneath the colourful small flowers and strategically positioned stems.

"Thank you. I love it."

"Pleasure," he said as he removed his surgical gloves. "Can I take a photograph?"

Shaking her head, Lori said, "Not a chance!"

Laughing, he guided her back through to the main store. "Maybe next time, princess."

"Maybe," she conceded. "Now how much do I owe you? This has been more than the auction lot was for."

"You're good, princess. No charge," he replied. "But can I ask a favour?"

"You can ask," answered Lori, curious to know what he wanted from her.

"A friend's coming into town next month. He's coming to do a tattoo for me. I've not much bare skin left, but I need something quirky. About three inches by three inches. Can you come up with something?"

"Me design a tattoo for you?" laughed Lori, totally taken aback by the request. "Whereabouts on your body dare I ask?"

"My butt cheek," he confessed almost blushing. "One cheek's done already."

The tattoo parlour was filled with the magical musical sound of Lori's laughter. Wiping a tear from her eyes, she nodded, "I'll do it on one condition."

"And that is?"

"You send me a photo of the finished article."

"Deal, Mz Hyde," said Danny, shaking her hand. "I need it for the 4th July."

"Not a problem," giggled Lori. "Now I need to hurry. I'm late for collecting Jake's sister at the ferry terminal."

"Drive safely, princess," he said, handing her the wallet of aftercare instructions and a jar of cream. "Till next time."

"Bye, Danny."

Instead of cooking dinner for Lucy and the boys' last night in Rehoboth, Lori had booked a table for dinner at a family restaurant in town. Their table had been booked for seven thirty but by seven there was still no sign of Jake. She tried calling him but his phone went straight to voice mail. Through in the sun room, she could hear the boys telling their dad about their trip on the Lewes-Cape May ferry. Since Rob had arrived an hour before, the boys had been stuck to him like glue, regaling him with tales of the adventures they had had all week.

Eventually, at quarter past seven, Lori's phone rang. It was Jake.

"Where are you?" she asked, trying hard not to sound exasperated.

"Just leaving JJL. I'll meet you there," he replied, the phone reception crackling loudly.

"How long will you be?"

"No more than a half hour. Order for me if you have to, li'l lady."

"Ok," agreed Lori. "You better have a good explanation for being so late."

"No excuses, Lori. It's been a long fucking day. Nothing's gone right, but Gary has decided to stick with us," he explained wearily. "I'll tell you all about it later."

The restaurant was packed when they entered just after seven thirty. Having taken Lori's name for the reservation, the hostess showed them to a circular table in the centre of the restaurant. She gave them a minute or two then returned to take their drinks order.

"What's good to eat in here, Lori?" asked Rob as he perused the extensive menu.

"Everything," she replied honestly. "I've never had a bad meal here."

"I think I'll go for a steak," said Lucy before asking the boys what they wanted.

Just as the hostess came back to take their food order, Jake came rushing in.

"Sorry, guys," he apologised, slipping into the empty seat between his fiancée and his sister.

"You're just in time," said Lori, handing him her menu. "I was going to order you a fillet steak."

"Actually, can I have the flounder please?" requested Jake without looking at the menu.

Efficiently the waitress took the rest of their order plus Jake's drinks order and left the party to relax while they waited for their meal.

"How did recording go today?" asked Lucy, curious to hear all she could about Silver Lake.

"Slowly," grumped her brother. "We've had better days. Lots of technical glitches today. Blown fuses that blew one of the amps. Bust strings. Wasn't our day today."

"How long do you have to go in the studio?" asked Rob, who was interested to determine how long the whole recording process took.

"At least three weeks," answered Jake. "Maybe nearer four. Then Dr Marrs has to work his black magic and mix it all. We'll be through by the end of July."

"Have you done any vocals yet?" Lucy asked.

"No," confessed Jake. "Drum tracks and bass are done. Rich and I are working on the guitar tracking. We should be done by the end of next week. Depends on how they work out. Vocals will take another week after that, I'd guess."

"Are the lyrics all written?" teased Lori, reaching under the table to put her hand on his thigh.

"More or less," he replied with a wink. "Now how did you get on with Danny, Mz Hyde?"

"Fine," she said with an impish smile. "I'll show you later."

Deliberately, she had worn a long, maxi dress that covered her freshly tattooed ankle and foot, but that also hung loosely over the fresh ink on her hip. She had shown Lucy her ankle design, but had kept the other one a secret. It was for Jake's eyes only.

"You didn't let him take a photo, did you?" Jake asked hopefully.

"No, but he's asked me to do him a favour," she answered. "He wants me to design a tattoo for him."

"For him?" echoed Jake genuinely surprised. "Danny can't have much bare flesh left."

"It's to be quite a small design," explained Lori. "Apparently he has a friend coming for the fourth of July and wants him to ink it then."

"And are you going to oblige?" asked Lucy curiously.

Lori nodded, then glanced at Jake as if she were seeking his approval.

"It's up to you, li'l lady," he replied. "Have you any idea what to do for him?"

"A few ideas," she said. "There was a condition to the deal."

"What?"

"He has to give me a photo of the finished tattoo," she said stifling a giggle.

"Nice touch, Lori," laughed Jake, understanding the irony of it. "Like it."

Both the boys fell asleep during the car ride back to the house after dinner and, while Rob helped Lucy put them to bed, Jake took Lori by the hand and led her through to the sun room. Politely, but firmly, he asked her to sit down. She tried to refuse, but giggles got the better of her and she collapsed onto the couch. Before she could even attempt to draw her feet up beneath her, Jake had grabbed them. He lifted the soft, cotton fabric of her dress and inspected the delicate tattoo. Flexing her foot and ankle, he nodded his approval at the way the design flowed with the movement.

"Beautiful," he said eventually. "Are you happy with it?"

"Delighted," replied Lori, admiring the design again.

"I thought you were getting the floral design that you showed me a while back," commented Jake as he got to his feet.

"I changed my mind. I was looking at the bracelet the band gave me last year for my birthday when I had it on the other day and decided I wanted something similar to that instead," explained Lori. "I designed it the next day and emailed it to Danny."

"Well, he's done a fantastic job as ever," commented Jake. "What are you planning for him?"

"Something quirky was the remit. I was thinking along the lines of the zombies I drew or a gargoyle."

"Or you could do something real cute and fluffy," joked Jake.

"The possibilities are endless here," giggled Lori.

Much later, as they got ready for bed, Jake noticed the white dressing covering Lori's hip.

"Confess your other sin, Mz Hyde," he said huskily as he reached out to draw her towards him. "What's this?"

Standing in her pale cream bra and panties, Lori giggled and tried to move out of his reach. He was too quick for her and had his arms wrapped round her before she could side step away from him. Gently, he peeled away the paper tape and lifted off the dressing. Under his fingers, he could feel Lori tense up.

"Very pretty," he said softly, gently kissing the skin around the fresh tattoo. "I think you're developing an addiction here, li'l lady. Two designs in one day?"

"Like you can talk, rock star," she laughed, running her finger over his dragon tattoo.

"True, but I've never done two in one day," Jake acknowledged, running his fingers through her hair. "Now come to bed so I can inspect this more closely."

♫

Tears flowed freely as Lucy and her family said their farewells to Jake and Lori next morning. They left with promises to meet up at Silver Lake's show at the end of July and, with a loud hoot of the horn and much waving, they were gone. Once all the breakfast debris had been cleared away, Jake said that he was going to take a run out to JJL for a few hours. First thing that morning, while Lori had been in the shower, he'd received a call from Dr Marrs asking him to come in.

"I'll be back for dinner," he promised as he kissed his fiancée tenderly.

"No rush, rock star," she replied. "I'm way behind schedule here. I could use a few hours peace and quiet."

"When's work starting on your attic studio?" asked Jake as he lifted his truck keys from the hook.

"That's on hold as of Friday. I got a call from the architect. He's trying to redesign it. Something to do with the weight of the glass and the structure of the roof," sighed Lori, a hint of exasperation in her voice. "I'm seriously considering abandoning the whole thing. The way he spoke, it sounds as though the whole roof would need to be redone."

"Not so good, li'l lady. Pity there's not more space to build something attached to the house."

"I used all the spare ground when I extended the house before," sighed Lori before quipping, "Back to the drawing board."

"Very funny! Now I need to run. I'll bring something in for dinner on my way back."

With the patio doors and French doors of the sun room wide open, Lori managed to fill the house with the fresh smell of the ocean while she sat at her drawing board. As the salty breeze wafted through, she was soon lost in the depths of the artwork on the board in front of her. Similar to her recent zombie piece, the current commission also had a dark edge to it. It was for Molton, the band who had given Silver Lake their first big break on the west coast, and was themed around dark temples with rooms filled with dreams and phobias. Initially, Lori had struggled with it, but having listened to the music sample a few times and spoken at length to Tori, the band's lead singer, she had developed a feel for what was expected. With hours of uninterrupted peace ahead of her, she hoped to break the back of the design by the end of the day.

Swinging the truck into the driveway in front of JJL, Jake spotted Kola's bike parked in the shade at the side of the building. It was unusual for her to be at the studio on a Saturday. From day one she had made it quite clear that weekends were for friends and family. Hooking his sunglasses into the neck of his T-shirt, Jake made his way into the building that was gradually becoming a second home.

"Morning," he called out, closing the door behind him.

"In here, Jake," called back Dr Marrs from the live room.

"No one else in yet?" asked Jake as he entered the cool live room.

"Just you today," stated Kola bluntly.

"Does someone want to tell me why?"

"Jason wants the vocal done on that new song you played him on Wednesday," explained Jim Marrs. "I've strict orders to get it done today and on his desk for Monday."

Shaking his head in disbelief, Jake asked if the other tracking was complete on it.

"Paul was in last night doing the drum tracking," said Dr Marrs. "And Grey came in too. Rich will be in tonight."

"Ok, let's get this party started," muttered Jake, obviously annoyed at the short timescale demanded by Jason. The Englishman's demanding arrogance got under his skin and he could feel himself growing angry.

"There's a part two to this," added Kola, shooting a dark look at the producer.

"And what would that be?"

"His royal highness wants an acoustic version ready too," stated the sound engineer.

"His wish is my command," joked Jake, bowing theatrically in a vain attempt to mask his frustration with humour.

After a brief debate, they decided to record all of Jake's guitar tracking for the song, then take a break before recording the vocals. Once he was settled on a stool, acoustic guitar in hand, the musician's anger began to abate. The song, now tentatively titled Out Of The Shadows, was so new that, each time he played it, Jake was tempted to change parts. After he had tweaked several sections, Dr Marrs halted him abruptly.

"No more changes, Jake," he cautioned. "Time's against me here. This has to fit with the drums and bass track that I already have."

"Sorry, Jim," apologised Jake with a sigh. "Want me to go back to the original version?"

"Stick with where we are," relented the producer. "But no more changes."

"Deal," agreed Jake.

It took them another hour to record the acoustic guitar track, but eventually both producer and sound engineer were happy. With the first part in the bag, Kola announced she was going out for coffee and donuts. While she was gone, Jake set to work rehearsing the non-acoustic version of the tracking. Again he was tempted to make changes, but a dark, growling look from Dr Marrs reminded him to leave things as they were. A hit of caffeine was enough to re-focus him and it wasn't too long before they had the guitar tracks in the bag. From the control room, Dr Marrs gave him the thumbs up, then called through to suggest they stop for a late lunch. At Jake's suggestion, the three of them piled into his truck and, deciding that Milford was closer than Rehoboth, headed up the highway in search of an eating house. There was a brief, heated, childish debate about who wanted what that was cut short when Jake pulled up outside Bob Evans.

It was quiet inside the air-conditioned restaurant with only a handful of tables occupied. Their hostess was a mature lady who teased them about looking like rock stars. This tickled Kola's sense of humour, causing her to giggle uncontrollably into the menu.

"I wouldn't have thought you'd have been in a rush to stop around here?" commented Dr Marrs as they ate. "Wasn't it near here you were shot at?"

With his mouth full of salad, Jake nodded.

"Shot!" exclaimed Kola sharply. "Tell me more, Mr Power."

"Not much to tell," began Jake, trying to play it down. "We were playing an open air show sponsored by a local radio station last summer. A kid took a shot at me. Hit me on the outside edge of my knee. I tried to play on but I only lasted about three songs. I've still got a two-inch scar on my knee to prove it."

"Jesus," muttered Kola, almost choking on her burger. "You tried to play on? After you took a bullet? Are you crazy?"

"I didn't want to let everyone down. I went to the side for some medical treatment, but there wasn't anyone there. One of the crew threw me a roll of duct tape. I taped my thigh up tight and went back out. The guy brought me a stool, but we wrapped it all up short."

"You're insane," declared the sound engineer with a laugh. "Totally insane."

"It seemed like the right thing to do at the time."

"How did it feel going back out there next time round?" asked Dr Marrs curiously. "Weren't you scared?"

"Terrified," confessed Jake openly. "Once we were part way through the first number I was fine though."

"Still insane," muttered Kola. "Crazy musicians!"

They were back at the studio for four o'clock and, after a shortened warm up routine, Jake was ready to make a start on the vocal track. As with the guitar tracking, he opted to do the acoustic version first. He kept it very clean, exactly the same as when he had sung it for Jason. There was a natural warmth to the tone of his voice and both Kola and Dr Marrs nodded appreciatively when he was finished. At the producer's request, Jake sang it through three more times. Recording the non-acoustic styled vocal ran just as smoothly.

"Thanks for that, Jake," called Dr Marrs warmly. "We're done here."

"Glad to hear it," joked Jake, reaching for his bottle of water. "Do you need me back out here tomorrow?"

"You're good till Monday," assured Jim Marrs. "Unless you want to come in."

"I'll see what tomorrow brings," suggested Jake as he gathered up his belongings. "Lori and I might take a run out in the afternoon."

"We'll be here."

"Right, I'm out of here," declared Jake. "Don't stay too late, guys."

In the half light of dusk, Lori sat out on the deck, surrounded by lit candles. She had opened a bottle of wine after Jake had called to say he was on his way home with some Chinese food for dinner. Sipping her wine, Lori listened to the noise of the waves crashing in on the beach. One of the neighbouring houses was having a party and she could hear the bass rhythm of their music, accompanied by loud voices. It sounded like teenagers having fun. A typical summer beach resort evening soundscape. Silently, she reflected on the progress she had made workwise during the day. In a few short peaceful hours, she had accomplished more than she had for the last week or more. She hoped Jake's day had gone as smoothly and productively. When her current project was complete, the Silver Lake art work was next in her schedule.

So lost was she in her thoughts that Lori never heard Jake's truck pull up out front. When he stepped out onto the deck behind her, she let out a squeal of fright.

"Sorry, li'l lady," he apologised, setting the bag with their food down on the table. "Didn't mean to scare you."

"No harm done," she laughed. The enchanting, musical sound made him smile. "Just a little spilled wine. I was miles away."

"How was your day?" asked Jake, as he sat across from her. "Productive?"

"Very," replied Lori as she poured her fiancé a glass of wine. "Yours?"

"Same," he answered. "Jason wanted a rush job on one of the new tracks. Paul and Grey did their bit last night. Rich is going in tomorrow."

"And is your bit done?"

"All done," he declared proudly, raising his glass. "Jim Marrs is in for a long weekend. Kola too."

"Poor guy," sighed Lori then turning her attention to the bag of food in front of them she asked. "What did you pick up for dinner?"

"Your favourite noodle dish."

As they ate, they chatted about how the recording was going, the themes emerging from the record and the timescales for the remaining tracks to be completed. A few of Jake's comments gave Lori flashes of insight for her forthcoming commission. She had asked him about the track Jason wanted rushed through and he confessed he had written the lyric about Grey's situation.

"Has he realised?" asked Lori quietly.

"I don't know," confessed Jake a little awkwardly. "He's obviously heard the lyrics, but I don't know how closely he listened."

"Maybe you should tell him." suggested Lori, concerned that the rather private bass player might be offended by the sentiment.

"Let me play it to you and you can judge for yourself," countered Jake. "Once you've heard it, if you think Grey will be angry, I'll call him."

Lori tidied up the dinner debris, then settled herself on the couch in the sun room while Jake fetched a guitar from the basement. His favourite acoustic was out at JJL so he opted for one he occasionally used on stage. It was a more expensive instrument with beautiful mother of pearl inlays, but he hadn't developed a close relationship with it yet. Stretching his long, denim clad legs out in front of him, Jake settled himself on the floor, leaning back against the closed patio doors. He refined the guitar's tuning, flashed a smile at his fiancée then began the gently picked intro to the song. The warm tone to the vocal when Jake began to sing sent tingles down Lori's spine as she sat entranced by what she was hearing. Instantly, she could tell why Jason was so excited by the song. Jake had written something truly special. Despite her initial concerns, the lyrics were beautifully subtle and, if you didn't already know the bass player's personal circumstances, then you wouldn't guess it related to him. When he finished the song, Jake sat still with his head bowed, his blonde hair falling carelessly over his face.

"That was fantastic," enthused Lori, a huge smile lighting up her face. "Stunningly beautiful."

"Not going to offend Grey then?" asked Jake looking up slowly.

"Not at all," assured Lori. "But answer me one question."

"What?"

"Is he falling for Kola?"

"He's not said as much, but I suspect so," replied Jake, laying the guitar back in its velvet lined case. "I also suspect the feelings are mutual."

As she had anticipated, Lori received a phone call from Jason early on Monday morning. She was still finishing her first coffee of the day when the phone rang. The Englishman was polite but cut straight to the point.

"Mz Hyde, I need a design for Silver Lake's next single by Friday noon," he stated bluntly.

"Jason, I've a midweek deadline on the Molton cover," replied Lori, her tone equally blunt. "And I'm not finished it yet."

"Fine, but I need a cover for their single by Friday."

Taking a deep breath and counting to ten before she spoke, Lori stated, "If I do this, then the fee is double due to the unrealistic timescales here and the design will be quite straightforward. Nothing overly complex or detailed."

"Double!" exclaimed Jason sharply. "It's your boyfriend's band. What happened to mate's rates?"

"Not applicable when you expect at least a week's work in two days, Jason."

There was silence on the line for what felt like an eternity.

"Alright, Lori, you win," conceded the Englishman. "Speak to Gary and the band. Get a feel for what they want, then call me."

"Leave it with me, Jason," replied Lori, feeling pleased with herself for holding her ground.

With Jake out of the house planning a late night at JJL laying down guitar tracks, Lori set to work finalising her Molton commission. Barely stopping to eat, she was still at her drawing board when Jake finally came home at midnight. The design was almost finished. When he saw how pale and tired she was, he insisted she call it a night.

"I need another couple of hours," protested Lori, as he lifted her off her chair and carried her through the house. "Please, Jake."

"You're exhausted, li'l lady," he stated firmly. "I promise I'll waken you when I go out for my run in the morning but you need sleep."

Realising it was futile to resist, Lori snuggled into his shoulder and allowed him to carry her off to the bedroom. In her heart, she knew he was right. She was mentally and physically exhausted from focusing on the detailed drawing. There were so many layers to the design that drew the viewer's eye into the tunnel of rooms that it was a challenging piece to focus on for long periods of time. Gently, Jake sat her down on the bed and, before she could protest, he slipped her jeans off her and removed her T-shirt. With warm, nimble fingers, he removed her underwear, then carefully slid the T-shirt she wore to sleep in over her head. Pulling back the lightweight summer duvet, he settled her down like a mother would a child, tucking her in.

"Sweet dreams, li'l lady," he whispered, kissing her forehead, her eyes already closing.

"Night, rock star," she mumbled sleepily.

By the time Jake had removed his own clothes and climbed into bed beside her, she was fast asleep, a half smile on her face.

Sun was streaming into the Mercedes as Lori drove out to JJL the next afternoon. With the Molton project emailed off for approval, she had decided to lunch with Maddy and the twins before heading out to the studio to talk to Gary and the band. Lunch had been chaotic out at the farmhouse. Both she and Maddy had tried to eat their salad while balancing a grizzling baby on their lap. The twins, at ten weeks old, had had their first vaccinations and were grumpy and out of sorts. It was with a pang of guilt that she had left her friend with the babies, but she knew she had to get out to the studio and time was short enough on this impromptu Silver Lake project. Having parked the car beside Jake's truck, Lori made her way into the building. A cool blast of air met her in the entrance porch and the building beyond was delightfully cool inside. From the foyer, she heard Rich and Jake playing a powerful sounding duet. Trying to be as quiet as she could, Lori slipped into the control room beside Jim Marrs.

"Hi," she said softly, taking a seat beside him at the mixing desk. The vast array of buttons, switches and dials never ceased to amaze her.

"Afternoon, Mz Hyde," replied the producer curtly. "Were we expecting you?"

"Surprise visit to get some inspiration for his Royal Highness' rush job," joked Lori with a smile. "If I'm interrupting though I'll go."

"Too late," commented Dr Marrs. "You've been spotted."

Looking through to the live room, Lori saw Jake and Rich waving at her like two naughty school kids.

"Sorry," apologised Lori, trying hard not to giggle at their antics.

"No harm done," sighed the producer. "We were due to take a break. You've got thirty minutes, Mz Hyde. Not a minute over."

"I'll be quick," promised Lori sincerely. "Thanks for this, Jim."

"Go on through before I change my mind."

As she reached the door into the live room, Jake opened it and wrapped her in his arms. Nuzzling into her neck, he whispered "Boy, am I glad to see you, li'l lady."

"Rough day?" she asked quietly.

"Something like that," he sighed softly. "Anyway, what brings you out here?"

"The car," she joked with a mischievous giggle.

"Very droll, Mz Hyde," he groaned. "I heard Jim say you've got thirty minutes. You'd better get in here quick."

After a quick round of greetings and a general grumble about the lack of progress, Silver Lake were ready to listen to Lori. Keeping it brief, she explained that she wanted something quite stripped back and bare for the single cover design, but if there was to be a theme for the remaining album artwork then she wanted to pick up on it as soon as possible. Grasping her dilemma, the band exchanged glances. There were shoulder shrugs and a couple of non-committal grunts.

"Guys," began Lori, sounding a little desperate. "I'm looking for a hint here. I'm quite happy to go with my own interpretation, but I felt you might want some input."

"You're right," acknowledged Rich as he lifted a bottle of water. "We're just a little frazzled just now. What were you thinking of doing?"

"I've had two thoughts," revealed Lori calmly. "One was to use photography for a change. A black and white shot of either sunrise or sunset shadows. The other idea was to create a "character" for the album and have him or her emerge from a dark place into bright sunlight. Something a bit creepy and evil looking."

"I like the sound of them both," confessed Grey with a yawn from his reclined position on the couch at the side of the room. "As long as it doesn't look like me or Kola."

Jake blushed, then said, "You knew?"

"Yup," said the bass player. "Don't shit yourself, Jake. I'm flattered. It's an awesome song."

"I like the idea of a creepy character," said Paul. "A kind of Gollum thing. Something we could tie back to the Celtic knot and stuff."

"Perhaps," agreed Lori hopefully. "I just don't have much time to play with here."

"When does Jason need it for?"

"Friday," she stated. "And we're already almost through Tuesday."

"Can you come up with a Silver Lake imp in that time?" asked Jake, taking her hand. "I kind of like that idea. We could carry it through the album cover, merchandise. You know, all that shit."

The boys nodded in agreement.

"Ok, imp it is," said Lori, relieved that a decision had been reached." Leave it with me."

"And you're sure you can do it in the time frame?" checked Rich. "It's not too big an ask?"

"I'll do it," promised Lori with a smile. "Now get back to work, boys. Dinner at the house on Friday?"

"Deal," called Grey from the couch. "I'll bring beer."

"Bring Kola," invited Lori, with a wink to Jake. "I'll see you all later."

Leaning heavily on her cane, she walked out of the live room without a backwards glance. Once back out in the hallway, she met Gary, who was chatting on his cell phone. She started to head past him, but he reached out to stop her and mouthed, "Wait a minute, please."

Lori nodded and took a seat on the smart couch that dominated the small reception area. Within a few seconds, Gary had sat down beside her and was clearly winding up his call. Stuffing the phone back into his pocket, he apologised for delaying her.

"No problem," replied Lori warmly. "You ok?"

"I think so," replied the band's manager. "I've decided to stick with Silver Lake. I was just cancelling the other job."

"And are you ok with that?" asked Lori, noting the confusion written all over his face.

Gary nodded. "It's the right decision."

"You don't sound too sure," commented Lori, trying to get him to open up to her. "I sense a but."

"It's a stupid but," he laughed, looking embarrassed. "I'm homesick for England."

"Why not go back for a few days?" she suggested. "The boys would understand."

"I'm needed here until the end of August. Jason has me under strict orders to be working for this band twenty-four seven," Gary explained quietly. "I'm going to call my sister. See if she'll come out in August. Maybe I'll be able to fly back with her for a week or so. I miss my young brother too."

"I hate to see you unhappy, Gary," began Lori. "But there's not a lot I can do, is there?"

"You're doing it, Lori. You're listening," he said with a sad smile. "Don't say anything to Jake or the others. I'll be fine in a day or so."

"I won't," she promised. "But I think you should tell them. They'll understand. They've all got family."

"Maybe," he conceded, then changing the subject, asked if she'd started on the design for the new single.

"No, but I have a plan and some inspiration," she replied. "I'm heading home now to start work on it. Come over on Friday night. The boys are all coming. I'll reveal the design then."

"Sounds good to me," said Gary smiling. "Scott'll be back by then too. Can I bring him along? He's out in LA on a video shoot until Thursday."

"The more the merrier," declared Lori, getting to her feet. "I'll see you both on Friday."

"Looking forward to it."

There were discarded sketches scattered all over the sun room floor when Jake arrived home after dinner. Pausing to gather them all up, he saw that they were various incarnations of the Silver Lake imp. Some of them were really evil looking characters, but none of them were finished off. Carrying the pile of half-finished drawings, he wandered out onto the deck where Lori was sitting, focussed on the sketch in front of her.

"Evening, li'l lady," he said softly, his voice a little husky after spending the previous two hours making a start on the vocals. "Are you winning yet?"

"Yes," she replied, without looking up.

"Can I see?" asked Jake hopefully, trying to sneak a peek over her shoulder.

"Not yet. Patience, rock star."

Ok, I can take a hint," laughed Jake backing off. "I'm going to watch TV. Can I get you anything?"

"No thank you," replied Lori only half listening to him.

In front of her, in the half dark and candlelight, the wizened face of the Silver Lake imp was taking shape. After many false starts, she had finally settled on a male imp with a wistfully wrinkled and scarred face. At first, she had wrestled with the colour of his eyes before deciding the whole face looked best with milky white cataracts over the eyes. She had clothed him in a midnight blue, tattered, hooded cloak with a brooch holding it fastened at his chest. The brooch was a miniature version of the circular Celtic knot that she had given to Jake just after they met. Eventually, she was satisfied with her creation.

On the table beside her, the candles had almost burnt out and the air had grown chilly. Gathering up her sketches and pencils, Lori headed back indoors. Jake was stretched out on the larger of the two couches sound asleep, a baseball game playing on the TV. He looked incredibly peaceful in slumber. It was unusual for him to nap like this, but Lori guessed it had been a long day out at JJL. Trying to be quiet, she reached for the remote to turn off the game, but accidentally knocked over an empty glass with her foot. The clatter startled Jake.

"Wha'? Who won?" he muttered sleepily.

"Game's still on," replied Lori, resisting the temptation to hit the red button. "You were asleep, rock star."

"Long day and a bit of a migraine," confessed Jake sitting up. "Did you find our imp?"

"I think so," she replied with a smile. "Now, bed for you, rock star."

"Can I see him?"

For a moment Lori hesitated, then decided to let Jake take one quick look at the character she had created. Passing him her sketchbook, she watched to gauge his reaction."

"Wow!" exclaimed Jake, his eyes lighting up with enthusiasm. "He's a powerful creation."

"Will he do?" she asked, praying that the answer was a resounding "yes".

Handing her back the drawing, Jake declared, "I think he's perfect. He's ugly. He's vulnerable. Yet there's a like-ability factor there."

"Thank you. Now, not a word to the others, please."

"I'll try," promised Jake with a smile. "I love how you got the knot design into his cloak. He's amazing."

"Well, he'll have to stay secret for another couple of days," warned Lori, her tone harsher than she had intended. "Now, time to call it a night."

♫

The first streaks of dawn were lighting the sky on Friday morning before Lori finally finished off the cover artwork for "Out Of The Shadows". Despite Jake's protests, she had refused to stop work until the design was finished. Working at night when the house was quiet and creaking occasionally, helped her to create the eerie, dark half of the design. She had created a scene where the imp was emerging from his cave dwelling into the evening sun. In contrast to his short, ugly, twisted form, she had drawn his shadow as a tall, muscular figure. Light and dark; short and tall; ugly and beautiful. The contrasts pleased her. As she scanned the finished piece and emailed it to Jason, she prayed he liked it. She forwarded a copy to Gary, asking him to share it with the band. Satisfied that her work was done, Lori crawled off to bed.

The gentle strains of Metallica's "Enter Sandman" roused Jake from sleep at seven thirty. Reaching to silence the alarm, he was relieved to find Lori asleep at his side. She had worked late on Wednesday night and had looked completely exhausted the previous night when he had called it a day at midnight. Now, sleeping beside him, she looked pale and drawn, an ethereal quality to her beauty. Silently, he slipped out of bed, picked up his running gear and crept out of the room. Having dressed in the main bathroom, Jake headed out for a run before it was time to drive out to the studio. Pounding out a few miles along the sand in the cool morning sunlight recharged the batteries to his soul. As he ran, his mind raced ahead to the schedule for the day. Despite the rough start to the week, Silver Lake had completed about half of the guitar tracking and were ahead of schedule. They had revised their plan of attack for the coming week to allow some rehearsal time for the record company event in Philadelphia. It might only be a short three song set, but they were under strict instructions to be note perfect.

A rogue wave broke over his feet as he ran, the cold rush of water, bringing him back to the present. First thing in the morning, the beach was a beautifully, idyllic place to be. So quiet.

Only seabirds for company. With a heavy heart, Jake turned after twenty minutes and ran hard and fast back towards the house. Skipping breakfast, he showered and changed, grabbed his satchel and headed off to JJL, leaving Lori a scribbled note. "We'll be here for dinner by 6. J x"

On the drive out to the studio, Jake ran through some of his vocal warm up exercises. When he had left the studio the day before, the plan had been for him to do vocals for most of the day as Rich couldn't come in until after lunch. Neither Grey nor Paul were scheduled to be there, so they had declared their intention to spend the day fishing at the beach. As he swung the truck into his preferred parking space, a day's fishing sounded heavenly.

"Morning," called Kola as he stepped down from the truck.

"Morning," replied Jake then noting the tray she was carrying added, "I hope there's a coffee and some breakfast there for me."

"Sure is."

Once inside, they sat in the control room with Dr Marrs, listening to some of the tracks that Jake was to sing the vocals for. In the corner, the white board suddenly didn't look so bare - each of the tracks had at least three squares scored off. Only three out of the fifteen had the vocals crossed out. "Out Of The Shadows" was the only completed song. Sipping his latte, Jake asked, "What's the plan for the day?"

"Vocals for tracks twelve, seven, four and one," stated Dr Marrs firmly. "In that order. No messing. No frills. Then we'll see if we have any time left."

"And Rich is doing backing vocals when he comes in?"

"If you're done by then," said the producer, taking the last donut hole out of the bag. "How long do you need to warm up?"

"Give me half an hour," Jake suggested getting to his feet. "I was warming up in the truck on the way out here but it's way too early for this shit."

"You've got thirty minutes, Jake," stated Jim Marrs with a grin. "I'll leave you to it. I need to go and call Gary."

Recording vocals always gave Jake a buzz and, suitably warmed up, with the lyric sheets stacked in front of him, he was eager to get started. He had expressed a preference at the outset of the project to be alone in the studio to record the vocal tracks this time round. Some of the new material was stretching and he wanted a degree of privacy to record those tracks in particular. When he reviewed the running order for the day, he appreciated that the producer had picked a pretty smart schedule. The mid to lower range more straightforward tracks were first, with the higher more complex songs left for the end, when his voice would be as warmed up as it was going to get. Tracks twelve and seven were two of the heavier numbers and, initially, he felt self-conscious performing in front of Kola and Dr Marrs. After three false starts at the first one, Jim Marrs called through. "Turn round, Jake. Don't face us. Find your own space in that room. Ignore us."

"Easy for you to say, my friend," he laughed nervously. "Easy for you."

"Just try it."

A simple suggestion, thought Jake, as he repositioned himself. With his back to the control room, he started again. Instinct soon overruled his nerves and he was quickly lost in the song. With the occasional request or instruction from Dr Marrs, Jake focused himself on the work to be done. A couple of times during tracks seven and four, he was the one to halt proceedings and request that they try things differently.

In the control room, both sound engineer and producer sat in awe of the talent on display in front of them. Having worked with Silver Lake previously, Dr Marrs knew what Jake was capable of but Kola confessed that she had never really heard him sing before. As the time passed, she grew more and more star struck as Jake's vocals surpassed expectation with every verse. Just as they were about to tackle the final track of the session, Rich arrived, sneaking silently into the control room. Track one was a complex song for Jake to sing. It started with a high ghost-like intro verse then quickly moved into the main body of the song at a deeper faster tempo. Immediately after the guitar solo, the final vocal section returned to the ghost-like quality. The lyrics were about an apocalypse; a total destruction of something; the ruination of a community and the after effects. Eventually, after a couple of takes Jake called a halt.

"Have you got what you need back there?" he asked, hanging his headphones up on the mic stand.

"Sure have," called back Rich.

At the sound of the guitarist's voice, Jake turned round, "How long have you been back there?"

"Long enough," declared Rich, grinning at him through the glass. "That was fucking awesome, Jake! Can't wait to do that one live."

"It'll be a tough one," admitted Jake, heading towards the control room. "A real tough one."

"Nothing to a man of your talents, Jake."

Blushing profusely, Jake yelled back, "Get your ass in here and let's get back to work!"

A constant ringing noise wakened Lori sharply. Still more asleep than awake, she reached for her cell phone.

"Hello," she mumbled sleepily.

"Mz Hyde?" came Jason's voice, for once sounding a little hesitant.

"Jason!" she replied, instantly more alert. "Sorry, you woke me."

"Apologies," muttered the Englishman. "Is it not mid-afternoon there?"

Glancing at the clock, Lori agreed, then explained that she had been up all night finalising the design for the single.

"And worth every second of lost sleep, Mz Hyde," he declared enthusiastically. "It's fabulous! The possibilities here are endless."

"Thank you."

"Have the band seen it yet?"

"I mailed it to Gary to share with them," she answered, as she sat up in bed. "Jake's seen the imp character, but not the final cover."

"I'll get feedback from Gary. I hope they love it as much as I do. Is this theme going to carry over onto the album art?"

"That was the plan," she said. "I just wasn't sure you'd like it."

"Love it, Mz Hyde!" he enthused. "And I don't say that too often. Need to run. I'll be in touch via email with the full remit for the album pieces."

"Fine. Run the numbers through David first," suggested Lori. "If the numbers don't look good, he'll negotiate with you on my behalf."

"I'll make sure he approves it all first. Talk to you next week. I assume you're coming up to Philadelphia?"

"Probably not," said Lori softly. "I'll see you soon though."

Placing her phone back on the night stand, Lori let out a sigh of relief. In all the time she had worked for Jason, she had never heard him so enthusiastic about a design. Still smiling like the cat who'd got the cream, she headed into the shower.

Deciding that she had earned a few hours off, Lori fixed herself a sandwich and took it, along with her sketchpad, out onto the sundeck. While she had been working on the band's imp design, she had come up with an idea for Danny's tattoo. In the midst of her work, she had all but forgotten the deadline that was looming on that particular commission. With the sun beating down on her damp hair and bare shoulders, she set to work. The idea she had conceived was a little quirky, leaving her unsure if Danny would like it. She debated with herself, then opted to prepare two designs for him to choose from. It didn't take her long to do a Celtic knot-style design, based on images of intertwined tattoo guns. This was her "safe" design and, although it was her fall back, Lori was really pleased with it. With the first design completed, she started on the "real" one, her preferred option. The design was a bit of a twist on the imp idea. She had opted to draw a beautiful, fairy princess, stepping out of an ornate doorway. If the design was inked as it was drawn, then the depth perspective would make it look as though she was stepping out of the tattoo artist's butt cheek. She deliberately chose to draw a very feminine figure, clothed in a dress of shades of blue, her one concession against making it overly "girly."

Just as she was putting the final touches to the drawing, she heard Jake's truck pull up in front of the house.

"Lori!" he called from indoors a few moments later.

"Out here!"

Still wearing his sunglasses, Jake stepped out onto the deck, looking every inch the rock star in his tight jeans, black band T-shirt and boots.

"Lord, it's hot out here," he declared as he came over to sit at the table.

"It's gorgeous," sighed Lori, laying her pencil down beside her sketchpad. "Do you like this one?"

She turned the fairy design towards him.

Lifting his sunglasses up, Jake admired the drawing, then asked if it was for Silver Lake.

"No," she giggled. "It's my tattoo design for Danny."

"It's brilliant! He can't have much skin left to ink. Any idea where he's putting it?"

Still giggling, Lori replied, "His butt."

Jake threw back his head and laughed. "Perfect! And you asked for a photo of the finished tattoo? Love your style, Mz Hyde!"

"I've done a second one as a backup," confessed Lori, turning the page over to reveal the tattoo gun Celtic knot. "I'll give them both to him."

"That's clever," admired Jake approvingly. "If he's got enough skin left, I can see him going for both."

"I thought we could drop them in to him tomorrow. Are you still free tomorrow?"

"That's the plan," replied Jake. "I could talk to him about my next addition."

"Have you decided on something?"

"I keep changing my mind," admitted Jake. "I was thinking of adding to the music on my arm, but I'm not sure. Or I could add something to my sword."

"I could design you a butt tattoo," teased Lori with a mischievous glint in her bright, blue eyes.

"Perhaps," he mused with a smile. "Now, I'm going to get changed and go for a swim before the others get here."

"Who's all coming?" asked Lori as she tidied up her sketching materials.

"The rest of the band, Dr Marrs, Kola, Linsey and, I think, Paul's bringing Maddy with him. Gary was going to pick up Scott. I'm not sure if Todd is planning to drop by. He was hoping to pick up an extra shift at work," rhymed off Jake. "Do we have enough food?"

"I hope so!" giggled Lori. "There's plenty of burgers and chicken. I bought some ribs the other day. If anyone wants shrimp, they'll need to bring it with them."

"Rich said Linsey was bringing a seafood salad. I'll call Jim Marrs and get him to stop off and pick up some shrimp."

The roar of Kola's Harley Davidson sent chills through Lori as the sound engineer pulled up out the front around dusk. Almost everyone else had arrived, the BBQ coals were hot and Jake and Grey were ready to play chef for the night. Hearing Kola arrive, the bass player excused himself and darted round to the front of the house, Sensing Lori's anxiety, Jake came over to sit beside her on the sun lounger.

"So, when do we get to see the cover for our single?" he asked, in an effort to distract her mind from thoughts of motorbikes.

"Gary didn't share it with you then?" she asked, looking over at the band's manager.

"Not yet," he replied. "I was waiting until we were all here. I've had it printed off poster sized. It's in the car."

"Go and fetch it, boy!" snapped Maddy, feigning anger. "And be quick about it!"

"Yes, ma'am," laughed Gary, getting up from his seat on the deck.

"Nice to know you're still calling the shots, boss," teased Jake.

"Someone needs to keep that boy on his toes," laughed Maddy as she took a large mouthful of wine. The twins had been left in the care of Grey's mother and, when she had arrived, Maddy had declared her intention to party.

At that moment Grey returned with his arm protectively around Kola's slender waist. "Who lit the fire under Gary?"

Laughing, Jake pointed at Maddy.

"Figures," muttered Grey, stopping to take a lite beer out of the cool box for Kola. "You know everyone, don't you, Kola?"

Nodding, she said shyly, "I think so."

"No need to be shy around here," said Grey, grinning over at Lori. "The gracious Mz Hyde is used to us all."

"Ain't that the truth," declared Lori, trying and failing to stifle a giggle.

"Ok. Listen up a minute," called Gary from the doorway. "Lori, do you want to do the honours?"

"No," she replied, blushing slightly at the knowledge her design was about to make its public debut.

"Here, I'll help you," offered Jake, crossing the deck towards the band's young manager.

Having taken a corner each, on a count of three, Gary and Jake unrolled the poster-sized copy of the single cover.

"Wow!" exclaimed Grey. "He's ugly!"

"He's fabulous," declared Rich and Linsey in unison.

"Perfect as ever, Mz Hyde," Maddy complimented warmly. "So much for keeping it simple."

"Thanks," said Lori, her cheeks now scarlet. "He just kind of evolved."

Leaving Gary holding the entire poster, Jake stepped round for a closer look. He drank in the design in front of him, then went straight over to Lori and kissed her full on the lips, adding to her embarrassment.

"Maddison's right, li'l lady," he whispered. "That's perfect."

"Let's have a toast," interrupted Rich loudly. "Here's to the talented and beautiful Mz Hyde!"

"To Lori!" agreed the others in a loud chorus.

"And to Silver Lake," added Lori with a smile. "And to rock and fucking roll!"

Much later, after they had all eaten their fill and the leftovers had been cleared away, Rich and Jake fetched two guitars from the basement. They had just begun to play when Todd arrived with Kate, apologising for being so late. While Lori rustled up two plates of food for them, Jake sent Todd to fetch himself a guitar. Relaxed in the warmth of the summer night, Jake and Rich coaxed the teenager into playing with them. After some encouragement, Kate was persuaded to sing a few numbers. As the youngsters revelled in the luxury of jamming with Silver Lake, Maddy whispered to Lori, "Those kids have got real talent."

"I know," agreed Lori smiling warmly. "Jim, when are they due into JJL for their studio slot?"

"End of the month," replied the producer. "I've got their time mapped out already."

From his seat in the corner, Scott was surreptitiously videoing the impromptu performance. No one appeared to have noticed him until Maddy reached over and tapped him on the shoulder. "No sneaky You Tube or Facebook videos, sunshine."

"Not at all," he promised, looking a little sheepish. "Jason wants me to film the band off duty for a DVD release to accompany the new record."

"I'm watching you," warned Maddy sternly.

"Yes, ma'am," replied the young filmmaker.

Oblivious to the video camera, Jake had coaxed Kate into doing a duet with him. The young girl was reluctant at first, but Jake won her over with one of his famous "Power" smiles. While Todd and Rich played, Jake and Kate duetted on "Highway To Hell". Her confidence growing, Kate then sang a rendition of U2's "Beautiful Day". Her voice rang out clear and strong over the acoustic accompaniment from the two Silver Lake guitarists. When the song was over, she said shyly that she would leave the rest to the professionals.

"Don't sell yourself short, young lady," scolded Maddy sternly. "You could out-perform Mr Power here any day."

The shy teenager had no answer to that and sat quietly, not knowing where to look. Shortly before eleven, Todd lay down the guitar he had borrowed and said that they would have to leave – curfew was looming. Once the young couple had left, Rich and Jake sat playing quietly. The others were scattered around the spacious deck, sprawled on sun loungers and chairs, chatting casually. The perfect relaxed Friday night after a long week in the studio. Watching Jake and the others, Lori smiled quietly to herself. Seeing them all chilling out gave her a happy warm feeling inside.

Rehoboth was busy next afternoon as Jake and Lori walked hand in hand along the boardwalk. Both of them had slept late after the party the night before, but surprisingly, both had wakened feeling refreshed and clear headed. They had arranged to meet Grey and Kola for an early dinner, but had to visit Danny at the tattoo parlour first. When they reached the main avenue, Lori apologised that she needed to rest for a few moments. The walk along the sand and then the boardwalk had taken its toll on her and she could feel her leg beginning to protest. When she asked for a seat, Jake began to fuss.

"I'm fine," she promised him sincerely. "I just need a minute or two."

"We should've driven in," muttered Jake, sitting on the bench beside her.

"Nonsense. I'll be fine in a moment," assured Lori, taking his hand. "Remember the first time we went to visit Danny?"

"Sure do," grinned Jake. "It was after my last shift at the pizza place."

"Yes," recalled Lori with a smile. "And I had to take a cab into town to meet you. At least this time I've made it here under my own steam."

"True," acknowledged Jake, hugging her. "I just worry about you. I don't like to see you in pain, li'l lady."

"Stop worrying, Jake. I'm fine."

They sat people watching for a few minutes, then began to head up the street towards Danny's shop. It was almost closing time when they arrived and the diminutive tattoo artist was finishing up his last client of the day. Taking a seat on the bench, Lori and Jake waited until he was done and had flipped the "open" sign over to "closed".

"Well, good afternoon," he greeted them enthusiastically. "My two favourite celebrity clients."

"Cut the crap, Dan," laughed Jake, shaking the ink artist's hand.

"To what do I owe the honour?"

"I come bearing gifts," giggled Lori, reaching into her bag for the envelope containing the two designs.

"Ah, princess," sighed Danny, accepting the large envelope. "I thought you'd forgotten."

"Would I dare?"

"Obviously not."

"I did two for you," commented Lori, a bubble of anticipation growing inside her.

Carefully, he opened the envelope and pulled out the two designs. He inspected the tattoo gun Celtic knot design first and nodded approvingly. When he saw the second design, his eyes lit up instantly.

"Naughty, Mz Hyde," he commented, raising one eyebrow. "And perfect."

"I wasn't sure if that was what you had in mind or not when you said quirky," explained Lori, relieved that he liked the design.

"To be honest, princess," he announced. "I love them both. I'm just not sure where to get the gun knot done. It's a wonderful mark for my art."

"Well, they are both yours to do with as you please," she said warmly. "Just remember the second part of the deal."

"Yes, I know," he laughed, sliding the designs back into the envelope. "You want photos of the finished article. Although why you want a picture of my butt is beyond me. Now, Jake, when are you coming back to sit on my throne?"

"Soon," promised Jake. "I did want to ask you something."

"What?"

Standing up, Jake quickly removed his T-shirt and pulled his hair out of the way. With his back to Danny, he asked, "Is there any scope to add a bit onto the pommel of the sword?"

"Kneel down, Jake," instructed Danny bluntly. "No way can I see that high!"

"Sorry," apologised Jake, kneeling in front of his friend.

The tattoo artist inspected the large sword tattoo before commenting. "I guess you could add something on, but it might take the design quite far up the back of your neck. If it were me, I wouldn't mess with it, but it's your call, Jake."

"Ok, back to the drawing board," sighed Jake, getting up from the floor.

"What did you want to add?" asked Danny.

"A circular Celtic knot. The design Lori did for our first album cover. It's kind of grown to symbolise the band," he explained, reaching for his discarded T-shirt.

"You could put it on your chest," suggested Danny. "Over your heart."

"I could," mused Jake, glancing down at his bare chest. "Not sure how it would look there."

"Here's a thought," began Danny. "Send me the design. I'll prepare a transfer for it. We can draw it on in detail. If you don't like it, I'll wash it off. If you do, we ink it in. No charge to you for the trial run."

Glancing over at Lori as if seeking her approval, Jake replied, "Sounds like a plan to me. How long do you need?"

"How about coming in on Friday afternoon?"

"Thursday might be better for me. We're rehearsing Friday out at JJL. I can slip away easier on Thursday."

"I'll stay late for you. Be here no later than five thirty. Get the design to me by Monday night."

"Perfect. Thanks, Dan."

"Pleasure as always," he replied. "Maybe I'll get a picture of this one."

"Unlikely," laughed Jake, pulling on his T-shirt. "I meant to say, that's a beautiful job you did on Lori's ankle. I'm impressed."

"I was pleased with that one myself," Danny admitted. "Fine work's a challenge, but a reward too when it turns out as well as that did."

"I love it," added Lori. "We'd better make a move if we're going to be on time for dinner, Jake."

"Yeah," he agreed, as he draped his arm around her shoulder. "I'll email that design over, Dan, and I'll see you on Thursday."

"Looking forward to it."

When they entered the restaurant a short while later, Grey and Kola were already seated at a table waiting for them. There was no sign of Becky, which surprised Lori slightly.

"Sorry we're late," apologised Jake, taking a seat.

"Wouldn't expect anything less of you, Mr Power," joked Grey.

"Ok. Ok," laughed Jake. "I know, I'm always late."

"We were at Danny's," explained Lori. "He kept us chatting."

"More ink?" asked the bass player.

"Not for me," answered Lori with a smile. "Well, not yet. I was dropping off two designs he'd asked me to do."

Quickly she explained about the deal she had done with the tattoo artist and about the designs she had presented him with. Jake then added that he was planning the next addition to his "ink library".

"Do you have any, Kola?" asked Jake, in an attempt to get the shy sound engineer to join in the conversation.

"A few," she confessed coyly. "I like angels."

"She has a stunning set of wings," added Grey, much to her embarrassment.

Sensing it was time to change the subject, Lori asked where Becky was.

"My mom's got her again tonight," replied Grey. "I'll pick her up tomorrow after lunch."

"He doesn't think she's ready to meet me," stated Kola calmly. "He doesn't want me to confuse her."

"That's part of it," confessed the bass player. "It's still early days, angel."

Fortunately, the waitress approached at that moment to take their order, saving Grey from having to defend himself further. Once they had ordered, Lori asked Kola what had brought her to the east coast.

"I needed my own space," replied the younger woman. "LA is great, but I wanted to step out of the shadow of my family. Plus my brother was already here."

"Is there something you're not confessing here?" asked Jake, intrigued by her answer.

"My dad's in the music business. I wanted to be recognised for my own efforts and not for being his daughter."

"So who's daddy?"

"Jake," growled Grey softly. "Leave it."

"It's ok," interrupted Kola, touching his arm. "My dad, Nick, plays guitar for the metal band Black Ashes."

Both Jake and Lori exchanged glances. Black Ashes had been a huge "big hair" metal act in the 1980's.

"I've done some work for them," admitted Lori. "Interesting guys."

"When did you do stuff for them?" asked Grey, keen to take the spotlight off his date.

"Just after college," Lori began, then went on to explain which album cover she had done for them. "They liked their angels too, as I remember."

"Dad still does," laughed Kola, finally relaxing. "He's got a full set of burnt wings tattooed on his back. My mom hated it."

"Are they still playing?" asked Jake. "I've not come across them for a while."

"Occasionally," answered Kola quietly. "Keeping them clean and sober long enough is the challenge there."

"I hear you," sympathised Jake. "Did you never fancy being in a band?"

"No," she said instantly. "Never."

"Ah, raw nerve. Sorry," apologised Jake, feeling a little guilty for putting her back on her guard again.

"No need to apologise. I prefer the technical side to the performing."

It was still early when their meal was over, but sensing that Grey and Kola wanted to spend time alone, Lori suggested that they get a cab home. Both the bass player and the sound engineer invited them to join them for a few drinks, but, before Jake could accept, Lori said she really needed to get home. When the cab arrived, they said their goodbyes, promising to meet up the following weekend after the Philadelphia gig. Once in the car, Jake asked if she was ok, his voice full of concern.

"I'm fine," said Lori softly. "They just needed time on their own."

"Oh!" said Jake, the penny suddenly crashing down. "I guess."

"Grey must really care about that girl if he's prepared to leave Becky two nights running," observed Lori.

"I hadn't thought, but when you put it like that, li'l lady," admitted Jake with a smile. "She's a sweet girl. Really shy."

"Well, let's see how they get on," said Lori quietly. "Grey looks happier than I think I've ever seen him."

"I won't disagree there."

♫

Recording moved on swiftly at the start of the week out at JJL. More and more boxes were filled in on the white board. By the time they called it a day on 4th of July, they had fully completed ten out of the fifteen tracks and the remaining five were more or less there. Silver Lake had made a conscious decision to focus on the guitar tracking, to allow Jake to rest his voice for the short set planned for Saturday. None of them had made plans for the holiday. Jake and Rich worked late on into the night, rewriting two of the guitar solos at Dr Marrs' request. Eventually, they had the newly written parts recorded and headed home for a few hours rest before they were due back at the studio for rehearsals. Jason had emailed through the final details for the weekend's event. The venue had been changed and they were now lined up to play on the roof terrace at the record company's office block. The band had already decided on what to play during their short set and spent a few hours on Thursday running through the three numbers. Late afternoon, Jake laid down his guitar and declared he was leaving for the day.

"Once more on Out Of The Shadows," said Rich as he watched Jake lift his bag to depart.

"Sorry, guys," he called back over his shoulder. "I've an appointment in town. I'll be in first thing though."

Before any of them could stop him, he made good his escape. Despite the late afternoon traffic, he made it to Danny's just after five. The tattoo artist was waiting for him and, as Jake entered the shop, he instructed him to flip over the "open" sign.

The sun was setting by the time Jake pulled into the driveway. His chest was throbbing under the white dressing. Killing the engine, he lifted his bag and the envelope that Danny had given him and climbed out of the truck. As he came round the side of the house, he found Lori lying on one of the sun loungers. At first glance he thought she was asleep, but he noticed the ear buds and realised she was listening to her iPod. When she heard his feet on the decking, she sat up.

"You're late, rock star."

"Sorry. Danny took longer than I expected. What's for dinner? I'm starving," replied Jake, kissing her on the forehead.

"There's some cold roast chicken and salad," said Lori starting to get up.

"Stay where you are, li'l lady. Have you eaten?"

"Hours ago," answered Lori, subconsciously rubbing her thigh.

"I'll fix myself a plate and be right back."

A few minutes later, Jake returned with a plate piled high with chicken salad and two bottles of beer.

"What were you listening to?" he asked as he sat down at the table.

"A few advance tracks for my next commission," she replied, rolling up her earphones around her iPod. "Trying to listen out for some inspiration. How was your day?"

"Fine. We were playing through the tracks for Saturday," answered Jake, through a mouthful of chicken. "Oh, I've got something for you."

"What?"

"Danny gave me an envelope for you. I left it on your desk."

"Is it what I think it is?" asked Lori, getting slowly and deliberately to her feet.

"Are you ok?" asked Jake, noticing the grimace of pain she was trying to hide.

"More or less," confessed Lori, rubbing her thigh. "I slipped in the bathroom this morning. Got a bruise to prove it and I've pulled something."

"Did you get yourself checked out?"

"I'm fine, Jake," she promised firmly. "I'm just a bit stiff from sitting. Trust me, I can tell when I've done some damage."

"Are you sure?"

"I'm sure," she insisted as she limped into the house.

A few seconds later, Jake heard the wonderful musical sound of her laughter. When she stepped back out onto the deck, Lori had two photographs in her hand and was still giggling. Unable to speak, she handed the photos to Jake.

"Dear Lord!" he exclaimed before starting to laugh.

The first photograph was a picture of the fairy princess that had been expertly inked onto Danny's butt cheek. Whoever had tattooed it had truly done a beautiful job. They had managed to capture the fragility of her gossamer wings and the detail of her dress. The second photograph was the tattoo gun Celtic knot. It too had been expertly inked and was adorning the back of Danny's left hand.

"The knot looks great," said Jake, handing the photos back to her. "I'm glad to say, Dan didn't offer to show me the other one."

"And how did you get on with him?" asked Lori with a smile. "Did you add to your ink gallery?"

"What do you think?" teased Jake with a mischievous grin.

"I can see the outline of the dressing through your shirt," Lori observed. "Reveal all, rock star."

"Later," said Jake softly. "Let me finish dinner first and relax for a while."

Midnight had come and gone before Lori announced that she was going to bed. They had sat out on the deck chatting before moving indoors to watch a movie. It hadn't escaped Jake's notice that Lori swallowed two painkillers with the second bottle of beer that he had brought her. As she undressed in the soft light of the bedroom, he saw the huge bruise on her thigh.

"That's one hell of a bruise, li'l lady."

"Quite impressive, isn't it?" she commented as she slipped into bed. "Now come here, rock star, and let me remove that dressing."

Deciding to oblige and not to tease her any longer, Jake knelt on the bed beside her and allowed her to peel away the paper tape that held the dressing in place. Underneath, the skin was still red and puffy, but Danny had done an expert job at reproducing the Celtic dragon knot design. He had added some extra shading, creating more of a 3D effect. The fresh tattoo had begun to crust over and there were spots of blood on the discarded dressing.

"Nice," said Lori, running her index finger over it gently. She paused for a moment before adding, "Will your guitar strap catch it?"

"Probably," he agreed. "I can always put a dressing over it if it does."

"Are you pleased with it?"

"Sure am," smiled Jake, getting off the bed to finish getting undressed. "Needs something on the other side to balance it though."

Laughing, Lori lay back on the pillows. "You're addicted!"

"Perhaps. Now, let me take a closer look at that bruise of yours, li'l lady."

Carefully Lori rolled onto her right side and let Jake inspect the purple bruise. He ran his warm hand ran gently over it, then ran his finger down the fading lines of her scars. Despite her best efforts, Lori still flinched when he touched the scarred skin.

"Relax, beautiful," he whispered as he began to kiss her gently at first, but his hunger for her quickly becoming obvious.

Responding to his touch, Lori rolled over onto her back and ran her fingernail down his well-muscled stomach, pausing as she reached the edge of his fair pubic hair. Jake moved to sit across her and began to kiss her breasts, teasingly biting her nipples hard, causing her to take a sharp intake of breath. Under his touch, her skin was smooth as silk, her gentle feminine musk only serving to arouse him further. Unable to resist her any longer, he entered her slowly, trying to avoid causing her any discomfort. Beneath him, she moaned softly and raised her hips, encouraging him to thrust deeper inside her. Rhythmically, they moved as one as Jake stroked her to the precipice of orgasm. Feeling her moist and ready for him, he moved faster and harder, penetrating deep into her womanly darkness. Both of them were lost in the pleasure of their mutual orgasm as Lori gasped then called out his name.

Spent, Jake moved to lie beside her, putting a protective arm around her and drawing her close.

"I love you, Mz Hyde," he said huskily.

"Love you too, rock star," purred Lori sleepily.

Saturday marked day five of an official heat wave and, as the band prepared to leave JJL, they debated who was driving with whom and whose vehicle had the most reliable air conditioning. Eventually they decided that Jake and Gary would travel with Rich, while Grey and Paul would follow in Grey's truck. With everything packed into the back of the truck, they set off for the city. It was an easy drive. The highway heading away from the beaches was quiet. As they drove into the city centre, almost two hours later, the traffic quickly grew congested, causing Rich to swear under his breath as he fought his way towards the record company building. It was a relief to finally pull up in the underground parking lot.

Upstairs on the roof terrace, several small gazebos had been erected to shade the invited guests from the blazing July sun. A slightly larger version had been hastily erected over the small stage. Silver Lake had just enough time to set up and complete a hurried sound check before Jason summoned them to meet the first of the VIPs to arrive. He introduced them to the promoters behind the open air festivals they were scheduled to perform at and also to the prospective promoter for their planned winter trip to the UK and Europe. Having exchanged pleasantries with numerous people, Jake excused himself and went off in search of a quiet space to warm up. He was on his way through the corridors when he met his young sister, Lucy, coming towards him.

"What are you doing here?" he asked as he hugged her tight.

"Gary invited me in my capacity as admin for your fan page," she giggled. "I thought he would have told you."

"Fan page?"

"Yes. It's been officially linked to the record company. We only set it up online last month, but there are about three thousand fans registered for it so far," explained Lucy proudly.

"Show me later, little sister," said Jake, shaking his head incredulously. "I need to watch the time and I need to warm up. I'll catch up with you later."

When Jake returned to the roof terrace about three quarters of an hour later, his fellow band mates were posing for photos with Lucy, the Philadelphia skyline providing a perfect backdrop. Spotting her brother milling around with the record company suits, Lucy called him over to join them. As he posed for photos, Jake heard a familiar voice call out, "Nice to see you've kept your shirt on, Mr Power."

It was Dan Crow, lead singer with Weigh Station.

"Don't want to get sunburnt," joked Jake as he shook the older man's hand. "Are you guys playing today?"

"No," replied Dan, with a shake of his tousled head. "We did the 4th of July street party thing. I'm just here to make sure you behave."

"Too fucking hot to do anything else."

Their conversation was interrupted by Jason, who invited the company chairman to step up to the mic to say a few words. A tall, well-muscled man of around fifty stepped forward, taking the microphone from the Englishman. He spoke eloquently as he delivered a potted history of the record label's past twenty-one years, highlighting the highs and lows. After about fifteen minutes, he declared that it was too hot to delay proceedings any further and invited Silver Lake to take the stage. The band walked out onto the small platform to a polite round of applause.

"Good afternoon," said Jake, stepping forward to the mic. "Damn, it's hot out here!"

This raised a louder cheer from the small crowd.

Without further delay, Silver Lake launched into Dragon Song, their loud hard rock music echoing out over the city rooftops. As he sang, Jake could sense the invited guests weren't wholly appreciative of the heavy, powerful, rock number. As the last notes sailed off towards the Liberty buildings, Jake introduced their second number. "This is the new single from our forthcoming album. You'll be glad to hear, it's a lot quieter. This is Out Of The Shadows."

Out of the corner of his eye, Jake saw Dan standing beside Lucy, nodding in time to the music, as they premiered the new song. This time the invited audience seemed more engaged and the band were all relieved to see both Jason and the chairman smiling. Knowing that this number was going down well allowed the band to relax a little and enjoy the performance.

Once the applause faded away, Jake said, "A Silver Lake set always ends with Flyin' High and this one's no exception."

As the band made to step off stage a few minutes later, Jason came forward and halted them. Quietly, he whispered a suggestion to them, then beckoned Dan forward. Unable to decline under the circumstances, Silver Lake agreed to perform with the Weigh Station front man unrehearsed. The older man came up on stage and, after a few moments of debate, they agreed to play "Simple Man" a classic song they all knew and one that was easy for Dan and Jake to share the vocal chores on.

"Ok, folks, totally unrehearsed," joked Jake as he adjusted the mic. "Be gentle with us."

Ever the professionals, the four members of Silver Lake, plus their invited guest, delivered a solid version of the Lynyrd

Skynyrd classic, earning them a resounding cheer for their efforts.

"Thank you and good afternoon," said Jake when they were through.

He was almost relieved to set down his guitar and to step down from the small stage in exchange for some shade. The blistering heat was searing through him. Lucy was among the first to come over to congratulate them, enthusing about the new single. Hugging her, Jake said, "I take it you liked it then, little sister?"

"Loved it! Can't wait to hear the rest of the new album," she enthused. "When is it out?"

"We've not even finished recording it yet," laughed Rich, coming over with a glass of juice.

"Late September," added Gary, joining the group. "Maybe early October."

"That's months away!" protested Lucy shrilly.

"Patience, little sister," teased Jake. "Patience."

Looking round, Lucy suddenly asked, "Where's Lori? I thought she'd be here."

"Not this time," replied Jake, lifting a glass of juice from the tray of a passing waiter. "I think she was planning on working today. She's got deadlines to meet."

Before they could continue their conversation, Jason approached and led Jake and Rich away to meet one of the promoters and his star struck teenage daughter. For the next hour or more, the band mingled with the invited guests, signing autographs, posing for photos and chatting to journalists. All part of the rock and roll game, thought Jake as he finished off another version of the same conversation he'd been having all afternoon. Politely, he excused himself and walked over to where Gary was deep in conversation with a journalist.

"Ok, time's up," said Jake quietly, whispering into the manager's ear. "Let's wrap this up."

"Give me half an hour," replied Gary, obviously keen to continue his conversation with the girl in front of him.

"Ten minutes," countered Jake bluntly. "Rich and I will meet you back at the car."

"Ten minutes," agreed the band's manager reluctantly.

An hour later, Jake hugged his young sister as they said their goodbyes in the underground car park. She had shown him the online fan sites on her cell phone before eliciting a promise from him to share some of his day to day thoughts and photos with her for inclusion on her "official" fan page. With promises to meet up at the end of the month, Silver Lake pulled out of the garage in convoy, waving goodbye to Lucy as they left. It took them a while to negotiate the city centre traffic, but soon they were clear of the chaos and out on the highway.

"Am I glad to be out of there," sighed Rich as he concentrated on the road ahead. "There's a limit to the amount of polite smiling I can deal with in this heat."

"Same here," agreed Jake from the back seat. "Why do I always attract the women wanting hugs and autographs? And kisses and photos?"

"It's your striking, good looks, Mr Power," said Gary in jest. "And your long golden locks."

"Don't forget the twinkling hazel eyes and Power smile," added Rich with a laugh. "It was the same at school. Female teachers and students loved him."

"Cut it out, guys."

"Seriously, guys," began Gary, adopting a more serious tone. "Today was fantastic. Jason is really pleased with that set. I spoke to a couple of potential promoters looking to set up more shows. Painful it may have been but that PR stint will pay dividends."

"As long as Lord Jason is happy," sighed Jake, stretching out. "He's hard fucking work."

"So what's the plan for tonight?" asked Rich. "Are we eating at your place, Jake?"

"I'll call Lori when we are nearer home. We can BBQ. Unless you have a better plan?"

"Suits me," answered Rich. "Can't make it a late one though. Dr Marrs wants us in early again tomorrow."

"On a Sunday?" quizzed Gary looking confused.

"Vocals," revealed Jake with a sigh. "It's just the two of us who are in. Apparently he has a plan."

"Should I be worried?" asked their manager, craning his neck round to look at him.

"Relax, Gary," assured Jake. "He just wants us to try a couple of different vocal styles on one of the tracks, then we'll get on with the rest as planned."

"Where was Scott today? I kind of missed his camera in my face," asked Rich, changing the subject.

"Vegas. He's due back on Monday," explained Gary. "He had hoped to be back for today, but his project in Vegas ran over schedule."

"Then we'll be one big happy family again," laughed Jake, glancing back and waving to Grey and Paul in the truck behind them. "I have to admit, it felt good to play live again, even if was hot as hell out there."

"Same here," agreed Rich, drumming on the steering wheel in time to the song playing on the radio. "Three weeks until our first outdoor show of the run."

"You guys had better work out the set soon," warned Gary bluntly. "And remember to include some of the new stuff, but not too much."

"Yes, boss," stated Rich and Jake in unison.

"I give up," muttered Gary, pulling his baseball cap down over his eyes. "Waken me up when we reach the beach."

Within minutes, the band's manager was sound asleep, snoring gently under his hat. In the back seat, Jake struggled to get comfortable, his long legs cramped in the confined space. The fresh tattoo on his chest was annoying him too. It was itchy. He had kept it covered over while they had been playing but now reached under his T-shirt to pull off the dressing, unable to tolerate the itch any longer.

"You got new ink?" enquired Rich, watching his friend struggling in the rear view mirror.

"Yeah. Saw Danny on Thursday."

"Ah, the mystery late afternoon appointment," mused the guitarist. "What did you get?"

"I'll show you when we get to the house," promised Jake, gently rubbing his chest. "It's the Silver Lake knot design. Dan did an amazing job on it."

"That's a stunning job he did on Lori's ankle," commented Rich. "He's quite skilful. I could be tempted to pay him a visit."

"Very skilful," agreed Jake nodding. "Ask Lori to show you the photos he gave her. She designed two tattoos for him and he had them done on 4th July."

Their easy banter continued as Rich drove down I-95 then onto Route 1, The Coastal Highway. Traffic was in their favour again. The weekend beach visitors had all driven down either on Friday night or early morning. Some of the day trippers looked to have packed up early due to the heat as the opposite carriageway was busy. Jake stole a glance at the thermometer on the dashboard. It read that it was 94F outside, hot even for July. When they reached Dover race track, Jake reached into his pocket for his cell phone. With practiced ease, he called Lori.

"Hey, li'l lady," he said warmly as she picked up the call.

"Hi. How was Philly?" asked Lori brightly.

"Hot as hell. Great set though. Lucy was there," answered Jake. "Did you know about this online fan page stuff she's set up?"

"Of course," giggled his fiancée. "Maddy and I helped her. Maddy is the co-admin for it all."

"I might have known!"

"How far away are you?" asked Lori.

"About an hour at the most. We've just passed Dover Downs and the traffic's been ok so far," Jake replied. "Can you light the grill in about a half hour?"

"Sure," agreed Lori, before adding, "If you want anything other than burgers, can you pick it up on your way in?"

"Will see what we can do. Need anything else?"

"Better pick up some beers," suggested Lori. "And a bag of ice."

"Not a problem, li'l lady. See you in an hour."

"Love you, rock star."

Slipping the phone back into his pocket, Jake sat back and relaxed, watching the scenery go by. In the front, Gary was still sound asleep. It never ceased to amaze him how their manager could sleep anywhere anytime. Cat napping was never something Jake had been good at and he seldom slept in cars or on planes. His mind began to wander back to thoughts of recording after they drove past JJL.

"Hey," Jake called through to Rich. "I thought the Blues Brothers back there were stopping to drop off the gear at the studio?"

"Change of plan. Grey said he'd drive out later on and drop it off," replied Rich.

"Ok. I'd better call them and check if they are stopping by for dinner," sighed Jake, reaching back into his jeans pocket for his phone.

Quickly he called Paul, exchanging a few playful insults with him before confirming that they were both coming for something to eat, but that neither of them could stay late – family commitments. Jake had to loosen his seat belt to get the phone back into his pocket. He was reaching to grab the belt again when he caught sight of a large, dairy tanker out of the corner of his eye.

"Rich!" he yelled. "Watch out!"

The tanker was charging straight through the stop light at the intersection with Route 9. It was charging straight towards them, swaying as the driver tried to make the turn too fast. Heeding Jake's warning, Rich attempted to swerve out of its path.

The sickening scream of metal on metal filled the car.

Like a rag doll, Jake was flung across the back seat, cracking his head off the side window as Rich wrestled with the steering. Howls of tearing metal drowned out everything else.

In seemingly slow motion, the car slewed across the carriageway, spinning out of control as the weight of the tanker ripped off the front quarter. Engine noise roared, then there was silence.

The car had come to a stop.

Dazed and with a hot, fiery pain in his left shoulder, Jake kicked open the twisted door and stumbled out onto the road. In the driver's seat, Rich was slumped over the airbag, blood running from his forehead onto the white inflated cushion. As he gazed round, searching for Gary, Jake gradually realised the front of the car was missing. Debris from the crash was scattered across the highway. His eyes followed the wreckage, coming to rest on the toppled tanker. Milk was flooding out of its fractured side.

"Gary!" screamed Jake, clutching his elbow as a bolt of pain shot through his shoulder dropping him to his knees. "Gary!"

Cars all around on both sides of the highway had come to a silent standstill. No one was moving. As he scanned the wreckage, Jake was vaguely aware of Rich beginning to groan in the remains of the car behind him. Jake's eyes followed the tracks of broken and bent bits of car like a trail of breadcrumbs. The reality of the scene suddenly hit him. The passenger seat was under the tanker.

A cold chill descended on the blazing hot highway.

A hand touched his right shoulder, jolting Jake back to the present. He staggered to his feet as Grey reached out to steady him.

"The tanker," spluttered Jake. "Gary! I can't find Gary!"

"Paul's called 911," said Grey, his voice remarkably calm. "Are you hurt, Jake?"

"My shoulder. My ribs," mumbled his friend, unaware of the blood running down his cheek from a deep cut below his left eye. "Where's Gary?"

"Let's sit you down until the paramedics get here," suggested the bass player, guiding Jake away from the wreckage.

"Rich!" yelled Jake, spinning and staggering round out of Grey's reach. "Where's Rich?"

"I've got him," called back Paul from beside the wreckage of the car. "He's ok, Jake."

"Come on," said Grey firmly, leading Jake over to the side of the road away from the debris. "There's nothing you can do."

Sirens were already wailing in the distance, rapidly growing louder as they approached the scene of the accident.

Shock was setting in and Jake began to shake uncontrollably as Grey guided him over to the grass verge. Carefully Grey helped his friend to sit down on the short, burnt grass. The movement jolted Jake's injured shoulder and ribs. He groaned as the pain swept through him, then blacked out, slumping across the grass at Grey's feet. The next thing Jake was aware of, was the two paramedics working on his shoulder. One of them was trying to explain to him that the shoulder was dislocated and that they were going to attempt to pop it back into place. The pain from the manipulation and his damaged ribs caused everything to go fuzzy then black as Jake lost consciousness for a second time.

Crouched down on the grass verge, Grey looked on in complete disbelief at the carnage and tragedy that surrounded them. Firefighters and a team of paramedics were over at the toppled tanker working frantically. Another team of paramedics surrounded the car as they worked on Rich. The bass player could see Paul standing watching, his face pale and wet with tears.

"Sir," said one of the crew working on Jake. "We've sedated your friend here to keep him still for now. We're about to transfer him into the rig. Do you want to ride with us?"

"I don't know," replied Grey shakily. "What about Rich? Are they ready to move him too?"

"Let me check."

A few seconds later the medic ran back over to him, calling out that they were ready to move the guitarist too. He confirmed that they were taking them both to the emergency room at Beebe."

"Paul and I will follow you in the truck," said Grey calmly. "Any word on Gary?"

"Not yet," replied the medic solemnly. "But it doesn't look good. He's trapped under the tanker and they can't get to him. As soon as we hear, we'll let you know."

"Thanks," mumbled Grey, feeling a lump of emotion swelling in his throat. "I'll call Jake's fiancée and get her to meet us at Beebe."

"No need," said the medic. "The police have that in hand. Your friend gave them the contact details. Now, we really need to get moving."

Silently Grey nodded, as he watched an unconscious Jake being stretchered into the back of the ambulance. A single tear slid down his pale tanned cheek.

♫

After Jake had called, Lori had settled back on the sun lounger to read another chapter of her book. She had spent the afternoon quietly sunbathing in her bikini, confident that no one was going to drop by and disturb her. When she reached the end of the chapter, she slipped her bookmark into place and closed the book over. "Time to light the coals," she thought, as she got to her feet. The decking boards were hot under her bare feet as she crossed the deck to the BBQ. A plastic chest sat at the side of the deck with the charcoal and BBQ fluid inside. Trying not to cover her bare skin with charcoal dust, Lori tipped the remains of the bag into the tray, scattering the lumpwood evenly. She sprayed it lightly with lighter fluid, then tossed in a lit match. Small flames licked up, gradually spreading out evenly over the bed of charcoal. Satisfied that it would stay lit, Lori headed indoors to wash her hands.

As she turned off the tap, the front doorbell rang.

The noise sounded alien in the quiet house. No one ever rang the bell. Pausing to lift one of Jake's shirts, that he'd left hanging on the back of the kitchen chair, Lori slipped it on over her bikini as she limped down the hallway. She could see two dark shadows through the frosted glass pane. Taking a deep breath, she opened the door. Two police officers stood on the top step – one male; one female.

"Miss Hyde?" asked the male officer politely.

"Yes," replied Lori, feeling the blood drain from her face. "What's happened? Is it Jake?"

"There's been an accident out on Route 1. I'm sorry to inform you that Mr Power was in one of the vehicles involved."

"No!" she exclaimed sharply, shaking her head. "No!"

"I know it's a shock, Miss Hyde," began the female officer softly. "He's been taken to the medical centre. We don't know his exact condition, though."

Tears flowed freely down Lori's cheeks as she stared at the two officers in complete disbelief. Her legs were trembling and she gripped the edge of the door tightly to steady herself.

"We're here to take you out there," added the other officer.

"Or to escort you, if you'd prefer to drive yourself."

"Jake," sobbed Lori quietly. "Not Jake."

"Miss Hyde," said the female officer, reaching out to touch her arm. "The sooner we get you to the medical centre, the sooner you'll see Jake. Do you need me to help you fetch anything before we go?"

"Give me a minute, please," replied Lori tearfully. "I'll grab my purse."

Turning her back on the officers, Lori stumbled down the hallway to the bedroom to fetch her bag. Catching sight of herself in the mirror, she grabbed her sarong off the bed and tied it around her waist. She slipped her feet into a pair of flip flops, lifted her bag and her cane then left the bedroom again. Remembering her cell phone, she detoured through the kitchen before returning to the front door.

"Ready," she whispered sadly as she stepped out of the house, pulling the door closed behind her.

As she sat in the back seat of the police car, tears flowed soundlessly down her cheeks. Her chest was tight with a sickening knot of fear and panic. Reaching into her bag with trembling hands, Lori pulled out her phone and called Maddy. The line was busy. Before she could decide who to call next, the phone began to ring. Grey's number came up on the small screen.

"Grey!" she sobbed as she answered it. "Is he ok?"

"He's knocked about a bit, Lori, but I don't think it's too bad," replied the bass player, trying to sound positive. "We've just arrived at Beebe. The doctor is with him just now."

"How bad?" demanded Lori sharply, the phone shaking in her quivering hand.

"Lori, he walked out of the wreck. Lord knows how! He was talking to me. He's hurt his shoulder pretty bad and his ribs. There's a nasty cut on his cheek. They're working on him just now. Try not to panic, sweetheart. Are you on your way here?"

"Yes," whispered Lori tearfully. "The police came to the house. I'm about twenty minutes away."

"I'll meet you at the door to the ER," promised Grey warmly.

"What about Rich?" asked Lori, suddenly remembering that he had been driving.

"They're bringing him right now. I've not spoken to him. Paul stayed with him while I was with Jake. I think he's pretty much the same as Jake though. There's no word on Gary yet," he explained, images of the carnage they had left behind on the highway flooding his mind. "It doesn't look good, Lori."

"No," she sobbed. "This isn't happening."

"I know," he agreed, emotion cracking in his own voice. "Look. I need to try to call Linsey. I'll see you in a few minutes. I'll wait right by the door for you."

"Ok," whispered Lori. "Ok."

The first person Lori saw, as the police car pulled up outside the medical centre, was Grey. True to his word, he was standing in the shade beside the entrance, talking on his phone. Spying Lori stumble out of the car, assisted by the police officer, he quickly ended the call and ran over to her. Wrapping his arms around her, the bass player held her tight for a few moments, whispering soft reassurances to her as she sobbed into his chest. While he held her, the police officers discretely said that they would catch up with them inside, leaving them to make their own way into the emergency room. Keeping an arm around Lori's shoulders, Grey guided her through to the small, family waiting room where Paul was sitting with a cup of coffee. Hearing Lori's cane clicking on the floor, he jumped to his feet and embraced her tightly as she came into his reach. Both of them were trembling and just held each other for a few moments.

"Where is he?" asked Lori, bravely trying to keep her emotions in check.

"They took him down the hall to do some x-rays," explained Paul, his voice trembling. "I was told to wait here."

"And Rich?"

"He's here somewhere. I saw them wheel him down the hallway a few minutes ago."

"Any word on Gary?" asked Grey, dreading the answer.

Paul shook his head and fresh tears filled his eyes. "He didn't make it."

Feeling her legs go weak, Lori sank down onto the nearest chair. "No! Tell me he's here too!"

"Lori, I wish he was," sighed Paul. "One of the police officers broke the news to me just after Grey went out to fetch you. Said he hadn't stood a chance. That he wouldn't have suffered."

With sobs wracking her body, Lori sat rocking backwards and forwards, her face buried in her hands. Both grieving musicians moved to sit on either side of her; both putting their arms round her shoulders. Lost in their own private grief, the three of them sat silently for what felt like an eternity. In the background, the buzz of hospital life continued. A phone was ringing loudly. A young child was screaming, obviously in pain. At the nurses' station, a man was yelling about the waiting time. After a while, Grey went to fetch them all a drink from the vending machine at the end of the hallway. Sipping their coffee from Styrofoam cups, they slowly told Lori as much as they could about the accident. They held her as she cried fresh tears, trying their best to console her and answer her questions.

"Miss Hyde?" asked a young male voice.

A junior doctor stood in the doorway with a chart in his hands.

"Yes," said Lori, looking up through a veil of tears.

"Mr Power's going to be ok," he said reassuringly as he came to sit across from them. "He's back from radiography and we're waiting to admit him."

"Admit him?" echoed Lori, looking confused.

"We want to keep him under observation for twenty-four hours as a precaution," explained the doctor. "He's a lucky man, all things considered. He's dislocated his shoulder but the paramedics relocated it at the scene. His x-rays are clear. Nothing's broken. No internal injuries. His ribs are quite extensively bruised though. There's also a nasty cut below his eye that needs to be sutured and he's had a bang to the head. He was sedated at the scene so he's quiet and a bit drowsy."

"Can I see him?" asked Lori, wiping away a tear.

"Of course," said the doctor, before turning to Paul and Grey. "Have either of you managed to contact Mr Santiago's family?"

"Not yet," replied Grey. "How is Rich?"

"He's on his way back here from radiography. He'll be admitted for a few days. His nose was badly broken by the impact and needs surgery to realign it correctly. There's hairline fractures to his cheek bones, but nothing appears to be displaced. Apart from that, he's got a cut above his eye that needs attention and extensive bruising to his ribcage and chest. They've both been incredibly lucky."

"Can we see them now, please?" pleaded Lori, getting shakily to her feet.

"Certainly," said the doctor. "If you could follow me please, ma'am."

The doctor led them down to the end of a short corridor lined with curtained off cubicles, then pulled aside the pale blue curtain.

"We've kept them both together," he explained, stepping aside to let Lori enter.

Nervously, Lori moved past him into the cubicle, the curtain catching on her sarong, exposing the full length of her thigh to all three of them. In front of her, Jake lay propped up on several pillows, his left arm in a blue sling and his eyes closed. His ashen face was still blood stained. A few stumbling steps took her to his side and, as Lori took his hand in hers, fresh tears glided silently down her pale cheeks.

"Hey, li'l lady," said Jake drowsily, struggling to open his eyes. "Don't cry."

"Oh, Jake," she sobbed. "Are you ok?"

"I've been better," he admitted, trying to sound "normal".

"The doctor told us," said Grey, joining them. "Sounds like you and Rich have been the lucky ones."

"Well, we're still here," mumbled Jake, squeezing Lori's hand. "They just told us about Gary."

"I'm so sorry," whispered Lori tearfully. "I don't know what to say."

"I don't think he would have known much about it," replied Jake, his voice thick with emotion. "It all happened so fast. He was asleep up front when the tanker hit us."

From the other side of the enclosed space, Rich spoke for the first time. "It could easily have been all of us."

Hastily Lori turned round and hurried over to his bedside. Trying to smile, she asked if he was ok.

"I'll live," he said, forcing a weak smile back at her. "They've scheduled surgery for tomorrow morning to rebuild my nose. I thought airbags were meant to protect you?"

"It did," stated Grey bluntly.

Before they could continue with their conversation, a small nurse came into the cubicle.

"Sorry to interrupt, folks," she apologised as she pulled on a pair of surgical gloves. "Time to suture those cuts, boys."

Both Jake and Rich groaned.

"You're first, Mr Power."

"Christ," sighed Jake. "My lucky day."

"I'll be gentle with you," she promised kindly. "And I'll do a neat job. Need to preserve those rock star looks of yours."

The nurse proved to be as good as her word. She worked swiftly and efficiently while Lori sat silently holding Jake's trembling hand. After a few short minutes, the nurse declared she was done.

"How many was that?" asked Jake, curious to learn the extent of the damage.

"Six," she replied, as she removed her latex gloves. "You'll need to come back to visit us in about ten days to get them removed. It's deep but it's a nice clean cut. I don't think there will be too much of a scar."

"Thank you," said Jake, forcing a weak smile.

"Ok, Mr Santiago," she called across the room. "Your turn next."

As she approached Rich's bed, Paul declared, "I can't watch. Can I get anyone a coffee or something?"

All of them declined his offer.

"I'll go and call Maddy instead," muttered Paul, desperate to avoid watching the nurse work on Rich.

"I'd better call my mom and tell her to keep Becky tonight," said Grey. "Can I trust you guys to behave until I get back?"

"I'm not going anywhere," said Jake closing his eyes. His head was pounding and waves of nausea were washing through him.

"Too damn right you're not," stated Lori firmly, finally feeling a little more in control of her emotions.

Sleepily, Jake opened his eyes again and smiled at her. For the first time, he noticed Lori was wearing her bikini with his shirt over the top of it.

"I see you left in a hurry, li'l lady."

"Something like that," mumbled Lori, suddenly self-conscious about her state of undress. "I was scared. I just wanted to know you were alive. The police didn't have too many details when they arrived to fetch me. It was Grey, who let me know you were still with us."

"I'd have called if I could," apologised Jake quietly. With a weary sigh, he added, "I still don't believe this has happened. He was there one minute and then...."

Tears welled up in his eyes and he turned his face away from Lori, not wanting her to see him cry.

"Baby, it's ok to cry," she whispered softly.

"There was nothing, absolutely nothing, we could do. If Rich hadn't reacted as quickly," a sob caught in his throat. "We could all have been killed."

Getting to her feet, Lori gently reached out to hug him. Ignoring the pain, Jake struggled into a sitting position and wept openly into her shoulder. Silent, painful sobs wracked his battered body. Tenderly, Lori smoothed his hair, rubbed his back and held him as he wept. Seeing her strong rock star grief stricken was tearing her apart, but she knew she had to be strong for him. As his tears subsided, Lori kissed him on the cheek and helped him to lie back against the pillows.

On the far side of the cubicle, the triage nurse had left and Rich was quietly watching his friend unravel. When he saw Jake sink back onto the pillows, he called over, "Hey, you ok, buddy?"

"I don't know," admitted Jake looking over at his band mate. Ignoring Lori's protests, he swung his legs over the side of the bed and struggled to stand up. Rather unsteadily, he staggered over to sit in the chair beside Rich's bed. "You?"

"I'm not sure," confessed Rich, reaching out to touch his arm. "One minute he was there, then he was gone. He never uttered a sound."

"Boys," interrupted Lori, sensing they needed a minute alone. "I'm going to the ladies' room. I'll be back in a few minutes."

She slipped out of the curtained off cubicle, leaving them to talk in private. Out in the corridor, she met Paul on his way back. She stopped him, suggesting that he give the two musicians a moment or two in private.

"I guess," he sighed, running his hands through his tousled, spiky hair. "I've spoken to the police. Given my statement. They said they don't need me to hang about. Are you ok if I head home to Maddy and the kids? She's frantic."

"Of course. I'll be ok here."

"Will you explain to the guys?"

"Go home, Paul," instructed Lori firmly. "Maddy needs you more right now."

"Thanks," he said sadly. "What a shit end to an awesome day."

Without another word, he turned and headed towards the exit, his head bowed and shoulders hunched, grief draped all over him. Slowly, Lori made her way down the hallway to the ladies' room. When she came out of the stall and had washed her hands, she stood leaning on the sink, gazing into the mirror. Her face was flushed and blotchy from crying. Her hair was dishevelled. Rummaging in her bag, she found a hairbrush that allowed her to at least rectify that. She had an eyeliner and a lip gloss that helped to make inroads to improving her overall look. There was nothing she could do about her attire, but now that she had calmed down sufficiently, she was aware that her own scars and her bruise were poorly disguised by the thin sarong. Adjusting her clothing as best she could, she took a deep breath and headed back out into the corridor. Grey was waiting outside for her.

"They're about to move the boys to a private room upstairs," he explained. "I thought I'd better come and find you."

"Thanks. Did you track down Linsey yet?"

"Yeah. She's out of town at her sister's. She'll be back first thing tomorrow," replied the bass player as they walked down the corridor. "I let her talk to Rich. He's still got my phone."

"And are you ok?" asked Lori softly.

"I guess. I don't think it's hit me yet. I'll see the guys settled upstairs, then head home. Mom's keeping the little one until the morning," he replied, suddenly sounding and feeling weary. "What about you?"

"Now I've seen Jake, I'm a lot calmer," admitted Lori with a weak smile. "It's all so hard to take in. Hard to believe. I can't believe Gary's gone."

She stopped and turned to face Grey. "Has anyone called Scott?"

"I'll call him when I get home," promised Grey sadly. "He's out of town until Monday. Nothing he can do anyway."

"I know, but he deserves to know."

"True," acknowledged Grey.

By the time the staff had transferred Jake and Rich to a small private room on the first floor, the two injured musicians were exhausted. Both of them had detested being transported by wheelchair, but neither of them were in a fit state to argue with the two burly hospital porters. The small private room was laid out with the two beds facing each other. There was a comfortable chair and a locker beside each bed plus two chairs and a small table in front of the window. Once the nurse had seen them both settled into bed, she left to fetch Jake a late dinner. He protested that he wasn't ready to face food, but she insisted that he had to attempt to eat a little.

"Guys, I need to head home," said Grey, reaching for his truck keys. "I've a few calls to make."

"Take Lori home will you," said Jake as he lay back on the pillows with his eyes closed.

"No," protested Lori sharply. "Not yet."

"Grey, take her home," stated Jake firmly.

"Jake," began Lori, fresh tears welling up in her eyes. "I can get a cab in a while. Don't send me away yet. Please?"

Taking her hand, he kissed it gently, then looked her straight in the eyes. "Please let Grey drive you home. Call me when you get there, then I'm going to try to get some sleep. My head's pounding. The world's spinning. I've asked the nurse for something to help. I'll be out of it before you know it."

"But I don't want to leave you here," she protested, knowing in her heart that it was pointless to even try to persuade him. "I hate leaving you like this."

"You look exhausted, li'l lady. Go home. I'll be right here when you come back in the morning. Promise."

"Come on, Lori," said Grey, taking her arm. "Let's leave these guys to get some rest."

Having said an emotional good night to Jake, Lori allowed Grey to lead her out of the hospital to his truck.

In the dark a few hours later, neither Jake nor Rich were sleeping. Both of them had gone over and over the crash repeatedly, trying desperately to make sense of it all. Despite the pain medication that had been administered, they were both in agony. Most of it a pain that no amount of medication could touch.

At the beach house there wasn't much sleep going on either. After Grey had dropped her off, Lori had gone in and called Lucy to tell her about the accident. It had been a heartbreaking phone call to make. Both girls had sobbed through it. Lori had just ended the call when the phone rang again. This time it was Maddy and there were more tears. When she eventually went down to the bedroom, the bed felt huge and cold and lonely without Jake sprawled out beside her. Lori finally curled up round one of his dirty T-shirts from the laundry basket, inhaling the familiar scent of his deodorant mixed with sweat. Wrapped in "essence of Jake", she fell into a restless nightmare–filled sleep.

When she awoke a few short hours later, the sky was growing light. The first thing she did was send a message to Jake's phone to check if he was ok. When there was no answer after an hour, she called the medical centre. The duty nurse assured her he was fine and had had a restful night. She advised he would likely be discharged after the doctor's morning ward round.

There were a handful of journalists lurking outside the medical centre when Lori pulled into the parking lot shortly after nine. Taking a deep breath, she stepped out of the Mercedes, lifted out the back pack she had brought, containing a change of clothes for Jake, and walked confidently towards the main entrance. The press reporters tried to block her way, but she held her head high, maintained her silence and somehow mustered enough courage to walk through them. With the doors closing automatically behind her, she could still hear them calling her name. There was no one at the main reception desk, but there was a security guard over at the coffee machine. Lori approached him, explained about the unwanted press attention and asked that he ensure they were gone by the time Jake was discharged.

Up in the room on the first floor, Jake was picking at the breakfast tray in front of him. Two orderlies had come to collect Rich an hour earlier to take him to the operating room to have his nose reconstructed. The guitarist had been anxious about the surgery and Jake had promised that he would wait at the hospital until he was back safely. As he sipped the cold coffee, the door opened and Lori breezed in.

"Morning, rock star," she said, kissing him gently on the cheek. "How are you this morning? Where's Rich?"

"He's in surgery. They're fixing his nose," replied Jake, wincing in pain.

"You ok?"

"Sore. Tired," he sighed, running his hand through his hair. "I just want out of here."

"I know that feeling," agreed Lori, taking a seat beside the bed. "Has the doctor been in yet?"

"He's due in any time but I promised Rich I'd hang about until he came back up."

"Did you get any sleep?"

"Not much," admitted Jake. "Every time I closed my eyes, I saw it all happen again and again."

"I know that feeling too," sighed Lori softly, remembering her own accident all too clearly. "It gets easier in time."

Changing the subject, she prattled on about calling Lucy and about bringing him a change of clothes. She was saved from making a complete fool of herself by the arrival of the doctor. Much to her great surprise, it was John Brent, who entered the room. He did a double take when he saw who his patient was.

"When I saw the name on the list it never clicked. I'm sorry, Jake," he apologised, setting the chart down on the bed. "How are you this morning?"

"Ok, I guess," answered Jake, struggling to sit up a bit. "Feel like I've been hit by a truck."

"No need for humour, Mr Power," chastised the doctor. "I've read these notes. You have to be in quite some considerable pain."

"Hurts like hell," he confessed, closing his eyes as a stab of pain shot through his ribcage.

Realising she was in the way, Lori excused herself, saying she was going to fetch a coffee. Jake asked if she would bring one back for him too.

As the door closed behind her, the doctor looked Jake straight in the eye. "No need for the brave face now. Do you need any pain medication before I examine you?"

"No. The nurse brought some with breakfast. I took the two pills, but they've not kicked in yet."

"I'll be as gentle as I can then," promised the doctor.

Even the gentlest touch to his ribcage caused Jake to flinch. Dark purple bruising stretched round from his chest and across his back. The left hand side was more deeply coloured than the right. As he moved, every inch of him ached- the muscles in his neck were stiff, his hips throbbed dully too. Removing the sling, Dr Brent cautiously tested the range of movement in Jake's injured shoulder.

"I expected that to be worse than it is," he commented as he put the sling back in place.

"Old injury," replied Jake, rubbing his aching shoulder. "It's popped out a few times over the years. I first did it falling off my bike as a kid."

"Be careful with it," cautioned the doctor, scribbling on the chart. "If it comes out of place again, we may need to look into it further. It might need surgery."

Jake nodded without commenting.

"How's the headache? Any blurred vision? Nausea?"

"Head's sore, but I'm ok. Feels like a migraine. Lack of sleep isn't helping. Eyes are ok. The sick feeling passed last night," replied Jake sounding weary.

"You're good to leave then," said John Brent warmly. "Lots of rest over the next few days. No strenuous activity whatsoever. Keep that sling on. I'll slot you in for an appointment on the 16th. The nurse will take those stitches out then too. If you need anything before then, call me. I'll leave a script for some anti-inflammatory and pain meds. Follow the pain management regime to the letter until I see you."

"Thanks, John," sighed Jake with a weak smile. "Am I ok to wait around until they bring Rich back?"

"Of course. Take your time getting ready. I suspect you won't have much choice though. Let Lori help you."

Right on cue, the door opened and Lori returned with the two cups of coffee balanced one on top of the other. The doctor grabbed the top cup and set it down safely on the bedside locker, scolding her for carrying them like that.

"Relax, John," she said with a mischievous smile. "I had only piled them up till I got the door open."

"Well, I don't need you in here with burns, Mz Hyde," he chastised, picking up the chart. "I've signed the discharge papers. You're free to take Jake home."

"Thanks," said Lori, relieved by the news. "I just want him home safely."

"Look after each other," suggested the doctor. "Jake, I'll see you on the 16th."

At Jake's suggestion, Lori took their coffees over to the two seats at the window. It took all of her will power not to try to help him as he walked stiffly across the room. Every inch of him hurt as he took each step, reminding him just how badly shaken about he had been by the crash. With a grimace of pain, he lowered himself into the seat opposite his fiancée. He sat back with an audible groan.

"You ok?" she asked, passing him the tall waxed-paper cup.

"I don't know. Every bit of me hurts," he replied, lifting the cup with a trembling hand. "Have you heard anything from Linsey?"

"She called while I was at the coffee shop downstairs. She should be here in about twenty minutes," replied Lori, taking the lid off her own cup. "Maddy called too."

"I'd better take a shower before Linsey gets here," Jake said. Looking slightly embarrassed, he added, "I might need some help with that, li'l lady."

"Do I get to wash you, rock star?" teased Lori playfully, trying to lighten the mood.

"Perhaps. Let's see how I get on," he replied, smiling at her. "Can you unfasten this fucking sling for a start?"

With the sling removed, Jake sat and finished his coffee, then walked slowly towards the bathroom, holding his arm protectively across his chest. Silently Lori fetched the backpack that she had brought and took the toiletries and clean clothes into the bathroom for him. She set them down on the stool that sat just inside the door and told him to yell if he needed help. Returning to her seat by the window, she listened to the sound of the running water. In the background, she was vaguely aware of the hum of normal hospital routine. The sound of Jake calling her name jolted her back to reality. As quickly as she could, Lori limped over to the bathroom and stepped inside. Jake stood naked and dripping wet in the middle of the floor, the towel clutched in his hand.

"What's wrong?" asked Lori concerned.

"I can't get dried off," he confessed, passing her the towel. "Be gentle. Everywhere hurts."

Tenderly Lori dried him, trying not to let the extensive bruising to his normally strong body distress her. As soon as she touched his back and ribs, she heard him take a sharp intake of breath. Apologising for causing him extra pain, she moved to dry the rest of him. Eventually he was dry enough to begin to get dressed. With Lori's assistance he managed to get his boxer shorts and jeans on. She had brought him a white cotton shirt and very gingerly slipped it on over his injured shoulder.

"Can you button it up, please, li'l lady?"

"Of course."

"I feel like a baby," he muttered, as she nimbly fastened the mother of pearl buttons.

"Don't be so hard on yourself," said Lori, kissing his damp bare chest. "Come on. Let's go and get your hair combed through. You look like a scarecrow."

"Thanks," he grumbled as she held the bathroom door open for him.

Linsey was sitting on Rich's empty bed when they stepped back into the room. Her face was pale and her eyes bloodshot from crying Lori noted as she hugged her tight.

"I thought he'd be up from surgery by now," commented the art teacher tearfully.

"I'm sure he won't be much longer," Lori said, trying to sound reassuring.

"Is he really ok?"

"Linsey, he's alright," replied Jake, as slid his arm slowly back into the sling. "Lori, can you fasten this fucking thing?"

While Lori secured the sling, then began to comb out his long, wet, tangled hair, Jake filled Linsey in on the details of the accident. Several times he paused to compose himself, not prepared to let her see him getting over emotional. Before he could finish the sad tale, the door opened and an orderly, accompanied by two nurses wheeled Rich back into the room. With an arm around Linsey to stop her from rushing over and getting in the way, Lori watched the medical staff help the battered guitarist back into bed.

"He's still a bit groggy," explained the nurse as she ticked off his chart. "I'd let him sleep for a while."

"Thanks," said Jake, the little colour he had draining from his face as he watched his friend.

Breaking free of Lori's embrace, Linsey rushed over to sit beside Rich, tears streaming down her cheeks.

"Hey, babe," he mumbled through the post-anaesthetic fog.

"Oh, Rich," she sobbed. "Your poor face."

Both the guitarist's eyes were black and swollen. His nose was taped after the surgery and there was a ragged line of stitches above his left eye.

"It doesn't matter," he said. "It'll heal."

Coming over to stand at the other side of the bed, Jake put his hand gently on his friend's shoulder. "I'll call you later. We're going to get out of here, buddy. Leave you to rest and catch up with Linsey."

"Ok," sighed Rich reaching up to take Jake's hand. "You take care of yourself. Don't overdo it."

"He won't," interrupted Lori warmly.

When they reached the reception area, Lori asked the security guard to check that the journalists had left. He nodded and headed outside, returning a few moments later to say the coast was clear. A blast of hot air hit them as they left the building. The heat wave was continuing and the late morning temperature was already touching ninety. The short walk to the car left Jake shaking and breathless. Very gingerly, he lowered himself into the passenger seat, then sat patiently while Lori fastened the seat belt for him. They drove back to the beach house in virtual silence, Jake staring out of the window, lost in his own grief-stricken world. To break the silence, Lori switched on the radio and the car was filled with the midday news report about the band's accident. Immediately she reached to turn it off.

"Leave it," stated Jake plainly.

The newscaster kept to the facts, didn't over dramatize the

events, declaring there had been two fatalities and that the road had now fully re-opened to traffic.

"Guess the truck driver didn't make it," commented Jake, closing his eyes on the tears stinging at them.

"Have you spoken to the police yet?" asked Lori, reluctant to keep talking about the tragic events of the day before.

"Briefly," he answered, still staring out of the window. "They never said if they needed any more from me. Two officers spoke to Rich and I last night just after you left."

"Did they give you any idea what happened with the tanker?"

"Not really. One of them said the driver was in the ER with a suspected coronary. If he's dead, we may never know."

"I guess," sighed Lori sadly as she turned the car into the driveway. "Home sweet home."

Neither of them knew what to do when they entered the house. Knowing it was pointless to fuss over Jake, Lori left him to wander from room to room while she took the backpack and plastic bag, that the hospital had given them with the remains of his clothes from the day before, down to the bedroom. From there, she heard the screech of the sun room's patio door opening and guessed Jake had stepped out to get some air.

Out on the sundeck, Jake stood gently breathing in the warm, salty, ocean air, glad to be rid of the clinical smell of the hospital. Now that he was home, he didn't know how he was meant to feel. He didn't know what he was supposed to do. Inside, he felt numb, still not truly believing that it had all happened. He expected Gary to call at any minute. Slowly, he wandered over to the BBQ grill. A pile of ashes covered the bottom of it, left to burn out when Lori had rushed off to the hospital. Trailing a finger through the soft, grey, powdery ash, Jake felt a tear slide down his cheek. Closing his eyes, images of the tanker careering towards the car filled his head. A cold shiver ran through him, despite the warmth of the sun's rays on his back. In his pocket, his phone began to vibrate. It was Grey's number on the screen.

"Grey," he said calmly as he picked up the call.

"Hey, I was just checking to see how you were today. Didn't want to call too early."

"We just got home," said Jake, lowering himself carefully onto the sun lounger. "I feel like shit if I'm honest."

"Sore?"

"Like you wouldn't believe."

"What about Rich?" asked the concerned bass player.

"He's still in the hospital. He'd just come back from surgery when we left. Linsey's there. He was ok, I guess. Looks hellish. His eyes are black and almost closed. That cut over his eye is nasty."

"You were both a bit of a mess when I left last night," joked Grey, trying to lift the melancholy mood.

"I guess," agreed Jake, before adding, "Are you busy today?"

"No. Why?"

"Want to come over? It might help if we're all together for a few hours," suggested Jake.

"If you're sure you're up to it. I'll need to bring Becky."

"That's fine."

"Alright. We'll be over in an hour or so."

Ending the call, Jake dialled Paul's number. The phone rang out, then went to voice mail. Muttering, he hung up and tried Maddy's number.

"Jake!" she screamed almost instantly down the phone. "Oh, Jake, are you ok?"

"Deaf in one ear now as well as battered and bruised," he answered.

"Sorry, darling. Are you home?"

"Yes. We got back a few minutes ago. I just spoke to Grey. He's coming over in an hour. Do you guys want to come over too?"

"Are you sure? Shouldn't you be resting?"

"Yes, but I feel like I need to see everyone. Get everything out in the open," he replied.

"Let me round up the meatballs and Paul and we'll be right over," she said warmly. "I spoke to Jason earlier. He's coming down to JJL tomorrow."

"Thought he might be down," groaned Jake. "If he wants to see me, he'll need to come out here. I'm not straying too far for the next few days."

"I don't know what the plan is. When I find out, I'll let you know," promised Maddy. "Now, we'll see you both in an hour or so."

Indoors Lori began to empty the bags, tears welling up in her eyes as she saw Jake's torn bloodstained clothing. His T-shirt was in tatters where it had been cut off. His jeans had been expertly cut up the sides. Only his socks and boots were intact. There was a small plastic bag containing his wallet, some loose change and a handful of guitar picks. Laying the small bag on the nightstand at Jake's side of the bed, she gathered up the ruined clothing, took it through the house and out to the trash. It may have been her imagination, but it had reeked of death. Realising the time, she fixed them both a sandwich and poured two glasses of iced tea.

Stepping out onto the sundeck, carrying the plates, she found Jake lying propped up on one of the loungers, his cell phone in his lap.

"I brought you some lunch, rock star. You hungry?"

"Not really," he confessed. "But I'll eat it."

Setting the plate on his lap, Lori set the other one down on the table and went back indoors for the iced teas. Jake was nibbling on the soft Italian bread sandwich when she returned.

"Grey called," said Jake between mouthfuls. "He's coming over for a while. Paul and Maddy are coming over too."

"I thought you were meant to be resting?" Lori began to protest. The look on his face told her it was pointless to continue.

"I need to see them, li'l lady. Get seeing them over and done with. Get all the awkwardness out of the way."

"I understand," she replied, realising that some company might just be good for both of them. "Just don't overdo things."

"I'm not moving from here," he said with a smile full of pain. "It hurts like hell to move."

"You'd better not. John said you were to rest."

A short while later, just as Jake had dozed off under the shade of the parasol, Grey and Becky arrived. They came round the side of the house, as Lori was taking the lunch dishes indoors. She indicated to them both to be quiet and to follow her indoors. Once in the kitchen, Grey gave her a hug and asked if she was alright.

"I'm fine," she assured him. "I'm just worried about Jake."

Turning to Becky, she said, "You need to be really gentle with Uncle Jake for now, honey. No hugs today."

"I know. Daddy said already," replied the little girl seriously. "I drew him a picture to make him feel better."

She showed Lori the colourful drawing.

"It's me and Uncle Jake on the beach."

"He'll love that, honey," said Lori, smiling warmly at the little girl. "You can give it to him when he wakes up."

"Can I watch TV until then?"

"On you go," laughed Lori, as the little girl skipped into the sunroom in search of the remote control.

Grey and Lori were still sitting in the kitchen when Paul and Maddy arrived with the twins. Both babies were wide awake and contentedly sucking their thumbs as Paul carried them through in their car seats. There were fresh tears, as the two girls hugged each other.

"We'd better go outside," said Lori, after she had fetched everyone a drink. "I don't want Jake getting up to come looking for us."

Quietly, they all made their way out onto the sundeck. The babies' car seats had individual sun shades, but Lori asked Paul to put up the big umbrella to make sure they were out of the intense July sun. When she saw Jake lying asleep, looking pale and bruised, Maddy began to cry again.

"Emotion, Maddison?" said Jake sleepily as he opened his eyes. "Should I be worried?"

"Oh, Jake!" she exclaimed, wiping away a tear. "How can you joke at a time like this?"

"Sorry," he apologised as he struggled to sit up a bit. All of them saw the pain etched into his face as he moved.

"You ok there?" asked Grey, sitting down on the deck beside the lounger.

"I'll live," muttered Jake, reaching over to rub his shoulder. "How are you guys today?"

"Been better," confessed Paul. "I still don't believe this is all real."

They all agreed that they felt the same, prompting a fresh discussion about the accident and more tears, as they mourned the loss of their friend. From her seat at the table, Lori realised that Jake had been right to invite everyone over. Getting all the grief and emotion out in the open seemed to be helping all of them come to terms with the tragedy. Gradually, Jake began to ask questions about Gary's family and the funeral.

"His sister and brother are flying in tomorrow from England," said Maddy, fiddling with her bracelet. "Jason called them. He's collecting them in Philadelphia himself, then bringing them down here late tomorrow afternoon. Paul's collecting Scott at BWI tomorrow night."

"What about the funeral?" asked Jake.

"Probably won't be for a week at least," answered Paul softly. "We'll need to wait until his body is released by the coroner."

"Oh, what a fucking mess," sighed Jake, shaking his head.

"And then there's the album. And, shit, we're meant to play that festival on the 27th."

"Don't worry about any of that today," scolded Maddy sharply. "Leave that stuff up to me to fix."

"But you're still on meatball leave," pointed out Grey, raising one eyebrow at her. "Or has that changed?"

"I promised Jason I'd help out in the short term," revealed Maddy. "We've not discussed it all yet. I'm meeting him either tomorrow when he gets here or on Tuesday. I've spoken to Jim Marrs too. He can work on the mixes for the completed tracks he's got for now. We'll just need to play the rest by ear. The important thing here is getting Jake and Rich back to full health."

"Amen to that," sighed Grey.

When it came time to cook dinner, Grey and Paul stepped in as chefs, insisting that Jake supervise from the sun lounger. The two girls took the twins indoors to feed and change them, before setting the table for dinner. Bored with the cartoon channel, Becky was pleading with her daddy to be allowed down onto the beach. As Grey attempted to scold her for asking, Jake declared that he needed to stretch his legs for a few minutes and that he would take her for a short walk. Ever so gently, Becky took his hand and the others watched as he walked slowly barefoot down the path onto the hot sand.

"He'll be fine," whispered Maddy, noticing the worry on Lori's face. "Don't panic. He probably just needs a few minutes to himself."

"You're right," replied Lori, shifting a wriggling Wren onto her other hip. "I just hope he's not too long down there."

The beach in front of the house was deserted, the heat having chased the day-trippers home early. Once out of sight of the house, Jake let go of Becky's hand and watched as the little girl ran and jumped towards the water's edge. She had kicked off her sandals as she ran and splashed happily in the wet sand, allowing the waves to trickle in over her feet. It struck Jake just how full of life she was, seemingly oblivious to the pain and grief of the adults around her. Feet caked in sand, she ran back up the beach towards him and took his hand again.

"Come into the water, Uncle Jake," she pleaded, smiling up at him. "It'll make you feel better."

"Not today, princess," he replied. "I've got my jeans on. I'll get them wet."

"I could roll them up for you," she said, determined not to be beaten.

With a smile, Jake said," What the hell! Roll them up, Becky."

Her small hands clumsy, the little girl knelt in the sand in front of her favourite "Silver Lake uncle" and rolled his jeans up to mid-calf length. Happy with her handiwork, she led him down to the water's edge, then slowly out into the shallows. The ocean was relatively calm. No breakers crashing in today, just small gentle waves.

"I'm sorry you got hurt," said the little girl sincerely. "And I'm sad that Gary got killed."

"Me too," replied Jake, digging in the soft, wet sand with his toes.

"Maybe he's with my Mommy," continued Becky with all the innocence of a child. "She could buy him a drink at the bar in Heaven."

Jake started to laugh, then grabbed his ribs as a spasm of pain wracked through him. "Oh, don't make me laugh, Becky. It hurts too much to laugh. But, you know what? I reckon you're right. Your mom will be taking care of him. Maybe my mom's fixing them both dinner."

"That would be a good thing," said the little girl seriously. "My Mommy was a rotten cook."

Trying hard not to laugh, Jake took her hand and they walked a little way along the beach.

"Will you have a scar when the doctor takes the stitching out?" she asked, staring at the black fuzzy stitches under his eye.

"Probably."

"Like Lori's?"

"Not as nasty as Lori's, princess," he answered, recalling that the little girl was one of the few folk who had seen the full extent of the scarring to Lori's thigh. "It'll fade once it's healed over. Uncle Rich is going to have one too. His cut is above his eye. He needed more stitches than me. It's a bit of a mess."

"He could grow his hair to cover it," she suggested helpfully.

"Maybe," said Jake softly. "Come on, princess. Time to go back. I'm getting sore and I'm hungry."

Hand in hand, they walked back along the shoreline, splashing each other in the shallow water. Despite being rolled up, Jake's jeans were soon soaked up to the knees. The short walk had done him the world of good. His heart was still heavy with grief, but Becky had helped him to see that all was not totally lost. She ran on ahead up the beach to the house, remembering to pick up her sandals on the way. By the time Jake reached the path, Lori was on her way down to look for him, Wren still nestled on her shoulder.

"I was getting worried," she said softly.

"Relax, li'l lady," he replied, putting his good arm around her and hugging her gently. "I'm fine. Becky helped me to see things in a different light. There's a wise woman inside that little girl."

"There is?"

Jake nodded, before declaring, "I'm hungry. Is dinner ready yet?"

"Almost."

Although Jake sat at the table with the others for dinner, they all quickly saw that he was in incredible pain and tiring rapidly. With the meal over, Paul and Maddy announced that they needed to get the little ones home. Picking up on their lead, Grey too said he needed to head off. Only Becky protested about having to leave so early.

"You can come back later in the week, princess," promised Jake, giving her a gentle hug. "I'm going for a soak in the tub, then I'm going to bed. You wore me out down on the beach."

"Come on, angel," instructed Grey, hoisting his daughter into his arms. "You need a good scrub in the tub too."

With everyone gone, the house and its surroundings seemed unnaturally quiet. Lori had brought them both a glass of wine out onto the deck. They sat together, listening to the gentle rhythm of the waves swooshing in down on the beach. In the dusky light, Lori noted how pale and drawn Jake looked. His earlier bravado was gone along with their guests.

"Bath time," he said as he finished off his wine.

"Probably a good idea. Might help to ease off your muscles a bit. There's a bottle of muscle soak in the cabinet. Add a little of that. Its herbal stuff I bought when I came down here at first," replied Lori, watching him wince as he stood up. "Want me to come and talk to you?"

Jake shook his head. "I could use some time on my own, if you don't mind, li'l lady."

"I understand," she said, reaching out to touch his hand. "Yell if you need me. I'll be out here for a while longer."

"Can you unfasten this sling for me?" he asked. "It's annoying the crap out of me."

"You need to keep it on for a few days at least," scolded Lori, as she reached to unfasten it for him. "Doctor's orders."

"I know. I know. But, it's annoying the fresh ink on my chest. I'll put it back on before I go to bed. Promise."

She watched as he walked slowly through the sunroom, holding his left arm protectively under the elbow.

Steam and a strong smell of eucalyptus and lemongrass filled the en suite bathroom. As the tub filled up, Jake stood naked in front of the full length mirror, inspecting the bruising to his battered body. Quite an impressive collection, he thought to himself as he found another one on his left hip. He was still amazed that his eye hadn't gone black. His cheek bone, below the gash, was tender to the touch. Taking extra care not to slip on the damp, tiled floor, he climbed into the bathtub and very slowly lowered himself into the hot water. Gingerly, he lay back and rested his head on the edge of the tub. Eyes closed, he lay there allowing the heat from the water to seep into his weary body. Breathing deeply caused him some pain but gradually, as his muscles began to relax, so did his breathing.

Part of him felt guilty for telling Lori that he needed time alone; part of him relished the quiet, secluded calm of the bathroom. It was the first chance he had really had to be alone to try to take stock of all that had happened over the last thirty-six hours or so. His mind was haunted anew with the images, sounds and smells of the crash. Images of the aftermath, of the paramedics and the ER all flooded in, threatening to overwhelm him. Memories of the police officer interviewing him in the dim light of the ward, forcing him to relive the full horror again while his wounds had still been raw and open. The herbal heat of the water surrounding him gently teased out the worst of the pain.

As he relaxed, his thoughts moved to Rich and a fresh wave of guilt washed over him as he thought of his friend, still lying in the hospital alone. He felt for Grey and Paul too, who had had to watch the whole drama unfold in front of them, totally helpless to do anything about it. His mind wandered to Gary's family and to the long journey they were due to make in the morning. He didn't envy them that one. Gary had been a very private person, rarely talking about the family he was homesick for. Lord alone knew what he was going to say to them when he met them.

With a smile, he thought back to his brief walk along the sand with Becky and her child's directness and innocent wisdom. The vision of Gary propping up the bar with Grey's late wife made him smile. Happy memories began to seep in as he recalled working and drinking with Gary and the rest of the band. The vision of him passed out on the sun deck after they had all celebrated the arrival of the twins tugged at his heart.

Deliberately, Jake tried not to think about the amount of work left to be finished out at JJL. He tried not to worry about the string of festival appearances that Silver Lake had lined up. Rubbing his injured shoulder, he wondered how long it would be before he could play guitar again. The joint throbbed hotly under his touch. Testing it, Jake tried to move it and was rewarded with a fresh bolt of pain.

As the water grew cooler, he reached over and twisted the dial to release the plug. He lay in the tub until the last of the water had drained away, then gently eased himself up and onto his feet. The movement caused fresh ripples of pain to flow through him, but, ignoring them, he climbed out of the bath and reached for the towel. He managed to wrap the large, pale green, fluffy bath sheet around his waist, then he draped a smaller towel over his shoulders.

When Lori came into the bedroom, she found Jake stretched out on top of the bed, sound asleep, still wrapped in the damp towels. He looked calm and relaxed, his breathing deep and even. Trying not to disturb him, she got ready for bed as quietly as she could. He was still sleeping like a baby when she turned off the lamp.

The bed beside her was empty when Lori awoke next morning. The damp towels lay in a heap on the floor. A gentle aroma of freshly brewed coffee wafted through from the kitchen. Wearing only her T-shirt, Lori wandered through the house in search of Jake. He was sitting at the kitchen table, chatting on the phone, a half drunk mug of coffee going cold in front of him. From the half of the conversation that she could hear, Lori couldn't determine who he was talking to. Trying not to make too much noise, she poured herself an OJ then went through to the sunroom, not wanting to intrude on her fiancé's call.

"Morning," said Jake from the doorway a few minutes later.

"Morning, rock star. How do you feel today?"

"Sore, but more tuned in," he replied, still cradling his arm. "Can you help me with that fucking sling, please? My shoulder's not feeling so great."

Lifting the discarded sling from the couch, Lori helped him to slide his arm into it and secured the fastener.

"Who was on the phone?"

"Dr Marrs," answered Jake, adjusting his arm's position in the cradle of the support. "He was checking up on me."

"You're not thinking of going out to JJL, are you?"

"No," he said, shaking his head. "Not for a few days. Jim said Todd had turned up out there. Sounds as though he was in a bit of a state. Jim's showing him the mysteries of mixing."

"So what do you feel up to doing today?" asked Lori, almost dreading the answer in case it was an activity that she would be forced to veto.

"As little as possible. We could maybe go out and see Rich later. I'll call him first though," replied Jake, much to Lori's relief.

"I need to do some work this morning," began Lori. "But we could take a run out to Beebe this afternoon if Rich wants us to."

"Sounds like a plan," he sighed resignedly. "I think I'll head down into the basement for a while."

An air of calm descended on the beach house over the next two days. The July heat wave continued unchecked. As the hours ticked by, Lori tried to give Jake the space he needed to grieve and to begin to heal. There were moments when he was irrationally angry and frustrated; there were others when he was emotional and quiet. He disappeared down to the basement for hours at a time, emerging tired and in search of pain medication. Lori worked on her Silver Lake project but, struggling to remain focussed, she made little in the way of progress. Their phones rang red hot throughout the first day and eventually Jake switched his off, leaving it lying silent in the bedroom. News from the hospital brightened up Tuesday as Rich called Lori to say he was being discharged the following day. Via Maddy, Lori learned that Gary's family had arrived safely and that Scott was back in town. Reluctant to return to the apartment, he was staying out at the farmhouse with Maddy and Paul for a few days.

As they sat out on the deck after dinner on Tuesday evening, Lori's phone rang again. Before its ringtone aggravated Jake, she answered the call. It was Jason. They exchanged pleasantries and she updated him on Jake's condition.

"Do you think you could make lunch tomorrow?" asked the Englishman hopefully. "If you can't, I'll understand, but Alice and Tom are keen to meet you both."

Deducing that Alice and Tom were Gary's brother and sister, Lori glanced over at Jake before replying, "Where did you want to meet? And when?"

"I thought we could have a private lunch at the hotel around one," he replied calmly.

"Are the rest of the band coming?"

"Just your good selves," said Jason before adding. "They met Paul and Grey earlier on for dinner and Scott's here just now."

"Ok. We'll be there. If anything changes, I'll let you know," promised Lori, unsure if it was too soon to expose Jake to fresh grief.

"Thanks, Lori. I appreciate this."

"What have you committed us to?" asked Jake as she set her phone down on the table.

"Just lunch tomorrow," she answered. "Is that ok?"

Slowly Jake nodded, then asked, "With Jason and Gary's family I assume?"

"Yes. They had dinner with Grey and Paul. Scott's there too. It'll just be us tomorrow."

"Guess I've no choice," he conceded with a sigh.

Next morning, dark storm clouds were brewing and an oppressive heat hung over the Delaware beaches. With Lori's help, Jake had dressed in a pair of smart, black jeans and a white shirt. His shoulder was feeling stronger, but he knew he still had to keep the sling on. He flinched as Lori helped to secure the fastening. As they drove out to the hotel on the outskirts of town where the band had launched their last album, he hid his emotions behind his sunglasses. Having parked as close to the front door as she could, Lori checked if he was ok.

"Not really," he commented, unfastening the seat belt.

"We can go home, Jake," she said softly. "No one expects you to be a hero here."

"It's fine. I need to see them sooner or later," he said with a sigh as he opened the door. "Show time, Mz Hyde."

The air conditioning felt beautifully cool as they entered the foyer. Jason was sitting near the entrance, waiting for them. His face paled visibly when he saw Jake. The usually calm and collected businessman looked emotional and more than a little flustered. Gone was his English stiff upper lip persona. He hugged Lori tightly and thanked her for driving all the way out to the hotel.

"Jake," he began, reaching out to embrace the musician then pausing.

"No offence, Jason, but no hugs," said Jake, forcing a smile.

"How are you?" asked the Englishman, a genuine warmth in his usually cool voice.

"Sore, but I'm getting there," replied Jake. "I've bruises to rival Lori's art work."

"I'm so sorry," sighed Jason sadly. "I hate to see you like this, Jake. It's all so unfair."

"Have you seen Rich yet?" asked Jake. "He's a bigger mess. Or at least he was when I saw him on Sunday."

"I haven't seen him yet," confessed Jason. "But I spoke to him on Monday and again earlier this morning. I'm hoping to see him tomorrow or Friday."

"How long are you staying here for?" asked Lori, taking Jake's hand and squeezing it gently as if to say "it's ok, I'm still here."

"For as long as I need to," said Jason. "Now, are you sure you feel up to this?"

Jake nodded, then added," There's never going to be a good time or a right time, is there?"

"I guess not," agreed Jason with a smile. "We're in the small dining room through here. Tom and Alice are really anxious to meet you. Seems you both made quite an impression on Gary."

The small dining room seemed vast with only one of its dozen tables laid. A young woman and a teenage boy sat holding hands, watching as Jason escorted Jake and Lori through from the foyer. The young woman bore a striking resemblance to Gary. She bit her lower lip nervously as she stood up to greet them.

"Alice?" said Lori warmly, before Jason began to fluster his way through an awkward introduction.

The woman nodded and reached out to hug Lori, "You must be Mz Hyde."

"Only when I'm working," replied Lori, hugging her tight. "Today it's Lori."

"You're exactly as Gary described you," commented Alice, unshed tears glistening in her eyes.

"Thank you," said Lori, taking the woman's hand. "And this is Jake. Please don't hug him."

Tears spilled down Alice's cheeks as she took a step towards Jake. Disregarding the pain, he put his good arm around her and held her as she wept.

"I'm so sorry, Alice. So very sorry," he whispered hoarsely, his voice thick with emotion.

"Thank you," she said with a shy, sad smile. "You're taller than I imagined."

"Six three the last time I looked," joked Jake awkwardly. "Maybe six four on a good day."

"And every bit as charming as Gary said," added Alice before blushing. "Let me introduce you to Tom."

The teenage boy barely glanced up at the mention of his name. He looked pale, his eyes bloodshot and tear filled.

"Tom!" said Alice sharply. "At least say hello!"

"Leave him be," said Lori softly.

"He's really struggling with all of this," Alice explained, wiping away a stray tear. "He's only seventeen. He idolised Gary.

It's probably hit him the hardest."

"It's hit us all pretty hard," acknowledged Jake, taking a seat at the table beside the boy.

Following his lead, the two girls sat down while Jason went off in search of a waitress to take their lunch order. There were a few moments of awkward silence before Alice asked Jake how he was feeling.

"Tender," he replied. "Nothing broken, but it all hurts like hell."

"And your poor face," sympathised Alice, indicating the neat line of stitches.

"Doesn't matter," said Jake, suddenly self-conscious. Taking as deep a breath as he dared, he asked "Is there anything you want to ask me about the crash?"

"I don't know. Grey and Paul told us all about it. We've spoken to the police too this morning. Apparently the tanker driver had some kind of seizure at the wheel. He seized again in the ER, triggering a major heart attack."

"I hadn't heard that," sighed Jake, running his hand through his hair nervously. "Explains his speed through the intersection."

"They've released Gary's body," added Alice, her voice barely above a whisper. "Jason's helping to arrange the funeral. We want it to be a cremation. I think we'll take him home after."

"I think that's a nice idea," said Lori hesitantly. "He missed England."

"I know," sighed Alice wistfully. "But he loved America and he loved the beach here. We'll need to get to see it."

"That's not a problem," replied Lori warmly. "Come over to visit us anytime. We live right on the beach."

"Oh, he loved your house!" enthused Alice. "Told me all about the BBQs out on your sun deck."

"And did he tell you about sleeping off his hangover on it too?" asked Jake was a smile. "We shared some good times together."

"Thank you for all that you both did for him," said Alice as her inner strength crumbled and her grief flooded through. "I'm glad he was with such good people when he was taken."

"SHUT UP!" screamed Tom, leaping violently to his feet, sending his chair crashing to the floor. "Just shut up!"

Before Alice could stop him, the boy had stormed off out of the dining room. Emotion and grief got the better of her and Alice slumped over the table, sobbing helplessly. Reaching out to comfort her, Lori mouthed silently to Jake, "Go after him."

Jake found the boy outside in the hotel's private garden, beside the small swimming pool. He was sitting on the edge of the pool with his feet dangling in the water. Awkwardly, Jake pulled off his own shoes and socks, then rolled his jeans up as far as he could. He placed his shoes beside a sun bed, then walked over to sit at the poolside beside the angry, grief-stricken teenager.

"Mind if I sit with you?" he asked quietly.

"If you must," muttered Tom sourly.

Thunder clouds rolled overhead as they sat in silence. At the first flash of lightning, Tom flinched beside him.

"It might be an idea to go back indoors before the storm hits," said Jake, glancing up at the blackening sky.

"I want to see where he died," stated Tom bluntly. "Then I don't want to talk about his death again."

"Ok," agreed Jake, trying to keep his tone soft and even. "We can go there after lunch. It's not far."

"You'll take me?" asked the boy, staring at him with piercing blue eyes.

"If that's what you want. Lori can drive us out there."

Large drops of rain began to fall, casting circular patterns on the otherwise calm pool.

"Why Gary and not you?" demanded Tom sharply. "He was going to bring me over here. He was going to take me on the festival tour with you. He was going to spend time with me."

Tom's tears fell as hard and as fast as the rain pouring down on them. Gently, Jake reached out and put an arm around the grieving teenager. The boy's head was heavy on his shoulder as his tears soaked into the white cotton of Jake's shirt.

"I don't know why, Tom," he said, tears running down his own pale cheeks. "A few seconds later and the truck would've missed altogether. If we'd driven faster. If we'd driven slower. If we'd been in the other lane on the highway. I've asked myself a million times."

"I never said goodbye," sobbed the boy, trembling in Jake's

embrace.

"None of us did," Jake sighed sadly. "He told us to waken him when we got to the beach. We never got him there."

In the dining room, Alice had regained her composure and both she and Lori were waiting anxiously for Jake and Tom to return. They had sent Jason in search of them and he had returned saying they were sitting by the pool in the storm. At the Englishman's request, the staff had delayed lunch and a waitress now stood discretely by the door, waiting for the signal to bring their meal out. Both the girls had ordered on behalf of the boys in their absence, Lori conscious of the fact that Jake only had the use of one hand. Polite conversation was drying up as the time ticked by.

Eventually the door creaked open and a sodden Jake led Tom towards the table. Alice rose to begin to make a fuss of her young brother, but with one dark look and a shake of the head from Jake, she quickly sat back down.

"Sorry about that, folks," apologised Jake as he sat down.

Jason nodded over to the waitress.

"Wet out there?" asked Lori, passing Jake a napkin to dry his face.

"Just a bit," he replied with a smile. "Storm's cleared the air, though. Should be clear by the time we've eaten."

As the waitress served their coffees at the end of their meal, Jake said, "I've agreed we'll take Tom out to the intersection when we're done here."

A silence descended on the table. Tears welled up in Alice's eyes.

Taking a deep breath, Lori spoke first, "Ok. I can park at Lowe's and you can walk across, I guess."

"I'm not going," stated Alice sharply. "I can't face it."

"I'll stay here with you," said Jason smoothly. "There's a few things we need to go over."

"Jake," began Lori, trying to mask the concern she was feeling. "Are you ready to go back out there?"

"Only one way to find out," he answered, keeping his gaze lowered towards the table.

Lowe's parking lot was quiet when Lori pulled in. Slowly she drove to the far end and parked the Mercedes in one of the boundary spaces facing the Coastal Highway. In the passenger seat beside her, she could see Jake begin to tremble and then take a breath in an attempt to compose himself; in the back seat, Tom sat staring out at the traffic. Trying and failing to ignore his physical pain, Jake climbed slowly out of the car, then stood back while Tom unfolded himself from the rear seat.

"Come on, sunshine," he said warmly. "Time to say our goodbyes to your brother."

Lori too had stepped out of the car. She stood watching silently as Jake and the young boy walked across the damp but burnt grass boundary of the parking lot. There was a small pile of flowers laid at the edge of the sidewalk. Traffic flowed through the intersection and down the highway; a steady rhythm of commuter life. The asphalt where the tanker had tipped over was still discoloured slightly, but apart from that, there was no other sign that anything untoward had happened there. Closing his eyes for a moment, Jake could see the whole tragic scene replay in front of him. Memories of Grey bringing him over to sit in front of where he now stood flooded back. A wave of nausea washed over him. Oblivious to the world around him, Jake turned away from Tom, retching, then vomiting onto the grass. The pain from being so violently sick dropped him to his knees. In an instant, Lori was at his side.

"You ok?" she asked, crouching down beside him.

His stomach heaved again and the last remnants of lunch were deposited onto the grass.

"Sorry, li'l lady," he apologised, his voice strained. "Check Tom's ok. I'll be fine in a minute."

Lori glanced over at Tom, who was standing staring out blankly across the intersection. Turning her attention back to Jake, she said, "He's ok. Come on, let's get you back into the car."

"No!" snapped Jake sharply. He paused, then added, "Sorry. I didn't mean that, Lori. Can you help me up?"

Putting a steadying arm around him, she helped her fiancé to his feet. Once he was sure he wasn't going to be sick again, Jake walked over to Tom.

"You seen enough?" he asked, holding his bruised ribs. Being sick had caused him more pain than he would have believed possible. His rib cage was screaming in agony.

"There's only cars," said the boy vacantly. "It's as though he never was. As though there was no accident. Gone. Driven over. Forgotten."

"Never forgotten, Tom," assured Jake sincerely. "We'll never forget this. Never."

"Some dying flowers," continued the boy morbidly. "That's all?"

"More than I thought there would be," admitted Jake, as another wave of nausea swept through him. His legs were shaking and he was feeling light headed. "I'm going back to the car. Come back when you're ready."

With his legs trembling beneath him, Jake walked unsteadily back to the car and, without complaint, allowed Lori to help him back into the passenger seat.

"Want a mint?" she asked, offering him a strong mint from the small tin she carried in her purse.

"Thanks," replied Jake, taking two of the small round sweets. "I'm sorry, Lori."

"What are you sorry for?" she asked, placing her hand on his thigh. "I'm so proud of you, Jake. It can't have been easy coming out here so soon."

"Harder than I thought," he admitted with a weak smile. "Do you have any painkillers? I'm in agony."

Quickly she rummaged in her bag and found a small bottle with some Vicodin in it. Without hesitation, she opened it and passed him two pills. "Sorry, I've no water or juice."

"Doesn't matter," he muttered as he swallowed the pills with ease. "I'm not even asking why you're still carrying those pills."

"They've been in my bag for months. I've not touched them for at least four months," replied Lori defensively.

"I'm just glad you had them, li'l lady," sighed Jake, leaning back against the head rest. "I feel like shit."

"I'll be back in a minute," stated Lori evenly. "I need to get you home."

Before Jake could utter a word of protest, she had left the car to walk back over to where Tom was still standing, gazing out at the flow of traffic.

"Tom," began Lori quietly, putting a hand on his shoulder. "I don't mean to rush you, but I need to get Jake home. He's in real pain. Are you ready to leave?"

Nodding, the boy said, "Sorry, I didn't mean to make him throw up."

Tears welled up in his eyes.

"It's ok," replied Lori. "Neither of us were to know how he'd react. Are you ok?"

"Kind of," he said, turning to follow her back to the car. "I thought I'd feel close to Gary out here, but I didn't feel anything."

"I'm sorry."

"Thank you for driving me out here," he said as they reached the car. "At least I've seen it for myself. It's just a road junction though."

When they arrived back at the hotel, Lori insisted Jake remain in the car while she escorted Tom back to the suite where his sister and Jason were waiting. Alice was full of apologies when she heard what had happened out at the intersection. She began to berate her young brother, but Lori stopped her, saying that the boy had needed to see the place for himself and that no harm had been done. As she turned to leave, Jason said he would come down with her. Once they were in the elevator, he asked if Jake was really alright.

"I don't know," Lori admitted, her voice full of emotion. "He wasn't ready to go out there. Wasn't ready to face that yet. He did it for Tom. I guess, he really did it for Gary."

"I couldn't have done it," confessed the Englishman as the lift reached the ground floor.

"Me neither," agreed Lori. "I took almost a year to go back to the scene of my own accident."

"Look after him, Lori," said Jason, hugging her tight.

"I intend to," she replied. "Any decision on when the funeral will be? I assume that's what you had to discuss with Alice while we were out."

"Monday at two o'clock at the chapel with the crematorium out on the Coastal Highway," revealed Jason, his face paling at the sudden realisation of the location.

"I'll let Jake know," promised Lori quietly. "He would want to be there no matter where it was."

"Thanks. I'm sure we'll see you both before then. Alice wants to see Rehoboth and she needs to sort out Gary's things. Scott's meeting us tomorrow. She also wants to go out to JJL to see where he was working."

"Call if you need us," suggested Lori. "Now, I really need to go."

"Thanks," he called, as the elevator door closed behind her.

Long, early evening shadows were being cast as Lori pulled up outside the house. Beside her in the passenger seat, Jake let out a sigh before opening the door and hauling his battered body out of the car. When Lori came into the house a few moments later, he had disappeared. Standing in the dining room, she noticed the basement door was shut tight. As she listened, she could hear him moving about downstairs. With a heavy heart, she turned and went through to the kitchen.

♫

Time dragged painfully by over the next four days for everyone involved with Silver Lake. The band had met up for dinner on Saturday out at the farmhouse. All of them had been relieved to see Rich. Both he and Jake were noticeably quiet and subdued. On Sunday, Jason had brought Alice and Tom out to the beach house for a couple of hours. They had been to the apartment in the morning, had lunched with Scott in town, then dropped by to see Jake. As soon as they arrived, he took Tom down to the basement, closing the door behind them. The others could hear the muffled soft strains of guitar music and assumed he was giving the boy a tour of the rehearsal space. When they emerged an hour or so later, Lori was relieved to see them both looking calm and relaxed.

"Can I ask you a huge favour, Jake?" began Alice as he came out to join them on the sun deck.

"Anything," he replied with a warm smile.

"Do you think you could play tomorrow at the chapel?" she asked, her eyes pleading with him. "If you're not up to it, I totally understand, but I think it's what Gary would've wanted."

"My shoulder's still a mess," began Jake hesitantly, "But I'm sure I can play something. I'll stock up on pain meds first."

"I don't want to cause you any pain," she said anxiously. "You're already doing a reading for us."

"Alice, it's fine," assured Jake softly. "If that's what you and Tom want me to do, that's what we'll do. Did you have something special in mind?"

"We'll leave that up to you."

Come Monday morning, Jake was still unsure what was appropriate to play. He had lain awake most of the night, running over countless possibilities in his head. Finally, he had narrowed it down to two choices before he had drifted off into a restless sleep. It was late when Lori came through to waken him. She had brought him a mug of coffee and sat with him while he drank it. He had used the last mouthful to wash down two painkillers. The bruising to his rib cage and back had faded out to a dirty green-yellow colour; the stitches on his cheek felt tight and ready to be removed.

"Do you have a black scarf I can use as a sling today?" he asked, passing the empty mug to Lori. "I'm not wearing that hideous hospital thing a minute longer."

"I think so," she replied going over to search in the dressing table drawer. After depositing most of the contents on the floor, she found what she was searching for. "Will this do?"

Jake nodded. "Looks ideal."

A couple of hours later, dressed in a black shirt and his best black jeans, Jake asked for Lori's help to tie the scarf in place as a makeshift sling. It took her a couple of attempts to get the lengths right, but finally he was comfortable with it. Lori too was dressed in black, the colour setting off her golden blonde hair and beach tan.

"You look beautiful, li'l lady," he complimented, kissing her tenderly.

"You don't look so bad yourself, rock star," she whispered. "There's a glint of the old Jake in your eyes again."

"I'll be glad when today's over," he admitted. "It's going to be tough to say goodbye."

"I know," she agreed sadly. "It's never easy."

Cars were already filling the parking lot when Lori drove up to the funeral chapel. A space had been reserved for them at the side of the building. Several journalists were gathered outside as she and Jake walked silently past them into the cool tranquillity of the building. In the vestibule, Rich, with dark glasses hiding his face, and Linsey were waiting for them. As they exchanged comforting hugs in greeting, Grey arrived with Kola, closely followed by Paul and Maddy. A few seconds later, they were joined by Dr Marrs, Todd and a sombre looking Scott. A member of staff politely ushered them into the chapel, directing them to their seats in the rows reserved for them. The chapel was full, a testament to Gary's popularity. Friends had flown in from Britain and several other countries. A few of the musicians he had worked with had also made the effort to be there to say goodbye.

On the stroke of two, the mourners were asked to stand as Gary's casket was carried in. Two single white roses rested on top of the plain oak coffin. Behind them, Alice and Tom walked in slowly and silently took their seats in the front row. The reverend, who was conducting the service, signalled for them all to be seated, then delivered a warm, heartfelt eulogy. It was light hearted and created a true reflection of the person Gary had been. Scott was the first to step forward to do a short reading, a Bible passage requested by Gary's elderly parents. The young film maker spoke calmly and clearly, his English accent ringing round the chapel.

After the first and only hymn, Jake stepped up to the lectern, a piece of paper in his trembling hand. He looked out across the gathered mourners, spotting friends and colleagues. Taking a deep breath to try to steady his quivering emotions, Jake began,

"Do not stand at my grave and weep;
I am not there. I do not sleep.
I am a thousand winds that blow.
I am the diamond glints on snow.
I am the sunlight on ripened grain.
I am the gentle autumn rain.
When you awaken in the morning's hush
I am the swift uplifting rush
Of quiet birds in circled flight.
I am the soft stars that shine at night.
Do not stand at my grave and cry.
I am not there. I did not die."

His voice cracked with emotion as he recited the last two lines. Wiping away a tear, he murmured, "Thank you," and walked back to his seat, with his head bowed.

The preacher led the congregation in a short prayer and blessing, then announced that there would be an acoustic performance to end the ceremony. Carefully, Jake eased his arm out of the makeshift sling and passed the scarf to Lori. Keeping his head bowed, he walked back out to the front of the chapel, pausing for a brief moment beside Gary's coffin. A chair sat to one side with one of his acoustic guitars on a stand beside it. He took a moment or two to settle himself with the guitar resting on his knee. Focussing his attention, Jake stole a glance over towards Tom and Alice. He could feel everyone's eyes on him. Perhaps it was his imagination, but he could feel Gary standing behind him. Only at that moment did he finally decide which of the two songs that had been on his mind was going to be the one he played. The delicate, familiar strains of The Beatles "Yesterday" filled the chapel. Jake's husky, unrehearsed vocal was perfect. Beside him, the curtains closed softly around the casket. His voice wavered and a tidal wave of emotion hit him as he sang, "Why'd he have to go?"

Seeing that he was struggling, the assembled group of Gary's friends one by one joined in. Their united, strong voices gave Jake the strength to finish the song. When it was done, he sat where he was, eyes cast downwards to hide the tears that were flowing freely down his cheeks. The minister delivered a final blessing over them all, then came forward to shake Alice and Tom by the hand. Soundlessly, brother and sister led the mourners out of the chapel, their final goodbyes said.

Rich was the first person to reach Jake. Putting his arm around his friend's shoulder, he said, "That was amazing. I could never have held it together to deliver that one."

"Thanks, buddy," said Jake with a sad sigh. "I wish I hadn't had to. That was tough."

"You nailed it. Gary would've loved it."

"I hope so," sighed Jake, setting the guitar back on its stand. "Let's get out of here. I need a drink."

At the front door, Alice and Tom were shaking hands and thanking each of the mourners for coming. Their faces were pale and strained. Silver Lake held back until the very end, Jake being last of all. When he finally stepped forward in front of them, Alice and Tom both reached out to hug him. All three of them stood in a tearful huddle for a few moments before Grey came back to say, "All local Silver Lake events end in one place. Let's head to the Turtle to toast Gary. I think we could all use a drink."

"Amen to that," said Alice, forcing a small smile.

The private function suite at the Turtle was crammed full when Gary's family and the band arrived. There was a table reserved for them in the corner and Jason had arranged for some champagne on ice to be waiting for them. When they all had a glass in their hand, the Englishman proposed a toast, "To Gary.

Always in our hearts."

"To Gary," echoed the others, clinking glasses.

Most of the mourners only stayed for one or two drinks, then slowly drifted home. At the corner table, Silver Lake were collectively reminiscing about past nights spent in the bar. Alice and Tom were soaking up each tale, using it as a salve on their grief. Once again, they were all relaxed and there was laughter in the air.

"This might be inappropriate," interrupted Jake after a couple of hours. "But let's go back to our house. We'll BBQ, play some music and party as though Gary was with us."

"Sounds like as good a plan as any to me," agreed Alice, already slightly drunk on the champagne.

Laughter and music filled the house. In the sunroom, Becky was camped out on the settee, watching the cartoon channel. Todd and Kate had arrived and been introduced to Tom. All three teenagers were huddled together on the other couch, watching YouTube videos of Silver Lake, some of which had been uploaded by Gary. Out on the deck, Maddy and Paul each had one of the twins nestled on their lap, both babies contentedly sucking on their thumb. While the others were relaxing on the sun deck, enjoying the late afternoon sun, Grey and Kola had slipped away, hand in hand, for a stroll along the beach.

"Jake," giggled Alice, her confidence boosted by the champagne and the wine she was now enjoying. "Can I ask you something personal?"

"If I say no, you're going to ask anyway, aren't you?" he teased playfully.

"Yes," she replied without hesitation. "Will you show me your tattoos?"

"All of them?"

She nodded.

"Ok, ma'am," he laughed as he stood up. Gingerly he slid his arm out of the scarf sling, then asked Lori to help him off with his shirt. Discretely he whispered to her to unfasten his jeans too. Stifling a giggle, she obliged. Alice watched as the tall rock star stripped in front of her until he stood there wearing only his boxer shorts.

"Your wish is my command, Miss York," he declared, flashing Alice a "Power" smile.

"Wow!" she exclaimed, her face flushing scarlet as she surveyed his ink gallery.

"Hey," called out Paul, causing Wren to jump with a start. "When did you get the knot done?"

"The Thursday before the crash," replied Jake, pulling his jeans back on. "Like it?"

"Yeah. We should all get one," suggested the drummer.

"I'm up for it," agreed Rich, admiring the tattoo design. "Once my ribs heal."

"Think Grey'll go for it?" asked Paul, shifting his daughter onto his shoulder as he stood up. He walked over to Jake, to take a closer look at the intricate design. "Nice!"

"Don't see why not," mused Jake as he slipped the sling back into place.

"Is there a story behind all of those?" asked Alice unable to take her eyes off him.

"Most of them," he admitted. "The cross on my back was the first when I was eighteen."

"What's the music on your arm?"

"Stronger Within," replied Jake, taking a seat on the sun lounger beside Lori. "It's the first song I wrote for Mz Hyde not long after we met."

"Do you have any, Lori?" asked Alice curiously.

"A couple," she revealed shyly. "My butterfly and my anklet." She raised the hem of her long skirt to reveal the delicate chain design.

"That's gorgeous!"

"If you want to get some ink, we can take you to see Danny," offered Jake. "He did them all."

"Oh no! Not for me. My folks never approved of tattoos," said Alice then turning to Maddy, she asked, "Did this Danny do yours too?"

"No, darling," purred Maddy with a smile. "I've collected mine from all over the world."

Conversation moved on to travel as they all talked about their favourite places. Maddy expressed a preference for the Far East while Lori said she loved London and Paris.

"I'd love to see New York," confessed Alice shyly. "This is my first trip to America."

"That's easily fixed," stated Lori warmly. "It's only a three hour drive from here. Well, maybe four, depending on traffic."

"I'm heading back to New York on Wednesday," added Jason, sipping his beer. "You're welcome to travel with me."

"And my apartment's empty, so you are welcome to stay there," offered Lori. "Stay as long as you like."

"Well, I suppose we could go for a few days," replied Alice. "Let me talk to Tom about it."

"How long are you planning on staying over here?" asked Rich.

"I don't know," she sighed sadly. "Gary had wanted Tom to see you guys do those festival shows. I am hoping we can stay long enough to at least see you guys play once."

An awkward silence hung in the air.

"That schedule is a bit up in the air," confessed Jake, running his hand nervously through his hair. "Maddison?"

"We need to talk about it, but not now," stated Maddy, her business voice creeping in. "I've a few calls to make but maybe we'll be back out there at the start of August. It depends on a lot of different factors. Primarily Rich and Jake's health."

After they had all eaten, Tom asked if he could walk back into town with Todd and Kate. They were heading for the boardwalk to meet up with Todd's friends. Much to his surprise, Alice agreed, asking only that he be back by nine thirty. With the three teenagers out of the way, the adults sat around the table chatting. The twins had fallen asleep. Wren was nestled on Jake's lap while Hayden was stretched out across Grey's chest. Becky had grown tired of watching TV and had cuddled in beside Lori. The little girl had eyed Kola suspiciously when she had sat next to Grey. In the background, Lori's iPod had been plugged in and music was flowing out from the sunroom.

True to his word, Tom appeared back on time, minus his two new friends.

"It's time we headed back to the hotel," said Alice, swaying slightly as she stood up. "Jason?"

"I'll drive you out there, but I'm staying at JJL tonight. Jim?

Kola? Do you guys need a ride?"

The producer and the sound engineer nodded.

As they all said their farewells a few minutes later, Jake cornered Dr Marrs, "Will you be about after lunch tomorrow, Jim?"

"Sure. Why?"

"I'll take a run out to JJL. I want to talk to you about an idea for the record."

"Fine. I'll see you then," agreed the producer, sensing that Jake didn't want to reveal his idea just yet. "Thanks for dinner, Lori."

"Any time, Jim," she called from her seat on the sun lounger.

Beebe Medical Center was busy when Jake and Lori arrived next morning. Their first port of call was the triage nurse. As they sat in line in the waiting room, Jake fidgeted, drumming his finger on his thigh, tapping his feet. Eventually the nurse called him through and, with a few expert snips, had the row of stitches removed. He ran his hand over the thin scar. It felt slightly raised, but smooth to the touch.

"You've been lucky, Mr Power," observed the nurse, taking her gloves off. "That'll fade in no time at all."

"Thanks," said Jake. "Next stop, Dr Brent's clinic."

"You take care now," she called as he stepped out of the cubicle.

When they walked round to the orthopaedic clinic, the waiting room was empty. While Lori took a seat, Jake went up to the reception desk. The young nurse on duty looked up and said, "Mr Power?"

"Yes," he replied with a smile.

"I'll show you through. Dr Brent's waiting for you."

"Morning, Jake," greeted the doctor as Jake entered the small office. "Take a seat."

Closing the door behind him, Jake sat in the chair beside John's desk. The doctor was typing an email and, as he hit send on it, he turned his attention to his patient.

"How are you?" he asked as he brought Jake's case notes up on screen.

"Fine, I guess," replied Jake awkwardly. "Ribs still hurt like hell. Shoulder's not too bad."

"Lost the hospital sling, I see," observed John with a wry smile.

"Sorry," muttered Jake, suddenly feeling self-conscious.

"Right, let's take a look at you. Do you need help with your shirt?"

"I can manage, thanks," replied Jake, unfastening the buttons. He winced as he moved his injured shoulder to slide his arm out of the sleeve.

"Stand up for me, if you don't mind," requested the doctor.

He examined Jake thoroughly. As he tested the range of movement in Jake's shoulder, he scribbled a few notes on his notepad, then said to Jake to put his shirt back on. Without being asked, he helped the rock star to get his injured arm into the sleeve then returned to his seat at the desk while Jake fastened the buttons.

"Well?" asked Jake, slipping his arm back into the makeshift sling.

"You're doing much better than I expected," commented the doctor as he typed up the notes he had taken. "The swelling and bruising to your ribcage is more or less gone. It'll take another couple of weeks for all the muscle damage there to settle. Have you had any further trauma to that area?"

"I threw up the other day," confessed Jake, embarrassed to admit it in front of the doctor. "Hurt like hell."

"I bet it did."

"Dropped me to my knees."

"What caused the nausea?" asked John.

Running his hand nervously through his hair, Jake looked at him. "I went back out to the intersection with Gary's young brother. The kid needed to see where his brother died. I don't know what happened. One minute I'm staring out at the traffic. Next thing I knew, I was chucking up on the grass verge."

"That's a common reaction," said the doctor softly. "Might have been a bit too soon to go back out there."

"Maybe but I had to face it sometime."

"I suppose so," agreed John. "And there's been no nausea since?"

"None."

"Good. And have you been using your shoulder or have you kept it supported?"

"I've used it a bit. Not too much," Jake confessed.

"How much?"

"I've played a bit of guitar, that's all. It's what I do!" stated Jake, his tone harsher than he meant. Quietly, he added, "I played at the funeral service yesterday too."

"That must have been hard."

"Toughest gig I've ever played," answered Jake, feeling his emotions slipping out of control at the memory of playing in the chapel.

"I'll bet," agreed John awkwardly. The doctor typed something into the computer. On his desk, the printer began to whir as it printed off two sheets of paper. "Ok, I'm guessing here but, I'd say you don't want to trail out here for physical therapy twice a week. You've dislocated that shoulder twice before in the past five years, so you know the score. Here's the exercises that I want you to start off with. Take it slowly. Don't rush it. Stick to the pain management regime for another week. Keep that arm supported. That shoulder doesn't feel like it's ready to take the weight yet."

"Thanks," said Jake, taking the printed sheets from him. "What about playing my guitar?"

"If I say no, you'll play anyway," countered the doctor with a smile. "Be sensible. Listen to your body. Short, and I mean short, practice sessions."

"I've an album to finish recording," laughed Jake. "We've a deadline to meet here and we've lost over a week already."

"Do not use the pain medication to extend the practice times," cautioned the doctor, handing him a script for more medication.

"I won't," promised Jake, genuinely meaning it.

"Ok. I'll see you back here in two weeks," said the doctor. "They'll sort you out with an appointment at the desk."

"Thanks, John."

As Lori drove out of the parking lot, Jake suggested they find somewhere to have a quiet lunch. With a knowing smile, she said she knew just the place and turned the car towards Lewes.

"Is this place new?" asked Jake as he climbed awkwardly out

of the car in front of the restaurant, swearing under his breath as he bumped his shoulder on the edge of the door.

"I'm not sure," replied Lori, locking the car. "Grey's mom told me about it the other week. She'd been here with one of her church friends."

Surprisingly, the restaurant was busy when they entered but the hostess quickly showed them to a table by the window. Together they browsed the unfamiliar menu debating what to select and had only just made a decision when their server returned with their drinks. With their food order placed, Jake raised his glass of sweetened iced tea and said, "Here's to you, li'l lady, for being so calm and patient with me for the last week or so."

Blushing, Lori lowered her eyes not wanting him to see the tears welling up in them. She felt him reach across the table and take her hand.

"I mean it," he said softly. "I don't know how I'd have got through this without you."

"You'd have found a way."

"Maybe," he conceded. "I wish I had half your empathy and patience."

"Don't sell yourself short, rock star. You were brilliant with Tom the other day."

"I wasn't so brilliant when we went out to the intersection," he muttered, still angry with himself for being sick in front of the boy.

"You realise we have to drive through there on the way back from the studio," said Lori calmly.

Jake nodded, then, in an attempt to lighten things, promised, "I won't throw up in your car."

"You'd better not!" she giggled. "If you do, you're cleaning up the mess."

"What was I saying about empathy?" teased Jake, kissing her hand. "I love you, Lori."

"Love you too, rock star."

Mid-afternoon temperatures were creeping up into the low nineties as Lori drove up the Coastal Highway. Over lunch, she had assured Jake that she had brought her laptop with her and had plenty to keep her occupied for a few hours while he met with Dr Marrs. It was almost three before she pulled off the highway and parked in a shady spot round the side of the main studio building. Both of them were mildly surprised to see Todd's beat up truck parked beside Kola's Harley Davidson. When they entered the reception area, they could hear someone playing guitar through in the studio. Instantly, Jake recognised the style of his protégé. He stood and listened for a few minutes, then couldn't resist the temptation to comment any longer. Taking Lori by the hand, he walked into the control room. Hearing the door, Jim and Kola turned round and silently mouthed, "Hello."

In the live room, Todd was totally focussed on the piece he was playing. Unaware of Jake's arrival, he stood with his back to the window, lost in the moment until he fluffed a section.

"From the top," called Jake, taking the teenager completely by surprise. "Don't rush that progression. Slow it down. Feel the music. Breathe through it."

"Hi," called back Todd, looking a little sheepish at having been caught practicing with the band's guitars.

"Hello, Todd," said Jake with a smile. "Now from the top, please."

There was no doubting that the boy had talent. This time the entire piece flowed almost effortlessly, earning him a round of applause from his small, select audience.

"Right, put the toys away," called Jake. "Could you re-tune that one back to the way I left it, please?"

"Sorry, sir," apologised Todd, guessing that he had overstepped the mark.

"No harm done," assured Jake as he turned his attention back to the producer. "Damn, he's good."

"He's amazing," agreed Jim Marrs with a nod. "He's been out here most of the last week practising. I've recorded some of it. He brought Kate out the other day. What a voice that girl has!"

"Two very talented youngsters," observed Lori, shifting her weight and leaning heavily on her cane. "I'm heading back out to the lounge to do some work. How long do you need here, Jake?"

"A couple of hours, li'l lady," he replied. "I'll see how my shoulder holds up."

"You're here to play?" asked Kola with her usual bluntness.

"That was the plan."

"But I thought," she began, pointing to the sling.

"I know, but I need to try something," interrupted Jake as Lori closed the door behind her. "I want to put an extra track on the album."

"What did you have in mind?" enquired the producer, his curiosity suddenly aroused.

"Let me show you and then you can let me know if you feel this will work," suggested Jake as he eased his arm out of the sling and headed into the live room.

"Are you sure you should be playing so soon?" asked Kola, noticing the grimace of pain that crossed his face as he crossed the room in front of the window.

"I'll be fine," he stated firmly. "Todd pass me the black Gibson will you?"

"Sure," replied the boy, reaching round to the guitar rack behind him.

Jake settled himself on a stool and accepted the guitar from Todd, careful to lift it with his right hand. While the boy plugged in the leads, Jake ran through a few chords. Biting his lower lip in an attempt to disguise his discomfort, he adjusted the tuning, then nodded over to Jim and Kola. Todd moved across the room to sit on the couch in the corner.

The piece began slowly, a delicate, slightly French feel to it, then Jake launched into a powerful heavy riff. He played with his head bowed to hide the tears that were welling up in his eyes. All in, the song lasted just over three minutes, ending with a reprise of the French air. By then end of it, he was spent, his shoulder screaming at him.

"Are there any lyrics to that?" asked Dr Marrs from the control room.

"No," replied Jake, massaging his shoulder gently. "I couldn't find the words. I think the music speaks for itself. What do you think?"

"I like it," admitted the producer. Jake sensed a "but" was coming. "In fact, I fucking love it!"

"Can we tag it onto the end?" asked Jake, feeling a sense of relief wash through him. "It needs a drum track and a bass line too."

"I disagree," stated Dr Marrs bluntly. "It's raw as it is. Full of pain. Filled with emotion. It's perfect as a guitar solo. Do you feel up to playing it again and I'll record this one?"

"Sure," agreed Jake, praying silently that the pain meds he had swallowed before he got out of the car would kick in soon.

Out in the lounge, Lori had fetched herself a coffee and was sitting at her laptop, working her way through her emails. With that mundane task dealt with, she brought out her sketchbook and began to play with some ideas that were forming for the Silver Lake album artwork. The imp had to be central to the design or at least a strong feature of it. She could hear Jake playing and recognised the music as the piece he had been working on in the basement over the last few days; the piece he had played for Tom when he visited the house. It felt good to know he was back in the studio, but she fretted that it was too much too soon.

Two hours became three and there was still no sign of Jake coming out of the studio. Todd had come out shortly before five, saying he had to go back into town to fetch Kate from work. When it reached six thirty, Lori packed up her stuff and went over to the control room. Quietly she slipped in, closing the door behind her. In the live room, Jake was putting the guitar back on the rack. His face was pale and there were deep lines of pain etched across it.

"He's just coming, Lori," said Jim warmly. "He's ok."

"Is he?" she asked sharply. "He looks exhausted to me."

"He is," muttered Kola. "But he wouldn't stop till he was done. The track's amazing. So raw. So much pain to it."

Sliding the sling back into place with an audible sigh of relief, Jake came through to join them. Putting his good arm around Lori's shoulder, he whispered to her, "I'm fine. Yeah, I'm sore, but I'm fine. Don't look so worried."

"If you say so," she sighed reluctantly. "Let's get you home."

Switching everything off, Dr Marrs asked, "Are you coming out tomorrow?"

"I don't think so," answered Jake. "I'll probably leave it till Thursday."

"Maddison was wanting a meeting on Thursday to re-jig the schedule. Has she called you?"

"I've not checked my phone" confessed Jake. "I left it back at the house."

"Ok. Talk to her first then let me know," suggested the producer. "I'll work on this tonight, after dinner. I'll email it over to you when I'm done."

"Thanks, Jim," said Jake sounding weary. "See you guys later in the week."

As soon as he sat down in the car, Jake leaned back against the headrest and sighed. Every inch of his body ached. His injured shoulder was throbbing. From the driving seat, Lori looked over at him and shook her head.

"You're worn out," she stated plainly.

"I'm not about to argue with you, li' lady," he said, pain creeping into his voice. "That was tough."

"Do you need any pain meds?" she asked softly.

"I'll survive. I don't want to take any just now," he replied, closing his eyes and allowing the pain to wash through him. "Let's just go home."

As she pulled out onto the highway, Lori could feel her own emotions fluttering. It had turned into a beautiful evening and she was looking forward to getting back to the beach to relax on the deck with a glass of wine. Beside her, she was aware of Jake fidgeting. The closer they got to the intersection with Route 9, the harder she prayed that the traffic lights would be in their favour. With the junction in sight, she asked, "You ok?"

"Not really," confessed Jake quietly. "Just keep driving."

Luck was on their side. The lights were green and Lori drove smoothly through and on towards home. Another ghost laid to rest.

♪

With two glasses of wine in her hands, Lori limped out onto the sun deck. On one of the sun loungers, Jake was stretched out, stripped to the waist, his injured arm resting across his tender rib cage. At first Lori thought he was asleep, but, when he heard her footsteps, he opened one hazel eye and smiled.

"There you go, rock star," she said, passing him the glass.

"Thanks."

"How's your shoulder?" asked Lori as sat down on the other lounger.

"Not so bad now. It's throbbing a bit," answered Jake wearily. "I was careful while I was playing. I sat down the whole time to keep the weight off it."

Sipping her wine, Lori said, "Do you want to tell me about the track you were recording?"

"I played that riff to Gary a few weeks ago and he loved it, but I never did anything with it. While I was in the hospital, I kept hearing it over and over and over in my head," began Jake haltingly. Pausing to sip his wine, he continued, "I wanted to add a tribute to him to the record. I wrote the piece around the riff, but I can't come up with any lyrics for it. I played it to Tom and he loved it. When I said to him about the lyrics, he asked if it had to have them. I admitted that I didn't know. Jim agrees it works well as an instrumental."

"Have the others heard it yet?"

"No," said Jake. "I just hope they understand. I wanted to get drums and bass on there, but Jim over ruled me. He wanted it stripped back. Bare, I guess. Raw was the expression he used."

"They'll understand," reassured Lori with a smile. "And if they don't, Maddy will help them to."

The kitchen in the house adjacent to JJL was excessively bright and modern. Its white wall mounted cabinets and stainless steel countertops contrasted starkly with the scarlet chairs and black hi-polish table. Coffee cups, a box of donuts and various electronic devices littered the table as Silver Lake gathered for their band summit. Gone was the "Mommy" Maddy; the "business" Maddy was back in full force. Once they were all assembled and had breakfasted on the donuts Grey had brought in with the coffees, she cleared her throat and began, "Ok, down to business, boys. We need to get this show back on track. The record needs to be finished and we need to salvage what we can from the shows Gary lined up."

Her tone was harsh and direct, taking them all a little by surprise.

"Maddy, I don't know when I'll be cleared by the doctor," Rich started. His voice was still more nasal than normal and a pair of sunglasses masked the bruising and puffiness around his eyes.

"I don't want to hear excuses," she snapped, casting a black look towards the guitarist.

"No one's making excuses, Maddison," said Jake calmly. "But, Rich, she's right. We need to get this resolved today. Get a plan together. A timeline agreed. We have commitments to honour or there's legal repercussions here."

"How long do we have to finish the record?" asked Paul, helping himself to the last donut.

"Today's July 18th. Dr Marrs is contracted till August 2nd. That gives us two weeks. I've spoken to him and he's agreed to extend us by a week maximum. Add to that the fact that JJL is booked out from August 12th. In an ideal world, you need it all recorded before the end of July."

"Right, now we're getting there," sighed Grey. "However, Paul and I are done. It's Jake and Rich, who have recording left to finish."

"Problem number one," stated Rich bluntly. "I can't sing my backing vocals right now."

"Agreed," acknowledged Maddy as she turned to stare at Grey. "Can you sing, Mr Cooper?"

"If I have to, I'll give it a go," agreed Grey with a laugh. "It could be a painful experience for you all."

"Well, Paul can't do it. Have you heard him sing?" laughed Maddy. "Or alternatively, we could hire a session vocalist?"

"No!" stated all four of them at once.

"Ok, no session guys," she noted calmly. "Jake, are you fit to finish off the lead vocal chores?"

"Probably not, but I'll give it my best shot," he offered. "And, if I take it easy, I can finish my guitar tracking."

"Same here," said Rich as he drained the last mouthful of coffee from his cup.

"So, can we be done by July 28th?" asked their manager, glancing round.

"Yes," answered Jake, sounding more confident than he felt.

"Fine. Progress," sighed Maddy. "Now, to the bonus track. Additional track. Tribute. Whatever you want to badge it as. Anyone object to it being on the record?"

All of them shook their heads silently.

"Fine. It's done and dusted. We'll add it in as an Easter egg."

"No," said Jake abruptly. "Don't hide it."

"I agree," added Paul as Grey and Rich both nodded. "Let's list it."

"Ok. I'll see what I can do," agreed Maddy, glancing down at her list of outstanding items. "Now to the festivals. We've pulled out of the first one on July 26th. The next one in the calendar is August 10th? Can we make that one?"

"How long a set?" enquired Rich, looking over at Jake in an attempt to gauge his reaction.

"At least an hour. Maybe a few minutes longer," she began. "I've got some of the scheduling emails, but Gary didn't copy me in on them all. I've been piecing it together for the last week, but there's still a few gaps I need to re-negotiate. Right now, we're looking at August 10th followed by 16th, 24th and September 1st. There's a tentative deal in place for September 6th. Jason's picking that one up with the promoter. If we get it signed off, that's a Friday night headline show so we need a full set. A full two hour show."

"Maddy, you're asking a lot here," began Grey, concerned that she was pushing them too hard too fast.

"It's ok," interrupted Jake, keeping his eyes cast downward. "We owe it to Gary to make this happen. He set this up. We shouldn't let him down."

"But if we're not fit to give a hundred percent," said Rich, taking his sunglasses off and revealing the full extent of the injuries to his face. "What the fuck do you suggest we do, Jake?"

"We give it a hundred fucking percent!" snapped Jake angrily. "Christ, we have no fucking choice!"

His angry outburst caught them all off guard. Scraping his chair back on the polished tile floor, Jake declared, "I need some air."

Out in front of the house, Jake sat on a beaten up rocking chair that was sitting in the middle of the burnt lawn. He could hear the traffic out on the highway. The painkillers he had taken first thing that morning had more or less worn off and his whole body ached. His heart ached too. Meeting as a band for the first time without Gary felt all wrong. Much as he admired Maddy and respected that she was only doing her job, it had been tough to sit round the table and talk business. Behind him, he heard the screen door squeak then slam shut. He recognised Maddy's quick, light step on the path. Approaching him from behind, the Goth laid her hand gently on his uninjured shoulder. "Hey, mister," she whispered warmly. "Are you alright out here?"

"Yeah," replied Jake sounding worn out. "I just needed a minute or two. It was getting way too intense in there."

Kicking off her trademark spike heels, Maddy sat down on the grass at his feet. They sat in silence for a few minutes, both of them listening to the world going by, before she said, "This is hard for me too. I miss my right hand man."

"I hadn't really thought about it like that," confessed Jake. "The last couple of weeks has really taken its toll on all of us."

"You can say that again."

"Are we done in there?" he asked, not wanting to return for more "round the table" debate.

"Yes," nodded Maddy, running her hands through her short, black, spiky hair. "I need to get home for the babies. I need to call Jason later and fill him in. I've to mail some photos to your sister for the fan page."

Laughing, Jake said, "I still can't believe she's doing all that for us. My little sister the rock groupie."

"Don't laugh," giggled Maddy. "She's doing a fabulous job for you guys. Have you seen the fan messages on that page?"

"No," admitted Jake. "I don't look that kind of thing up too often. She posted down a pile of cards and letters. I read some of those."

"Take a look at Lucy's page," suggested Maddy with a

knowing smile.

"Ok, boss," he agreed, flashing her one of his smiles. "I'll take a look later."

"I do need to ask one more favour," she said slowly. "If you say no, I'll understand. Rich already said no."

"What do you need me to do, Maddison?"

"Give a press interview."

The request hung in the air between them. The four small words had sent tremors of fear through Jake. Knowing that Rich had already refused added to the pressure he felt bearing down on him. Swallowing then sighing, he nodded.

"You'll do it?" Maddy asked, her eyes wide in surprise.

"Yes," he responded. "But it has to be controlled and on my terms."

"Name them."

Jake sat thinking for a few minutes. His heart was pounding at the thought of speaking to the media. His head knew it was the right thing to do for Silver Lake and their fans. In the past, he had enjoyed a very relaxed relationship with the local media and he had got on well with the British media on last year's tour.

"I'll meet them out here," he began. "In the studio. No more than four journalists. No video. I'll agree to photos. It can't last more than an hour."

"Sounds more than fair to me," agreed Maddy. "I'll hand pick them myself."

"One more thing," added Jake quietly. "If Lucy's fan page is generating as much support as you say then I want to put something on there first."

"Like what?"

"I don't know. A short video message?"

"I like that idea," replied Maddy. "And your sister will love it!"

"Is Scott around later on?" he asked, part of him already regretting the idea.

"I'll call him and get back to you on that."

"Ok," sighed Jake getting to his feet. "Time to find out if Grey can sing. Can you send him over to the studio? I'm heading over there before I change my mind."

Noticing the wave of pain that flashed across his face as he stood up, Maddy reached out to stop him. "You don't need to rush right in there, Jake."

"I know, but there's work to be done. I'll be fine," he assured her with a forced smile.

"Take it easy," she said as she dusted the grass off her short skirt. "I'll call you when I've spoken to Scott."

Jake nodded and walked off towards the studio.

It was cool and incredibly quiet in the studio. Jake had picked up a bottle of water from the refrigerator in the lounge and took a large mouthful of it to wash down the two painkillers he had attempted to swallow. A voice from the darkness of the control room startled him.

"I hope that wasn't a banned substance, Mr Power."

It was Kola.

"Not unless Walgreen's have banned Advil," joked Jake as she switched on the lights around her. "I've long since turned my back on the hard stuff."

"You?" she asked with obvious surprise.

"Ancient history," he muttered evasively, setting the bottle down.

Carefully, he picked his favourite cherry Gibson Les Paul out of the rack and carried it over to the stool in the centre of the room. Trying to set it up and plug it in one handed proved impossible. Moving his shoulder slowly, he eased his arm out of the sling. He plugged in the leads, then put the guitar on. Instantly, the weight and pressure of the strap sent fiery bolts of pain surging through him. Trembling, he sat on the low stool, taking the instrument's weight on his thighs. The pain subsided and he was soon lost in his own world as he warmed up and practised a few favoured routines. As he played, he saw Dr Marrs join Kola in the control room. The door to the live room opened. Grey came striding in to join him.

"You sure about this singing thing?" asked the bass player anxiously.

"Let's give it a shot," said Jake without pausing his practice. "Start with some warm ups."

"That caterwauling you do?"

"The very same."

Switching to "school teacher" mode, Jake slowly coached his friend through a basic vocal warm up routine. Initially the bass player was self-conscious, only too aware that his girlfriend was listening. Stopping him mid-scale, Jake suggested Dr Marrs took Kola out to lunch and then bring them something back. With the "audience" out of the way, Jake resumed the lesson. Gradually Grey's nerves subsided and, as he focussed on what Jake was demonstrating, he relaxed a little, revealing a half-decent voice. With both of them fully warmed up, Jake explained which tracks still needed backing vocals. There were three in total. Out of the five remaining half-finished tracks, these were the easiest vocally as the band had made a conscious decision that these would be more musically complex. While Jake was playing the lead guitar part for the first one, Kola and the producer returned from lunch.

"Not a good time to stop," commented Jake as Grey was heading for the door. "Jim, set up for track eight. We'll try this before we eat."

It was mid-afternoon before they finally paused to eat the sandwiches that Kola had brought back for them. Track eight's backing vocals had been completed though and Jake suggested he do his lead vocal next to allow Grey to rest his voice.

"I'm not taking chances here," stated Jake bluntly as Grey started to protest that he was fine. "You're not used to using your voice like that. We can't risk you straining it on day one."

Reluctantly, the bass player agreed.

"Guys," cautioned Jim Marrs, "Don't either of you overdo it."

"I hear you," acknowledged Jake, as he scrunched up his sandwich box and tossed it into the trash can. "Let's get track eight done and we'll call it a day."

"You look done in right now," stated Kola sharply.

Adjusting the position of the sling so that his shoulder felt more supported, Jake admitted, "Yeah, I'm sore and tired but this has to be done. I've not tried to sing properly since the accident. Let's give it a shot."

"And if it hurts your ribs too much?" she challenged, her dark eyes boring through him.

"I'll stop," promised Jake with a wink.

"Rock stars," she muttered in exasperation.

Track eight was one of the longer songs planned for the

record, its lyrics telling the story of a journey to fulfil your heart's desire. From the beginning, Silver Lake had hoped fans would see this as an anthem due to its powerful chorus. Vocally it didn't stretch Jake's range, but it was going to be a challenge to his power and stamina. There were a few long notes in there that would test his lungs.

Take one was a fiasco. Halfway through, Jake got the lyrics wrong, then got a fit of the giggles. Clutching his aching ribs and trying to stifle his laughter, he called through, "Let's try that again."

Take two ran smoothly until the last chorus. On the first line, something caught in Jake's throat, causing him to cough. The cough sparked a spasm of pain that shot through his ribs, almost bringing him to his knees.

"Enough, Jake," said Grey from the control room. He could see the pain etched on his friend's face, but he also recognised the look of determination in his eyes.

"Once more from the top," stated Jake as he took a swallow of water. "Last time for today."

With a slow nod of the head, Dr Marrs agreed with him. From the confines of the control room, the three of them watched as Jake composed himself. This time he nailed it. Note perfect. Word Perfect.

"Fantastic effort, Mr Power," declared Dr Marrs.

"Take him home, Grey," said Kola softly, as she watched Jake collapse onto the couch in the studio. "And good luck explaining this to Lori."

"Thanks," muttered Grey, searching in his pocket for the keys to his truck. "I'll see you guys tomorrow at some point."

Ever since Maddy had called around lunchtime to fill her in on the morning's meeting, Lori had been anxious. She had tried to focus on the plans for the Silver Lake artwork, but her mind was all over the place. After a couple of hours, she had called Jake's phone but it had gone straight to voicemail. By five thirty, she had left four messages and the lack of response was worrying her. When the phone rang a few minutes later, her heart skipped a beat, scared to answer it.

"Hey, li'l lady," came Jake's voice, sounding a little husky.

"Hey, yourself, rock star," she replied, trying and failing to sound cross. "I was getting worried."

"Sorry. We're just coming into town. Do you want me to bring something in for dinner?"

"If you want," she replied, relieved that he was alright. "Or I can fire up the grill?"

"I'm in the mood for steak sandwiches," he confessed. "And we've just pulled up outside the place."

"Fine," laughed Lori. "Can I have mine with onions, please? Is Grey staying to eat?"

She could hear their muffled voices in the truck then Jake finally replied, "Yes, but he won't be staying long. He needs to fetch Becky at eight. She's at a friend's house."

"Ok. I'll see you both when you get here."

Lori had just finished setting the table out on the deck when she heard Grey's truck pull up. It was a relief to hear the boys' voices as they walked round the side of the house. When she saw how pale and tired Jake looked, it took her all of her time not to comment. Instead of taking a seat, he kissed her gently on the top of the head and promised to be back out in a minute. As soon as he was out of earshot, Lori turned to Grey and stated, "He's exhausted. Why didn't you bring him home sooner?"

"I tried, Lori," sighed the bass player, taking a seat at the table. "But you try stopping him."

"I guess," she agreed reluctantly. "How'd it go?"

"Ok," began Grey. "The meeting was tough. Everyone's still a bit raw. Rich is really struggling."

"Maddy said that too when she called," said Lori as she opened up the bag of food and began to sort out whose was whose.

"We made good progress this afternoon though. And I've recorded my first ever backing vocals," announced the bass player proudly.

"You were fantastic today," complimented Jake from the doorway. "If you can still sing tomorrow, we could get those last two tracks done."

"Perhaps," mused Grey. "Let's see how you are in the morning, though."

After Grey left, Jake went indoors to fetch his laptop, remembering his promise to Maddy about looking up the fan page. He sat in the half-darkness out on deck, reading message after message from the Silver Lake fans. Some were purely wishing them a speedy recovery; others were sharing stories of their own losses. When Lori came back out to him, she found him sitting with tears in his eyes.

"This is incredible," he said, his voice filled with raw emotion. "There's hundreds of messages on here. For me. For Rich. For Gary's family."

"Your fans care about you all," she said, reading some of the messages over his shoulder. "Oh, I forgot to say Scott called. He's going to come over to do a video with you or something like that."

"Did he say when?"

"No. I said you'd call him back to sort it out."

"I'd better call him, then I'm going to bed," said Jake, shutting down the computer. "Today's been tough."

"You ok?" asked Lori, leaning forward over his shoulders to hug him gently. "Maddy was worried about you when I spoke to her earlier."

"I'm sore. Tired. Emotional," he revealed, kissing her fingertips. "I've felt Gary's shadow hanging over me all day. It's just been a surreal, long day and those fan messages have really blown me away."

"Maddy said you've agreed to talk to the media."

"Yup," he said quietly. "All part of the job. I'm dreading it, but it needs to be done."

"If you want me to be there with you…." she began.

"That would be good," said Jake, interrupting her swiftly. "I'd better call Scott before I change my mind about the whole damn thing."

Once the Silver Lake machine got rolling again, the pace picked up. With Maddy back at the helm, the boys had little choice but to stick to the timetable they had agreed on. Under the watchful eye of Jake, Grey stepped up and completed the remaining backing vocals in less than a day. This bought them back precious time for the four remaining lead vocal tracks and the remaining guitar tracking. After two long days in the studio, Dr Marrs insisted Jake took the weekend off, claiming he needed the time to work on the production. Much to the producer's surprise, there were no objections from the injured musician.

Late on Friday afternoon, just as they were packing up at JJL, Maddy dropped in with the twins.

"Jake," she called out from the control room. "Can you come through to the lounge, please? I need a word."

"On my way, boss," he called back.

In the lounge, he found Maddy sitting on the settee with both babies on her knee. Sitting down beside her, Jake offered to hold one of them for her. She passed him Hayden, who was contentedly playing with her car keys.

"What's up, boss?" he asked calmly.

"I've set up your press interview," Maddy replied.

"Where and when?" asked Jake, feeling a wave of nausea wash over him.

"Sunday afternoon. Here," she said softly. "I've hand-picked the journalists. Two of them are flying in tomorrow from London. There will be five of them in total, plus a sound recordist. It's still strictly limited to a one hour slot. Scott will do any photography that's required."

"I thought we said four?"

"We did, but I've called in a favour or two and got a slot on a UK rock station. The DJ is the fifth person. She's a personal friend."

"What time do I need to be out here?" asked Jake, hugging Hayden a little tighter, seeking some reassurance.

"Be here for one thirty. We'll start at two."

"Is it too late to change my mind?" asked Jake with a worried smile.

"Way too late, Mr Power."

"Guess we'll be here then," agreed Jake. "Lori's coming with me. Moral support."

"Someone else is coming for moral support too," added Maddy. "I spoke to Lucy earlier. She's driving down tomorrow morning for the weekend."

First thing on Saturday morning, before the heat began to rise,

Jake set off for a walk along the beach. Beside him, as he walked, the waves were crashing onto the shore, leaving a foaming trail in their wake. He had come out in his bare feet and walked along, allowing the cool water to wash over them. The rhythm of the surf helped to calm his nerves. It had been arranged that Scott would come out to the house mid-morning to film the video message for the fan page. As he walked, Jake went over and over in his mind what he planned to say. About a mile from the house, he stopped for a rest, sitting down on the soft sand, watching the rise and fall of the ocean swell. A part of him longed to be able to run out and dive into the waves for a swim. Common sense told him there was no way his shoulder would stand up to that. Taking a calculated risk, he had left the sling off, deciding to test how his shoulder felt after an hour or so without support.

Already it was growing hot under the July sun. He carefully removed his vest T-shirt before getting to his feet and heading for home. He was almost at the house when he spotted two young boys playing in the shallows, splashing each other and yelling loudly. Sitting on the sand, keeping a watchful eye on them was a young woman. It was Lucy. Although they had spoken on the phone several times over the last two weeks, he hadn't seen her since the day of the accident. Jake was almost beside her before she turned round.

"Jake!" she squealed leaping to her feet. "Oh, Jake!"

"Gentle, Lucy. Don't hug me too hard," he cautioned as she rushed towards him.

"You look great," she said, taking his hand instead of hugging him. "I'd expected you to look battered and bruised."

"Still a bit battered on the inside," he confessed, putting his good arm around her shoulders.

"And the scar's not too noticeable."

Touching his cheek and running his finger along the fresh red line, Jake had to agree that it could've been a lot worse.

Before they could continue their conversation, the two boys came running up the beach. They had obviously been well warned not to leap all over their favourite uncle, but instead danced round him, begging him to come into the ocean with them.

"Not just now, guys," said Jake, smiling at their infectious enthusiasm. "Maybe later, if my shoulder feels ok."

When they got back up onto the sun deck, they found Scott there, setting up his video equipment. The boys charged on ahead into the house, drying sand flying off their bare feet as they ran.

"Morning," called out Jake.

"Jake!" exclaimed Scott, nearly dropping the camera he was holding. "How you doing?"

"Good," replied Jake, realising he genuinely meant it. "I'm getting there. You?"

"I'm ok," shrugged the younger man. "It's weird being at the apartment. It'll be worse next week when Alice comes back for his things."

"That'll be hard," agreed Jake. "You know you can stay on there as long as you like?"

With a sigh of obvious relief, Scott smiled. "Thanks. I hadn't wanted to assume. I owe you one."

While the filmmaker finished setting up, they chatted through the plan for the video. As the press had been guaranteed an exclusive interview, they agreed there was little Jake could say. When Lucy came back out onto the deck with a juice for Jake, she suggested he keep it really short and just simply thank the fans for being there for them. As an afterthought, she suggested he could record extra mini-messages to go out for each of the festival shows, welcoming fans along.

"You'll wear me out," he teased as he drained the juice glass. "Let me go and put a clean shirt on then we can get started."

"Nothing too fancy, Jake," cautioned Scott. "Remember, we're going for the recovering at home look first."

"I hear you."

Half an hour later, they were all gathered out on the sun deck, all except the boys who had been taken into town by their father. At Lucy's suggestion, Rob had taken their sons into Rehoboth promising to buy them pizza and ice cream. Jake had changed into a clean T-shirt and shorts, taking Scott's hint about not being too dressed up to heart. His shoulder was protesting after being unsupported for a couple of hours so he had slipped his makeshift scarf sling back on. Feeling self-conscious, he sat down on the bench at the edge of the deck and let Scott fuss about as he set up the shoot. Both Lucy and Lori were sitting at the table with a coffee, casually watching.

"Relax, Jake," said Scott, noticing how tense the musician looked. "Would you rather I did some stills shots first?"

"No," replied Jake sharply. "Let's just get this done. I fucking hate video shoots and cameras. You should know that by now!"

"It's ok," laughed Scott. "I won't take it personally. Right, I'm ready whenever you are."

Recording the thank you message went easier than either of them could have hoped for. Two takes and they were done. Filming the four short videos to announce the live shows took longer. At the girls' suggestion, Jake changed shirt for each one to help make it look as though the recordings had been done at different times, then, jumping on that idea, Scott moved location for the shoot every time to a different part of the house. Finally, the last segment was filmed with Jake leaning against his truck out in the driveway.

Over lunch the four of them watched the playback, Jake cringing when he saw himself on screen.

"That's fabulous!" enthused Lucy, hugging her brother gently. "Thank you for doing all of this."

"I'd love to say it has been a pleasure," he grumbled. "When are you adding the thank you to your page, wall or whatever you call it?"

"As soon as Scott emails the video file," said Lucy. "The sooner the better. The page gets the most traffic over the weekend."

"Already sent it to you," commented Scott from the far end of the table. "And, Jake, the stills shoot's complete too."

"When?" asked Jake, looking bemused and not recalling being asked to pose for photos.

"Over lunch," revealed Scott, showing him the compact camera that had been hidden by his side. "On silent. No flash. You never suspected a thing."

"Sneaky bastard," declared Jake with a grin, relieved that he was done for the day.

"Can we see them?" begged Lucy.

"Let me get them onto my PC," replied Scott. "Give me half an hour."

While the girls cleared away the lunch dishes, Jake sat in the sunroom with Scott reviewing the photos. There weren't many, but with some clever editing, the photographer pulled an album together to pass over to Lucy. With his work done, Scott packed up his equipment and announced that he was heading home. He declined Jake's invitation to stay, saying he had "official" work to finish off, but promised to be out at JJL early the next day for the press interview.

Despite their best efforts to get out to JJL early, Jake and Lori arrived a few minutes later than planned for the interview. Their departure had been delayed, partly because Lucy and Rob decided to head home with the boys instead of Lucy coming out to the studio and partly due to the heavy traffic that was backing up the highway. As Lori parked the Mercedes in the shade beside the studio, she noted there were several cars already out front, mainly rental cars. Once the engine had stopped, Jake called Maddy to say they had arrived. She told him to stay put and that she would come round to brief him before he went in to meet the media personnel. A few seconds later, she came striding round the side of the building, her trademark heels clicking on the path.

"I was getting worried that you'd changed your mind!" she called out cheerfully. "You ok?"

"I'll be better once this is over," confessed Jake, getting awkwardly out of the car.

"He barely slept all night," added Lori, coming round to join them. "He's a nervous wreck."

"Yeah, I am," conceded Jake. "I'm just worried that I'll make an idiot of myself and get too emotional in there. It's still all so raw."

"I understand," sympathised Maddy warmly. "Remember, you are calling the shots on this one. If you need a break, we'll take one. If you don't want to answer a particular question, you don't have to. For what it's worth, they are all terrified of upsetting you."

With a jaded smile, Jake said, "Let's get this over and done with then I'm going home for a stiff drink."

All five of the journalists were chatting amiably over coffees in the lounge when Jake walked in, holding on tightly to Lori's hand. One couch had been deliberately left empty, but instead of sitting there, Jake pulled over a hard chair from the table and sat down. Both Lori and Maddy took a seat on the vacant settee.

"Jake," began Maddy. "Let me introduce you to Ben, Kurt, Kayla, Sam and, from London, Debbie and her assistant, Joe."

"Pleasure," said Jake quietly, an unexpected hint of shyness to his tone. "What's the plan here?"

"Well," started Debbie, her London accent sounding out of place in the room. "If I can ask you a few questions first off to cover enough for the radio slot that would be good."

"We're all agreed to share your responses to an extent. Saves you repeating yourself," explained Ben, his voice a surprisingly deep Texan drawl. "We're just honoured that you feel up to chatting with us this afternoon."

"The aim's to keep this as relaxed as possible," added Kayla softly. "And not to distress you or make you feel uncomfortable."

Glancing round at their anxious faces, Jake paused for a moment, swallowed hard then nodded, "Sounds like a plan."

"Are you happy for Joe to record the whole interview?" asked Debbie with a nod to the sound man.

"As long as we get to hear the tape before you air it," stated Maddy bluntly. "Management want final veto an all output from today."

"Let me grab a juice, then we can make a start," said Jake, forcing a nervous smile. "Lori, do you want something?"

"Just a water, thanks," she replied, smiling at him.

Once Jake had returned to his seat with a bottle of flavoured water, Debbie asked the opening question.

"First of all," she began with a warm, friendly smile. "Thank you for agreeing to this. We appreciate it's been a horrendous last couple of weeks for you and the band. I guess, the first question has to be, how are you? You're looking great."

"Thanks," replied Jake, nervously playing with the label on the water bottle. "I'm still a bit tender and bruised. All things considered, I got off lightly. Bruised ribs, mild concussion, a cut below my eye and a dislocated shoulder."

"And how is the shoulder? I see you've still got it supported."

"It's getting there. I've dislocated it a few times over the years and each time it takes a little longer to heal. It's amazing how many things you do with your left hand though. It's driving me insane."

"Any idea how long you'll be wearing the support?"

"Maybe another week or so. I've been exercising gently. Trying to build it back up. And, yes, before you ask, I have been playing my guitar a bit," he replied with a smile.

"And how's Rich? He wasn't able to be here today we understand," continued Debbie.

"He's on the mend. Rich broke his nose quite badly and had to have surgery to reconstruct it. I believe he has to have another procedure next week sometime. The gash above his eye has healed up and his bruises are fading too."

"I don't want to bring back the horrors of the 6th of July but are you able to tell us what happened?"

Looking to Lori and Maddy for some moral support, Jake took a deep breath before attempting to answer the question he had been dreading. "We were on our way home after the record company birthday celebrations in Philly. Kayla, you were there, weren't you?"

"Yes," replied the journalist softly. "I was talking to Gary when you came over to say it was time to go."

Blushing slightly as he recalled how blunt he'd been, Jake continued, "It had been a long, hot afternoon. We were all keen to get back down here. The plan was to meet up back at our house for a BBQ and a few beers. Grey and Paul were following behind us a couple of cars back. I'd just called them to check if they were still coming over to the house to eat. I had just put my cell back in my pocket when we came up to the intersection. I was in the back. Gary was sound asleep up front. That guy could sleep anywhere, anytime. Rich was driving." He paused for a moment, then continued, "Anyway, I looked over and saw the truck charging straight at us. It was swaying as it ran the stop light. I yelled at Rich to watch out. He tried to steer out of the way, but we didn't stand a chance. The tanker hit the front quarter of the car and the rest's a bit of a blur. I remember being thrown about. I remember the noise. I remember climbing out of the car. The door was twisted and I had to kick it open. There was debris everywhere. I was yelling on Gary when Grey reached me. He tried to keep me calm. Tried to get me off the highway. He got me over to the grass verge. As I sat down, I passed out. I remember the paramedics working on my shoulder to pop it back in as I lay on the grass. I vaguely remember being in the back of the ambulance, but that's pretty much it. I came to in the emergency room."

He could feel the emotion thickening in his throat. With trembling hands, Jake opened the water bottle and drank deeply from it.

"Did you realise how serious things were?" asked Debbie, wiping a tear from her cheek.

"They told us at the hospital that they hadn't been able to save Gary," answered Jake, his voice quiet and wavering slightly. "I think we all knew in our hearts though when we saw where the truck had landed. I just hope to God he didn't suffer. It all happened in just a few seconds. It's like slow motion at the time. It's like you are watching it happen to someone else. We were all helpless to do anything. The truck driver had apparently had a seizure at the wheel. He died shortly afterwards too." Jake paused to compose himself. "It's all too easy to torture yourself with "what ifs". If we'd stayed longer at the party or if we'd left earlier. If we'd stopped at our usual haunt for coffee. You can't afford to think that way. At least, I can't afford to think like that. It was a tragic accident. Two good men lost their lives, but it could have been so much worse."

"That's very gracious of you, sir," commented Ben in his slow Texan drawl. "Have you been back out to the site?"

"Yes," replied Jake, watching as Lori passed a tissue to the openly weeping Debbie. "It's on our road home. There's no way to avoid it. The first time we went back out was about a week ago. Gary's family are here from England and his young brother needed to see it. Lori drove us out there. That was tough. Really tough."

"I'll bet it was," sympathised the Texan.

Kayla took up the lead and commented, "I was at the memorial service last week. That was a beautiful reading and you did incredibly well to play too. How hard was that?"

"Incredibly hard," Jake admitted sadly. "Alice, Gary's sister, asked if I would play. There was no way I could turn her down. Deciding what to play was tough. It was only when I sat up at the front of the chapel that I finally decided on "Yesterday"."

"Perfect choice," Kayla concurred.

"There were a couple of songs on the short list that would've been appropriate too."

Composing herself once more, Debbie apologised for her emotional display.

"No need to apologise," reassured Jake warmly. "There's been a shit load of tears shed over the last couple of weeks. I've shed my fair share."

"No, I'm sorry," she said, wiping her eyes again. "I knew Gary really well back in London. He's left a huge hole behind in a lot of hearts."

"He had friends all over the world," Jake observed. "Everywhere he went, he met someone he knew."

"So what's next?" asked Debbie, changing tack. "I believe the record is almost finished and that there are plans for some live shows?"

"The record's almost done," began Jake, glancing at Maddy for reassurance on how much he could disclose. "We've got a week or so left here at JJL. There's a bit of guitar tracking to be done and some vocal tracks. We're taking it one step at a time. I can't put in a full day. The strength and stamina just aren't there. Also Rich can't sing right now so that gave us a problem. There's a few challenges there to be overcome but we'll do it."

"And the live shows?" prompted Kayla.

"Unfortunately, we had to cancel the first one up in Bethlehem. Gary had lined up four or five shows for us and we owe it to him to try and be ready for them. Sadly, there was no way we could be fit enough to play at Bethlehem. I feel bad about that. The first one we hope to make is scheduled for August 10th. We should be ok for then. We can work the set around any lingering health issues. We owe it to our fans to get back out there too."

"You released a thank you message to your fans last night on social media," commented Kurt, the youngest looking of the journalists. "There were over five thousand views showing against it by this morning. Does that surprise you?"

"The support and the messages from our fans have been incredible. We all really appreciate it. My sister is one of the admins for the fan site and she talked me into the video thing. I kind of felt I owed the fans something. Time to give a bit back," replied Jake, finishing off his juice.

"Will there be more personal messages of that style?" Kurt asked. "So many stars connect with their fan base via Twitter and Facebook these days."

"Maybe. I don't know," said Jake, feeling a little awkward. "I don't use social media on a personal level. I'm quite a private person and don't feel the need to share my entire life with the world. Lucy will no doubt try to convince me to share some stuff though. She can be very persuasive."

"Returning to the new album," said Dan, launching into his round of questioning. "What can the fans expect? Out of the Shadows has gone down really well since its release."

"To be entirely honest, I've not paid much attention to the single sales," confessed Jake. "It was released two days after the crash and was the furthest thing from my mind. It's not typical of the rest of the album. We've tried to develop our sound. Dr Marrs has been pushing us to try new things. Different arrangements. I hope the fans like it. We love it. There should be something on there for everyone."

"And will there be a UK tour this winter?" enquired Debbie. "We've heard the album is due out in early October and the rumour is that a UK tour will follow."

"We hope to play a few shows before Christmas," he replied, then gestured over to Maddy. "You'd be better asking the boss that one."

"We're working with a promoter to set something up," revealed Maddy. "Perhaps a few shows across Europe too. Watch this space."

"It's been a real rollercoaster of a year for Silver Lake," said Ben slowly. "You've been kind enough to tell us about the recent lows. What have been the highs?"

"Playing the UK shows last winter," replied Jake with little hesitation. "Particularly the London show on my birthday. That was so incredibly awesome."

"How do you keep it all in perspective?" asked Debbie. "This time last year you were teaching in a local high school as well as playing with the band. Then, by Christmas, you were playing to crowds of fifteen thousand plus. What keeps you grounded?"

"Good question," acknowledged Jake, stalling for time. "Lori keeps my feet on the ground. Friends too. Keeping it all in perspective can be a challenge. Kids are good at that."

Lori smiled at her fiancé as he continued, "I'll give you an example. The day I got home from the hospital, I couldn't settle. I needed to have people round me. It was a really scary, fragile feeling. Anyway, long story cut short, Paul and Maddy came over with their twins and Grey came over with his little girl, Becky. She's about six. She wanted me to take her down onto the beach like I usually would and wouldn't take no for an answer. Eventually I agreed to walk down on the sand with her for a few minutes. She ran on ahead, splashing in the waves like nothing had happened. She begged me to come into the water with her. I tried to explain to her that I was too sore. I even used the excuse that my jeans would get wet. She quite matter-of-factly rolled my jeans up and took me by the hand and led me down to the water's edge. As we walked, she said simply that she was sorry I'd been hurt, sorry that Rich had been hurt and sorry that Gary had been killed. Then, after a moment or two, she said maybe Gary was with her mommy in heaven and that her mommy would be buying him a drink at the bar. That made me laugh. It brought it home to me though that we all lose folk we care about, but that we can see a way forward too through the grief and the pain."

"I think that's a good place to end this," commented Ben with a smile. "Thank you for being so open and honest with us, Jake. Makes our lives so much easier."

"Pleasure," replied Jake, relieved that the interview was over. "Thanks for going easy on me."

As the journalists packed up, Kayla asked, "What about photos? Is your photographer here?"

"Not yet," answered Maddy, checking the time. She had expected Scott to be there, but there was no sign of him and no word from him. "We'll get them done and mail them on to you all."

None of the journalists seemed overly upset by this suggestion and, with a final round of thank you's, all bar Debbie and her sound man, left the studio.

"Are you free for a coffee or dinner tonight, Maddy?" asked the DJ hopefully. "I'd love to meet your twins."

"Come over to the farmhouse," suggested Maddy. "I need to get back quite sharp."

"If you're sure we're not imposing."

"Not at all," assured Maddy, gathering up her bag and cell phone. "Lori, do you guys want to join us?"

"Not tonight," replied Lori as she allowed Jake to help her up from the low couch. "We've plans for tonight."

"Ok. I'll call you tomorrow."

"I'll be back out here first thing," added Jake. "If you find Scott, send him out here late morning. He can do his photo shoot when we break for lunch. If we break for lunch."

A gentle breeze blowing in from the ocean caused the citronella candles to flicker, casting dancing shadows across the deck. Despite the lateness of the hour and the weariness that was blanketing him, Jake remained stretched out on the lounger. After dinner, Lori had left him alone while she went to do a couple of hours' work, promising to be back to share a nightcap with him. The bottle of Jack Daniels and two glasses sat untouched on the table. Staring up at the starlit sky, Jake reflected on the day. In spite of all of his anxiety, the interview had gone smoothly. It had been shorter than he'd expected, but he wasn't complaining about that. Talking about the events of the last two weeks had been tough. On the drive home, he had sent a short text message to Maddy saying he wasn't prepared to answer any more media questions about the accident. Chapter closed.

With the decision made, he felt a weight lift from his shoulders. Reclining on the lounger in the dark, Jake felt calmer and back in control of his emotions for the first time in days. His focus was back.

"You did a great job out there, Mr Power," whispered a quiet voice in his head. "Time to let go."

It wasn't the first time he'd imagined Gary talking to him.

Stiffly, he got up from the lounger and poured himself a generous shot of bourbon. With a silent toast to absent friends, he downed the fiery liquid in one gulp. As he poured a second shot, he heard Lori coming through the house.

"Sorry," she apologised as she stepped out onto the candlelit deck. "I lost track of time."

"There you go, li'l lady," said Jake, handing her a glass.

"What are we drinking to?" she asked softly.

"The past, the present and the future," He declared with a smile. "Time to let go. Time to move on."

"To the future," toasted Lori.

Together they sat on the lounger, listening to the steady beat of the surf. Gently, Jake put his arm around her shoulder and began to kiss behind her ear. His feathery kisses continued down her neck, then he ran his tongue along teasingly along her collar bone. Cupping her breast in his hand, Jake kissed her on the lips, his tongue slowly continuing to tease her.

"Time for bed?" suggested Lori between kisses.

"I want to make love to you out here," he murmured hoarsely, as he began a clumsy attempt to remove her top with one hand.

"Allow me to assist you, rock star."

Standing in front of him, Lori slowly removed her top, then slipped her cropped jeans down to her ankles, stepping daintily out of them. Wearing only her black lacy bra and panties, she motioned to her fiancé to stand up. Ever so carefully, Lori undid the knot in the scarf sling, then removed Jake's shirt. She swiftly undid his jeans, sliding them down his snakelike hips with ease.

"Think you can finish the job?" she teased as she removed the clip from her hair and shook it loose.

"I'll give it my best shot," he replied, expertly unfastening her bra with one hand. Ignoring the pain in his shoulder, he hooked his thumbs in the waistband of her panties and slid them down her slender, tanned thighs.

The thin cotton of his boxers failed to disguise his erection. Stepping towards him, Lori bit his nipples sharply, then ran her tongue down the centre of his well-muscled stomach, pausing at the waistband of his underwear. Pulling his shorts down, she continued to explore his body with her tongue until she reached his blonde pubic hair.

"Come here, li'l lady," he instructed, taking her by the hand and directing her back towards the lounger.

As soon as she lay down on the lounger, Jake was astride her and kissing her hard. The cool night air was electric with their desire for each other. In one careful movement, he was inside her. Their lovemaking was brief but all-consuming. Lori's orgasm swept through her the instant Jake penetrated her. Feeling her so wet and ready for him, he had immediately surrendered to his own climax. Lying side by side on the narrow lounger proved impossible and it was Lori who stood up first. She reached for Jake's discarded shirt, slipping it on over her cool naked skin.

"I wish that could've lasted longer," sighed Jake, rubbing his aching shoulder.

Kissing him on the cheek, Lori purred, "Come through to bed, rock star."

Out at JJL the air was blue by lunchtime next day. Straight after breakfast, Grey had picked Jake up and driven him out to the studio. Paul had collected Rich and the four of them arrived at the same time. A few minutes later, Dr Marrs came in with the obligatory tray of coffees and the five of them sat and worked out the schedule for the day. They decided to focus on the guitar tracking until lunchtime, then take a break before Jake did some vocals in the afternoon. Work commenced on the final guitar tracking for track three and, from the first note, it was as if someone was playing tricks on them – amps switched off; mics turned off; guitars slid out of tune. After an hour of mayhem, Rich's temper flared and he slammed his guitar down on the floor, yelling "For fuck's sake!"

"Easy, Rich," soothed Jake calmly. "Do you want to take a break?"

"No, I fucking don't!" snarled the guitarist. "I just need this shitty gear to fucking work!"

From the control room, Dr Marrs calmly called through, "Let's try that again, please, Mr Santiago."

Taking a seat on the couch in the live room, Jake watched as Rich took another five attempts to complete his share of the tracking to Dr Marrs satisfaction.

"Well done, buddy," complimented Jake when he was finished. "You ok?"

"No," snapped Rich, putting his head in his hands. "My head's pounding. My ribs are killing me. I can't breathe right through my nose. I feel like shit."

"Why not call it a day for today?"

"Maybe," sighed the guitarist. "I'll hang around for a bit. Watch you squirm when Scott gets here with his camera."

"Thanks," laughed Jake. "Jim, are you ready for me?"

"Ready when you are, Mr Power," called back the producer.

Taking his arm out of the sling, Jake picked up his guitar and settled himself on a stool to play his part for track three. No gremlins this time and he was done in two takes.

"How the fuck did you do that?" grumbled Rich as they

headed out to the lounge.

Jake shrugged, "Luck?"

"Harrumph," muttered Rich.

After a relaxed lunch in the lounge with the band, Scott took Jake outside to do the photo shoot to accompany the interview of the previous day. Once again, Jake found himself sitting in the old rocking chair on the lawn in the sun. Scott made the shoot easy for him by simply asking him to sit back and relax. After what felt like only a few minutes, the photographer declared he was done.

"Already?" asked Jake, sounding pleasantly surprised. "Thanks. That was painless."

"Pleasure as always, Jake," said Scott, sitting down on the grass in more or less the same spot as Maddy had sat a few days before. "Need a favour from you?"

"You do?"

"Lucy wants some shots for the fans. Just a few of the band off duty. If you all agree, I could use some of the ones I shot over lunch, but she was kind of hoping for some studio shots too."

"Time I had words with my little sister," muttered Jake, trying not to smile. "She knows I won't say no to her. Right, you've got ten minutes after I run through my warm up. No more."

"Thanks, Jake."

As the week moved on, the Silver Lake machine gathered pace once more. In the studio, the four musicians pulled together, supporting each other and, with their usual stoic professionalism, had the recording finished by July 26th – back on track. It was Rich who finished first, staying on into the small hours of the Friday morning. He was scheduled for minor surgery on the Friday afternoon and knew he had to stay till his work on the record was done. Next night, it was Jake who was still recording in the wee small hours. When he had arrived at JJL late on Friday morning, Dr Marrs had asked if he would re-record two of the earlier vocals. Having listened to it all again, the producer felt the vocal track needed a few changes and, after a brief heated debate, Jake surrendered, bowing to the producer's greater knowledge.

Back at the beach, Lori's focus was the artwork for the album. Her sketchbook was filled with different incarnations of the Silver Lake imp. The band still hadn't decided on a title for the album and that was hindering her progress. From the tracks she had heard, it felt as though it was going to be a very dark album with an emphasis on overcoming life's challenges. So far she had three rough sketches for the full cover. The first was of the imp cowering in a corner with a crowd of leering faces peering in the window of his hovel. Another was of him at the beach with a huge wave about to engulf him. The third, and her personal favourite, was of him crouched over a still pool, gazing at his own reflection, only the reflection staring back was a strikingly handsome man, a face that would match the "shadow" she had created for the single cover. While she waited with bated breath for the band to come up with a title, she worked on some ideas for the accompanying merchandising.

It felt good to be back in a routine. A sense of the mundane was helping them both to move on.

To celebrate the completion of the recording, Maddy arranged a Silver Lake dinner for Saturday night at their favourite sushi restaurant. The email invite had instructed everyone to be there for seven sharp or fines would be levied.

"Jake!" called Lori from the kitchen. "We're going to be late."

"Just coming, li'l lady," said Jake as he walked into the room. "And yes, I know we'll be late. Have you called a cab?"

"Yes," she replied with a smile. "It'll be here any minute."

"You look stunning," he complimented before gently kissing her on the forehead. "Beautiful."

"You don't look so bad yourself," replied Lori, admiring his skin tight jeans and black shirt.

"Thanks," he said, his cheeks flushing red. Lifting his makeshift sling from the table and handing it to her, he asked, "Can you stick this in your purse in case I need it later? I'll leave it off for now."

"Sure," she replied as they both heard a car draw up outside. "Time to celebrate, rock star."

When the cab pulled up outside the restaurant, Grey was standing at the door looking out for them.

"You'd better have a good excuse, Mr Power," he joked as Jake paid the fare.

"No excuses. Just late," confessed Jake with a laugh as they entered the crowded restaurant.

The Silver Lake party were all seated at a long table running the length of the restaurant. In their midst were Alice and Tom. All of them gave Jake a round of applause as he approached the table, hand in hand with Lori.

"Finally!" declared Maddy, trying to fake exasperation. "Grey, what's the fine up to?"

"Let's call it a round two hundred bucks."

"What!" exclaimed Jake in mock horror. "How about we call it a round of drinks for the table instead?"

"Sounds good to me," agreed the bass player, retaking his seat beside Kola.

When the waitress came over a few moments later, Jake ordered three bottles of champagne for them.

"A toast," he announced once they all had a glass. "To everyone who has helped to get this album finished."

"To absent friends," added Grey softly.

Dinner was a relaxed affair as they all laughed and reminisced together. Seated across from Alice and Tom, Lori asked how they had enjoyed their time in New York.

"It was incredible," marvelled Alice enthusiastically. "And your apartment is out of this world! We felt like film stars for the week."

"Thanks," said Lori, blushing slightly. "I'm glad you enjoyed your visit. It is an amazing city."

"I loved Central Park," sighed Alice wistfully. "Spending time there helped me to get my head straight."

"And I hear Jason took you to Vegas too?"

"Yes. Oh, what a fantastic place!"

"I don't want to go home," stated Tom sadly. "I wish I could stay here forever."

"When do you leave?" asked Jake, joining the conversation.

"Tomorrow night," replied Alice. "I need to get Gary's ashes home to my parents. We've been gone too long as it is."

"Time he went home too," agreed Jake, remembering how homesick his late friend had been.

"The band would like to invite you back in September," began Jason, realising the route the conversation was taking. "We'd like you to be our guests at the headline show on September 6th."

"I'm not sure," Alice started to say, more than a little over-awed by the offer.

"We'd love to," interrupted Tom with a huge grin. "Alice, it's what Gary would have wanted."

"I guess."

"Leave it with me," suggested Jason warmly. "I'll sort out the arrangements for you both."

"Where are Silver Lake playing?" asked Tom curiously.

"Good question," commented Jake, glancing at Jason. "We'd like to know too."

"House of Blues in Atlantic City," announced Maddy with a huge grin. "All signed and sealed as of four o'clock this afternoon. Full two hour set."

"That calls for more champagne!" declared Grey with a smile. "House of Blues? Can we fill it?"

"Only one way to find out," said Jason calmly. "Lots of promo work. Promise of new material. Strategic advertising. Tickets go on sale on Friday."

"Speaking of new material," began Lori tentatively. "Have you come up with a title for the album yet?"

"Ah, the million dollar question!" laughed Dr Marrs from the far end of the table. "How many hours have we spent debating that one?"

"Too fucking many," muttered Rich under his breath.

"Ah, raw nerve. Sorry, boys," apologised Lori, genuinely regretting her question. "However, if you don't give me a steer, you'll be selling it in a cover that looks like a brown paper grocery sack."

Although said in jest, the comment gave her inspiration for a fourth option for the cover. As a fresh debate commenced on the title, she sat doodling on her napkin before she forgot the image that had created itself in her mind. When their meal arrived, she slipped the napkin into her purse. Food for thought for later.

Over the meal, the band continued to throw suggestions into the mix for the album title. Eventually, after over an hour, they had it narrowed down to three possibilities. Borrowing a pen from Lori, Maddy took charge and wrote the three titles onto a napkin, then tore it into three pieces, screwed them up and dropped them into a clean, empty, water glass. While they all watched her, she shook the glass.

"Tom," she said, stretching across the table. "You can do the honours. Are we all agreed that whatever one Tom picks, we stick with?"

All of the band members nodded.

"I can't believe you're letting me do this," said the teenager with a huge grin.

After a teasing moment's deliberation, he made his choice and smoothed out the paper ball.

"Well?" asked Grey, impatient to know the outcome.

"Impossible Depths," announced Tom, holding up the paper napkin fragment for all to see.

"Like it," nodded Jake. "Fits."

"Got my vote from the start," Rich agreed with a smile towards Tom.

"Does that help our beautiful artist, though?" enquired Jason theatrically.

"Perhaps," replied Lori with a knowing smile. "You'll find out soon enough."

"Can I keep this?" asked Tom, still holding the piece of napkin.

"Of course, honey," answered Maddy softly.

"Is there space for you all to autograph it?" he asked hopefully.

"We can try," said Jake, taking the piece of soft tissue from him. "Write small, guys."

With the napkin autographed by all of Silver Lake, Tom passed it to his sister to store carefully in her bag. The three teenagers were growing restless at their end of the table as the meal ended. Sensing their desire to escape, Lori suggested, "Why don't we let the kids go down to the boardwalk for an hour or so and we could all go for a couple of drinks?"

"Sounds good to me," agreed Grey, signalling to the waitress to bring the check.

"If you don't mind," said Rich. "I'm going to call it a night. The pain meds are wearing off and my face hurts like hell."

"You ok?" asked Jake looking concerned.

"Yeah, I'm fine. Honestly," replied the guitarist as he stood up.

"The surgeon re-broke the bridge of my nose and my cheekbone, then re-set it again. Wasn't the original plan for yesterday, but was the best option apparently. I'd beg to differ right now."

"Come on, then," said Linsey. "Let's get you home for some more drugs, Ricardo."

When the waitress came over with the check, Jason accepted it, declaring that dinner was on him. Jake started to protest that he should pay part as he'd ordered the champagne, but the Englishman shook his head, insisting he had it covered. Once outside the restaurant, the three teenagers headed off towards the boardwalk, promising to be outside the Turtle by ten thirty. As the rest of them set off down the main avenue at a more leisurely pace, Jake discretely asked Lori to pass him the scarf from her bag. On the pretence of glancing in one of the T-shirt shop windows, Jake stopped to fix the sling back into place. Grey stopped alongside him while the others walked on ahead.

Alice fell into stride beside Lori and thanked her again for allowing them to stay at the apartment. For the first time, the English woman noticed Lori's cane and asked if she was alright.

"Legacy of an accident," explained Lori with a wistful smile.

"I never realised," apologised Alice awkwardly. "What happened?"

"I was hit by a motorcycle about eighteen months ago," replied Lori plainly, feeling she needed to tell Alice but part of her still unable to open up about it all. "I fractured my leg pretty badly. There's a lot of expensive metalwork holding it together."

"Oh, you poor thing," sympathised Alice warmly. "That must have been awful for you."

"It's had its moments," confessed Lori softly. "This is the best it's been."

"Best what's been?" asked Jake, catching up and putting his good arm around Lori's shoulder.

"My leg," explained Lori. "Alice was asking how I was."

"Ah, I see," he said softly, knowing how hard she found it to talk about it. "Well, if you hadn't messed up your leg, we might never have met."

"Pardon?" asked Alice, smiling. "I sense a story there."

As they walked the last few hundred yards along the boardwalk, Jake told Alice about finding Lori stranded on the beach and about helping her home.

"That's a beautiful story," she sighed as Jake finished. "So romantic!"

The bar was crowded when the Silver Lake party entered. Scanning the room for an empty table, Jake realised they were out of luck. A baseball game was showing on the TV screens and, as a result, there wasn't an empty seat in the place. They found a quiet-ish corner at the end of the bar while Jake ordered the first round of drinks. With his back to the crowded bar room, he was soon deep in conversation with Dr Marrs and Paul about the mixing for the album. Lori and Maddy were chatting animatedly with Alice about the pros and cons of life in Manhattan. All of them were relaxed; comfortable in each other's company; each still grieving, but finally beginning to move on. Shortly after ten, Maddy and Paul said their farewells, apologising that they needed to get back to the farmhouse and the twins. Gone was the brisk business Maddison, replaced with the mommy anxious about leaving the babies with Paul's sister for the first time.

"Maddy!" called Lori as her friend turned to leave. "Wait! I'll walk out with you."

Her friend took one look at her and just nodded, noting the pain in Lori's eyes. Once down the stairs and outside the bar, away from the others, Maddy put a protective arm round Lori and asked, "You ok, honey?"

"Just sore," sighed Lori, sounding exasperated. "I simply can't stand for any length of time anymore. I'll take a seat out here and watch for the kids coming back. I'll be fine."

"You sure, Lori?" asked Paul, sharing Maddy's concern.

"Positive," she replied, forcing a smile. "You two head home to the meatballs. Jake'll follow me out in a minute, I'm sure."

"Ok," relented Maddy, torn between waiting with Lori and going home to her babies. "I'll call you tomorrow."

"Night, guys," said Lori as she spotted an empty bench a few yards away.

"Night!"

Leaning heavily on her cane, Lori limped over to the empty white, wooden bench, cursing her damaged leg under her breath. With a sigh of relief, she sat down, almost immediately feeling the pain lessen. The boardwalk was busy with groups of teenagers and young couples enjoying the hot summer night. A few yards further down, she could see Tom with Todd and Kate and the other members of Hunt 'Em Down. They all looked to be laughing and sharing a joke. It made her smile to see Tom relaxed and happy- a dramatic change from the grief stricken, surly teenager she had first met. He turned and, spotting her sitting on the bench, waved over. A few moments later, it was Todd who came over to sit with her.

"You ok, Mz Hyde?" he asked, flopping down onto the bench beside her.

"How many times do I need to say it, Todd?" she laughed, trying to hide her discomfort from him.

"Always one more," he joked. "Seriously though, are you ok? You look a bit pale."

"I'm fine. Just sore from standing," Lori confessed, rubbing her thigh. "There's a ball game on so the Turtle's packed. No seats."

"If you're sure," he began awkwardly.

"I'm fine."

"That was a nice thing the band did for Tom over dinner. He's still talking about it."

"Yes, it was," agreed Lori, glancing over at the group of teenagers. "Sometimes Maddy surprises us all."

"She scares the crap out of me," Todd declared. "Those tattoos. The spiky hair and those heels!"

Lori laughed. "She's a kitten really. Believe me."

"I'll take your word for it," said the teenager with a smile. "You sure you're ok though? I don't want to leave you sitting here on your own if you're not."

"Go and have some fun. Alice'll be out looking for Tom in a few minutes. I'm fine here."

"As long as you're sure," said Todd standing up.

"I'm sure. And thanks for caring, Todd."

She watched as he loped off back along the boardwalk to join the others. Gently she stretched out her left leg, feeling the muscles protest at the movement. As she sat watching the world go by, she slowly bent and straightened her leg, easing off the pain with each movement. In her bag, she heard her phone "chirp". It was a text message from Jake asking where she was.

"Sitting outside on a bench, L x" she replied.

A second cricket chirp followed almost instantly.

"On our way out. J x"

It was almost ten thirty and Lori noted that the three teenagers were preparing to leave the group and head back over. With a smile, she watched Tom hug a petite, blonde girl then kiss her, before turning to follow Todd. Beside her, Lori felt someone sit down. It was Jake.

"Hey, li'l lady," he said warmly. "You ok?"

"Fine. How about you, rock star?" she asked, resting her head against his warm body.

"Wasted, if I'm being honest," confessed Jake with a lopsided grin. "I'm blaming the champagne."

At that the others joined them – the teenagers from one side; the adults from the other. There were hugs and a few tears as Alice and Tom bade them all goodbye. Alice held onto Jake a little tighter and a little longer than the others, then turned to hug Lori.

"Thank you," she said, tears gliding down her cheeks. "You've all been amazing."

"We'll see you both soon. In Atlantic City in September," replied Lori warmly. "Jason won't take no for an answer so I'd agree to whatever he suggests."

"Tom wouldn't let me say no," giggled Alice, glancing over at her young brother. "We'll see you soon."

With all their goodbyes said, Jake and Lori walked back along the boardwalk towards the house. Before they reached the end, Jake suggested that they walk the rest of the way home along the sand. After the buzz of the boardwalk, the pitch black beach was eerily silent. Only the gentle beating of the waves on the shore broke the silence. Walking in the soft sand was challenging, but Lori kept quiet, sensing that her fiancé needed the solitude of the ocean.

"Wonder what the beach at Atlantic City's like?" Jake mused, his voice husky from shouting to be heard back at the bar.

"You pleased with the news about that show?" asked Lori.

"Hell yeah," declared Jake without hesitation. "This is huge for us! We get to headline our own show in front of two thousand fans. If we fill the place, of course."

"You'll fill it," said Lori, confident that Maddy wouldn't have set the deal up if they weren't more than capable of selling out the venue. "Will you be ok to do a two hour set?"

"Should be," replied Jake, not sounding very certain. "I'll feel happier once I've seen John Brent on Tuesday."

"What about Rich?"

"He'll be fine. He only needs to stand and play," commented Jake as they turned up the beach towards the house.

The waiting room at the medical centre was packed when Jake arrived for his appointment. Lori had driven him out to Beebe but had dropped him at the entrance, saying she was going to do some shopping. As he had closed the car door, Jake had promised to call when he was ready to be picked up. Now, when he saw how many patients were waiting in line, he began to wonder if Lori had known he was in for a long wait. Unable to get a seat, he stood against the wall, near the door, silently praying that no one would recognise him. Almost an hour after his appointment time, the receptionist called his name and directed him towards the doctor's office.

"Morning, Jake," greeted John Brent as he walked in. "Apologies for the wait."

"No worries, John," said Jake calmly. "Has there been an outbreak of broken bones?"

"Summer break," joked the doctor. "Skateboard season too. Wrists. Elbows. Ankles. Knees. So how have you been?"

"Good," replied Jake, taking a seat beside the desk. "Ribs feel ok most of the time. Shoulder's a lot better. Still gets sore after a while."

"Ok, shirt off and let me get a look at you," instructed the doctor. "Have you been using that shoulder much?"

"A fair bit over the last week or so," confessed Jake as he carefully slid his shirt off. "We had to get the record finished so I've been playing quite a bit."

"Any trouble with it?"

"Some. I was careful. Sat down to play to keep the weight of it. Took regular breaks."

The doctor raised an eyebrow. "Really?"

"Really," laughed Jake. "And I've kept to the pain meds

regime. And I've followed the exercise plan you gave me."

"I'm impressed," complimented the doctor as he began to examine Jake's shoulder.

He spent a few minutes thoroughly testing his range of movement, then checked over his ribcage. As he asked Jake to take a deep breath, he noticed that the musician flinched.

"How much singing have you done?" enquired the doctor, running his hand down Jake's tender rib cage.

"Quite a bit. And, yes, it hurt like hell at times," replied Jake honestly.

"Ok, you can put your shirt back on, Jake," said John Brent before adding, "I meant to say before, that's some array of tattoos you have there."

"A life's work," joked Jake. "So what's the opinion?"

"On your tattoos or your injuries?"

"The injuries."

"You've healed really well, considering. I'm happy with your shoulder. The range of movement is good. Just be careful with it for a few more weeks. You might want to think about a neoprene shoulder support if you are playing for any length of time. Ease back on the pain meds. Only take them if you need them. I'm still a little concerned that your ribs are tender but there may have been a small fracture there that we missed. Singing will have put a strain on the muscles too, so that will hinder the overall healing process."

"I didn't have much choice, John," stated Jake bluntly. "It's my job and we had a deadline."

"I understand and I don't think you've done any long term harm. It's just taking time to settle down," reassured the doctor warmly. "You're good to resume normal activities."

"Can I drive?" asked Jake hopefully.

"Yes."

"What about running? Can I start training again?"

"Might be a bit too soon for anything intense. Gentle jogging to start with and see how it feels. If it hurts, stop."

"I hear you," said Jake.

"When are you next playing live?" asked the doctor.

"August 10th," answered Jake. "We've four open air festival shows coming up, then a headline show in Atlantic City in

September."

"Well, take care, Mr Power. Don't overdo it," cautioned the doctor with a warm smile. "When's the new album due out?"

"Start of October," replied Jake, a hint of pride creeping in. "Then the plan is to tour Britain and Europe in November and December."

"Busy schedule."

"Keeps us out of trouble," joked Jake.

"That remains to be seen," countered John playfully. "Hope it all goes well and, if you need me, just call. Lori has my cell number for emergencies."

"Thanks, John. Appreciate it," said Jake, shaking his hand.

When Lori pulled into the medical centre car park, she spotted Jake sitting on a low wall enjoying the sun. He was chatting on his phone as she stopped the car beside him.

"Sorry," he apologised, climbing into the passenger seat. "It was Grey checking up on the rehearsal schedule for this week."

"Normality resuming?" asked Lori hopefully.

"Sure is," he declared with a mischievous grin. "John gave me the all clear to resume normal activities."

"Glad to hear it."

"Me too," he admitted before glancing round at the pile of bags on the back seat. "Successful morning?"

"Retail therapy," stated Lori. "Before I shut myself away to finish the artwork for your album."

"Have you come up with something?"

"I think so. You'll just have to wait and see. Jason called earlier. He needs the main cover design by Monday at the latest."

"That's not giving you much time, li'l lady."

"I know, but I'll get it done. Are you guys rehearsing at the house?"

"That's the plan. Is it a problem?"

"No," replied Lori. "Actually, it might help as long as you're playing some of the new songs."

"We've still to work that bit out. The guys are coming over later to try to work out a set list."

Three days later as she was sitting at her drawing board, Lori was thinking that in future she might be more careful what she wished for. Silver Lake had been down in the basement all day rehearsing. The house had been filled with music – some old, some new- but it wasn't helping. In front of her, she had the album cover less than half done and she had four days left to complete it. Two days earlier, she had sent her rough sketches to Maddy and Jason, nominating her preferred option. They had both agreed that the one of the imp gazing into the pool was the best. Drawing the imp's outline had been easy and fun, as had the outline of his reflection, but now she was struggling. Reaching for her phone, she called Maddy.

"Hello," greeted her friend brightly. "You ok? I thought you'd be working."

"I'm trying to," sighed Lori, allowing her exasperation to show. "I want to change part of the design, but I'm not sure."

"What did you have in mind?"

"Instead of just the imp's handsome face being reflected, I want to add in other faces to the pool. Shadows almost. Ghosts," explained Lori, hoping her friend would be able to visualise where she was coming from. "Faces to reflect his character and the music."

"Can you do one with and one without?" asked Maddy, unsure if she liked the idea.

"I could scan it without then add in the faces," proposed Lori. "I don't have enough time to do both separately."

"Ok, go with that," agreed Maddy. "Will both be sharp enough to use?"

"Of course!" exclaimed Lori somewhat indignantly.

"I look forward to seeing them."

"Thanks, Maddy. I'd better get back to work."

"Don't work too hard, honey."

By the small hours of Monday morning, Lori had pulled together two separate drawings. Despite protests from Jake, she had worked late into the small hours each night, finding it easier to connect with the project after dark. The original version looked fabulous with the twisted imp staring at his "handsome" self reflected back up at him. On the whole, she was pleased with it, but she preferred her second take on it. The design was basically the same, but, as well as his handsome reflection, she had added several incarnations of his "ugly" self, as though they were receding into the depths of the pool, each more twisted and wretched than the last. As an afterthought, she drew in a tiny shadowy portrait in the bottom right hand corner. A portrait that was almost hidden within the design. Sitting back, she smiled as she surveyed both designs. Silently, she prayed that the band and the management loved them as much as she did.

When Jake wakened on Monday morning, the bed beside him was empty. It hadn't been slept in. Wearing only his boxer shorts, he padded through the house in search of his fiancée. Walking into the study, his heart skipped a beat as he saw Lori slumped over the desk. As he put a hand on her shoulder, she stirred under his touch.

"Hey, li'l lady," he whispered softly. "Let's get you to bed."

"Mmm," she mumbled without moving.

For a moment or two, Jake deliberated on whether to risk lifting her but common sense prevailed. He couldn't afford to aggravate his freshly healed injuries.

"Lori," he said a little louder and a little firmer. "Wake up. Let's get you through to bed."

"Wha' time is it?" she mumbled incoherently.

"It's still early. It's only just gone eight," replied Jake.

"I need to send the designs to Jason," said Lori, slowly sitting up.

"You need a proper rest," declared Jake, his tone sharper than his heart intended. "Grab a few hours' sleep, then you can send them through. You've got all day."

"Alright," she sighed as she ran her fingers through her tangled hair. "I'm beat."

Slowly she got to her feet, swaying slightly as a wave of fatigue engulfed her. Putting a supporting arm around her waist, Jake slowly guided her down the hallway. She stumbled several times, but eventually made it to the bedroom. Without pausing to take her clothes off, Lori collapsed onto the bed. Her pale complexion scared Jake a little, but he knew she was just overtired. Gently, he kissed her forehead and whispered a promise to waken her mid-afternoon as he draped the bedcovers over her.

Leaving her sleeping soundly, Jake grabbed a clean shirt and his cut-off shorts, then wandered back through the house. He pulled on his clothes while the coffee pot was preparing his first coffee of the day. Mug in hand, he went through to the study to sneak a look at the finished cover designs. Both of the versions were propped up on stands on the table beside Lori's desk. Jake's eyes were drawn to the original design first, then he turned to study the alternative one. The depths of the picture blew him away. Just as he was about to turn away, his eye spotted the tiny face in the corner. A lump instantly filled his throat and tears pricked at his eyes. Gary was staring back at him from the drawing. In minute writing underneath it, Lori had written "Finally at the beach. LH x".

The creak of the back door opening brought him back to the present. It was Rich and Grey, both early as usual.

"Hey, where's the coffee?" called Grey from the kitchen.

"Ssh," said Jake as he came back through from the study. "Lori's asleep. She was up all night finishing off our cover."

"Have you seen it?" asked Rich as he helped himself to a coffee.

"Yes, but I don't think we were meant to see it yet," replied Jake. "Come through and see what you think."

The two musicians followed him through to Lori's desk and stood in silence as they admired both designs. At first neither of them said anything, then Grey stepped closer to the second version. With a sad smile, he turned to face his fellow band mates. "Perfect. Absolutely perfect."

"That one gets my vote too," agreed Jake with a sad smile. "Lori's own tribute to him."

"Subtle and beautiful," added Rich, a catch in his voice.

Mindful that Lori was asleep upstairs, Silver Lake opted for an acoustic rehearsal during the morning. It had been after ten before Paul strolled in, apologising for being late. In true Silver Lake style, he was fined twenty dollars. As they rehearsed, the boys spent more time talking than playing so when Rich suggested breaking for an early lunch, no one objected. Early lunch evolved into a long, leisurely lunch out on the sun deck and, by the time Jake was due to waken Lori, all thoughts of rehearsing were long gone for the day.

Gently he sat down on the edge of the bed and gazed down at his sleeping fiancée. With her golden hair all tangled round about her, Lori was still sleeping soundly, her breathing deep and even. It seemed cruel to disturb her, but Jake knew she had to submit her artwork to Jason before the end of the regular working day. Smoothing her hair away from her face, he leant down and kissed her tenderly.

"Time to rise and shine, sleeping beauty," he whispered softly.

With a low moan, she stirred, then opened her eyes, flinching at the brightness of the room. As she wriggled and sat up, Lori asked what time it was.

"Just gone three, li'l lady."

"Aren't you meant to be rehearsing?"

"We were," he replied with a smile. "We stopped for lunch and never quite got going again. The boys are still out on the sun deck."

"I assume you all took a look at the designs."

Jake nodded, unsure if she was going to be pleased, or angry with him.

"And?" she asked curiously.

Wrapping his arms around her, Jake kissed her long and tenderly before replying, "It's perfect, li'l lady."

"Which one?"

"You know which one," he teased. "Now, is it not time you got up and shared them with the powers that be?"

"I guess," she sighed, relieved that he had loved the design. "I was thinking of just submitting one of them."

"Go for it. We've already agreed it's the one we want," said Jake, helping her to her feet.

"Let me grab a quick shower, then I'll send it off."

Within two minutes of her hitting "send" on the email to Jason, her phone rang.

"Hi, Jason," she greeted brightly.

"Mz Hyde, you are a genius!"

Blushing and stifling a giggle, Lori answered, "Met with approval then?"

"It's fantastic! Have the boys seen it yet?"

"Yes," she replied. "To be honest, there were two variations. They unanimously chose that one."

"I love it, Mz Hyde!" he enthused loudly. "Thank you."

"Pleasure as always, Jason," she laughed. "The merchandising designs will be with you by the end of the week."

"Perfect. Will you be at the festival at Columbia on Saturday?"

"That's the plan."

"Great. I fly back to New York on Friday. I'll likely see you there."

"See you on Saturday."

As the band's bus pulled into the showground on the outskirts of Baltimore, they were all peering out, trying to get a view of the crowd. It was a three-day annual rock event sponsored by a local radio network that always drew a huge crowd. This year looked to be no exception. Following the steward's directions, the driver negotiated the labyrinth that was the performers' enclosure before finally coming to a halt in the allotted space. For the rest of the day, this was now the Silver Lake camp. The back window of the coach had been fitted with a sun shade with the band's name emblazoned on it, announcing their arrival to all around.

"Ok, guys," began Maddy, her tone distinctly business-like and indicating clearly that they were to listen up. "It's just gone eleven. Go out and stretch your legs, but be back here before noon. Jake, Rich, there's two DJs coming to do a short interview with you at twelve. Live radio slot. Paul, Grey, you've to be at the TV station's stand by twelve thirty for a slot on their lunchtime show. I'll take you round there myself once Jake and Rich are set up for their interview. Sound check's at two on the practice stage at the rear. Show time is six o'clock."

"I thought we were on at four?" questioned Rich, raising his scarred eyebrow.

"Last minute line-up change," stated Maddy. "There's a VIP meet and greet for thirty minutes at four thirty."

"Hey, no one mentioned anything about that," Jake commented sharply.

"It was in the itinerary email last week, Mr Power," stated Maddy calmly. "You'll be fine. Photos and autographs for thirty minutes."

"I guess," muttered Jake, forcing a smile. "Come on, Lori. Let's go for a walk."

The August heat hit them as soon as they stepped off the air-conditioned bus. Holding Lori's hand, Jake led them through the maze of buses towards the backstage area. All around them there were people dashing this way and that; journalists conducting interviews; TV crews and photographers.

"Mz Hyde!" came a shout from under a large sun shade

emblazoned with the rock radio station's name.

Lori paused and turned round, recognising the voice instantly. It belonged to Leo, the bass player with the headline act, When The Chips Are Down. In the past, Lori had helped him build up a substantial guitar collection in her capacity as rock memorabilia expert.

"Leo, how are you?" she replied brightly. "Have you met my fiancé, Jake Power?"

"Ah, the voice of Silver Lake," declared Leo, coming over to shake Jake's hand. "Pleasure to meet you. Condolences about your manager. I met him a few times. Nice guy."

"Thanks," said Jake, somewhat caught off guard by his fellow musician.

"You guys fit to play today?"

"As we'll ever be," joked Jake with a grin. "It's going to be tough, but we'll be fine."

"Looking forward to hearing your set," said Leo sincerely. "Now, Mz Hyde, how are you? Beautiful as ever, I see."

"Leo!" exclaimed Lori, flushing scarlet. "I'm fine. You? Hope you're looking after that collection of yours."

"I'm good, thanks," he replied. "Looking to expand that collection in fact. You interested in sourcing a couple of axes for me?"

"Sorry, Leo, not my area anymore," apologised Lori. "I can give you a couple of names if you want."

"Can't I tempt you out of retirement, Lori?"

Jake watched her expression and wasn't surprised when she replied, "Email me the details and I'll see what I can do. No promises."

"You're a star, Mz Hyde."

As she walked through the VIP area with Jake, he teased her about giving in so easily.

"If he's after something easily found, I can do the negotiating via phone or email. If it's more difficult to trace, then I'll find someone to help and increase the price," she explained. "It's not a part of my past I'm in a hurry to rebuild, but business is business."

Before they finally made their way back to the Silver Lake bus, they were stopped several more times by fellow musicians wanting to pass on their condolences and good wishes. Although Jake had known Gary was a popular figure, he hadn't appreciated just how many people's lives he had touched. The other members of Silver Lake were all gathered outside the bus, sitting under a large sunshade at a picnic table. Each of them had had a similar experience as they had checked out the showground.

As Jake helped himself to an iced tea from the bus's fridge, Maddy called him back outside.

"Jake, meet Dom and Billy from WKYD," she said, introducing the two new arrivals. "Remember, it's a live interview and it's going out here as well as on the radio station."

"Hi, guys," said Jake, shaking their hands.

"Nice to meet you, buddy," said Dom as he firmly shook Jake's hand. "You ready to sit down and have a chat with us?"

"Sure," agreed Jake. "Rich, you ready?"

"Guess so," answered the guitarist, getting up from the table. He was wearing his sunglasses in an attempt to disguise the remaining bruising around his eyes. From behind their dark tinted lenses, he noticed the DJs flinch at the sight of the fresh scar across his forehead.

Together with Maddy, they made their way over to the radio station's marquee and temporary home for the weekend. Once they were settled at a table with their microphones set up, she bade them farewell, saying she had to rush back to fetch Grey and Paul.

The radio station tent was blaring Out Of The Shadows across the park and, as it played, the two DJs chatted to the nervous Silver Lake musicians in an attempt to put them at their ease. When the song faded out, Dom began, "And that was Silver Lake's latest single, folks. We've been joined by Rich Santiago and Jake Power from the band. Nice to see you boys looking so well."

"Thanks," replied Rich, conscious of the small crowd of press and fans that was gathering outside the marquee.

"Now, this is your first live show for a few months. What have you boys been up to?"

"Recording," said Jake warmly. "We've just finished our new album."

"And what can the fans expect from it? Out Of The Shadows is a bit different from previous Silver Lake tracks," commented

Billy.

"We think there's something for everyone on there," began Rich, beginning to relax. "We've really been stretched by our producer, Dr Marrs, and encouraged to try new things. We're really pleased with the new material."

"Does the record have a title yet?" Dom enquired.

"Impossible Depths," revealed Jake. "Although it's not all doom and gloom. It's a bit of a voyage of discovery."

"When's it due out?"

"October 14th, I think," said Rich, glancing over at Jake for confirmation. His fellow band member nodded.

"And will you be playing any new songs this afternoon?" asked Dom hopefully. "There's hundreds of fans out there living in hope."

"You'll have to wait and see," teased Jake, before adding, "We hope to throw in a couple of them."

"Now, we don't want to dwell on the tragedy that struck the band last month, but the fans are all keen to know if you guys are back to full fitness?"

After a brief pause and a glance over at Rich, Jake said, "To be honest, we're not a hundred percent yet, but we owe it to Gary and to each and every one of our fans to get out there and play. The support from our fans over the last few weeks has been amazing. We're playing for an hour later on. If it had been our full set, I think we would still struggle to make it through it."

"You've been moved up the bill to the six o'clock slot," Billy began. "It's shaping up to be a hot one out there today. Is the heat likely to cause any issues for either of you?"

"No more than usual," laughed Jake, trying to lighten the mood. "With my wrecked shoulder, I might struggle to get my shirt off if it gets too hot."

"I'm sure your legions of female admirers would help you, Mr Power," joked Rich playfully.

"Honestly, we can't wait to get back up on stage in front of the crowd and do what we do best," added Jake. "We'll be enjoying ourselves and we hope everyone else enjoys the show too."

"Thanks, boys," said Dom, winding the interview up. "We'll look forward to hearing you later this afternoon. Folks, this is Silver Lake's first single, Dragon Song."

Shortly before six, as they stood at the side of the stage, Jake wasn't feeling so confident. Their soundcheck had gone smoothly. Todd had done a fantastic job of preparing their guitars. They had tried out a couple of the new songs, but Jake had felt his ribs protesting as he sang with his full power. Adrenaline, plus the pain meds he had swallowed, were kicking in as he paced restlessly back and forth. The rest of Silver Lake were edgy and fidgety. Out on stage, the crew were finalising setting up. From his vantage point at the side of the stage, Jake watched Todd carefully slot a dozen picks into his mic stand. The crowd were beginning to chant "Silver Lake, Silver Lake, Silver Lake, Lake, Lake" and he could see his young protégé drinking in the atmosphere as he continued the final preparations with the rest of the crew.

A few moments later, Maddy gave them the nod. "Show time, boys!" she declared.

"Yes, boss," agreed Jake, giving her a hug.

"Get your ass out there," she laughed as she stepped back into the shade to stand beside Lori.

Silver Lake took to the stage to a deafening roar from the capacity crowd. With a wave to the fans, Jake and Rich launched into the intro to Dragon Song. All nerves vanished as Jake stepped up to the mic. His voice rang out across the crowd, strong and powerful, while behind him, Grey and Rich were playing back to back in front of the drum riser. After their second number, Jake paused to draw breath, then called out, "Good evening! You all still with us?"

A huge cheer came blasting straight back at him.

"I can't hear you!" screamed Jake, cupping his hand to his ear. "You still with us?"

This time the response was deafening.

"Damn, it's hot out here," he declared, wiping sweat out of his eyes. "This next one is our current single. This is Out Of The Shadows!"

As Rich began the distinct, delicate intro, the crowd went wild. Feeding from the audience's reaction, Silver Lake put their heart and soul into the song.

A few minutes later, Jake loped over to the side of the stage to change guitar. He grabbed his acoustic from Todd then walked slowly back to the centre of the stage, plugging himself into his radio pack and adjusting the strap as he went. His usual stool was missing from its mark. With a grin, Jake walked towards the edge of the stage and sat down.

"Time to slow it down for a minute or two," he announced. A stage hand appeared to move his mic stand into its lowest position. "We've had a rough few weeks as some of you know so this gives us a chance to catch our breath too.

The crowd cheered wildly.

Casually, Jake began to strum the guitar as he looked out over the vast sea of people. A familiar face near the front caught his eye, causing him to pause momentarily. It was his sister and, standing behind her was his brother, Peter. Regaining his composure, Jake said, "This is Stronger Within."

The fans lapped up the beautiful ballad, singing along enthusiastically to the anthemic chorus.

Before he began his second acoustic number, Jake teased the crowd by playing a little of the French air intro from his tribute to Gary.

"You might find that on our new record in a couple of months," he commented with a hint of sadness in his voice, before beginning to play Lady Butterfly.

Jake watched his young sister sing her heart out throughout the song as he played and sang. He still couldn't believe she was actually there in the front row of the huge crowd. At the end of the acoustic interlude, he ran back to change guitars again. He stole a few seconds to shout to Maddy to get security to bring Lucy and Peter backstage once Silver Lake were done.

After playing a familiar crowd pleasing rock classic, Jake said, "This is from our new record. This is Impossible. Be kind to us. This is new to us too!"

Impossible was one of the longest and heaviest tracks off the record. Despite its unfamiliarity, the audience went wild and Jake and Rich watched as a group of fans started moshing in the centre of the crowd, safely out of the reach of the security personnel.

All too soon, Jake found himself introducing Flyin' High and bidding the crowd a fond farewell until next time.

As the band left the stage to a thunderous cheer, Jake breathed a sigh of relief. Despite the strapping he was wearing, his shoulder was throbbing, his ribs were on fire, but he felt on top of the world. Beside him, Rich removed his sunglasses and wiped the sweat, or was it tears, from his eyes.

"He'd have loved that set," commented the guitarist with a sad smile.

"I hope so," sighed Jake, handing his guitar to Todd. "Great job, young man. Perfect."

"Thanks, Jake," replied the teenager, relieved to have survived his first set as guitar technician.

By the time the band had made their way backstage to the communal VIP hospitality area, the security guards had brought Lucy and Peter round to join them.

"I was looking forward to seeing When The Chips Are Down," teased Lucy as she hugged her brother.

"We can get you back out there for them," promised Jake. "Peter, how're you?"

"Great. Awesome set, young brother."

"Didn't know you were still here," commented Jake.

"Transferred to Dover permanently. Desk job," he explained. "Not much use for one-armed pilots."

"And we promised to be front row, didn't we?" laughed Lucy, hugging both her brothers.

"If I'd known you were there, I'd have joined you," said Lori, joining the group.

"You guys are crazy!" laughed Jake, lifting a bottle of water from a nearby table. "Completely insane!"

As the penultimate act took to the stage, the Silver Lake party retired to their bus for dinner. In true over-the-top style, Maddy had arranged for a silver service seafood banquet to be laid on for the band and crew. Two long trestle tables had been set up and the catering firm were standing by to begin service. All of them were starving and were soon tucking into blue crab and lobster. Several journalists and photographers were hovering about, but Maddy soon asked for the band to be left alone to enjoy their meal.

"Lucy," called Jake from the far end of the table. "Did you seriously want to see When The Chips Are Down?"

"Yes, I did."

"Peter, what about you?"

"I'm easy. I've never heard of them," confessed his older brother, almost sounding embarrassed by the admission. "I hadn't heard of any of the folks who played last night either."

"Last night?" echoed Lori curiously.

"Miss Lucy Lou here has us camping for the entire weekend," muttered Peter.

This revelation caused great hilarity and triggered no end of teasing, aimed directly at Lucy. Just as the joke was in danger of being carried too far, Jake intervened, "Come on then. Let's see if we can find you a spot to watch the headliners. Lori, are you coming?"

"I'll wait here," she replied, swatting at a mosquito. "You go on though."

"I'll see these guys sorted then be straight back," promised Jake, kissing her softly on the forehead.

As he started to leave, Maddy called out, "Bus pulls out at eleven, Mr Power. Don't get lost or be late!"

"I'll go with him," said Grey, standing up and stretching. "Fancy checking them out myself."

On the way back to the main stage, Jake and Grey were stopped repeatedly by VIP ticket fans wanting photos and autographs. Seizing the opportunity, Lucy too photographed the guys with their fans, adding to her collection to share on the fan page. By the time they reached the side of the stage, the headliners had already started their set. Neither Jake nor Grey had seen them perform before and watched as closely as Lucy did. From the expression on Peter's face, he wasn't enjoying the band. After half a dozen songs, he tapped Jake on the shoulder and indicated he was going back to the bus.

"Can you stay with Lucy?" Jake asked Grey. "I'll head back with Peter."

"Sure. I'll bring her back safely," promised Grey with a wink.

"See you back at the bus."

In a few moments, Jake had caught up with his brother. They made their way slowly back to the Silver Lake camp.

"How do you cope with all of this?" asked Peter seriously,

when they were half way back and had been stopped another half a dozen times by fans.

"What do you mean?"

"All the attention. Performing. The travelling."

"It's what I've spent twenty years working for," replied Jake honestly. "Yeah, it's tough at times, but the buzz you get out on that stage makes it all worthwhile."

"You were quite something out there earlier," complimented his brother with a proud smile. "That crowd would've done anything you asked."

Jake blushed, then shrugged his shoulders before admitting, "Today was tough."

"Didn't show."

"That's a good thing," agreed Jake wearily. "If that set had been any longer I'd have struggled big time. My ribs are killing me."

"When's your next show?"

"Friday night," replied his brother. "Somewhere in upstate New York."

"Is it a full set?"

Jake shook his head, "No. Another short one. Next full show is in Atlantic City on September 6th. Want to come?"

"Would love to."

"I was going to call Simon and Dad too," continued Jake hopefully. "It's a big show for us. Thought perhaps you'd all like to be there."

"No idea where the old man is but I'm sure he'll come if he can. Same for Simon."

"Well, I can only ask," said Jake as they arrived back at the Silver Lake party.

Life over the next three weeks picked up pace as the promotional work for Impossible Depths began in earnest. Now that she was back in the driving seat, Maddy was pushing Silver Lake hard and soon lined up numerous interviews and radio slots for them. The three other festival weekends that had been booked passed smoothly. Twice she managed to get them moved up the bill. Working flat out took the band's minds off any lingering thoughts of the accident. By the start of September and, after their last outdoor show, both Jake and Rich agreed that they finally felt as though they'd returned to full fitness.

After the final festival appearance, Jason called a band meeting at the record company offices in Philadelphia. It was the first time that Silver Lake had been back there since July. It was the final ghost they had to lay to rest. As before, they had driven up in two cars – Grey travelling with Jake and Rich, while Maddy and Paul drove up together. Walking back into the city centre building felt a little surreal, but they were soon directed to a meeting room that none of them had been in before. When Jake entered, with Grey and Rich following closely behind him, he was surprised to discover they were the first to arrive. At the conference table, Jason was sitting chatting with an older gentleman with long, snow white hair, tied in a braid that stretched down his back. As the three members of Silver Lake clattered into the room, both of them looked up.

"Boys," called out Jason. "Come on in. Grab a seat."

The three of them sat at the opposite side of the table to the Englishman and the long haired stranger.

"Is Maddison with you?"

"She's on her way," replied Grey, helping himself to a glass of juice from the pitcher on the table. "They left just after us, I think."

"Good. Good," replied the Englishman. "I'd like to introduce you to Jethro Steele. Jethro, this is, from left to right, Rich Santiago, Grey Cooper and Jake Power."

After a round of handshaking and polite greetings, Rich cut to the chase, "No offence, Jethro, but where do you fit in?"

Before Jason could answer, the white haired Jethro replied, "I'm here to support your manager."

"This should be interesting," mused Grey softly.

"Jason," began Jake, his tone sharper than he had intended. "Does Maddison know about him?"

"In a roundabout way. She knows I've been looking for someone to support her for the tour of the UK and Europe. I may have brought the start date forward a little here."

Before any of them could say anything else, the door opened, allowing Maddy and Paul to enter the room. Much to the band's amazement, when she saw the white haired man, Maddy screamed, "Jethro!" and rushed to hug him.

"Easy, Maddison," he said, hugging her back.

"Jason," she exclaimed shrilly. "You never said it was Jethro you were talking to?"

"Didn't I?" replied the Englishman innocently. "Must have slipped my mind."

"Ok, what's the deal here?" asked Rich, looking from Maddy to Jethro then to Jason.

"It's ok, boys," said Maddy, taking a seat next to Jethro. "We're old friends. If I have to accept help from someone, I can't think of anyone I'd rather work with. Trust me on this."

"I showed Maddison here the ropes on her first world tour," explained Jethro grinning mischievously. "She was a fast learner."

"And you guys work well together?" asked Rich curiously.

"Beautifully," declared Maddison enthusiastically.

"Ok, then," sighed Grey, still somewhat bemused. "Looks like Jethro here made the team. Now can we get down to business?"

Business lasted for several hours as they laid out the plans for the run up to the album launch on October 14th and the plans for the winter tour. In addition to the sixteen European dates, Jason had tagged five US dates onto the start of the tour schedule. All five were east coast dates, but he hinted that he was trying to secure a couple of west coast shows too.

"Jason," began Jethro, having listened to the heavy schedule that had been laid out. "When do you expect these boys to recharge their batteries?"

"There's down time built in," stated Jason bluntly.

"Not hellish much," countered Jethro, fingering the end of his long white braid. "By the time you factor in all the album promotional work and the fact that these boys have families, you're stretching them pretty damn thin here."

"I agree," said Maddy, scanning the list of dates again. "Can you delay the west coast shows until some point in the new year? Late January maybe?"

"Potentially," conceded Jason sourly.

"If you postponed them until the new year," began Rich, reviewing the schedule, "perhaps you could extend the run into the Midwest too?"

"Leave it with me," stated the Englishman calmly. "I'll make a few calls and see what's feasible here. Now, is everything in place for Friday?"

"We've a full run through planned for Wednesday," said Jake, running his hands through his hair nervously. "There's press stuff set up for most of Thursday afternoon and Friday morning as I recall."

"Plus a VIP session on Friday afternoon," finished off Maddy.

"I'll be down on Friday," said Jason. "I've a few VIPs to bring along myself."

"Jethro," asked Maddy hopefully. "Are you coming along?"

"Purely to watch, Maddison," he replied warmly. "That's if I'm invited, boys?"

"We'd be honoured to have you along," said Grey theatrically.

"Then I guess I'll see you all in Atlantic City then," he agreed as he got to his feet. "Maddison, I'll call you tomorrow."

Thunder clouds had gathered over Rehoboth as the band drove back towards town. Having dropped Grey and Rich off en route, Jake was glad to have a few minutes alone to mull over the day's developments. Common sense told him that Maddison needed help with the management of the band; his heart wasn't ready to see someone else fill Gary's shoes. Seeing Maddy welcome Jethro into the fold had made it a little easier, but Jake still felt like a traitor for liking the eccentric Jethro. As he turned the truck into the driveway, the first flash of lightning lit up the charcoal grey sky, bringing him back to reality. Torrential rain began to fall as the thunder rolled overhead.

Dripping and soaked through from the short run round the side of the house, Jake stumbled into the kitchen through the back door. From the sunroom, he could hear Lori clattering around, muttering about the storm.

"You ok, li'l lady?" he called as he dumped his bag on the kitchen table.

"Two hours work ruined!" she grumbled as she came through, clutching her damp sketch book.

"Can't you dry it off?" asked Jake, trying not to smile at her obvious anger.

"No I bloody can't! The colours have all run!"

"Come here," suggested Jake, reaching out to wrap his arms round her. "Did you know that you're beautiful when you're angry?"

"Hmph," she growled as she succumbed to his embrace. As she felt the damp warmth of his body against her, Lori felt her anger begin to melt away. "How did the big meeting go?"

"Interestingly," he replied, kissing the top of her head. "I'll tell you all about it after I've been for a run."

"A run? In that rain?"

"Yup," he said softly. "It'll be good for my soul. I won't be long."

Rain was still lashing down as Jake set off along the beach at a leisurely pace. Gradually, he had been building up the distance and intensity of his runs, but decided to take things easy today, not wanting to risk aggravating his ribs before the band's Atlantic City show. Waves were crashing onto the shore beside him, causing him to dash back up the sand every few minutes as the foaming water surged towards him. Jake breathed in the fresh salty ocean air and, breath by breath, he felt all the frustrations of the day exhale away into the storm. Now that he had cooled off and got things back into perspective, he realised that Jethro was maybe what Silver Lake needed. Someone totally different to Gary; someone who knew Maddison, and, as he had already demonstrated, someone who would stand up for them. Gary would have approved of him, Jake reasoned by the time he turned towards home.

As the house came into view, the rain stopped as suddenly as it had begun. A watery sun tried to force its way through the hazy clouds at the tail of the storm and, as Jake sat down on the edge of the deck to remove his sodden, sand encrusted sneakers, he spotted a rainbow arching over the house. His mother had always told him that rainbows signified that all would work out just fine.

Carrying his wet shoes and socks, Jake wandered through to the kitchen to fetch a drink of water. A glass sat waiting for him with a Post-it note stuck to it. "Run out to the food store. Lx". Still smiling, he stood at the window, drinking the cool water, watching the rainbow fade away. Leaving the empty glass in the sink, he headed through the house to take a shower.

As he stepped out of the shower, he heard the back door open and Lori calling hello to him. Pausing only to wrap a towel round his waist, he hurried through to see if she needed help with the groceries.

"You need a hand, li'l lady?" he asked as he walked into the kitchen.

Before Lori could reply, the door opened again and Todd and Kate entered carrying the rest of the brown paper grocery bags.

"Hi, Jake," called out Todd brightly, while Kate flushed scarlet at the sight of the semi-naked rock star.

Trying to suppress a giggle, Lori explained, "I met these two at the store so I invited them for dinner."

"So I see," acknowledged her fiancé, feeling his own colour rising. Holding on tight to the towel at his waist, he added, "I'd better go and get dressed."

As he retreated hastily down the hallway, he could hear the two girls giggling.

When he returned to the kitchen a few minutes later, Lori and Kate were deep in conversation while Todd was sitting at the table, idly flicking through a guitar magazine.

"How long until dinner?" Jake asked.

"About an hour," commented Lori as she switched on the oven.

"Perfect," he declared. "Todd, school's in."

"I've not got my guitar," began the young musician, closing the magazine.

"Not a problem," said Jake, heading towards the basement. "Plenty of toys down here."

While Jake switched on all the lights and selected two guitars to use for the lesson, Todd took a seat, rummaging in his pockets for a pick.

"Have you kept up your practice?" asked Jake as he handed his protégé a black Gibson SG.

"Yes, sir," replied Todd with a grin. "Just ask Kate's folks."

"Not out staying your welcome there?" Jake enquired as he settled himself on the stool with his latest acquisition.

"A bit," admitted Todd, before adding, "But I leave for school next week."

"Of course," exclaimed Jake, suddenly realising the dates. "Have you got everything set up for that?"

"Yes, sir. Lori's been great. I got the keys to an apartment last weekend. Kate and I are driving over to see it tomorrow. I'll move my gear in next week and classes start September 14th."

"And you're still ok for this Friday?" checked Jake, conscious for the first time that he was losing his guitar tech.

"Wouldn't miss it."

"Glad to hear it," sighed Jake as he tweaked the tuning on his guitar. "Well, if this is the last lesson for a while, let's make it count."

Upstairs, Lori had put Kate to work setting the dining room table for dinner. The younger woman had finally stopped blushing after seeing Jake half-naked and both women had giggled about it at Jake's expense. As she laid out the cutlery, Kate had commented that she and Todd were driving to Baltimore next day to check out Todd's new apartment.

"When do you leave for school?" Lori asked, passing her a large bowl of salad to take through to the table.

"Next weekend. My parents are driving me," she replied, a hint of sadness in her voice.

"I never asked," began Lori curiously. "What are you going to study?"

"Humanities at Princeton," Kate answered quietly.

"Good school. You don't sound too thrilled about it."

"I am," gushed Kate. "But I don't want to give up on the band. We've played a few shows. The studio slot at JJL was awesome. I hate seeing all of that coming to an end."

"I can understand that," sympathised Lori, giving her a hug. "But with that voice of yours, you will soon find an outlet for it at Princeton."

"Maybe," sighed Kate with a smile. "But it won't be the same."

Much later, after a second thunderstorm had passed through, Jake and Lori lay side by side on the couch, half-watching TV. Their young dinner guests had left early, wanting to spend some time alone before heading back to Kate's house. As she snuggled into Jake's chest, Lori said, "You never told me how the band meeting went."

Twisting her long, blonde hair through his fingers, Jake sighed. "It was fine. Jason laid out the schedule. Laid down the law as usual. He's hired a guy to help Maddy with the tour."

"Who?" asked Lori, sensing that Jake wasn't thrilled by this fact.

"An old guy called Jethro Steele."

"Jethro?" echoed Lori loudly. "I haven't seen that old devil in a long time! You'll be fine with him. Maddy adores Jethro."

"I got that impression," agreed Jake softly. "It just felt wrong."

"Is he coming on Friday?"

"Yes, as far as I know."

"Give him a fair chance, rock star," she advised warmly. "He's no Gary. No one can replace Gary but I think you'll like Jethro's style when you get to know him."

"I know you're right," Jake acknowledged. "He seems like a nice guy. He stood up for us against Jason earlier. Told him straight that the schedule was overloaded. Jason backed right off. I've not seen that happen before."

"Speaking of schedules," began Lori, changing the subject. "I've been thinking."

"Should I be worried?" teased Jake, tickling her gently.

"Maybe," she giggled, swiping at his hand. "When do you guys get back from Europe?"

"Last show's December 18th. Why?"

"I was wanting to arrange something for before Christmas."

"What?" asked Jake, his curiosity aroused.

"Our wedding," she answered. "I thought we could get married in New York on December 22nd."

"But that's…." he began as she put a finger to his lips to shush him

"What better way to put it behind me once and for all? It's a date I'll never forget but I'd rather remember it for all the right reasons, not the wrong ones."

"December 22nd? You're sure?"

"Positive," stated Lori before kissing him tenderly.

"Sounds perfect to me, li'l lady," he agreed, kissing her back.

"I don't want a huge affair though. Let's keep it small. Simple," she said between kisses. "I thought we could have the ceremony at my apartment."

"Are you sure? We could book out a hotel or a restaurant?"

"I've given this a lot of thought, Jake," she whispered. "A small private wedding will be perfect."

"Mmm, intimate," he teased as he kissed her again. "I like the sound of that."

"Jake!" she squealed. "You're incorrigible!"

"Can I tell folk we've set a date?" he asked hopefully.

"Not yet. Let's get it all booked first," Lori suggested. "I'll make a few calls tomorrow. If I can get the basic bookings made, we can tell everyone after the show on Friday."

"I guess I can keep quiet till then," conceded Jake with a contented sigh.

♪

Atlantic City was busy, built up, noisy and hot. Despite numerous visits in the past, Lori had never been a fan of the town, preferring quieter, more family orientated resorts. As Jake navigated through town, she cringed inwardly. The band had been booked into the Showboat Hotel and had arranged to meet up at an artisan sandwich bar in the complex for lunch. Having checked in and left their bags in their room, Jake took Lori's hand and they went in search of the rest of the Silver Lake party.

Walking into the sandwich bar, a little after two, Jake spotted Grey at a corner table with Becky and his mother, Annie.

"Ah, the late Mr Power," joked the bass player as they approached the table.

"Afternoon, all," greeted Jake, flashing a smile at Becky. "And I'm not late. We never agreed a time."

"No fine this time, then," laughed Grey. "The others just left. Rich and Linsey have gone for a walk. Paul and Maddy went upstairs to let the twins take a nap."

"When's our first interview?" asked Jake as he pulled over a chair.

"Maddy said to meet in the bar at three," Grey replied. "Think we're back to back from then until seven."

"Oh joy!" Jake sighed, rolling his eyes and making Becky giggle. "Guess we'd better grab some lunch."

Once their meal was over, Annie announced that she was taking Becky for a walk along the boardwalk.

"Do you mind if I join you?" asked Lori. "I could do with stretching my legs."

"Please come, Lori!" squealed Becky excitedly. "Grammy said she'd buy me ice cream."

"You're more than welcome to join us, dear," added Annie. "You can help me keep this young lady entertained."

"And keep my mom out of the casinos," teased Grey with a wink towards his mother.

"I'll do my best," laughed Lori as she got to her feet. "Where will we meet you guys?"

"Back at our room is probably easiest," suggested Jake,

checking the time. "We can all go to dinner together."

"Ok. We'll see you upstairs at seven."

"If there's any change of plan, I'll call you," promised Jake. "Have fun out there, ladies."

Compared to the familiar boardwalk in Rehoboth, the boardwalk in Atlantic City felt like the strip in Las Vegas. Holding on tight to Becky's hand, Annie led them confidently away from the hotel towards one of the shopping malls. The warm September sun beat down on them as they walked.

"I'm not going too fast for you, am I, my dear?" asked Grey's mother after a couple of hundred yards.

"A little," admitted Lori, feeling a little embarrassed. "I'm stiff after the car journey."

"Sorry," apologised the older woman. "I'm so used to charging along at full speed."

"It's fine," assured Lori, relieved that their pace had eased. "Are you looking forward to the show?"

"Do you know, I am," laughed Annie. "I've never really seen the boys play before. Grey's arranged seats for us so Becky can see it all properly."

"I think the band have blocked out a few balcony seats for guests," said Lori. "I'm sure that's where Jake suggested I watch from. I've never been in the audience before either. Side of the stage is as close as I usually get."

"Will you sit beside me?" asked Becky, dancing in front of Lori.

"If I can," promised Lori taking the little girl's hand.

Back at the hotel, Grey and Jake had met up with their fellow band members in one of the hotel's bars. Ever efficient, Maddy had printed off interview schedules for them. Their first slot was in the bar with the local newspaper's journalist. It was only a half hour slot, then they were scheduled to do a second half hour slot for a local TV station in the concert venue next door. At five o'clock they had a live radio phone-in interview before they ended their official duties with a British journalist who had arranged to meet them in one of the hotel's cocktail bars.

By the time Maddy guided Silver Lake into the cocktail bar for the final session, they were all flagging. It had been an intense afternoon for all of them, especially Rich and Jake. Questions had been varied, bordering on the bizarre and the thought of facing a further barrage wasn't inspiring any of them.

"Take a seat over there," instructed Maddy, pointing to an empty table. "I'll get us all a drink. You've earned it."

"Just water for me, Maddison," called Jake as they took their seats round the table.

"Look who I found propping up the bar," called Maddy as she returned with the tray of drinks.

Jethro was following behind her, carrying a cup of coffee.

"Afternoon, boys," he said with a smile. "Mind if I join you?"

"Be our guest," welcomed Jake, flashing him one of his "Power" smiles. "When did you get here?"

"A couple of hours ago," replied the silver haired man, stirring his coffee. "Hate the place. Too much razzmatazz!"

"It's a bit full on," conceded Rich, accepting his bottle of beer from Maddy.

Before they could continue their conversation, Maddy spotted the journalist that they were due to meet. It was Debbie, the same person who had interviewed Jake after the crash. When she spotted Silver Lake, she waved and gesticulated that she was going to the bar first. A few minutes later, she dashed over to join them, almost spilling her soda in her haste.

"Sorry to keep you guys waiting," she apologised. "I over ran with my previous interview, then got lost trying to find this place."

"Not a problem, honey," replied Maddy warmly. "This is their last stop for the day."

"Oh, I wish it was mine!" sighed the journalist. "I've to dash back to New York after this to do another interview, then I'm on the first flight to LA in the morning."

"Well, we'll leave you to it," said Maddy. "Boys, be good. Jethro, can I speak to you for a few minutes?"

With their management team discretely seated a couple of tables away, Silver Lake sat back to answer the journalist's questions. As anticipated, Debbie asked a fairly standard array of questions and the band did their best to make their answers sound fresh and enthusiastic.

"Thanks," she said after about half an hour. "Now, if you don't mind, I have a few extra easy ones for you. The magazine I write for back in England does a spotlight on artists and their favourite things. We'd like to feature Silver Lake in that slot when your tour hits the UK."

"Ok, young lady, do your worst," yawned Grey, feigning boredom.

"I'll be gentle," giggled Debbie, fishing in her bag for the list of questions. Spreading the sheet out in front of her, and with a glance round the table at each of them, she began with, "Favourite pastime or hobby?"

"Fishing," said Paul with little hesitation.

"Messing about with old engines," Grey added. "I love tinkering with old cars and trucks."

"Rich?" prompted Debbie.

"Probably playing my guitar," he confessed.

"Jake?"

"Going for a long run along the beach," answered Jake before challenging, "And yours?"

"Interviewing rock gods," laughed Debbie, jotting down their answers. "Next, favourite book?"

"Lord of the Rings," replied Jake instantly.

"Same here," echoed Grey.

"I'm not much of a reader," admitted Paul sheepishly. "I like DC and Marvel comic books. Love Batman. Shit like that."

"Philistine!" joked Jake playfully. "What about you Rich?"

"To Kill A Mockingbird," replied the guitarist.

"Oh, I love that book!" Debbie exclaimed enthusiastically. "Favourite colour?"

"Colour?" quizzed Paul scornfully, raising his eyebrows at the young English woman. "Black, I guess."

"Blue," added Jake, visualising Lori's eyes.

"Black," revealed Grey bluntly.

"Oh, I'll say red, just to be different," laughed Rich. "Is it favourite food next?"

"Almost," giggled Debbie. "It's least favourite food."

"Pizza," declared Jake emphatically.

"Lamb," said Grey, wrinkling up his nose. "Hate the smell."

"Olives," answered Rich.

"Zucchini," finished up Paul.

"Ok, one last one," began Debbie, trying not to giggle. "How old were you when you lost your virginity?"

"What?" Grey roared with laughter. "You can't ask us that!"

"I just did," challenged Debbie with a coy smile.

"About nineteen," confessed Rich, blushing at the memory.

"Who says I've lost mine?" teased Jake with a wink.

"Mr Power," growled Grey. "Confess."

"Senior year in high school. Guess I was about eighteen."

"Yeah, Same," added Paul quickly, trying not to embarrass himself.

"I was seventeen," boasted Grey. "And she was twenty-three."

"Thanks, guys. You've been great sports," said Debbie, putting her things back into her bag. "I hope the show goes well tomorrow night. I'll try to get you booked into my radio show when you come over to London. Maybe you could play a couple of numbers for me too?"

"Set it up with Maddison or Jethro," suggested Rich, shaking her hand. "I'm sure they'll work something out."

With their press commitments met for the day, the band breathed a collective sigh of relief and ordered another round of drinks. As Jake brought the tray back from the bar, Maddy and Jethro came back to join them.

"What's the plan, boss?" Jake asked, passing out the glasses.

"Dinner's booked for eight thirty," replied Maddy, checking the time. "Scarduzio's."

"Count me out," declared Grey, downing his beer. "I've a date with my princess. I'm eating with Becky and my mom."

"We might be a few minutes late," confessed Maddy. "I want to get the twins settled before we come down to dinner."

"Who's watching them?" asked Jake, sipping his glass of iced water.

"My sister," Paul replied. "She's got the room that connects to ours."

"Twins?" queried Jethro looking quizzically at Maddy. "You?"

"Wren and Hayden," she said proudly. "They're almost five months old."

"Well, I'll be......" laughed Jethro. "Who'd have thought I'd live to see the day!"

"You can meet them tomorrow," promised Maddy. "I'll bring them along to lunch. Now I'd better run upstairs and check on them. Paul, are you coming up?"

"Right behind you."

"Not much surprises me anymore," admitted Jethro once Maddy and Paul were out of earshot. "But that sure as hell did. Twins? Maddison?"

"Wait till you meet them," said Jake with a laugh as he reached into his pocket for his phone. "They are cute and adorable."

"I'll bet. Is the lovely Mz Hyde with you?" enquired the older man curiously. "I've not seen her for about four years."

"I'm just about to call her," replied Jake, dialling his fiancée's number. "She should be back upstairs by now."

Ten minutes later, as Lori entered the bar, Jethro was the first to notice her arrival. An afternoon of walking the boardwalk had taken its toll and she was leaning heavily on her cane. The older man watched as she limped towards them, concern written all over his lived in face.

"Lori, darling," he said, hugging her tightly. "As beautiful as I remember."

"Jethro!" giggled Lori, kissing him fondly on the cheek. "You haven't changed a bit. Hair's a bit longer."

"Just an inch or three," he laughed, reaching for his long, snow white ponytail. "Looks like you have a tale to tell me, Mz Hyde."

"Another time," said Lori softly. "Don't look so worried. I'm fine. Honestly."

"Are you sure?"

Taking a seat next to Jake, Lori said, "Just the legacy of an unfortunate accident. Plus, I've overdone it a bit today."

"Can I buy you a drink?" he asked, sensing that she wasn't about to tell him anything further.

"A dry, white wine would be lovely," she replied with a warm smile, then, turning her attention to the others asked, "How was your afternoon?"

"Long and repetitive," groaned Rich, trying and failing to stifle a yawn. "Yours?"

"Exhausting," admitted Lori, subconsciously rubbing her

aching thigh. "Grey's mom walks way too fast for me!"

"She's a character, isn't she?" said Jake, draping his arm casually around her shoulders. "Did you keep her out of the casino?"

"Almost," said Lori with a giggle. "Don't tell Grey but we got back here before five. Becky and I have been watching TV while Annie headed down to the casino for a couple of hours."

"Did she win?" asked Rich, already sure of the answer.

"A thousand dollars."

"She's a piece of work," Jake declared with a smile. "I'll guarantee she'll be back down there tonight. And, Lori, she always wins!"

Their relaxed, good humour continued through dinner. Feeling more comfortable among them, Jethro relaxed a little and happily told tales of previous tours and of working with Maddy. As the waitress served dessert, he began to reminisce about meeting Lori, much to her embarrassment. She cringed and giggled helplessly as he recalled a rather drunken, rowdy after show party in Las Vegas.

"We're seeing a new side to you tonight, Mz Hyde," teased Jake. "A dark side!"

"That was the first incarnation of Mz Hyde," protested Lori still laughing. "From what I remember that was a hell of a party. Didn't Maddy and I dance on top of the limo that arrived to take us back to the hotel?"

"I do believe you did," concurred Jethro with a smile.

"I'd forgotten about that night," giggled Lori. "That must have been about six years ago."

"Nearer seven. That was the last tour I touched any alcohol on. I've been sober ever since," stated Jethro with more than a hint of pride in his voice.

"Kudos to you," replied Rich, eyeing his own beer. "I couldn't turn my back on the odd beer or two."

"It was stop drinking or die," said the older man plainly. "And I'm way too young and good looking to die just yet!"

"Isn't everyone?" commented Jake quietly, a sombre cloud hovering over the table. Running his hand through his hair, he smiled over at Lori, then said "Jethro, tell me more about my fiancée's exploits. I'm seeing a whole new side to Mz Hyde tonight!"

"Well, there was one party," began Jethro, winking over at Lori. "We were in Canada somewhere and it was near Christmas...."

"Don't you dare, Jethro Steele!" squealed Lori shrilly.

"Go on," encouraged Jake.

"We were all staying in log cabins for a couple of nights between shows. There was this huge hot tub...."

"Jethro!" Lori practically screamed. "No!"

"I'll save that one for another night, Jake," said Jethro with a mischievous grin.

"I'll look forward to it, sir," laughed Jake, taking great delight in watching Lori squirm with embarrassment.

"It's ok, Mz Hyde," Jethro assured her softly. "I'll not embarrass you any further in front of your young man, but I still have those black string bikini bottoms if you ever want them back."

Both Rich and Jake roared with laughter as Lori flushed scarlet between them.

"What's the hilarity?" asked Paul as he re-joined the table. "Am I missing something here?"

"No," snapped Lori, her cheeks still rosy. "Not a thing. Where's Maddy?"

"She's staying up in the room. The twins are playing up," explained the drummer, signalling to the waiter to come over. "What's good to eat? I'm starving."

Conversation slowly settled to the schedule for the following day and then onto the set list for the show. Both Jake and Rich voiced their concerns about lasting the full two hours. They were all in agreement that it had been too long since they had had the opportunity to play a full set. Subconsciously, both musicians began to run their fingers over their freshly healed scars.

"If it's not too forward of me to suggest this," commented the older man calmly. "Only you know the full set list. Agree beforehand what numbers you can afford to let go if it gets too much out there. As long as you still play for at least ninety minutes with an encore, every fan will go home happy. Add in an acoustic track if it buys you a bit of a breather."

"We've got two acoustic numbers in there already," said Jake, running through the set list in his mind. "I guess we could tag on another if need be. Three's one too many in my book. Plus, it doesn't really give me a breather if I need one."

"Or buy a bit of time by playing with the audience," suggested Lori. "Talk to them a bit more between songs, but not too much."

"We'll be fine," stated Rich, not sounding entirely convincing. "Once we get out there, adrenaline and the crowd will get us through it."

Thunderstorms were forecast for the New Jersey shore, according to the breakfast news programme as Jake and Lori got ready next morning. Maddy had instructed them all to be down for breakfast for nine o'clock. Jake was determined not to be late. Fastening the belt on his jeans, he asked Lori what her plans for the morning were.

"Jason's asked me to do an interview about the artwork I've completed since I resurrected Mz Hyde. It's for an industry documentary that he's got Scott working on," she replied as she brushed her hair. "I'm dreading it."

"Is Scott filming it?"

"Yes, but I don't know who the interviewer is. No idea about the list of questions either," revealed Lori anxiously. "Guess I'll find out at ten."

Wrapping his arms around her, Jake said, "I wish I could be there for you, but we're back to back with press stuff in the venue all day."

"I'll be fine," said Lori, sounding less than convinced. "Now, we'd better get down for breakfast before Maddy is yelling at you, rock star."

With a protective arm around his fiancée's shoulder, Jake guided her through the large dining room towards the table where Maddy and Paul were seated. The twins were between them in two high chairs, contentedly chewing on pieces of toast. Little Wren let out a squeal of delight when she saw Jake much to his embarrassment.

"Your daughter is eyeing up my man," joked Lori as they took a seat at an adjacent table.

"Takes after her mom," commented Paul with his mouth full

of cereal.

"Lori," began Jake, still smiling at the baby girl. "What can I get you for breakfast?"

"OJ would be a start."

"You need to eat too."

"Bring me a croissant or something like that, please," she answered. "I'm not really hungry yet."

By the time Jake came back over from the buffet, they had been joined by Rich and Grey. As the waitress served them all fresh coffee, Lori spotted two familiar faces entering the dining room. It was Alice and Tom. When they saw the Silver Lake group, they waved and headed towards them.

"Morning," greeted Alice a little shyly. "Can we join you?"

"Of course," agreed Jake warmly. "When did you guys arrive?"

"We've been here all week," answered Alice as she sat at the next table. "When did you guys get here?"

"Yesterday lunchtime," replied Lori. "How are you both?"

"Better than last time we were over," said Alice with a sad smile. "It was nice to fly over for a happy reason this time."

"Glad you both made it," said Grey, looking genuinely pleased to see them both.

"Tom," said Jake. "You ok?"

"Yes, thanks," replied the teenager a little awkwardly.

"Feel up to doing some work today?" Jake asked, winking over at Alice. "We could use an extra pair of hands."

"Sure," agreed the teenager, looking to his sister for approval.

"Great. Come with us after breakfast," said Grey, stirring sugar into his coffee.

"What about you, Alice?" asked Lori. "Do you have any plans?"

"Not really. We're to meet Jason in the lobby at three, but that's all until the show," replied the English woman.

"You are more than welcome to tag along with me, if you want," suggested Lori hopefully. "I've to do an interview and could use some moral support."

"Interview?" queried Maddy sharply, as she wrestled Hayden out of the high chair. "What interview?"

"Blame Lord Jason," muttered Lori sourly. "It's for a

documentary on rock art or something. Scott's filming it, but I've no idea who's asking the questions. There's been no brief. Nothing."

"Be careful, honey," cautioned Maddy, sounding a little concerned. "If you're not comfortable with the line of questioning, stop the interview."

"Don't worry, I will," stated Lori bluntly. "So, Alice, do you want to tag along? We'll be done in time to meet the boys for lunch."

"I'd love to!"

The studio suite had been reserved for the interview. Scott was finalising the camera setup when Lori and Alice arrived. He suggested that they take a seat while they waited for the interviewer to arrive. The two women had only just settled themselves on a low settee when the door opened and a young woman burst in, carrying a large coffee cup.

"So sorry I'm late," she apologised. "Traffic's horrendous out there today. Oh! I'm Jen, by the way."

"Lori Hyde," said Lori, standing up and shaking the girl by the hand. "This is my friend, Alice York. Moral support."

"Pleased to meet you both."

"Can you fill me in on the plan for this morning?" asked Lori, trying to disguise her nerves. "Jason was a bit vague about the details."

"It's nothing too formal, Mz Hyde. Just a résumé of your career," replied Jen. "Both halves."

"Ok," agreed Lori, sitting back down. "And I reserve the right to decline to answer anything too personal."

"Mz Hyde," said Jen, sitting on one of the round backed chairs beside the couch. "It's not my intention to make you feel uncomfortable."

"Ladies," interrupted Scott brightly. "Can I do a few test shots before we start?"

"Where should I sit?" asked Alice anxiously. "I don't want to be in the way."

Indicating a seat over by the window, Scott suggested Alice observe from there.

Half an hour later, with a pot of coffee on the table, Jen was ready to start the interview. Her casual chatter while they had finished setting up had helped to put Lori at her ease. Now, though, seated at one end of the curved couch, Lori could feel her nerves beginning to rattle. With a nod to Scott, Jen started the interview, "I'd like to introduce you to one of the most high profile album artwork designers in the music world over the last ten years. Hers is a story of two halves. Hopefully today we'll get the whole story when we chat with the legendary Mz Hyde."

At being declared "legendary", Lori struggled to stifle a nervous giggle.

"If I've done my research correctly, you completed your first album cover while still in college. Is that correct?" began Jen, checking the sheaf of notes in her hand.

"Yes," nodded Lori, regaining her composure. "The class tutor set us a project in our final year to get a professional commission and to produce a finished piece before the end of the semester. My dad had a few contacts. People he'd leased property to. I submitted my portfolio to a few folks. I was lucky. Very lucky. I got two commissions that way and completed them both before the end of that semester."

"The first of those was for Weigh Station, I believe."

"Yes. The first of several," replied Lori, beginning to relax a little.

"That album was in the Billboard top ten, wasn't it?"

"Top five," corrected Lori smiling. "Great record. I still play it."

They chatted about various projects Lori had worked on during the first incarnation of Mz Hyde; they debated their favourites from that period and agreed to disagree on a few.

"Now, you retired Mz Hyde about three years ago. Why?" asked Jen, keen to learn the reason.

"I needed a change. A new challenge," explained Lori, fingering her engagement ring. "The rock memorabilia side of my business was taking off and taking more and more of my time. The art commissions I was being offered were repetitive. Nothing new in them to excite me. No challenges. It felt stale. I needed a break from it all so I retired Mz Hyde."

"And was the intention always to return at some point?"

"I'm not sure," admitted Lori honestly. "Looking back, I was burnt out. I never ruled out a resurrection, but I never gave it much thought either. At that time, I was passionate about what I was doing with the memorabilia. Enjoying the travelling. I get a kick out of sealing the deal and sourcing the piece."

"It's been over a year since Mz Hyde returned and, from the volume of work you've produced in that short time, is it safe to say she's back to stay?"

"For now," laughed Lori. "It's been a very busy year or so, but I've loved every minute of it."

"So why did you step back into the ring?"

Subtly worded, but it was still the question that Lori had been dreading. With a glance at Scott for some reassurance and conscious that Alice was hanging on her every word, Lori took a deep breath and began, "It felt like the right time and the right thing to do. I hadn't drawn anything for a long time then I did a small design as a gift. I guess from there I rediscovered my passion for creating a piece of art."

"Was this around the time you relocated away from Manhattan?" pressed Jen gently.

"Yes."

"Can you tell me a bit about that first piece by the second incarnation of Mz Hyde?"

"It was never meant as a Mz Hyde piece. It was an intricate Celtic knot design with a dragon entwined in it. Originally it was given as a gift but it has subsequently been re-used in several guises," replied Lori, conscious that she was being evasive.

"And you gifted it to Jake Power from the band Silver Lake?" Jen asked directly.

"Yes," said Lori, smiling at the memory of how thrilled Jake had been with the simple present. "The design belongs to him. Silver Lake used it as the cover of their first CD. It's appeared on Paul's drum head. Now it's incorporated into the imp design on Out Of The Shadows. It's the brooch that holds his cloak in place."

"Is there any truth to the rumour that the band all have it tattooed too?"

"You'd need to ask them that," laughed Lori. "I couldn't possibly divulge that information."

"Now you mentioned the imp design. It's been nominated for

a few music industry awards, I believe. How did he come about?"

Keeping it brief, Lori explained about the rush job for the single cover and how the imp had evolved from there.

"Can we expect to see more of him?"

"Most definitely. I can't say too much but watch out for the band's new record next month. He's already on some of the merchandise for tonight's show."

"And what does the future hold for Mz Hyde?" asked Jen, folding up her question sheet, indicating that Lori's ordeal was coming to an end.

"A slightly quieter few months. I've a couple of commissions in the pipeline. I also want to do another jewellery collection before Christmas. And, if the right opportunity presents itself, who knows!" answered Lori.

"Thank you for your time today."

"Pleasure."

A "thumbs up" from Scott was the final signal that Lori needed to relax. With the filming complete, he took a few stills shots of Lori with Jen then declared that she was free to make good her escape. Politely, Lori and Alice said their goodbyes, promising to catch up with Scott later. Once out in the hallway, Lori let out a long sigh.

"You didn't enjoy that one bit, did you?" commented Alice bluntly.

"Not really," Lori confessed. "But it comes with the territory. I just didn't feel ready to let it get too personal."

"I think you handled her beautifully," praised Alice. "Now, how about a strong coffee to recover?"

Checking the time, Lori noted they were due to meet the band for lunch in less than an hour. "How about we get some fresh air?" she suggested. "Assuming the storm hasn't hit."

"Fine by me."

Dark thunder clouds were gathering to the south of the area as the girls stepped out onto the boardwalk. For the moment, though, it was still dry and sunny. Slowly they meandered along, enjoying the warmth of the September sun.

"I wonder how Tom's getting on?" mused Alice almost to herself. "He's been so excited about being with the band. About seeing Todd. All he's talked about since we got here is Jake."

"He'll be fine," reassured Lori. "Jake'll look after him. Todd was due to arrive first thing too. How's Tom been since you went home?"

"He's had his moments," Alice confessed. "He starts a course at college when we go back."

"Todd starts next week too."

"I know. They've kept in touch all summer," revealed the English woman. "It's helped him a lot."

"And what about you?" asked Lori, pausing and looking straight at the young woman by her side. "Is Alice ok?"

"Alice has her moments too," she confessed sadly. "I miss him so much, Lori."

"We all miss him. I've watched the boys struggle with it day in day out. Especially Rich, although he doesn't say much."

"I've spoken to him on the phone a few times," said Alice, a tear sliding down her cheek. "He blames himself."

"I know," sighed Lori. "You can't go through life thinking "what if?" It'll destroy you. Hard as it is, you have to move on. You can't dwell in the past. I just hope Rich can reach that point soon."

"Is Jake ok?" asked Alice, wiping away her tears. "He's always so caring when I talk with him."

Lori nodded, "We've talked. He tends to work these things out through his music though. He still has his moments when he thinks I'm not watching. He tries not to let it show to make it easier for everyone else. He paints on that Disney Power smile."

Alice burst out laughing. "Disney Power smile?"

"Yes," replied Lori. "The public smile that hides the private person. The Disney smile. You'll see it this afternoon if you go along to the meet and greet session. It's taken him a while, but he's finally mastered it."

"Learned the technique from you, did he?"

"Yes," conceded Lori. "I'm an expert at it."

"I noticed earlier on as you fielded those questions," teased Alice as they both turned to head back to the hotel.

The first drops of rain were starting to fall.

"Some subjects are off limits. The Hyde Disney smile masks that."

Efficient as ever, Maddy had arranged a "family and friends" lunch back at the hotel. It was a relaxed buffet affair and, as Lori entered the room with Alice, the first person she saw was Lucy. Beside her at the table were her brothers and her father. Spying Lori, she leapt up from her seat and ran over to greet her future sister-in –law.

"Hi. We were getting worried about you," she cried, hugging her tightly.

"Hi, Lucy," said Lori. "We went to get some fresh air. Where's Jake?"

"Over at the buffet. His nephews are helping him to choose his lunch."

After greeting the Power men, Lori excused herself and headed towards the buffet. As she was piling some green salad onto her plate, Jake came up behind her.

"You ok, li'l lady?" he asked softly. "Scott said it was a tough interview."

"I'm fine," she assured him. "She didn't ask anything I wasn't expecting. I didn't answer the questions I wasn't comfortable with."

"Good for you," said Jake as he helped himself to some salad. "Are you coming over to sit with the Power contingent?"

"Of course. I'll be over in a minute," promised Lori.

It was the first time in almost six years that the entire Power family had sat round the one table. Overexcited at being in the hotel and at the thought of going to the concert, Sam and Josh were running about with Becky in the far corner of the room. Someone had found some balloons to entertain them and they were playing happily together, too excited to eat lunch. It gave the adults a few precious minutes to catch up with all the family news.

"Am I going to need ear plugs this evening, son?" asked Colonel Power with a grin. "I recall how loud you boys were the last time I heard you play."

"Probably," laughed Jake between mouthfuls. "Full stage set is a bit louder than we were at the launch party."

"I'll vouch for that," seconded Simon, remembering his trip to see Silver Lake in London. "What's the chances of Peter and I watching from the general access area?"

"Sure," shrugged Jake. "See Maddy. She'll get you in. There's plenty of reserved seats up in the balcony though."

"So what's the plan till show time?" asked Peter.

"We've a meet and greet session and sound check," said Jake, swallowing the last of his lunch. "We'll be done about four, four thirty, I'd guess."

After a quick debate, the other three Power males agreed to head to the casino for the afternoon. Lucy said she had promised the boys a couple of hours on the beach before the show. With security passes dished out to everyone, they agreed to go their separate ways until late afternoon.

On the other side of the dining room, the twins were stealing the show. Little Wren had been scared of Jethro, wailing loudly every time she saw him. Her brother, on the other hand, was a little braver, allowing the older man to hold him very briefly. As soon as their meal was over, Maddy reluctantly handed the babies back into the care of Paul's sister, promising to run back to the room at dinner time. With her children safely out of the way, the "business Maddy" returned and brusquely shepherded the band into the venue.

Already there were fans gathering outside and the lucky hundred VIP ticket holders got a cheer as they were escorted in out of the rain just after three o'clock. Fresh from the morning's video shoot, Scott had set up a photo area with a Silver Lake backdrop. The band patiently posed with each fan for a souvenir photograph. From her seat at the far side of the hall, Lori could see the "Disney Power" smile in full use and nudged Alice to point it out. Both girls laughed loudly, causing Jake to look over at them with a puzzled expression. Once the photos were completed, the band spoke to each fan for a moment or two, signed autographs, posed for even more photos and, to their great surprise, received numerous gifts. With the intimate part of the afternoon completed, the band made their way onto the stage to start their sound check.

While they were getting themselves sorted out, a small group of fans spotted Lori sitting at the side of the general access area. Before she knew what was happening, she was being asked to autograph various articles ranging from the fans' VIP tickets to their copies of Out Of The Shadows. Obligingly, she signed everything that was presented to her, then politely excused herself. With Alice in tow, Lori retreated to the sanctuary of the backstage area. Not wanting to miss the sound check, the two girls made their way to the side of the stage, arriving just in time to hear the band rehearse the opening to "Dragon Song."

Out on stage, Silver Lake were relaxed and joking quietly with each other, all too aware that their VIP guests were watching their every move. They ran through a few of the trickier bits for the evening's set and, with the help of their stage crew, adjusted the various settings until they were all happy. Before they brought the sound check to a close, Jake whispered something to the others, who nodded in agreement.

"Ok, folks," called out Jake. "We've decided to treat you to something a little special."

A resounding cheer went up.

"We're going to try one of the songs that will be on our new album for you. This is Engine Room."

The song Silver Lake had chosen was one of the heavier tracks on the album. Both Rich and Grey launched confidently into the intro, a riff that immediately caught their small audience's attention. Jake's vocal for the track was strong and powerful but with an edge of menace and darkness to it. Seeing the small crowd's positive reaction made all of them smile and relax a bit. As they finished the number, two of the VIP fans yelled, "More. Play another one, Jake."

"No more, ladies," he said, shaking his head.

"One more," they pleaded loudly.

Paul and Grey had already darted off stage and Jake could see that Rich had handed his guitar over to Todd and was poised to follow the others. Not wanting to disappoint the fans, Jake said, "Just a little teaser then. This is just between us."

With his back to the hall, he began to play the tribute track that they had named At The Beach. His hands were trembling as he played and he stopped less than a quarter of the way through the instrumental number.

"That's it, folks," he announced, trying to disguise the emotion in his voice. "See you guys back out here tonight."

Before anyone could stop him, he left the stage, wiping a tear from his cheek.

"Gary," he thought to himself. "That was for you, buddy."

Backstage, Jake walked in on a debate about the set list. Lifting a bottle of water from the fridge, he listened as Maddy debated heatedly with Rich and Grey over the proposed changes. Screwing the lid back on the now half empty bottle, Jake calmly but firmly said, "Stop this right now, folks."

"Tell Maddison she's out of line," snarled Rich angrily.

"You're all out of line," stated Jake, keeping his tone as level as he could. "Maddison, you don't want us to play Same Day New Life, is that correct?"

"Correct," snapped their irate manager sharply.

"Why?"

"It's out of place in the set list. Plus, three acoustic tracks together is too many," she explained, running her hand through her spiky hair in exasperation. "It's not what the fans have paid to hear. It's not what they want."

"Ok, I hear you. Boys, you want to keep the acoustic slot to three?"

"Yes," snapped Rich, with a glance towards Grey. "It gives you and I the breathing space we need. I'm worried that the whole set is too much for us to play."

"Can I suggest a compromise?" offered Jake. He saw and understood both sides of the argument.

"Throw your thoughts in," sighed Grey. "It can't make this fuck up any worse."

"Let's substitute Same Day with At The Beach," suggested Jake, almost instantly regretting the idea. "It still gives Rich a three song break and it gives me a few minutes to catch my breath. Maddison's right here, by the way. Three acoustic songs together is too many. I've said that right from the start."

An awkward silence hung in the air as they all stood looking at each other. It was Maddy, who spoke first, "Are you sure you want to play that one live?"

"No," confessed Jake openly. "But, I've just played part of it out there and those guys lapped it up. This was the big show that Gary was setting up for us. It kind of feels right to try to play it out there tonight."

"He's right," agreed Grey, looking over at Rich. "Well, Ricardo, what do you have to say?"

"I don't know," replied the guitarist, shaking his head. "It's a huge ask of you, Jake. Can you hold it together to play that out there tonight?"

Shrugging his shoulders, Jake said, "All I can do is try."

Without any further comment, Jake turned and walked out of the dressing room. He had no idea where he was going. He wandered down the corridor, eventually stopping at the fire exit. There was a stairway leading up to the left, marked "Staff Only." With a deep sigh, he sat down on the bottom step and put his head in his hands.

Back in the dressing room, Lori and Alice arrived to find the band still talking about the set changes. Anxiously, Lori looked round for Jake. When Grey filled her in on what had just happened, she sank down onto one of the couches, not believing what she was hearing.

"I'm sorry, Lori," apologised Rich, coming to sit beside her. "I started it. I was out of line. Jake was just trying to find the compromise. Trying to find the right answer to keep the peace."

"No need to apologise to me," she sighed. "But you never saw him out there playing the first part of it."

"That tough?" asked Maddy, regretting her own challenge to the agreed set.

Lori nodded.

Before any of them could say anything else, the door opened and Jason waltzed in with the promoter and two record company executives. If he realised that he had walked in at a bad moment, he never let on. With his usual flamboyance, he held court in the room as he introduced everyone. In the midst of everything, Jethro too had arrived and immediately noticed Jake's absence. Casually, he made his way across the room until he was standing behind Lori. Leaning over the back of the couch, he whispered softly in her ear, "Go and find the boy."

Excusing herself a few moments later, Lori got up and, leaning heavily on her cane for support, slowly made her way to the door. If anyone noticed her depart, they never said. The backstage area was a warren. She had no idea where Jake had gone. Trying to think logically, she guessed he would have tried to get as far away from the dressing room as he could. Following her gut instinct, Lori headed down the corridor to the very end, then was faced with a choice. Left or right? She listened to see if she could hear anything that would give her a clue. In the distance, she thought she heard something. It came from further down the left hand passageway. When she looked more closely, she could see the fire exit door and what she thought were the toes of a pair of Converse.

When she reached the end of the passage, she found Jake

sitting on the step, his head still in his hands. He looked up when he heard her cane on the concrete floor.

"Penny for them, rock star?" she asked softly as she sat down beside him.

"They're not worth it," he muttered hoarsely.

"You ok?" asked Lori, putting an arm around his shoulder.

"Yeah," he sighed, laying his head on her shoulder. "I just needed some space. All the press stuff. The meet and greet. The sound check. I didn't need the Rich and Maddy show on top."

"He's apologised," said Lori, hugging her fiancé tight. "You're all on edge. It's understandable. Rich feels bad about earlier as does Maddy."

"I just hope I can hold it together to play the damn thing."

"You will," she stated confidently. "I have complete faith in you. We all do."

"I don't know if I can play it straight after the two acoustic songs. They choke me up most times. At The Beach straight after them would kill me," he confessed.

"Split them up," suggested Lori. "Bring the acoustic slot forward, then play At The Beach nearer the end."

"That might work," conceded Jake with a nod. "What time is it?"

"Just after five," replied Lori, checking her watch. "Jason had just arrived with some suits before I came looking for you."

"Guess I'd better head back."

"Only if you're up to it."

"Come on, li'l lady," said Jake, getting up from the step. Helping her to her feet, he added, "It'll help knowing you're in the audience tonight."

Seated in the front row of the balcony, slightly to the left of the stage, a few hours later, Lori felt sick with nerves. On one side of her, Becky was sitting patiently waiting to see her daddy and her Silver Lake uncles; on the other side was Alice, equally excited at finally getting to see the band play live. When she had returned to the dressing room with Jake, there had been a few awkward moments until he cleared the air between himself and Rich. The four members of the band had discretely discussed tweaking the set further and, by the time Jake had gone to complete his vocal warm up, peace and harmony had been restored.

The support band, a recently signed act to JR Management, had played a solid forty-five minute set, the perfect warm up, and the crowd were buzzing. A gradual chant of "Silver Lake, Silver Lake, Silver Lake, Lake, Lake," began to build. Behind them, Lori could hear the fans pick up the chant. She glanced along the row at the rest of the band's invited guests. Linsey and Kola had arrived earlier and were sitting on the other side of Grey's mother. Lucy and her family were just beyond that. A tap on her knee brought her back to the moment. Eyes wide, Becky asked, "Why's everyone shouting?"

"They're trying to hurry things up," said Lori with a smile. "They all want to see your daddy as much as you do."

"Can I shout too?"

"Go for it, honey," laughed Lori as the little girl enthusiastically joined in the chant.

A few tiny flashes of light were the only hint the crowd needed. The roar, as the lights went up and Silver Lake launched into Dragon Song, almost lifted the roof off. As Jake stepped forward to the microphone, he looked straight up to the area where they were seated, then his focus returned to the song and the crowd in front of him. The fans sang along enthusiastically, their warm welcome melting away the last of the band's nerves. From her seat, Lori could just see Jethro and Maddy at the side of the stage.

After their second number, Jake called out, "Good evening, Atlantic City!"

The crowd cheered wildly.

"I can't hear you!" bellowed Jake. "Good evening, Atlantic City!"

He was rewarded with a resounding roar of appreciation.

"Ok," he grinned. "Much better. We're going to play a new one for you now. This'll be on the new record. This is Engine Room."

The reaction to the new song was fantastic. The fans almost immediately picked up on the chorus and were soon singing along.

Watching Jake and the boys command the stage made Lori's heart swell with pride. Seeing them perform from the fan's perspective, she wholly understood the magic that was being spun in front of her. Her rock star came to life out on that stage – a far cry from the emotional Jake of a few hours earlier. He had the capacity crowd eating out of the palm of his hand.

Six songs in and the lights dimmed for a moment before a single spotlight focussed on Jake perched on a stool centre stage. Lori just caught a fleeting glimpse of Todd scampering off stage, having handed over Jake's precious acoustic guitar.

"Still with me, Atlantic City?" he asked as he settled himself on the stool. The crowd cheered back. "Time to catch our breath a bit. Those of you who've seen us before will know the next two numbers mean a lot to me. Tonight they're even more special because "Lady Butterfly" is out there among you. If you know the words, please sing this with me. Lori, these are for you."

Beside her, Becky was jumping up and down "Uncle Jake's singing just for you, Lori!"

"Sh," said Lori, feeling her cheeks flush with embarrassment. "Let's listen to the song, honey."

Out on stage, Jake gazed out over the room full of Silver Lake fans and smiled. As he began the gentle intro to Lady Butterfly, he watched the audience in front of him light up as the fans held their cell phones high in the air. When he began to sing, they were each hanging on his every word. This was the kind of moment he had dreamed of and, knowing that Lori was out there among them, made it all the more precious. Stronger Within went down just as well with the fans as they sang along in perfect harmony with him. When the song ended, Jake stood up and bowed to the crowd before blowing a kiss towards the balcony.

"Thank you. That was beautiful. Very special."

A quick change of guitars and the rest of the band were back out on stage for the next section of the set. The audience went wild when they played Out Of The Shadows. Once they were finished that one, the tenth on the set list, Jake and Rich were moving into untested territory from a fitness perspective. Another two songs later and the moment Jake was dreading was upon him. Physically, he was beginning to struggle. His shoulder was throbbing; his ribs were aching; his heart was pounding. As the lights dimmed, he accepted his change of guitar from Todd. With trembling hands, he plugged the black Gibson into his radio pack.

Behind him, his fellow band members had gathered in a line in front of the drum riser, their heads bowed.

Unsure what was coming next, the crowd started their customary Silver Lake chant. Up on the balcony, Lori was on the edge of her seat, watching anxiously, as Jake stepped forward.

He rubbed his sweating palms dry on his jeans, then grasped the microphone with both hands.

"We'd like to take a moment now, folks," he announced, his voice ringing our clear and true across the packed hall. "Some of you may know we lost a dear friend back in July. He was instrumental in setting tonight up for us."

Avoiding looking up at the balcony, Jake continued, "His family are here as our guests. We wish he was here too. Gary, wherever you are buddy, this is for you. This is At The Beach."

The dedicated fans in the audience cheered Jake on as he took a step back.

Head bowed, his blonde hair hiding his face, he began to play the delicate French air intro to the piece before launching into the heavy frantic riff that ran through the instrumental. His long, slender fingers flew over the frets with graceful ease as he immersed himself in the solo performance. Focussing on getting through the next few minutes, he tried to block out the memories that were tumbling unbidden into his mind. Jake was all too aware of his three band mates standing silently behind him, paying their own quiet tribute to their late friend. His emotions threatened to spiral out of control as the number reached the final section, a return to the gentle French theme echoing the start. With tears blinding him, Jake made it note perfect to the very end. Emotionally, as well as physically, he was spent. As the last notes drifted out over the audience, he raised his head and faced them, his cheeks wet with his tears.

The crowd, who had been stunned into silence, erupted.

Up on the balcony, everyone, Lori included, her own cheeks wet, was on their feet cheering. Behind Jake on stage, his three friends were also applauding him. At the side of the stage, Maddy was sobbing openly into Jethro's shoulder.

Having taken a deep breath, Rich walked forward, accepting his guitar back from Todd en route, and stepped up to his mic, "Atlantic City, give it up for the incredible Jake Power!"

While the fans continued to cheer, Jake took a bow, then walked across the stage to the drum riser for a drink of water, taking his time and using the few precious moments to compose himself.

"Thank you," he said humbly when he returned to his usual centre stage spot. "This next one is off the new album. Ironically perhaps, this is Impossible."

By the time Silver Lake reached the last song of their encore, the ever popular, Flyin' High, Jake was exhausted- physically, mentally and emotionally. He felt himself going through the motions at the end of the show, flicking picks out into the crowd, reaching out to shake hands with those lucky fans in the front row, then, with a final wave, he led the band off stage.

Up on the balcony, Lori watched him disappear into the darkness at the side of the stage. Around her, the fans were beginning to filter out, heading for the exits, some of them still chanting "Silver Lake, Silver Lake, Silver Lake, Lake, Lake."

"Do we go and see Daddy now?" asked Becky, trying to stifle a yawn.

"Yes, we do," promised Lori, giving her a hug. "Let's wait till most of the people are away though."

"They were fantastic!" enthused Alice, standing up and gazing round the venue at the departing sea of rock fans. "Gary would've been so pleased with that set."

"Yeah, I think he would," agreed Lori with a wistful smile. "And with Tom for his technical support."

"I couldn't see him. Was he on stage?" asked Alice.

"He was down the back of Paul's drums most of the time," replied Lori. "I saw him passing fresh sticks up a few times."

"He'll live off this for months!"

"I hope so," said Lori as she stood up and reached down to pick up her cane. "Let's go and find the boys. Becky, take your Grammy's hand, please."

Once safely off stage and in the dressing room, Maddy was the first to reach out and hug Jake. With tears in her eyes, she whispered, "That was incredible. I've no idea how you did that."

"Thanks, Maddison," he said, kissing her cheeks.

Passing him a towel, Grey declared, "That was quite something, Jake. Quite something."

"I couldn't have done it," stated Rich, his own voice thick with emotion. "It was tough enough just standing out there while you played."

"You'd have managed it, Rich," stated Jake, drying himself off with the towel. "That said, I'm not doing that again. Tonight was a one off."

"Never say never," cautioned Paul, handing him a bottle of water. "The fans loved it."

"Hmm," muttered Jake as he wandered off towards one of the smaller dressing rooms.

It took Lori and the others almost twenty minutes to thread their way through the venue and round to the dressing rooms. As soon as she saw him, Becky flew at Grey, hugging him tight. Lifting the little girl into his arms, he kissed her forehead and asked if she'd enjoyed the show.

"It was awesome!" she said seriously.

Looking over at his mother, Grey asked, "Too loud for you, mom?"

"A bit," she confessed. "But what a show!"

Glancing round, Lori asked, "Where's Jake?"

"He's through getting changed, I think," said Rich, pointing towards the smaller dressing room at the back.

Knocking the door first, Lori entered the small room. Jake was sitting on a hard plastic chair, legs stretched out in front of him, head back and eyes closed.

"Hey, rock star," she greeted softly, closing the door behind her.

"Hey yourself, Mz Hyde," he said, opening one eye.

"You were incredible out there."

With a worn out smile, he conceded, "It felt pretty special."

"You ok?"

"I will be," sighed Jake, sitting up straight. "I'm fucked. My ribs are agony. My shoulder's screaming at me. I'm beat."

"At The Beach was beautiful," commented Lori, reaching out to take his hand. "You did Gary proud tonight."

"That was hard. Damn hard."

"But it came straight from the heart," she said warmly. "Everyone around us got that. It was perfect."

"Thanks."

A knock at the door interrupted them. The door opened and Grey stuck his head round, "Sorry to ruin the moment, but Maddy's wanting us to get cleaned up and cleared out."

"We'll be out in a moment," promised Jake.

As Grey closed the door over, Lori said, "Let's not mention the wedding tonight. Doesn't feel right."

"You sure?"

"Positive," she nodded as her fiancé got to his feet. "Tonight's about the band, not you and me."

"I guess you're right," he agreed, giving her a sweaty hug. "Ok, let's join the party. I don't know about you, but I need a drink."

Duty called for the band for the next couple of hours as they dined with their invited guests and the various VIPs that Jason had brought along. Obligingly, they all chatted politely and posed for photographs then shortly before two in the morning, Maddy rounded the boys up.

"Time to make good our escape," she whispered to Lori. "Head back to the studio suite. I've secured it for us to relax together for a few hours."

It took the band a while, but eventually they had each excused themselves and filtered away from the after show party. Not surprisingly, Jake and Lori were the last to leave. On the way up in the elevator, Jake put a protective arm around her and kissed her gently on the top of the head.

"One drink, li'l lady," he yawned. "Then I'm heading to bed."

"I've heard that before," laughed Lori, snuggling into him. "Let's see how this goes."

"You still sure about keeping the wedding news quiet?" he asked. "If it's only us then we could announce it."

"You're desperate to tell them, aren't you?" she teased as the elevator doors opened. "If the right moment comes up, you can tell them."

"Love you," whispered Jake with a sleepy smile.

Entering the large suite, Jake and Lori found everyone

sprawled about the room, relaxing with a drink. The TV was playing one of the many rock music channels. All of them looked exhausted. In one corner, Todd, Kate and Tom were huddled round a laptop, looking for fan videos online of the show. Rich was lying across the curved couch where Lori had sat during the interview that morning. On the floor beside him, Linsey sat curled up, her head resting on his thighs. Across the room, on one of the over-sized armchairs, Kola sat on Grey's knee sipping a beer.

"Lively bunch," commented Jake as he poured a drink for Lori and himself.

"It's late. It's been a long fucking day," muttered Rich, sounding more asleep than awake.

"It has been a long day," agreed Jake as he passed a glass of wine to Lori. "What's the plan for tomorrow?"

"Relax and head home," sighed Maddy from her seat by the window.

"My mom's staying on till Monday," added Grey. "Says I kept her out of the casino for too long."

"Where is she?" asked Lori, scanning the room.

"With Becky, I hope," replied the bass player.

"She's probably got Becky with her at a slot machine," teased Paul.

"It wouldn't fucking surprise me," muttered Grey, scowling at the thought.

As Lori sat down on the only empty chair in the room, she said, "Alice, what are your plans?"

"Stay on here for a few days," replied the English woman, trying to stifle a yawn. "We fly home on Wednesday."

"Ah! I meant to speak to you about that," began Jake, as he sat on the floor at Lori's feet. "Tom and I have it all planned out."

"You do?" replied Alice and Lori together.

"You're coming back with us tomorrow. Tom and I have an appointment on Sunday morning," explained Jake with a conspiratorial wink over at the teenager. "I'll drive you both to the airport on Wednesday."

"Jake," began Lori. "We can't leave until after lunch tomorrow."

"Why?"

"I've arranged for us to have lunch with your family before

they all head off," she explained. "Is that ok? Alice, you and Tom are more than welcome to join us."

Alice burst out laughing. "Jason's invited us to lunch."

"Lori," called out Rich, trying to maintain a serious expression. "Can we come to lunch? I'm feeling left out over here."

Giggling, Lori launched a cushion at him before declaring, "Jake, if we can't even organise this, how the hell will we organise a wedding?"

Jumping on the throwaway comment, Maddy asked, "Have you two set a date?"

Realising what she'd said, Lori blushed, then nodded.

"When?" squealed Maddy loudly.

"December twenty second," revealed Jake with a grin.

"But that's….." started Maddy, staring at Lori.

"I know," she interrupted. "At least this way I'll remember the date for a positive reason."

"Explain, Mz Hyde," said Rich looking bemused.

"It's the second anniversary of my accident," replied Lori quietly.

"Shit. Sorry," mumbled the guitarist. "Fuck. I feel like a jerk now."

"It's ok, Rich," said Jake. "You weren't to know. So, are you all free that day?"

A chorus of "Yes" almost deafened them.

"This calls for champagne!" proclaimed Maddy theatrically.

"Not tonight, boss," answered Jake. "I'm wiped out. How about we arrange something for Sunday night?"

"Deal," agreed Maddy. "Come out to the farmhouse. We'll throw a party for a change."

It was almost four thirty before Jake and Lori headed back to their room. Both of them were completely and utterly exhausted. Once there, they both undressed, collapsing into bed in virtual silence. As she snuggled in close to Jake, Lori asked, "Are you happy now that it's all out in the open?"

"Yes," he replied sleepily. "Are you?"

"Yes," she purred, her eyes closing. "Love you, rock star."

"Love you too, li'l lady."

Both of them slept late; slept through their ten thirty alarm call. They slept through the reminder call at ten forty-five. It was Jake's phone ringing that finally roused him just after eleven.

"Wha'?" he mumbled sleepily as he answered the call.

"So you are still alive?" snapped Maddy harshly. "I've had reception on the phone. They were worried when you ignored your pre-booked alarm calls."

"Never heard them," said Jake, sitting up in bed. Every bit of him ached and his head was pounding. "We're both fine. No need to panic, Maddison."

"As long as you're ok," she replied, her tone somewhat softer. "You need to be checked out by twelve. The bill's already taken care of. Hand the key card in on your way out."

"Yes, boss."

"Ok. We're heading home. We'll see you tomorrow afternoon. Come over about four."

"See you tomorrow, Maddison."

With their bags safely stowed in the trunk of the Mercedes, Jake and Lori went to meet Jake's family for lunch. They had agreed to meet Tom and Alice at three in the hotel foyer, giving themselves plenty of time for a leisurely lunch. When they walked into Johnny Rocket's together, the rest of the Power family were already seated and waiting for them. Jake's two nephews began waving madly at them as they approached the table.

"You're late and I'm hungry," complained Josh, as Jake and Lori sat down.

"Sorry. We slept late," confessed Jake, his voice sounding a little hoarse. "How's everyone today?"

"Dying," declared Peter, who was sitting with his sunglasses on.

"Likewise," muttered Simon. "But I won three thousand bucks last night."

"Don't give them any sympathy," cautioned Lucy with a smile.

"And how are you, son?" asked Colonel Power warmly. "When did you two stop partying?"

"Tired," confessed Jake. "It was after four before we headed to bed, I think."

"I'll be glad to get home," added Lori, her voice sounding tired. "It's been an intense couple of days."

After they had ordered their meal and the waitress had returned with their drinks, Colonel Power asked, "So what's next for the band?"

"We've a few days free then its promo stuff right through to mid-October and the record launch. The tour starts on November 17th in New York then we head to Europe around November 27th. We fly home on December 19th," replied Jake, feeling even more exhausted at the thought of it. "We have a date for you all to put in your schedules. Keep December 22nd free."

"Why?" asked Lucy, not daring to hope it was for what she was thinking.

"We're getting married," said Lori, smiling over at her fiancé.

"Really?" cried Lucy, eyes wide with excitement. "Where?"

"Really," assured Jake, putting his arm around Lori's shoulder. "It'll be a really small private wedding in New York."

"Congratulations, both of you," said Ben Power, glowing with pride.

Conversation throughout the rest of the meal was monopolised by wedding talk. Jake's brothers playfully cautioned against it while Lucy interrogated Lori for details. She offered to take Lori wedding dress shopping and to help in any way she could.

"The planning's still in the very early stages," said Lori eventually when she could get a word in. "We would like to involve the boys, though if that's ok with you and Rob?"

"Sure," agreed Rob, realising there only was one answer. "Doing what?"

"Maybe Sam could do a reading? And Josh could be ring bearer?" suggested Jake looking at his two young nephews. "Nothing too complex."

"It's a deal," said Lucy. "What about bridesmaids? And the best man?"

"Still working that out," answered Jake, "Now, enough questions for one day, little sister. Just make sure you all keep the date free."

By the time everyone had said their goodbyes and Jake and Lori had met up with Alice and Tom, it was almost four o'clock before they were heading away from Atlantic City. Traffic down towards Cape May and the ferry terminal was light, making the journey easier. During the ferry crossing, Jake excused himself and went to sit on deck on his own for a while. The intensity of the last two days, plus the show itself, had taken its toll on him. He was in desperate need of some private time. In the last of the day's September sun, it was cool on deck. Selecting a quiet spot in the sun, Jake lay out along one of the white benches and closed his eyes. His ribs were still aching and he gently ran his hand over them as he took a few deep breaths of the clean ocean air. The ache only served as a lingering reminder of the last two months. It struck him as odd that he could look at his reflection in the mirror every day and barely notice the scar below his eye, but that the ache in his ribcage brought it all back. Playing At The Beach had brought it all back too; had almost brought it all crashing down, but there was no denying that the fans had loved it. Paul's words about "Never say never" came back to haunt him. If need be, could he play it live again?

Having all of his family there had been strange. A good kind of strange he decided as he lay staring up at the sky. Lunch had been his first proper family meal since his mother's funeral. Seeing his two brothers tired and hungover, with their dad looking on in disgust, had brought back teenage memories of being at home in the kitchen with his mom claiming, "The boys are just tired, Ben" as his brothers sat suffering from the excesses of the night before. It made him wonder what she would have thought of the band. What would she have thought of Lori? What would she have had to say about their wedding? Before the maudlin mood took hold completely, Jake got up and went to stand at the guard rail, watching the waves. He loved the ocean. It soothed his soul.

Leaving the girls to enjoy a leisurely, late breakfast out on the sun deck, Jake drove Tom into Rehoboth on Sunday morning for their mystery appointment. In bed the night before, Jake had explained to Lori that he had arranged for Danny to do him a favour and open up for a couple of special commissions. As he parked the truck round the rear of the tattoo parlour, he spotted Todd running up the street.

"Am I late?" Todd gasped as they come round the front of the building.

"Not any later than us," joked Jake with a grin. "Now are you two sure about this? It's a huge commitment. If you want to back out, now is the time to do it."

"Sure," stated both boys in unison.

"Alright," said Jake, leading the way into Danny's shop.

As he opened the door to the tinkling of the wind chime, the familiar smell hit him. Hearing them enter, Danny appeared from the back of the shop.

"Good morning," he called out cheerfully.

"Morning, Dan," replied Jake. "I've brought you two tattoo virgins."

"Ah, fresh, unblemished skin!" laughed the diminutive tattoo artist, rubbing his hands together in front of him. "Welcome to my lair, boys."

Both of the teenagers exchanged nervous glances, then looked to Jake for reassurance.

"He's kidding, guys," laughed Jake, recalling how anxious he had felt about getting his first tattoo. "Dan, I have an order for two more Silver Lake knots. One for each of them. Same template as mine."

"Same as Mr Santiago too," commented Danny. "He was in last night. I thought he was the last of you. Miss Addison even paid me a visit, although hers is smaller and in a more discrete location."

"Maddison was in?"

"A few weeks back. Mid-August, I think. Are these specimens the last?"

"Has Scott been in?" asked Jake curiously.

Danny nodded, "He was in the same day as Grey and Paul. Can I expect Mz Hyde too?"

Shaking his head, Jake said, "I doubt it, but you never know."

"And what about you? Am I inking you today too?" enquired Danny, a hopeful edge to his tone.

"Not today."

"Pity," murmured the ink artist. "Right, who wants to sit on one of my thrones first?"

Todd stepped forward tentatively.

"Have you decided where you want the design, Todd?" asked Jake, feeling somewhat responsible for the boy.

"Same place as yours," replied his protégé as he took his jacket off.

"Tom?"

"Same," replied Tom. "I've ideas for my upper arms for another time."

"Ok, Dan, they're all yours," declared Jake. "I've a few errands to run. I'll be back in a few hours."

"I'll be gentle with them."

When Jake returned to the shop, he found Todd sitting on the bench, watching the finishing touches being put to Tom's tattoo. Taking a seat beside him, Jake asked if he was alright.

"Now I am," replied Todd. "I felt like shit at first. Nerves I guess."

"You'll be fine."

As Tom carefully pulled his T-shirt on over the dressing on his chest, Jake handed Danny a bundle of cash. Without bothering to count it, the smaller man stuffed it into his pocket.

"So when will I see you back on my throne?"

"I don't know," said Jake. "Don't worry, I'll be back. I've just not worked out the next one yet."

"Well, I'll be waiting to photograph the next one," joked Danny as he handed the boys their aftercare leaflets and a jar each of his magic healing cream.

"We'll see," laughed Jake. "Now, I need to get these two home. Thanks for this."

"Anytime, Mr Power."

Once outside, Jake invited Todd back to the house, but he declined.

"I'm heading up to Baltimore this afternoon. Classes start on Tuesday and I've paperwork to submit tomorrow first thing," Todd explained.

"Ok," acknowledged Jake warmly. "Take care. I'll call you during the week. Remember, if you need anything, call Lori or I."

"I will," promised Todd, giving him a hug. "Thanks for everything."

"You're welcome," said Jake. "Remember to keep November 22nd free. You're working for me that night."

"Will do," promised Todd.

Leaving him to say goodbye to Tom, Jake went round to the start the truck, A few moments later the passenger door opened and Tom clambered in.

"Alice is going to murder me," he laughed as he plugged in his seat belt.

"You didn't tell her?"

Tom shook his head.

"I'm not taking the rap for this," declared Jake as he started the engine. "You're on your own with that one."

The girls were still out on the deck chatting when Jake led Tom round the side of the house. Both of them looked up at the sound of their footsteps.

"Hi," called Alice. "Good trip into town?"

"Yeah," agreed Tom, taking a seat at the table. "Said goodbye to Todd. He starts college on Tuesday."

"I thought he was coming to the party?" commented Lori, looking up at Jake.

"Apparently not. He's heading up to Baltimore this afternoon. I told him to call one of us if he needs anything," Jake replied. "When's the boss expecting us?"

"Soon. She called earlier. I said we'd be no later than three," said Lori before adding, "How was Danny?"

"Same as ever. He was asking when you were coming back to see him."

Looking over at Tom, Lori asked, "Well, where did he put it?

Glancing nervously at his older sister, Tom swallowed before replying, "Same place as Jake's."

"And Todd?"

"Same," replied Jake, watching to gauge Alice's reaction.

"What are we talking about here?" she asked sharply. "What's been put where, Tom?"

"I got a tattoo," stated the teenager bluntly. "In memory of Gary. Same one the band all have."

"A tattoo!" yelled his sister. "Why in God's name did you do that?"

"I wanted to," said Tom, looking to Jake for moral support.

"Alice," began Jake calmly. "It's ok. It's all been expertly done. Each of us got one to remember Gary by. It was important to Tom to be included. I set it up with Danny. He's done a fantastic job."

"Let me see it," demanded Alice, glaring angrily at Jake.

Taking his shirt off, Tom carefully peeled the dressing off to reveal the raw design on his chest.

"You've got one the same?" she asked Jake without taking her eyes off her young brother.

"Identical," replied Jake. "Here, I'll show you. I got mine done first. Two days before the crash. After, the guys decided they would get the same design done to remember Gary by. Even Maddy has it inked somewhere."

Slipping his T-shirt over his head, Jake moved round to stand beside Tom. When she saw the healed Celtic knot, Alice sighed, "Put your shirts back on."

"Don't be angry, sis," said Tom, patting the dressing back into place. "This was important to me."

"Fine," muttered his sister. "It's done now. Don't let Dad see it. He'll kill you. He detests tattoos."

Cars were lining the driveway out at the farmhouse with several already parked in the front yard, including Kola's Harley. Wishing he'd brought the truck, Jake carefully reversed Lori's Mercedes onto the grass under the shade of a large oak tree. As they all climbed out of the car, they could hear music coming from the rear of the building. Taking Lori's hand, Jake led them round to the back yard.

"Afternoon," he called out loudly.

His fellow bandmates were already there, beers in hand, as were most of their road crew from Atlantic City. In the shade, Jethro was sitting contentedly on a rocking chair with Hayden on his knee.

"What's up, Jake?" yelled Grey with a grin. "You're not late!"

"Very funny."

"Jake!" called Maddy from the French doors. "I've a young lady here looking for her favourite uncle."

"Afternoon, boss," he said as he strode towards the house. "Where's my little Wren?"

"In the playpen," answered Maddy, stepping aside. "You're about the only person she'll go to without screaming the place down."

"I'm honoured."

With Wren snuggled into his shoulder, Jake wandered back out to join the party. The baby eyed the other guests with suspicion, burying her face into Jake's hair if anyone tried to talk to her. Both Paul and Maddy were busy playing at being the perfect hosts and, once everyone had arrived, including several people that neither Jake nor Lori recognised, Maddy called out shrilly, "Folks, can I have your attention for a moment?"

Soon all eyes were on her. Smiling over at Lori, Maddy said, "I got a call last night with two pieces of exciting "hot off the press" news. The first is that Jake here has been shortlisted as top new rock vocalist by MMR magazine."

A cheer went up and Jake felt his face redden in embarrassment.

"The second news," began Maddy, "is that Mz Hyde has also been shortlisted for her artwork on Dragon Song and for her zombie drain cover and for the last Weigh Station artwork."

Another huge cheer went up as Lori stared at her friend in complete disbelief.

"Your invites will be in the mail but the award ceremony is in New York on September 25th," finished Maddy, raising her glass. "To Jake and Lori!"

Chaos reigned over the party for the next half hour as everyone congratulated them both on their nominations. Eventually, Lori made her way over to Jake and wrapped her arms around him. Adjusting his hold on Wren, he put an arm around Lori and kissed her on the top of the head, "Congratulations, Mz Hyde."

"Likewise, rock star," she said with a giggle. "Guess we'd better dust off the glad rags."

"Can't I wear my jeans?" protested Jake.

"I doubt it," replied Lori. "I've been to that ceremony as a guest before. It's black tie. You may need to invest in a tux."

"That'll be the day," muttered Jake, loathing the thought of wearing a tuxedo. It reminded him of his high school prom night and that had been an unmitigated disaster.

Running his hand round the inside of his shirt collar, Jake viewed his reflection in the mirror. From her seat at the dressing table, Lori giggled.

"Glad you think this is funny, li'l lady," he growled as he undid his black silk tie. "There's no way I'm wearing that!"

"Relax, Jake. Stick the tie in your pocket for now."

"Remind me why I had to wear a suit?"

"Invite states formal dress," she replied, standing up and smoothing out the front of her dress. "That means a suit not jeans."

"Now, you look stunning," he complimented with a proud smile.

After a lot of debate between frocks, Lori had opted to wear a long, fitted black dress with a plunging neckline. It was more revealing than her usual choice but she had decided it was more appropriate for the occasion. The skirt of the dress was slit up to the thigh at the right hand side and, as she walked over to lift her bag and cane, Jake caught a glimpse of smooth sun-kissed skin.

"I'm losing the ponytail too," he muttered, untying the leather cord at the nape of his neck.

"Just be yourself tonight," soothed Lori, passing him the hairbrush.

"I'd be happier if I wasn't performing," he admitted as he dragged the brush through his long sun-bleached hair.

At the last minute, Weigh Station's management had contacted Jake and requested that he perform Broken Bottle Empty Glass with Dan. Weigh Station were scheduled to receive a lifetime achievement award and their three song performance was to be the finale for the evening. They had had time for one quick rehearsal at lunchtime but that was all that time had allowed.

"Time to go," said Lori softly. "Show time."

She had booked a limo to drive them across town to the Times Square hotel where the ceremony was being held. At first Jake had protested, but she had swiftly explained that it was expected.

As the limo pulled up outside the building, Jake took note of the crowds that were gathered behind the security barriers and also of the long, plush, red carpet.

"You never mentioned red carpet, Mz Hyde," he hissed nervously.

"Sorry. Must have slipped my mind," she replied with a mischievous wink. "Now remember, I need you to help me out of the car."

A uniformed attendant opened the door before Jake could reply. Taking a deep breath, he stepped out to a barrage of flash bulbs and screaming fans. He turned and offered a steadying arm towards Lori then discretely shielded her from view with his body position until she was out of the car. He hovered beside her until she had positioned her cane and was ready to walk across to the open doorway at the far end of the crimson runway. Keeping a protective arm around her waist, Jake guided Lori into the foyer, followed by cheers from the Silver Lake fans among the crowd. Once inside, just out of sight of the public, a journalist from the magazine approached them.

"Good evening," she purred. "MMR is delighted you could join us this evening."

"Thanks," smiled Lori. "It's an honour."

"And you're both nominated for awards. I think that makes you our only celebrity couple where that's happened," commented the journalist. "And, Jake, how are you feeling about guesting with Weigh Station later on tonight?"

"Nervous," confessed Jake, holding onto Lori a little tighter. "It's an honour to be invited to play with them. I've been a huge fan of theirs for a long time."

"Speaking of fans, there's a few of yours lined up outside. When can they expect something new from Silver Lake?"

"The new record comes out October 14th and we're playing a few shows mid-November," replied Jake.

"And, Mz Hyde," continued the journalist, returning her attention to Lori. "Have you done the album cover for Silver Lake this time round?"

"Yes," said Lori calmly. "But we're keeping it under wraps a little longer."

"You've received three nominations across two categories.

Were you surprised?"

"Completely," answered Lori honestly. "I only brought Mz Hyde back to life just over a year ago, so to be recognised for three covers in that space of time is just amazing."

"Three diverse covers too," commented the reporter. "I shouldn't ask, but do you have a favourite?"

"No," said Lori, shaking her head. "That's like asking a mom to pick her favourite child."

The journalist laughed politely, then spotting her next celebrity arriving out of the corner of her eye, said, "Thank you for your time. Good luck for tonight and, Jake, I'm looking forward to hearing more from you later on."

"Thanks," said Jake, guiding his fiancée towards the ballroom doorway.

A uniformed hostess greeted them at the door and led them through the maze of tables to one at the right hand side in front of the stage. The round table seated ten and another three couples were already chatting over a glass of champagne. Both of them recognised Tori from Molton and, to her right, Leo from When The Chips Are Down.

"Jake Power," declared Tori loudly. "Looking hot as ever!"

Blushing, Jake replied, "Evening, Tori. You look stunning."

"And Lori!" exclaimed the singer. "Love the dress!"

"Thanks, Tori," said Lori, taking a seat. "Need to look the part."

"Stunning as always," complimented Leo, raising his glass towards her. "Have you found my axes yet?"

"No," replied Lori. "I'm waiting for an email from a contact in Italy. One might be in a private collection in Milan. If it is, then it won't be for sale."

"Everything's for sale, Mz Hyde," he stated theatrically. "We just need to agree on a price."

"Do you guys know Zack? Drummer with Time March," introduced Tori.

"Pleasure," said Jake, shaking the long haired drummer's hand. "Loved Sands Of Time."

"Cheers," replied Zack. "It's why I'm here. Rest of the band are overseas. We're nominated for best new metal band off the back of it."

Before any of them could continue the conversation, the final couple arrived at the table. To Lori's surprise, it was Jason and Dr Marrs. The flamboyant Englishman was soon dominating conversation and pouring champagne for everyone. Being among familiar faces helped to settle Jake's nerves, but, conscious that he had to sing later, he declined a refill to his champagne flute with a polite, "Maybe later."

Shortly after eight, the compere for the evening took to the small stage and welcomed them all to the tenth annual MMR Magazine awards as voted for by the readers. From the programme that lay in the centre of the table, Lori guessed they were in for a long night as she scanned the list of award categories.

For the third year in succession, Tori lifted the award for MMR Rock Goddess. Having accepted her accolade, she remained on stage to present the next category. With her usual confidence, she read out the list of nominees then opened the matte black envelope tantalisingly slowly, "And the winner of the MMR award for the best new rock voice is the wonderful Jake Power from Silver Lake!"

"Shit," muttered Jake, feeling himself flush scarlet as all eyes were suddenly on him.

Everyone at the table was congratulating him as he got to his feet to go up to collect his award. Running his hand nervously through his hair, Jake walked up the steps towards Tori. She hugged and kissed him as she presented him with his crystal statuette.

"Thank you," said Jake humbly, holding the award up high. "My first ever! Thank you!"

"Ladies and gentlemen, the awesome Jake Power!" roared Tori, taking him by the hand and leading him from the stage.

A few minutes later, they arrived at the first of the two categories that Lori was nominated in. It was the MMR award for the best metal album cover. Holding her breath, she listened as the list of nominees was read out by Nick from Black Ashes. The iconic guitarist was older than the last time she had seen him, his black hair now streaked with grey. She noted his hands were shaking badly as he held the envelope.

"That's Kola's dad," Lori whispered to Jake.

He looked at her in disbelief but, before he could whisper his reply, the elder statesman of metal was opening the envelope.

"And the winner is Mz Hyde."

Her zombie drain design had won!

Taking her time, Lori got to her feet and, trying not to lean too obviously on her cane, she carefully negotiated the steps up to the stage. Chivalrously, Nick came over to take her arm, making a theatrical gesture of helping her. He bowed low before her as he presented her with the statuette.

"Thank you!" called out Lori to the assembled guests as she admired the modern crystal design. "Not a bad result for a design inspired by my laundry."

Everyone in the room laughed.

"You can do my laundry anytime, Mz Hyde," joked Nick with a wicked, slightly creepy, laugh.

"I'll pass on that opportunity, kind sir," laughed Lori, discretely stepping out of his reach.

She had barely sat down again at the table when Dr Marrs stepped up to present the next award.

"And to follow on from the award for best metal cover, we now have the nominations for the MMR award for the best rock album cover," he announced to the crowd. "I've been honoured to produce all three of the albums on this list. In no particular order, the nominees are…"

Nudging his fiancée, Jake said, "I wouldn't get too comfortable, li'l lady."

Lori giggled nervously and turned her attention back to Jim Marrs on stage.

Teasingly slowly, he edged the card out of the black envelope, read it, then nodded approvingly. With a small smile of satisfaction, he announced softly, "And for her outstanding efforts on Weigh Station's album, the winner is Mz Hyde."

"Told you," whispered Jake as he kissed her on the cheek.

With a flash of thigh, Lori got up from the table again and made her way towards Jim Marrs. The producer came partway down the steps to greet her and led her up onto the stage to a standing ovation and a thunderous round of applause from the invited guests.

"I think we all want to hear a few words from you this time,

Mz Hyde," prompted the producer.

Having presented Lori with her second statuette, Dr Marrs called out, "Ladies and gentlemen, I give you Mz Lori Hyde!"

With no speech prepared, Lori took a deep breath as she stepped forward to the microphone. "I'd just like to say a huge thank you to everyone who has welcomed me back as Mz Hyde. To all the fantastic artists I've had the privilege to work with in the past few months. And thank you to everyone who voted for my designs. It's been quite some year and it's an honour to be standing here. Thank you."

Placing a protective arm around her waist, Dr Marrs accompanied her back to the table. Jake stood up as she approached. Wrapping his arms around her, he hugged her tight as the flash bulbs from the press photographers went off like fireworks around them. Nuzzling into her neck, he whispered, "I'm so proud of you. Love you, li'l lady."

"Love you too, rock star."

A few minutes before the end of the award categories, one of the backstage staff came over to fetch Jake. With one last sip of champagne, he slid back his chair and slipped away from the table to prepare for his appearance with Weigh Station. Up on the stage, the editor of MMR was preparing to welcome Weigh Station out to accept their MMR lifetime achievement award. The veteran British rock band took to the stage to a standing ovation from the audience. With his usual theatrical flamboyance, Dan bowed to the guests. Accepting their award, he stepped up to the microphone and declared, "We've managed twenty-five years together. This award marks the start of the next twenty-five! Thank you one and all!"

The heavy, red velvet drapes behind them opened up to reveal the remainder of the stage, set up for the live set. Handing their awards to a member of staff, Weigh Station began to sort themselves out as the compere quickly ran through the extensive list of "thank you's."

"To bring tonight's proceedings to a close, ladies and gentlemen, it gives me great pleasure to introduce Weigh Station!"

The opening chords of one of the band's biggest hits had the crowd back on their feet, cheering loudly. As ever, Dan was the consummate professional, playing the room as if it were a sell-out stadium show. Sweat was running down the side of his face by the end of their first number. Wiping it away, he quickly introduced their second song, a slower rock ballad. At moments during the vocal, Lori detected that he was struggling a bit and wondered if age was catching up with his voice.

"We'd like to bring out the voice of the future to close the show with us," said Dan, his own voice noticeably hoarse. "It gives me enormous pleasure to welcome Jake Power out here."

From behind the velvet drapes, Jake stepped out onto the stage. He had abandoned his suit jacket and looked every inch the rock star in his dark suit pants and waistcoat with his crisp white shirt open at the neck. Clapping him on the back, Dan stepped to the side, allowing Jake to take centre stage. With a nod to the band, they began the intro to Broken Bottle Empty Glass. Despite the lack of rehearsal, Jake felt confident as he started to sing the hoarse, rasping lyrics. There was a warmth to his tone that hadn't been there before, but it lent itself to the song. In front of him, the small audience remained on their feet. He could see Lori standing, with a steadying hand on the table, watching his every move. As he brought the song to an end a few minutes later, he beckoned Dan forward.

"Ladies and gentlemen, give it up for the legendary Weigh Station!" roared Jake with a huge grin.

"And show your appreciation for the incredible voice that is Jake Power!" added Dan. "Thank you and good night."

The two singers exchanged a few private words, then Jake jumped down off the stage to re-join Lori. A member of staff had brought his suit jacket back to the table during the performance. Lifting it off the back of the chair, Jake put his hand on Lori's shoulder and declared, "Time to go, li'l lady."

"Where to?" she asked curiously, as she allowed him to lead her out of the room.

"Private party," he replied with a wink.

"Jake, I thought we agreed….." she began to protest.

"Shh," he interrupted. "Trust me."

It took longer than Jake anticipated for them to make it outside to their limo. The hard-core fans had waited all evening and begged both of them and the other departing celebrities for photos and autographs. Obligingly, they posed and signed their way down the red carpet runway, eventually making it to the waiting car. Sliding into the back seat, Lori watched as Jake leaned forward and gave an address to the driver.

"Rock star, where are we going?" she asked as he settled himself back on the seat beside her.

"Home," he replied, reaching over to kiss her.

"But I thought...."

"Shh," said Jake, kissing her teasingly again. "It's a private party. Just you and me. It's all arranged."

When the limo pulled up in the underground garage at the apartment building a few minutes later, the driver got out to open the door for them. Slipping him a generous tip, Jake said, "Remember the route I gave you. We want the press to think we partied like rock stars all night."

"Yes, sir," agreed the driver, pocketing the cash. "I believe I got you back here for four, sir?"

"Perfect. Thank you," said Jake, putting his arm around Lori's shoulders. "Night."

With a nod to the concierge as they passed through the lobby, they headed into the elevator hand in hand. As the doors slid smoothly shut, Jake pulled Lori into his embrace and began to deliver soft, sensual kisses to her neck, then worked his way round to her ear, nibbling it gently. When the door opened, he led her across the tiled hallway into the apartment. In the few short hours that they had been out, the entire lounge had been filled with bouquets of flowers. On the coffee table, between two large vases of red roses, sat a large champagne bucket with two bottles chilling in it. Two crystal champagne flutes stood beside it.

"How did......?" began Lori gazing round, eyes wide in wonder.

"I knew you had won at least one of the awards after rehearsal," revealed Jake softly. "One of the organisers asked me if the steps were going to be too much for you and what table would it be easiest to seat you at."

"And you never said!" exclaimed Lori.

"When we arrived, Jim told me he was presenting his award to you," added Jake. "So when you received the first one, I already knew you were getting the second one."

Laughing, Lori sat down on the nearest couch. He never tired of hearing her musical laugh.

"And you ordered the flowers before you came back here to get ready?"

Jake nodded.

"I love you, rock star," declared Lori. "Now, are we opening this champagne?"

Expertly, Jake wound the cork out without a huge bang, then carefully poured them each a flute, more bubbles than alcohol.

"Congratulations, Mz Hyde," he toasted as he sat beside her.

"Congratulations to you too."

Their awards were sitting on the table in front of them and as they sipped their champagne, Jake joked about them having "His' n' Hers" MMRs.

"Lord knows where we're going to put them," giggled Lori as she snuggled closer to her fiancé.

"Windowsill in the bathroom," he suggested, taking her glass from her.

"Perhaps," she mused.

Before she could suggest an alternative, Jake had reached over and begun to kiss her. His initial kisses were teasing and feathery then she felt the tip of his tongue between her lips. She needed no second invitation. Lifting her, as though she were a doll, Jake laid her on her back on the couch, amidst the soft plump cushions. With a sharp bite to her lower lip, he turned his focus to her décolletage. Nibbling his way along her exposed collar bones, he then ran his tongue down into her cleavage.

"I want to make love to you right here, li'l lady," he murmured, slipping his hand up inside the skirt of her dress. "This slit skirt has been turning me on all night."

As Lori arched her back, Jake slid her black lace panties down her thighs. Holding them aloft like a trophy, he commented, "A black lace thong? Naughty, Mz Hyde."

Blushing, Lori said, "No panty line that way."

Casually he dropped them onto the floor, then stood up to remove his suit pants.

"Leave the shirt and vest, rock star," she instructed with a wicked grin. "They've been having the same effect on me as the slit has on you."

"Your wish is my command."

With his shirt unbuttoned, Jake moved back over beside her and slowly raised the soft fabric of her dress to reveal her slim tanned thighs. Tickling her with his hair, he slowly kissed his way up her inner thigh, then returned his attention to her cleavage. As he licked the curves of her breasts, Lori could feel his erect penis pulse against her.

"Make love to me," she pleaded softly, running her hands down inside his shirt.

He needed no second invitation and entered her hard and fast. His urgency took her breath away, but two could play rough. Reaching up, she began to kiss his bare tattooed chest, then bit his left nipple hard.

"Like that, is it tonight, li'l lady?" he goaded quietly.

In the heat of their lovemaking, Jake manoeuvred her off the couch and, with her skirts tangled up around her back, he continued to thrust powerfully inside her as they lay coupled together on the floor. With a primal growl, Lori responded to his demands, and as she arched her pelvis up, encouraging him to penetrate deeper inside her, they climaxed simultaneously. Moaning softly, Lori felt her orgasm consume her in crashing waves as Jake collapsed on top of her. Spent, they lay together hot, sweaty and panting.

"Wow," sighed Jake, rolling over onto his side. "Where did that come from, naughty Mz Hyde?"

"Must be the effects of all of that champagne combined with the heady aroma of the flowers," purred Lori seductively. "Pour another glass and we can test the theory again."

The two empty champagne bottles lay on the floor under the coffee table, the glasses discarded beside them. Sunlight was flooding into the room. Wrapped in each other's arms, with Jake's suit jacket draped over them, both of them lay sound asleep on the floor.

An incessant buzzing noise wakened Jake. It took him a few minutes to realise it was his phone in his jacket pocket and that it was vibrating on his chest. He reached for it just as the vibration stopped. The missed call was from Dan but he'd left a voicemail. Slowly, Jake wriggled his other arm out from under Lori's neck, causing her to stir. Opening one sleepy eye, she asked, "What time is it?"

Looking at his phone, Jake answered, "Ten forty-five."

His fiancée groaned beside him.

"You ok?" he asked as he sat up. His back was aching after the night spent on the hard floor.

"Champagne's evil," she grumbled.

"Ah! Suffering?" mused Jake, feeling his own head pounding and a nauseous wave wash over him.

"You mean you're not?"

"A bit," he confessed. "I'll get us both a juice."

As he scrambled stiffly to his feet, Jake decided he was too old for spending the night on the floor. His back was in agony. Stretching and rubbing it, he hobbled through to the kitchen, still wearing his shirt and waistcoat. As he poured the juice, he heard Lori curse loudly as she got up from the floor. With a glass in each hand, he came back through to the lounge to find her sitting on the couch.

"Here, drink this, li'l lady," said Jake, passing her one of the glasses.

"I ache all over and my head's pounding," stated Lori bluntly as she sipped the ice cold orange juice. "It's been a long time since I've felt this rough."

"A hot shower will soon sort you out."

"Sounds like a plan," she muttered, abandoning her half-finished juice on the table. Stiffly she got to her feet, gathered the skirt of her dress in one hand and limped slowly towards the hallway. With a melancholy smile, Jake watched her go. Even hungover and dishevelled, she was truly beautiful in his eyes. With a sigh, he sat back and finished his juice. Remembering the voicemail, Jake picked up his phone to retrieve the message.

"Morning, Jake. If you're still in town, give me a call. If you can do lunch today that would be good."

Curious to know what the Weigh Station front man wanted, Jake called him back.

"Jake!" came the prompt and cheerful greeting from Dan. "Good morning to you."

"Morning, Dan. How's the head this morning?"

"Fine," replied the older man. "I was tucked up in bed, stone cold sober by two. You?"

"A bit rough but nothing that a hot shower and a strong coffee won't fix," admitted Jake, surprised to learn that the renowned party animal from Weigh Station had gone to bed sober.

"What's your plans for the day?" asked Dan, cutting straight to the chase. "I was hoping to catch up with you before I leave later."

"No plans as far as I know," replied Jake. "We could meet you for lunch around one."

"Just you and Lori?"

"Yeah. Where are you staying?"

"I'm at a friend's apartment down in the village," answered Dan, pausing to clear his throat.

"Where do you want to meet?"

"Somewhere quiet," said Dan.

"Why not come here?" suggested Jake, confident that Lori wouldn't object. Quickly he gave Dan the address.

"Thanks. I'll see you both around one."

Still curious to know what was going on, Jake left his phone on the table and headed downstairs in search of his fiancée. He could hear water running in the en suite. While he waited for her, Jake peeled off his shirt and waistcoat and put on the towelling robe that lay across the bed. He ran back upstairs to tidy away the empty bottles and dirty glasses from the night before, then called the concierge to arrange for lunch to be delivered for twelve thirty. Unsure what Dan would want, Jake opted for a mixed sushi platter from a nearby restaurant. When he returned to the bedroom, Lori was sitting at the dressing table, combing through her wet hair.

"Feeling any better?" asked Jake warmly.

"Ask me after I've had a coffee," she muttered.

"There's a fresh pot upstairs," said Jake. "We're also expecting company for lunch."

"What? Who?"

Quickly, Jake explained about the voicemail and his brief conversation with Dan. Both of them agreed it all seemed a little odd and when Jake added that his fellow singer claimed to have stayed sober the night before, Lori looked anxious. She had never known Dan to pass up the chance to party.

Punctual as ever, the Englishman arrived at precisely one o'clock. After instructing the doorman to send him up, Jake went out into the hallway to greet their guest. He too had showered and his long hair still hung in damp strands around his shoulders. The marble floor felt icy cold under his bare feet as he stood waiting for the elevator door to open.

"Jake!" called out Dan cheerfully as he stepped out into the hallway. "Thanks for this."

"Pleasure," said Jake. "Come on through."

He led Dan through the living room and out onto the roof terrace. It was a warm day and Lori had decided they should make the most of the fall sunshine and eat outdoors. As they passed through the forest of flowers, Dan joked, "Who died?"

"Just a little private celebration," laughed Jake.

"Nothing less than Mz Hyde deserves," commented Dan, looking round. "Where is the beautiful lady?"

"Right here, Dan." said Lori from behind them.

She was carrying two platters of sushi and, having set them down on the small patio table, turned to hug her guest.

"Congratulations on your awards, princess," he said, kissing her on the cheek. "Long overdue recognition."

"Thanks, Dan. It was great to see you and the guys picking up your award too. Great set last night."

"Saved by our mutual friend here," added Dan, with a nod towards Jake. "That's kind of why I'm here."

Lori and Jake exchanged worried glances, then Jake said, "Grab a seat, Dan, then you can explain all."

Nodding silently, the older man sat down at the table. Sitting beside him, Lori said softly, "What's wrong?"

"Why should anything be wrong, Mz Hyde?" he asked, a lack of conviction in his tone.

"Call it a hunch," replied Lori.

"Women's intuition," he laughed, prompting a spasm of uncontrollable coughing.

Quickly, Jake ran to fetch him a glass of water and, as Dan wiped his hand across his mouth, Lori noticed a smear of fresh blood on his skin.

"Sorry," apologised the older man, sipping the water. "Guess I need to come clean."

He set the glass down on the table and turned to Jake. "Are you free on the 31st of October?"

"I think so," replied Jake, trying to recall what Maddy had lined up for the band. "Why?"

"I need you to come to London for a few days. We have our 25th anniversary show booked for 31st October at Wembley Arena. It's been sold out for weeks. We've already announced that it will be our last gig for a while. Thing is, I don't know if I can last the whole set," explained Dan plainly. "I need you there to step in if needed."

"I don't get it," said Jake, looking confused.

"Dan," said Lori, realising what her old friend wasn't saying. "How serious is this?"

"Bad," he stated. "Very bad. I've been diagnosed with lung cancer."

Both of them paled visibly at the news. It was Lori, who recovered her composure first.

Reaching out to hug Dan, she said, "I'm so sorry to hear that. So very sorry."

"It's ok, princess," he said with a sad smile. "I've known about the cancer for a while."

"Is it treatable?" asked Jake, stunned by the revelation.

"They're trying," answered Dan. "Treatment's worse than the cancer. So, Jake, can you be there to save an old man's hide?"

"Of course," said Jake without hesitation. "Whatever you need me to do."

"That's what I hoped you'd say," Dan said with a sigh of obvious relief. "Let's eat, folks. All this cancer talk is killing my appetite."

Over lunch, Dan explained that very few people knew he was ill and that he wanted to keep it that way. He definitely did not want the Weigh Station fans finding out. As they chatted, they tried to work out a cover story that would explain why Jake just happened to be there and able to step right into the role if need be.

"Why not publicise that he's to be your special guest then your fans will at least expect him to be there?" suggested Lori. "Say he's going to guest on the usual two songs by popular demand."

"And then, on the night, if you need me to do extra, pass it off as food poisoning or something," added Jake, helping himself to the last of the sushi.

"Maybe," nodded Dan, deep in thought. "Worst case scenario is that you have to do the whole show. Think you can do that?"

"If I have to," agreed Jake. "Send me the set list as soon as you have it."

"Thank you."

They chatted for another half an hour, then Dan rose to leave, claiming he had stolen enough of their day.

"Can I call you a cab?" offered Lori, getting up from the table.

"No thanks, princess. I'm going to take a walk in the park for a while, then I'm getting picked up at four thirty to head to the airport."

"I'll walk you out," she said, signalling to Jake to stay where he was.

The two musicians said their farewells then Dan followed Lori through the apartment, out into the entrance hallway. While they waited for the elevator to arrive, Dan hugged Lori tight and thanked her again for her hospitality.

"Can I ask you something?" she said. "Just between you and me?"

"Of course, my dear."

"How long have they given you?"

"Three to six months at best," replied Dan quietly. "How did…?"

"I can see it in your eyes, Dan," said Lori still holding him close. "I watched my mom and dad die that way. I know that look."

"Not a word."

"I promise," she said as the elevator door opened behind them. "Take care of yourself."

"A bit late for that," he joked feebly as he stepped into the small lift.

When she returned to the terrace, Jake was clearing the lunch dishes away. Seeing the sad look in her eyes, he set the plates back down on the glass topped table and hugged her tight. Tears stinging in her eyes, Lori snuggled into his chest, allowing herself to be held.

"You seem to be taking this very hard," whispered Jake,

smoothing her hair gently.

"Perhaps," she murmured quietly. "I've known Dan a long time, Jake."

"I know, li'l lady."

"And I watched cancer kill my mom and my dad."

"Took my mom too," whispered Jake, hugging her closer. "He's a fighter. If anyone can beat this, Dan can."

"I hope so," sighed Lori, gazing up into her fiancé's hazel eyes. "I really hope so."

A cloud had been cast over their trip to the city and, after breakfast on Friday morning, Lori asked Jake if he would mind if they cut the trip short and head home. Keen to return to the beach, he agreed on the spot. By lunchtime, they were packed and in the car heading down the Coastal Highway. They were on the outskirts of Dover when Lori's phone rang.

"Hi, Maddy!" she called brightly.

"Hi, yourself. How's Manhattan?"

"Behind us," giggled Lori. "We decided to drive back early. We're just outside Dover."

"Oh!" exclaimed Maddy in surprise. "Why the change of plan?"

"Long story," replied Lori with a furtive glance at Jake.

"Want to come over for dinner and tell me all about it?"

"I don't know," began Lori.

"Wren's missing her Uncle Jake," Maddy pleaded. "And I could use the company. Paul's gone fishing for the weekend."

"You've convinced me," agreed Lori. "We'll be there in a half hour, but we can't stay late."

"See you soon, honey."

Both babies were screaming when Jake and Lori arrived. From the driveway, they could hear their frantic wailing. Deciding not to bother with the front door, they headed round to the rear of the farmhouse where they found a rather harassed Maddison pacing up and down the deck with a baby on each shoulder.

"Come here, princess," soothed Jake as he took Wren from her mother. Confidently, he snuggled her into his shoulder, kissing her red hot cheek. "Teeth?"

Maddy nodded as Hayden let out another sharp scream. "Both

of them are teething. Wren's first tooth came through a week or two ago, but Hayden's first is still to break through."

"Let me take him," offered Lori. "You look fried."

"They were fine when you were on the phone but when they woke from their nap, they kicked off," explained Maddy. "Give me rock stars to manage any day!"

"Yeah," laughed Jake. "We've got all our teeth."

"Very funny, Mr Power," commented the band's manager as she passed her son to Lori. "So tell me all about New York?"

"It's a big city with lots of tall buildings and a park in the middle," quipped Jake, causing Lori to giggle uncontrollably.

Her laughter stopped Hayden mid-wail and he stared at her with his eyes wide.

"Too funny, Jake," muttered Maddy. "Lori, come inside and you can tell me all about it,"

Following her friend, Lori said, "Not much to tell really." Then, with a mischievous wink back at Jake, added, "It's a big city with lots of tall buildings and a park in the middle."

"I give up!" declared Maddy as she stormed indoors. "You two are crazy!"

Adjusting her one-handed grip on Hayden and leaning on her cane with the other, Lori followed her friend inside. "I'm sorry, Maddy."

"I guess I asked for it," laughed her friend with a weary smile. "Teething has killed my sense of humour."

Noticing that Lori was struggling a bit with the wriggling baby, Maddy reached out and took him back into her arms, "So where are your awards?"

"In a plastic bag on the back seat of the car," confessed Lori, taking a seat at the big kitchen table. "Pass me him back. I promise not to drop him."

Handing the baby back to Lori, Maddy commented, "I thought you were staying up there until Sunday?"

"Change of plan," replied Lori before adding, "We had a visitor yesterday."

"Oh? Who?" enquired Maddy as she filled the water reservoir for the coffee machine.

"Dan, from Weigh Station, came over for lunch. He wants Jake to sing with them in London at the end of October."

"And I take it that Weight Station's number one fan said yes?"

"Well, I couldn't say no," replied Jake as he walked in. "Where do you keep your diapers? Your daughter needs some personal attention."

"Through in the nursery," said Maddy. "Do you want me to take her?"

"It's ok. I've got this," replied Jake as he headed out of the kitchen.

"He never ceases to amaze me," sighed Maddy. "He'll make a great dad someday."

With the twins finally settled in their play yard in the family room, Jake and Lori helped Maddy to prepare dinner. As the band's manager drained the pasta, she asked who had been presenting at the MMR award ceremony.

"I got off lightly," laughed Jake as he laid the table. "Tori presented me with mine."

"I guess I drew a short straw with one," Lori admitted. "Nick from Black Ashes presented me with the first one."

"Kola's dad?" quizzed Maddy with more than a hint of surprise in her voice. "How is he?"

"Not great," stated Lori. "He was definitely high on something. He wasn't even clean. The odour was obnoxious"

"I couldn't believe it when I saw him," confessed Jake. "The guy's a mess. Poor Kola. No wonder she moved east."

"He was in a bad way the last time I saw him," said Maddy, adding sauce to the pasta. "Such a waste of talent."

While they were eating, conversation returned to the Weigh Station show.

"I've been running through the promo dates in my head," began Maddy. "The Weigh Station show might just fit in nicely. I'm sure you and Rich are scheduled to be in London on October 24th and 25th."

"That would tie in well," agreed Jake. "I'm not sure how much rehearsal time I'll need or will have time for."

"How many numbers are you doing with them?" asked Maddy, curious to learn more about the plan.

"That depends," said Jake, glancing over at Lori as if seeking approval.

"Depends on what?"

"Dan's sick," stated Lori sadly.

"How sick?"

"Maddison, he's got lung cancer," revealed Jake quietly. "But he doesn't want that becoming public knowledge. Personally, I think he's dying."

"Dying!"

Lori nodded. "I recognised the look in his eyes. I saw it with my mom and with my dad."

"Same here," agreed Jake. "Saw that look in my mom's eyes not long before we lost her."

"So you could end up doing the whole set?"

"Potentially," admitted Jake sadly. "I've no idea. Plan is to rehearse the full set and play it by ear on the night."

"Shit," muttered Maddy, shaking her head in complete disbelief at what she was hearing. "No pressure then, Mr Power?"

"I couldn't refuse," he replied. "Could I?"

"I guess not."

Changing the subject, Jake asked what the promo schedule was for the coming week.

"You're free all week until Saturday, maybe Sunday," announced Maddy, rising to clear the table. "Then we fly out to LA for two days, two days in Seattle, a one-night stopover in Phoenix then back here on Saturday the 12th to get ready for the launch on the 14th. Launch party's been moved to the record company offices in New York so we may need to drive up there on the Sunday."

"Where to after that?" sighed Jake, his mind seeing an endless stream of airports and faceless hotel rooms.

"A couple of days off, then we head over to Europe for some promo," she explained. "Mr Power, you really should read your emails more regularly."

"Yes, boss," laughed the musician, getting up to help her clear away the dinner dishes.

During the drive back to the beach house, Jake was noticeably quiet, his attention focussed on the road ahead. When they arrived, he took the luggage through to the bedroom while Lori fetched them both a drink. Having been shut up for a few days, the house felt stale and a little chilled. Carefully, she made her way down to the basement to amend the furnace to its winter settings. Jake had come down the stairs behind her with his guitar cases. Setting them down on the floor, he reached out to hug her.

"Are you ok, rock star?" Lori asked softly, resting her cheek on his chest.

"Yeah," he sighed as he smoothed her hair and gently kissed the top of her head. "Hearing Maddison rhyme off the schedule brought it home just how quickly this all snowballs."

"We'll be in New York for the wedding before you know it."

"Seems a long way off right now, li'l lady."

"Twelve weeks."

"Are you coming with us next week?"

Lori shook her head. "You're not the only one with work to do."

"But you'll come to London at the end of October?"

"Of course," promised Lori. "For a few days."

"And what about the tour?" asked Jake hopefully, dreading the thought of being away from her for almost a month.

"Maddy has that all sorted," she replied. "I'll meet up with you in Glasgow for your birthday and stay until after the Paris show. I've a wedding to organise, remember."

"What about the shows we play here before we go overseas?"

"I'll come to New York, Philly and Baltimore."

"Thanks, li'l lady," he said, squeezing her tight. "Guess we'd best make the most of this week off together."

♫

Rain battering off the windows wakened Lori next morning. Beside her the bed was empty, the sheets long cold. A glance at the clock informed her it was almost nine thirty; the aroma from the kitchen suggested Jake was making breakfast. Wearing only one of Jake's Molton T-shirts, Lori wandered barefoot down the hall in search of her morning caffeine fix. As she limped in, she spotted that her fiancé was on the phone. His expression was serious, but, from his tone of voice, she couldn't fathom out who he was talking to. Trying not to make too much noise, she poured herself a coffee, then took a seat at the table.

"Morning, sleepy," he said a few minutes later as he slipped his phone into his jeans pocket. "Fancy a trip to Dover later?"

"Dover? Why?" asked Lori curiously.

"That was Pete on the phone, begging a favour," began Jake, pouring himself a fresh coffee. "The band he had booked to play on the base tonight are stuck in Canada. Missed their flight and can't get here on time. He was looking for some help. Wants me to bail him out."

"Tonight?" exclaimed Lori. "That's short notice, Jake!"

"You're telling me!"

"Are you going to do it?"

"I need to clear it with Maddy first, then see if Rich is up for it. Paul and Grey are both away till tomorrow night."

"And if Rich isn't up for it?"

With a nervous laugh, Jake declared, "It could be the first and last solo Jake Power show!"

Giggling into her coffee mug, Lori asked, "How are you going to pull a set together at such short notice, rock star?"

"I'll figure something out," he muttered. "Somehow."

Half an hour later, Jake had been given the managerial seal of approval, on the condition that he didn't play any of the new, unheard material from Impossible Depths. Tracking Rich down proved to be more of a challenge. By lunchtime, Jake had left messages everywhere for his fellow bandmate but no one had seen or heard from him. Eventually, just after two, Rich called.

"Afternoon," he called out cheerfully. "You were looking for me?"

"Everywhere," grumbled Jake before quickly explaining about his dilemma.

"Shit. There's no way I can be back in time," apologised Rich. "I'm at my sister's in Florida until Thursday. When Maddy said we had a few days off, I jumped on the first flight."

"No worries. It was a big ask," replied Jake, feeling the nerves beginning to swarm in the pit of his stomach. "The Jake Power Solo Show is about to debut."

"You're going to do it?"

"Don't want to let Peter down. It took a hell of a lot for him to ask," said Jake. "I'll pull something together by tonight."

"Let me know how it goes, buddy."

"Will do," promised Jake. "See you when you get back."

Driving through the gates and security check at the airbase a few hours later stirred up old memories for Jake. Beside him in the passenger seat, Lori commented that it was the first time she had been to any kind of military base.

"I lived here for years," recalled Jake, a hint of sadness to his voice. "We moved off base when I was about twelve, I'd guess. Feels kind of surreal being back here."

It only took him a few minutes to find his way to the low building that housed the base's main bar. As promised, Peter was waiting outside for him, casually leaning against the wall under a lamp post. Recognising the truck, he stepped forward to greet them.

Lowering the window, Jake called out, "Hi. Where should I park?"

"Round the back. There's a couple of spaces back there. Will I send someone out to help with your gear?"

"Please."

Show time was set for twenty-one hundred hours and, with half an hour to go, the room was packed. Word had travelled fast across the base that their entertainer for the evening was the lead singer with Silver Lake. In a small room at the back, little bigger than a broom closet, Jake was pacing back and forth nervously. Before the bar had opened, he had set up his guitars and microphones on the small stage, but had barely had enough time for a sound check.

"Relax," said Lori as she wrapped her arms around his waist.

"Easy for you to say," he muttered, burying his face in her neck. "I've never played solo before. Never!"

A knock at the door interrupted them as Peter stuck his head round, "Can I come in?"

"Of course," said Lori before Jake could object.

Closing the door behind him, Peter said, "I can't thank you enough for doing this."

"Tell me that after I've played," joked Jake. "This is scaring the shit out of me."

"Why? There's only a couple of hundred folk out front, said Peter, looking and sounding genuinely surprised to hear that his young brother was nervous. "I've watched you play in front of thousands."

"Yeah, but there were four of us!" commented Jake, running his fingers through his hair. "I've never done it solo before."

"You'll be fine," assured Peter and Lori in unison.

"When this is over, big brother, you're buying me a stiff drink."

"Deal," agreed Peter. "Lori, do you want to come out and take your seat?"

"I'll be right out," promised Lori with a wink. "Let me grab my camera bag."

"Camera?" exclaimed Jake, eyes widening.

Lori giggled, "Miss Lucy's orders."

A couple of minutes after nine, Peter climbed up onto the low stage. For a second, he got a taste of how his young brother felt as everyone in the room turned to stare at him. Swallowing hard, he announced, "It gives me great pleasure to welcome someone very special out onto our humble stage. He's an international rock star. A local hero and my kid brother. Give it up, guys, for Jake Power from the mighty Silver Lake!"

To a rowdy cheer and a lot of whistling, Jake stepped nervously out of the shadows and onto the small stage. He settled himself on the stool that had been placed centre stage and reached for his favourite acoustic guitar. With a nervous smile towards the small audience, he bowed his head and began to play an acoustic version of Dragon Song. It wasn't a variation that Lori had heard before and she sat as mesmerised as the rest of the crowd. Jake's strong vocal rang out across the bar-room, showing no hint of the nerves that had been tormenting him all day.

As the cheers died away at the end of the song, Lori watched as her fiancé took a deep breath then let his shoulders relax. A good sign.

"Good evening," began Jake, gazing out across the crowded room. "For those of you who aren't familiar with Silver Lake, that was Dragon Song, our first hit single and standard show opener."

A loud, raucous chant of "Silver Lake, Silver Lake, Silver Lake, Lake, Lake," came from a group in the middle of the room.

"Whew, some fans!" laughed Jake. "I'm going to play a mix of stuff for you tonight. My brother didn't give me much notice for this so the set list is kind of fluid, shall we say. I've picked some fan favourites, some personal favourites and a few classics, just to be safe. Be gentle with me, folks. This is the first ever Jake Power Solo Show."

"First of many!" yelled an airman from the bar.

"Let's see how this one goes first!" said Jake. "Here's a Bon Jovi classic. Wanted Dead or Alive."

While Jake relaxed into his performance, Lori quietly slipped out of her seat and moved over to the side of the stage to capture the intimate moment for Lucy. It had been a long time since she had shot a show; a long time since she had done any professional photography. Her hands shook a little momentarily as she realised it was the first time she had ever attempted to photograph her rock star on stage. If Jake noticed her, he never let it show.

"Ok, folks. Still with me?" asked Jake after the sixth number on his list. The hastily handwritten set list was taped to the floor at his feet. Taking a sip from his water bottle, Jake reached over to change guitars. "The next two numbers are acoustic favourites in the Silver Lake set. Both of these are very personal to me, not just because I wrote them, but because they were written for a very special person in my life. The first one is Stronger Within and the second will be Lady Butterfly."

Watching as Lori lifted a different camera from the table in front of her, Jake added, "Mz Hyde, these are for you, li'l lady."

Swiftly, Lori set up the camera on a small table top tripod, pressed record, then sat back to enjoy Jake perform the two Silver Lake favourites. Perhaps it was the more intimate setting or the fact that the whole show was so stripped back, but Lori felt that she had never heard Jake perform the songs with such soul and passion. Around her, the audience was hanging on his every word. No one was singing along. It was simply her man and his music. As the final notes of Lady Butterfly died away, the place erupted and everyone was on their feet cheering.

"Thank you," said Jake humbly. "Now, how to follow that?"

He glanced down at his set list, then winked over at Lori.

"Can you guys keep a secret?" he asked, flashing the crowd a "Power" smile.

"Yeah!" came a call from the back of the room.

"We've a new record due out in a couple of weeks and I was warned not to play any of the new material but, what the hell! I'm among friends, right?" he said. "This is on the new record, just don't tell the guys I played this. Or our manager, Maddison. She'll skin me alive! This is a track called Depths."

Focussing his attention, Jake began to play a very soft, eerie intro piece and to whistle with an almost ghost-like quality. When the lyrics began, he kept his vocal soft but slightly higher in his range than the norm, maintaining a haunted edge as the lyrics spun a tortured tale of drowning and despair. From her seat, Lori recognised the lyrics, but not the arrangement. The song was more than half way through before the penny dropped – the album version was probably the heaviest track on Impossible Depths. If she was honest, she preferred this version.

When the song was over, Jake changed guitar again, "Now, remember that one was just between us. The album version's a little different."

Settling himself back on the stool, he introduced the next song, "I've been a huge fan of this band since I was a kid and was fortunate enough to get to share the stage with them on their last tour and again last week in New York. I've an enormous amount of respect for these guys. It was an honour to be asked to play and record this with them. This is Weigh Station's Broken Bottle Empty Glass."

Almost an hour later, Jake reached the final number on his list.

"Guys, you've been incredible tonight," said Jake sincerely. "When Peter called this morning and asked me to play here tonight, I almost refused. I'm glad I didn't. This has been a very special evening for me. Thanks to each and every one of you for being a part of the first ever Jake Power Solo Show. I'm going to leave you in true Silver Lake fashion. This is Flyin' High."

With a well-earned beer in his hand, Jake sat down beside Lori and his brother and said simply, "Well?"

"I don't know how you do it," declared Peter, shaking his head. "When I think of the wailing and caterwauling that used to come out of your room. How did you ever transform it into that?"

Laughing and blushing, Jake replied, "A lot of caterwauling practice!"

"I'll second that," giggled Lori as she placed her hand on his thigh. "You were amazing up there tonight, rock star."

"You're biased."

"No, she's right," said Peter. "I can't thank you enough for this."

"Couldn't see you stuck," answered Jake. "Did you get enough photos for Lucy Lou?"

"I hope so," said Lori. "And some video too. I'll sort it all out tomorrow."

"You didn't video Depths, did you?" he asked, panic rising in his voice.

Lori shook her head, "Your secret's safe."

Around them, the bar was beginning to empty. Only the table of bona fide Silver Lake fans were still drinking and chatting. They kept nodding and pointing towards where Jake and Lori were seated. Finishing his beer, Jake excused himself and stepped back up onto the stage to pack up his guitars. It was the catalyst the fan table needed and one of the younger looking fans came up behind him.

"Excuse me, Jake," he said politely. "My buddies and I were wondering if we bought you a couple of beers would you play another couple of songs?"

"Well, I don't know," began Jake. "It's getting late and we've an hour long drive home."

"Just a couple? It's not every day your rock idol plays your local bar," pleaded the young airman hopefully. "Please?"

"Idol?" laughed Jake, genuinely amused by the thought. "Ok. Buy me a beer and I'll be over to your table in a few minutes."

"For real?"

"For real. Just let me pack up some of my gear first," agreed Jake. "And, if you and your friends don't mind, I'll bring Mz Hyde over too."

"Thanks, sir."

With all bar one of his guitars packed up and stowed in the truck, Jake led Lori over to join the six young airmen at their table. As promised, a chilled bottle of beer was waiting for him.

"Thank you," said Jake, raising the bottle politely to them. "Did you enjoy the set?"

"It was awesome," declared one of them before blushing with embarrassment.

"Glad you enjoyed it. Now, you said I had to earn this beer," teased Jake. "Did you have something in mind for me to play?"

Suddenly, with their "idol" sitting among them, their earlier bravado evaporated and all six of them exchanged anxious glances before one of them said, "How about Out Of The Shadows?"

"Ok, guys," agreed Jake, lifting his guitar.

"Jake," interrupted Lori softly. "Any objections if I record this one for Lucy?"

"Go for it, li'l lady," he replied with a relaxed smile. "An exclusive to keep my little sister happy."

The six fans sat bewitched as Jake calmly played and sang the Silver Lake song just for them. Over at the bar, Peter was keeping an eye on them, smiling proudly at his young brother. He knew the six young airmen well and guessed they would be bragging about this moment for weeks to come.

"Ok," declared Jake when the song was done. "Anything else?"

"I saw you guys play Atlantic City and you played an amazing solo," began one of the boys. "Could you play it?"

With a heavy sigh, Jake stared down at his guitar, then looked over at Lori for reassurance. She could see a mix of emotions in his eyes and was unsure as to how he was going to react to the request.

"Big ask," he eventually said, pausing to take a mouthful of his beer. "I declared that night after the show that I'd never play it again. Paul said "Never say never." Looks like he was right."

"If it's too big an ask…."

Jake shook his head. "I'll give it my best shot."

"Why's it so hard?" asked one of the six bluntly.

His friend hit him hard on the shoulder and told him to "Shut the fuck up."

"Sorry."

"It's ok," said Jake quietly. "The solo's on the new record as a tribute to our friend and manager, Gary. He was killed out on the Coastal Highway at the intersection with Route 9. The last thing he said was to waken him when we got to the beach. We never got him there. It's called At The Beach."

Before any of them could say another word and before his nerve gave out, Jake began the delicate French air intro. Without a word, Lori left the camera recording.

Keeping his head bowed, Jake allowed his hair to cascade over his face. Hidden under this veil, he focussed on the acoustic version of At The Beach. He was still acutely aware of everyone's eyes on him, but he remained calm, keeping his emotions in check. Part way through the number, he felt composed enough to raise his head and smile at Lori. The ghosts of the song were being laid to rest as he played. For the first time, he enjoyed playing it. In his head, he could still hear Gary, still see him smile. When the song returned to the lilting French air, Jake bowed his head again, but this time there were no tears, only smiles.

"Well done," whispered Lori when he finally looked up.

"Thanks," he said simply, reaching over to kiss her. Laying his guitar against the chair, he lifted his beer and drank deeply from the bottle.

Peter chose that moment to come striding over. "Guys, the bar manager needs to lock up in ten minutes."

"Time for one more?" asked one of the airmen hopefully. "Mz Hyde, you choose one."

"Your call, li'l lady," agreed Jake, winking over at the airmen. "Bet I know what she'll pick."

"Oh, you do, do you?" giggled Lori, knowing full well that he expected her to request Simple Man. She paused for a few seconds, then said, "How about Bad Company's Shooting Star?"

"Lord, I've not played that for years!" exclaimed Jake as he reached for his guitar. "But, your wish is my command, Mz Hyde. Jesus, I hope I can remember the words!"

He began the intro, then paused, unaware that the camera was still recording. "This could be a fail of epic proportions."

With a deep breath, he started the song again. From the looks on his young audience's faces, it was obviously a song most of them were unfamiliar with. Only one of them seemed to know it. When Jake reached the final chorus, the boy joined in, harmonising perfectly.

"Well done," complimented Jake with a nod towards the younger man.

"Thanks. My dad loves that song."

"Christ, now I feel old," laughed Jake, passing the boy his guitar pick. "On that note, I'm done, guys."

While Jake went to put his guitar back in its case, Lori discretely switched off the camera. The six younger men finished their drinks and rose to leave.

"Can I borrow all of you for a moment?" asked Lori as Jake returned to the table. "Last photo of the night. Peter, can you come over here too?"

"Yes, ma'am," sighed her future brother-in-law.

With the seven members of the air force grouped together and Jake positioned in the centre, Lori expertly fired off a few shots.

"Anyone else need a keepsake photo?" she asked.

"Can you email me a copy of that one?" suggested one of the boys.

"Sure. I'll send it over to Peter tomorrow," promised Lori. "Guess it's time we headed home, rock star."

Guitar case in hand, Jake draped his other arm around his fiancée's shoulders. "Thanks for the beer, boys. I'll see you around. Stay safe."

"I'll walk out with you both," offered Peter.

Beside the truck, in the dark, Jake hugged his brother.

"Thanks for inviting me along tonight," Jake said sincerely. "It's taught me a few things. Laid a few fears to rest."

"Will you come back another time? Maybe bring the rest of the band?"

"Don't push your luck," joked Jake. "We'll see in the spring. Things are a bit busy over the next few months."

"Safe journey home, guys."

"Night."

The highway was quiet as Lori drove them back towards Rehoboth. She rarely drove Jake's beloved truck, hating its manual transmission. As they had exited the base, bidding the security guards on the gate good night, Jake had turned on the radio to a local classic rock station. The original version of Simple Man was the first song they heard. Sitting in the passenger seat, Jake began to laugh.

"What's so funny?" asked Lori as she wrestled the truck up a gear.

"I was so sure that was what you were going to ask me to play back there."

"Never assume," giggled Lori, filling the cab with the sound of her musical laughter.

Jake smiled across at her. "You enjoyed that show tonight, didn't you?"

"More than I thought I would," confessed Jake reflectively. "I felt a bit naked up there on my own at first. It was quite intense."

"I thought it was fantastic."

"As long as the audience went home happy, I've done my job," he sighed. "I'm wiped out now, though."

Later, still entwined in each other's arms after making love, Lori ran her fingernail lightly round the Silver Lake knot inked on Jake's chest. A tremor ran through him as her tender touch tickled and he pulled her closer to prevent any more tickling. Gently, he kissed the top of her head.

"Time to get some sleep, li'l lady," he murmured sleepily.

"Can I confess something first?" said Lori, nuzzling closer into him.

"What have you done, Mz Hyde?"

"Videoed more of tonight than you think," she whispered nervously. "I recorded all three songs that you played for those guys at the end, but I also recorded three others from the main set.

If the quality's ok, I'd like to share them all with Lucy."

"You're devious," he said sleepily. "You know I'm too tired to argue with you."

"I love you, rock star. Night night."

With all the household chores taken care of and Jake dispatched to the food store, Lori settled herself at her desk, with a fresh mug of coffee, to transfer the photos and video from her cameras. Uploading the files onto her laptop was the easy bit. Taking her time to study each photo, Lori pulled off a separate folder of the images she wanted to use. Her plan was to edit them, then create an album for Lucy to use on the fan site that reflected Jake's solo show. Some of the shots lent themselves to a monochrome look and, with a filter duly applied, Lori was secretly proud of the results. Happy with the photographs, she turned her attention to the video files. Even at college, video had held little attraction for her, but she had the appropriate software to help convert and enhance the files.

"Lori!"

Jake's call from the kitchen half an hour later interrupted her train of thought.

"Through here," she called back from the study.

"Guess who I ran into at the Giant?"

"Who?"

She listened as she heard footsteps coming through from the kitchen.

"Me," said Scott sounding almost shy as he appeared in front of her desk.

"Perfect timing!" declared Lori with a relieved smile. "I was just about to call you for help. I thought you were still out of town."

"I was meant to be," replied the young British filmmaker. "Last minute change of plan. I flew back last night. Project's on hold."

Coming through to join them, Jake added, "I thought you might want Scott's input with some of the stuff from last night. Was I right, li'l lady?"

"Spot on," replied Lori, getting to her feet. "Scott, take the helm. I'm losing the battle with these video files."

"What's the problem?" he asked, coming round to sit at the desk.

"I'll leave you both to it, shall I?" suggested Jake, realising he would just be in their way. "I'll put the groceries away, then fix lunch."

"Sounds good," answered Lori distractedly. "Can you put the laundry in the dryer too please? This shouldn't take too long. It's only a few files."

Leaving Scott and Lori discussing the videos, Jake returned to the kitchen. Moments like this made him appreciate how surreal his world could be. A few days ago, he had been on the red carpet and been centre stage. Now, he was grocery shopping and doing laundry. Normal everyday chores were the rocks that kept him grounded, he decided, as he stowed the chilled goods in the refrigerator. With a smile, he folded the empty grocery sacks and turned his attention to the laundry. As the dryer hummed away in the background, Jake busied himself in the kitchen preparing lunch. Deciding to make life easy for himself, he heated some soup and made some grilled cheese sandwiches. Nothing fancy.

"Lunch!" he called out a few minutes later.

He could hear Lori and Scott coming through from the study as he dished up the bowls of chicken soup.

"Not every day a rock star makes my lunch," joked Scott as he sat at the table. "Thanks, Jake."

"How are the videos looking?" asked Jake curiously.

"I'd better watch my back," teased Scott. "Lori's done an outstanding job considering the cameras she was using. We're almost done. Looks like you played a good set last night."

"Considering it was thrown together at a couple of hours' notice, it went well."

"Don't be so modest, rock star," said Lori. "You were brilliant last night. I have a feeling it won't be the last Jake Power Solo Show."

"Harrumph," muttered an embarrassed Jake. "We'll see."

After lunch, the three of them crowded round Lori's laptop to view the video footage. Watching himself on the small screen made Jake cringe, but he could see that the footage was simple and effective. The young film maker was right. Lori had done an excellent job. When they reached the film shot after the show, Lori had converted it to black and white. Between them, they had decided to leave in the casual conversation, creating a more intimate, relaxed atmosphere. The subtle lighting in the bar had cast shadows over the young members of the US Air Force, skilfully protecting their identities.

"I'm guessing my little sister's going to love these," said Jake when the film show was over. "Have you sent them on to her yet?"

"Not yet," replied Lori. "You're safe for a couple more hours. Maddy needs to approve them first. I've sent them on to her, along with the stills album."

"Ok. So which one of them is going to call me first?"

"My money's on Lucy," declared Scott with an air of confidence. "I need to go, guys. I've some editing to do for Jason for tomorrow. Thanks again for lunch."

"Any time," replied Jake. "I'll walk you out."

"Let me out through the sunroom," suggested Scott. "I'll head back along the beach. It's quicker."

"Bye, Scott," called Lori as the two guys headed through to the sunroom. "Thanks for your help."

"Pleasure, Lori."

A few minutes later, Jake came back through to the study. Sitting on the edge of the desk, he asked Lori what her plans were for the afternoon. Neither of them had anything urgent scheduled.

"Let's head out to Cape Henlopen and go for a walk on the trail," suggested Jake. "We can go for dinner on the way back."

"Sounds good," agreed Lori, delighted at the thought of getting some fresh air for a few hours. "Give me five minutes to finish up here."

Fall sunshine filtered through the pine trees as they walked slowly along the sandy trail. They were more than half way round the two mile loop when Lori asked if they could rest for a few minutes. On their right, there was a picnic bench set back in among the trees. Jake helped his fiancée to step over a fallen log that was blocking the path, then watched as she lowered herself onto the wooden seat with an audible sigh of relief. Sitting down opposite her, he watched as she massaged her aching thigh.

"I'm sorry," whispered Lori softly. "I just need a few minutes, then I'll be ready to walk the rest of the way."

"Stop apologising, li'l lady," said Jake firmly. "You should've said if this was too far or if I was walking too fast."

They sat in silence, listening to the gentle sounds of nature around them. A few other hikers and trail walkers strolled past, giving them a wave or calling out a polite greeting.

"It's so incredibly peaceful out here," sighed Jake, lifting his face to the sun. "The calm before the storm."

"You've a busy few weeks coming up," agreed Lori. "Any regrets?"

"Regrets?" echoed Jake looking confused.

"Regrets over how fast the band has taken off. Regrets about the pace of your life."

"None," he replied without hesitation. "Not one. Do you regret resurrecting Mz Hyde?"

"No," said Lori sincerely. "It still feels like the right thing to be doing. I've a couple of pieces to finish before the end of October but I'm already looking for my next project. Lin's looking for another jewellery collection before Christmas too."

"Guess we're both going to be busy," laughed Jake. "And there's the wedding to plan."

"That's almost done," she replied. "I've delegated some of it to David. Basic stuff. Have you thought about your best man yet?"

Jake nodded, "Best men. I've not asked them yet. Have you chosen a bridesmaid?"

"I was going to ask Grey if Becky would like to do it," said Lori with a smile. "I think she'd be perfect. If we're having Sam and Josh assisting too, the three of them will look great. I'm trying to keep it all simple."

"Simple works for me."

"We'll need to sort out your suit before you go to Europe. It'd be good if we could coordinate you and the guys with the two boys."

"Can we tie that in with the album launch in New York? We'll all be there anyway."

"Leave that thought with me," said Lori, lifting her cane and getting to her feet, "Let's get going, rock star."

As the path looped back on itself towards the car park, a chilly breeze blew in from the ocean, reminding them both that summer was over for another year. Noticing Lori shivering, Jake removed his jacket and draped it over her shoulders. Despite her protests that he would be cold, he insisted she wear it. They were in sight of the car when Lori's phone began to ring.

"Lucy?" guessed Jake as Lori pulled her phone out of her pocket.

Nodding, she said, "Hi, Lucy. I'm guessing you've seen the videos."

"They're awesome!" squealed Jake's sister down the phone. "Thank you so much!"

"Don't thank me. Thank your brothers," giggled Lori. "Did Maddy send you on the stills too?"

"Yes! I love them!" declared Lucy emphatically. "I'm not going to use them all at once though. Same with the video. I'll put the three individual songs online, but I'll hold the longer one back for now. Is that ok?"

"It's entirely up to you. Do you want to run it past the star himself?"

"Is he there?" asked Lucy excitedly.

Still giggling at her future sister-in-law's enthusiasm, Lori handed her phone to Jake.

"Afternoon," he said calmly.

"Peter said you were amazing last night!" gushed Lucy loudly.

"Hey, calm down, Lucy Lou," Jake laughed. "I think I've just gone deaf in one ear."

"Sorry," she apologised. "The videos are fantastic. You looked so relaxed. Totally chilled."

"Far from relaxed. It's a long time since I've felt quite so nervous."

"Is the Jake Power Solo Show going to be a regular feature?" she asked hopefully.

"Only within the confines of the house."

"Pity," sighed Lucy. "So what's next on the schedule?"

"We fly to LA in a few days for a week of promotional work. Radio stations. TV shows. You know the score, then we'll be in New York on October 14th for the record launch. Are you coming up for that?"

"I can't," she replied sadly. "I've got school. Maybe you could send me some video clips from the promotional stuff though, and the launch party?"

"We'll sort something out," he promised. By now they'd reached the car. "Look, I need to go, Lucy. I'll be in touch. Give those nephews of mine a hug."

"Will do. Tell Lori, I'll call her next week about wedding stuff."

♫

As Jake sat in the departure lounge at Philadelphia airport a few days later, Lucy's request for video clips came to mind. All four of them, plus Maddy were fidgety and keen to board their flight. The board still said it was delayed for an hour. It had been saying that for almost two hours. Taking his phone out, Jake videoed the board for a second or two, then turned the camera on himself.

"The rock'n'roll lifestyle! We've been hanging round here for nearly three hours. The kids are getting bored."

He turned the camera round to film his fellow band members. Rich was playing a game on his phone. Paul was reading a magazine and Grey was sound asleep.

"Best to let sleeping bass players lie," he added. "See you in LA, folks."

Taking a seat beside Rich, he sat trying to figure out how to mail the video clip to Lucy. He had just sent it off when the PA announced that their flight would be boarding shortly.

A misty cloud hung over Los Angeles as the plane came in to land several hours later. It had been an uneventful flight, but, after their long delay, all of them were keen to get clear of the airport and get some fresh air. Despite a further hold up in the baggage hall, they were still among the first passengers to walk through to arrivals. Leaning against the barrier, they found Jethro waiting patiently for them.

"Evening, folks," he called out with a lazy smile.

"Boy, are you a sight for sore eyes!" declared Maddy, hugging her fellow manager enthusiastically.

"Long day?"

"Eternally long," she sighed dramatically. "We're all starving. Airline food does not qualify as dinner."

"I've got a minibus waiting outside. Let's get to the hotel and then we can sort you guys out with dinner."

Once they had loaded all the luggage and various guitar cases into the back of the minibus, they were soon on their way across town. Jethro gave the driver details of their destination, then came back to sit among them.

"Change to our plans, boys and girl," he stated as he sat down next to Grey. "We've pulled out of one of the radio slots for tomorrow afternoon. Instead, you've been invited out to meet a new business partner. Lord Jason's orders."

"Who?" demanded Maddy, abruptly.

"He's set up a deal to get the boys' names on some guitars. Silver Lake signature models. We're going out to meet the folks tomorrow afternoon and play with their "toys"," Jethro explained as the three guitarists all looked at each other. "Tomorrow night we've been asked to attend a private party in North Hollywood. You've to play a short six number acoustic set."

"Are we playing at the two radio stations in the morning?" asked Rich, checking the copy of the itinerary email he had kept in his pocket.

"Yes. You and Jake are to play two numbers at each station."

"And the plan for Tuesday?" asked Jake, trying to recall the schedule.

"Back to back interviews till mid-afternoon at the hotel, then it's out to a regional TV station to guest on their weekly music magazine show. The evening's free after that, but remember it's an early flight to Seattle on Wednesday morning."

"Now I know why Lori was so insistent about staying home," muttered Jake, turning to stare out of the window."

When they arrived at the TV studios late on Tuesday afternoon, the four boys were flagging. It had been an intense couple of days, with the highlight being the visit to the guitar workshop. Their scheduled two-hour stop became a five-hour visit that included an impromptu jam session with some of the factory employees. Both Jake and Rich had warmed to the prototype guitars that had been designed for each of them. A custom made Jake P and a Santiago. Their feedback had been eagerly sought on the instruments. Rich had offered immediate constructive criticism on the hardware that was on the Santiago model and they had willingly agreed to alter it to his preferences. Both of them had been quizzed about their choice of finish and inlays for the neck. With a few further hardware tweaks needed on the Jake P, they were both more than happy to put their names to the instruments. They had each been gifted a guitar of their own choice from the existing custom stock room, including Grey, who fell instantly in love with the new bass. Having put the instruments through their paces back at the hotel, the three of them decided that these would be their weapons of choice for Tuesday's TV appearance.

The music magazine show was broadcast live for an hour across the west coast every Tuesday. There was one other guest band on the show, but Silver Lake were the only ones scheduled to perform live in the studio. When Jake walked into the green room half an hour before show time, he was stunned to discover that their fellow guests were Black Ashes. Recognising Nick from the MMR Award ceremony, Jake said a polite hello before joining Grey in the far corner of the room. The older guitarist followed him.

"I believe my little angel did the sound work on your new record," he said with a gravelly voice, his words slightly slurred.

"Yes, sir, she did," replied Jake, glancing at Grey. "She did a fine job too."

"Which one of you is she fucking?"

Feeling Grey tense up beside him, Jake said calmly, "Why should she be intimately involved with any of us?"

"Because her fucking bitch of a mother told me she was."

"Then it's up to Kola to tell you the rest," stated Jake, keeping his tone icy cold.

"You're all useless shits anyway," muttered the older man, swaying unsteadily on his feet. "She'll fuck you all before she's done. Whore just like her mother."

The two Silver Lake musicians watched him stagger his way over to join the other members of Black Ashes then take a long swig straight from a bottle of bourbon that was sitting on the table.

"You ok?" Jake asked Grey quietly.

"Yeah," muttered the bass player, staring across at Black Ashes. "Glad she wasn't here to see the state he's in."

"Not pretty, is it?" sighed Jake as he watched Jethro and Maddy walking towards them.

"What was that all about?" demanded Maddy as she reached them.

"Daddy was just asking after his little angel," growled Grey, glaring across the room.

One look from Jake told her to drop the questions. Instead, she asked if they were ready to play to open the show. It had been agreed with the TV show's producer that Silver Lake would play Out Of The Shadows to open the show, then close it with Engine Room and Dragon Song. During the show, all four of them would be interviewed by the young female guest presenter.

All too soon Silver Lake were on the small stage at the side of the studio awaiting their cue. They listened to the show's theme song being streamed through the PA then watched for their count to start playing. After a silent count of three, the band began to play Out Of The Shadows. When the song was over they set down their guitars and walked over to join the presenter.

"Silver Lake, it's a pleasure to have you on the show. Now, that was your current single Out Of The Shadows from your new record, Impossible Depths. When's the album out?"

"Next week. October 14th," replied Rich. "It's been a long time coming."

"What can the fans expect from the album? Is it much different from Dragon Song, your debut release?"

"We're really pleased with it," began Jake, sipping a glass of water. "It's heavier than Dragon Song but there's some softer tracks on there too. Our fans seem to like the ballads."

"And which do you prefer?"

"The heavier stuff," answered Grey with a grin. "Good strong pounding bassline."

"Rich?" she began. "What's your favourite track off the record?"

"Tough question," he replied, stalling for some thinking time. "It changes, but today it's Engine Room."

"Mine too," agreed Paul before adding, "But I do have a soft spot for one of the ballads too."

"Jake, you've been involved in the writing of all of the tracks on the new album. What's your favourite?"

"It's kind of hard to choose just one. Engine Room's fun to play. Depths is pretty special but it's a tough one to sing. Very intense. I'm proud of all of them," he replied.

"Do you prefer to sing the softer songs? The ballads?"

"Not always."

Now, you've a tour coming up next month, but there's only five US shows. When will we get to see more of you?"

"In the spring," promised Rich. "Our management are working out a schedule with a promoter so we hope to be in a position to announce more US dates before Christmas."

"Jake, we hear you've got a show coming up at the end of October in London with Weigh Station. Tell us a bit about that."

"Not much to tell. We're due to be in London for some promo events. Dan met up with my fiancée and I in New York last month and asked if I'd like to step out with them for their 25th anniversary show. I'm not sure what I'll be singing with them. I'll find out when I meet them in a few weeks. It's a huge honour to be asked to be a part of it. I'm a massive Weigh Station fan. Getting the chance to play with my idols is incredible."

"You're going to play again for us at the end of the show. What will you be performing?"

"Engine Room off the new record and our first single, Dragon Song," answered Rich.

"No Stronger Within?" asked the presenter, sounding dejected. "I'm disappointed. That's my favourite."

"Sorry," apologised Jake, smiling sheepishly.

"If we got you a guitar, could you play it for me just now?"

Exchanging glances with his band mates, Jake shrugged his shoulders, "I guess so. If it means so much to you."

"Ok. Let's take a short break and, when we come back, we'll be treated to an impromptu acoustic performance by Jake from Silver Lake."

During the brief commercial break, the other three members of Silver Lake retreated to the green room while Jake remained on set, waiting for someone to bring out an acoustic guitar. With less than a minute until they were live on air again, he was handed a stunning Taylor sunburst finish instrument. Much to his surprise, it was delivered to him perfectly tuned. He raised one eyebrow at the presenter and smiled, "I sense a conspiracy here, young lady."

Before she could reply, the commercial break was over.

"Well, folks, as promised, we've found a guitar for Jake."

"And you're sure you want Stronger Within?" he teased as he settled himself to play.

"Yes, please."

"Ok. I'd hate to disappoint a pretty girl. Here goes."

Within seconds the studio was filled with the gentle, acoustic strains of Stronger Within. The young female presenter watched entranced as he played and sang to her. When the song was done, Jake sat the guitar down at his feet.

"That was beautiful. Thank you."

"Pleasure. Glad you enjoyed it," he replied, running his hand nervously through his hair. "And that was a beautiful guitar you found me."

"We'd like you to accept it as our gift," she said smiling. "You were also voted hottest new body in rock by our viewers."

Flushing scarlet, Jake was lost for words. "You're kidding me, right?"

"Not at all," she giggled, as the huge screen behind them changed image to reveal photos of Jake stripped to the waist on stage in London with Weigh Station. "Here's the winning look for those who missed it."

"You're embarrassing me," protested Jake, cringing at the photos. "That all came about by accident. I was busy chatting at the side of the stage with my clean shirt in my hand. I almost missed my cue and had no choice but to step out there half-dressed."

"I don't think your female fans objected," she teased, then to bring the interview to a close added, "Thank you for being a good sport, Jake, and we'll look forward to hearing more from you at the end of the show. Now over to the red zone and the boys who have been joined by metal legends Black Ashes!"

With a brief glance over to the other interview set, Jake quietly lifted the guitar and retreated to the safety of the green room to join the rest of Silver Lake. When he walked in, guitar in hand, his fellow band mates were all standing facing the door, stripped to the waist. In the background, Maddy and Jethro were helpless with laughter.

"Very funny, guys," declared Jake, laying his new guitar down carefully. "Guess this is a good time to ask you all a serious question."

His band mates all stared at him, trying to keep their faces straight.

"If you swear to be better dressed," began Jake, grinning at them. "How do you all feel about being my best men in December?"

"Honoured," said Grey, stepping forward to hug his friend.

"You pick your moments, Mr Power," laughed Rich, clapping him on the back. "It would be a privilege to stand beside you with these guys."

"Count me in," added Paul with a lazy smile. "If I say no, Maddy'll kill me."

Before they could celebrate too much, a production assistant knocked on the door, "Two minutes, folks."

"Alright, boys," called Jethro, getting up from the couch. "Shirts on! Show time!"

Piece by piece everything was falling into place back in Rehoboth. With Jake away, Lori could settle herself to work uninterrupted. She had reviewed her schedule and worked out, with a little extra effort, she could meet her two deadlines early to allow her more time off before the tour and the wedding. Midweek, she had called Lucy to discuss the plans for the boys' outfits for the big day. Neither she nor Jake wanted the wedding to be too formal, but they had agreed on shirts, ties and waistcoats for all of the guys, including the two little guys. The two girls had chatted through a few ideas before Lucy finally asked, "When's Jake back?"

"Saturday," replied Lori, checking her calendar. "Late afternoon. Why?"

"Only a thought, but you could come up here on Friday night and we could go shopping first thing on Saturday," suggested Lucy hopefully. "You could be back before Jake arrives."

"Sorry, Lucy," apologised Lori, feeling a little guilty. "The boys are flying back into Newark. I'm meeting them in New York. I've already got a meeting set up for Saturday morning with David. Business stuff."

"Oh!" replied Lucy, failing to hide her disappointment in her tone of voice.

"The boys are getting measured for their outfits on Tuesday morning before we come back down here. They fly out again to Europe on Thursday night."

"When do you fly over to join them?"

"I fly out on the 23rd then we all fly back on back on Nov 2nd."

"Could you stop off here then?"

"Possibly," relented Lori, trying to salvage something out of this for Lucy. "Let me talk to Jake, but we could stay a couple of nights and finalise wedding things with you then."

"What about your dress?" asked Lucy. "Have you chosen it yet?"

"I've got a college friend designing it for me," explained Lori. "She's meeting me on Saturday for lunch. It should be ready for its first fitting."

"Any hints on the design? Colour?" asked Lucy hopefully.

"It's white. Very simple. Not too huge a skirt. I think you'll love it when you see it," revealed Lori. "But not a word to anyone!"

"Can't wait!" squealed Lucy excitedly. "What colour did you choose for Becky?"

"Midnight blue and silver," confessed Lori, deciding to take her future sister-in-law into her confidence. "The colour theme's blue and silver. Ties in with the band and with the theme Jake chose for our engagement party."

"Of course!"

"I just hope Jake's asked the boys about being best men by the time they come back," sighed Lori. "He hadn't found the right moment before they left at the weekend."

"He won't let you down, Lori," reassured Lucy warmly. "My brother loves you too much to do that."

"Thanks, Lucy. I hope you're right."

By the time Lori returned to her apartment on Saturday afternoon, she was exhausted. She had driven up to the city first thing, leaving before six and arriving in time to meet David at the Hyde Properties office at ten thirty. It had proved to be an intense two-hour meeting with him. For the first hour, she had gone through the board pack for the firm, signing off on the annual accounts. The second hour had focused on her Mz Hyde income. Much to her surprise, the accounts looked very healthy as she realised just how much she had produced since resurrecting her alter ego. The JJL investment was also paying dividends and

David was encouraging her to consider a sister venture with her two business partners. Sipping a strong coffee, she listened to the proposal for a second studio to be built on the west coast and signed the contract before she left, promising David that she would meet up with him on Tuesday to discuss wedding arrangements.

Having left Hyde Properties, Lori had hailed a cab to take her over to 7th Avenue to meet up with Kat, the friend who was designing her wedding dress. When she tried the dress on, it was a perfect fit. Over lunch, the two girls had discussed the decorative detail to be added to the dress, finally agreeing on a suitable design. In true Mz Hyde fashion, Lori had sketched out the design on a napkin in the restaurant. Agreeing that it was perfect for the occasion, Kat had slipped the napkin into her folio folder, promising to forward photos to her once the design had been added to the dress.

As she entered the apartment, Lori guessed she had a couple of hours to spare until Jake and the boys arrived. Their flight was due in from Phoenix about four thirty so she didn't expect them to arrive until nearer six. Dumping her bag, cane and coat in the hallway, she went through to the kitchen to fetch a glass of water. Her leg was throbbing, letting her know that she had pushed her limits for the day. After a quick search in the drawer, she found a strip of Advil, swiftly swallowed two, then limped through to the lounge. Kicking off her shoes, she lay down on the couch, feeling almost instant relief as she took the weight off her leg. With a smile, she remembered the last time she had lain stretched out there. It had been after the MMR awards. Still smiling at the memory of making love to Jake, she drifted off to sleep.

After five days of back to back interviews, Silver Lake were all dead on their feet. The damp weather in Seattle had reacted badly with Rich's compromised nasal passages, triggering an acute attack of sinusitis. By the time they had flown into Phoenix, he was in agony. Realising that over the counter remedies weren't helping, Jethro had taken the guitarist to the nearest emergency room for treatment. After a long, worrying wait, he had returned to the hotel with a course of strong antibiotics and anti-inflammatory drugs. While they had helped with the pain, they had upset his stomach and Rich had endured a miserable flight into Newark International Airport, spending most of it in the bathroom. As they waited in the baggage hall, he sat off to one side with his head in his hands. Discretely, Jake had gone over to sit beside him.

"You, ok, buddy?" he asked softly.

"Fuck knows," Rich muttered. "My face feels like it's been hit with a shovel and my guts are on fire. My whole head's pounding."

"Want me to call Lori to see if she can fix you up with another doctor's appointment?" offered Jake, unsure of what else to suggest.

"No. I'll live," replied the poorly guitarist. "I'll call my own doctor when we get out of here. Worst case scenario, I'll drive home tonight and come back up in time for the launch party."

"You're in no state to drive anywhere," stated Jake bluntly. "If you need to go home, I'll take you myself."

"Thanks. Appreciate the offer."

Their conversation was interrupted by Paul calling over to say they had gathered up all the bags.

On the drive from the airport to Lori's apartment, Rich fell asleep and, while he slept, the others debated what to do if the guitarist wasn't fit for the album launch. They all agreed that the album launch had to go ahead but, if need be, they would pull their planned live performance. With the decision made, the rest of them settled back to enjoy the ride into Manhattan. Jake had sent a message to Lori saying that they should arrive about six and was disappointed that she hadn't replied.

As the minibus pulled into the apartment block's underground garage, Rich woke up and declared he felt much better. It took a bit of reorganising and rummaging to sort out the luggage, but eventually it was only Paul and Maddy's bags that were left on board.

"We'll catch up tomorrow," called Maddy. "We're bringing the twins to lunch."

"I didn't know they were here," commented Jake as he lifted his guitars.

"Paul's sister's bringing them straight to my apartment," explained Maddy. "I can't wait to see my little meatballs. I've missed them."

"I'll bet," he agreed. "Give them a hug from us when you see them. Catch you all tomorrow."

With that, he closed over the door and waved them on their way. It took them two trips up and down in the elevator to shift all of their gear up to the lobby outside the apartment. When Jake led the way in, he was surprised by the silence. Directing the others downstairs to the bedrooms, he wandered through the house in search of his fiancée. The sight of her sound asleep on the couch with her hair half-covering her face made him smile. She looked so calm and peaceful. It seemed a pity to disturb her.

"Hey, li'l lady," he whispered as he knelt down beside her. Tenderly, he kissed her.

"Mm … Jake?" she murmured sleepily as she struggled to open her eyes.

"You alright?" he asked, kissing her again.

"Fine," answered Lori, rubbing the sleep out of her eyes. "It's been a long day. I drove up this morning. I've been up since four thirty. How was your flight?"

"It was a flight. Rich isn't feeling so great still. We might need to get him to a doctor," said Jake, his concern for his friend evident in his voice.

"What's wrong? I thought he got antibiotics in Phoenix?"

"He did, but they don't seem to be agreeing with him."

"Not so good," sighed Lori, sitting up and instinctively reaching out to rub her thigh as a sharp pain shot through her. Her reaction didn't go unnoticed but, before Jake could comment, she said, "I'm fine. The elevator was broken when I got to Kat's studio. I had to take the stairs. I'm paying for those ten flights now."

"As long as you're sure," said Jake, kissing her again, knowing it was pointless to argue with her. "Have you made any plans for dinner? We're starving."

Shaking her head, Lori replied, "I didn't plan anything. We can send out for whatever everyone feels like. Who's all here?"

"Rich, Grey and Jethro," revealed Jake as he helped her to her feet. "They're all downstairs."

"You go and find out what they fancy to eat and I'll set the table," suggested Lori with a smile. "Then you can all tell me all about your trip."

An hour later, with a selection of Italian pasta dishes spread out on the table beside two open bottles of wine, Lori sat back listening to tales of the various promo events. In between mouthfuls, Grey declared he was never moving to Phoenix having been terrorised in his hotel room by a huge spider.

"I'll stick to the Delaware shore," he stated. "Too damn hot in Arizona."

"Better than cold, damp Seattle," grumbled Rich as he picked at the plain macaroni dish in front of him.

"Personally speaking," began Jethro. "I prefer New York. It's nice to be back."

"And it's good to have you here," acknowledged Lori with a smile.

"Very kind of you to have us all to stay," continued the band's manager.

"Well, I couldn't have you staying in a hotel," laughed Lori. "It's nice to have a full house."

"What's the plan for tomorrow?" asked Grey, pouring himself another glass of red wine. "Did I hear Maddison mention lunch?"

Jake nodded. "Not a business thing. Just us. Not sure where though. She never told me that bit."

"Count me out for lunch," stated Rich, laying his knife and fork down. "I'm staying here all day. I plan on doing nothing until Linsey gets here at night."

"How are you feeling now?" asked Jake, conscious that his friend had barely touched his meal.

"Not as bad as I felt on the plane," Rich confessed. "But I've felt better."

"Do you need me to call a doctor?" offered Lori, concerned at how out of sorts the guitarist seemed.

"I'll be fine after a good night's sleep, Lori," he promised, forcing a smile. "But thanks for the concern."

"Well, if you need anything, just ask."

"Thanks," he said as he got up from the table. "I'm going to bed. Keep this party down to a riot and I'll see you all in the morning."

"Night, Rich," called Jake as they watched him head off down to the bedroom.

Once the dinner dishes had all been cleared away, the rest of them gathered in the lounge to watch TV. Grey had scoured the channels in search of a football game. While the three guys settled to watch the game, Lori fetched two large bowls of potato chips, then curled up on the chair with her sketchpad. She still had a jewellery collection to come up with before Christmas, so while the guys yelled at the football, she focussed on designing some earrings. Soon she was engrossed in a modern geometric design and was totally oblivious to the chaos around her.

In front of her, the design took shape and, satisfied with the pattern, Lori began to work it into a pendant design too. Working on the intricate design felt like therapy after her hectic day. After she had been sitting still for almost two hours, she was aware of a nagging ache spreading through her thigh. Despite her best efforts to ignore it, she knew she would have to surrender and take some more painkillers.

"Guys," she said, getting slowly to her feet, "I'm calling it a day. I'll see you all in the morning. Whoever is up first is in charge of making the coffee."

"Night, Lori," said Jethro, blowing her a playful kiss.

"I'll be down when the game's done," promised Jake, reaching to take her hand. He noticed the lines of pain etched into her face. "You ok, li'l lady?"

"Just sore and tired," she whispered, kissing his hand. "I'll take something for it when I get downstairs."

Jake nodded and watched as she limped heavily out of the lounge, paused to pick up her cane in the hallway then disappeared from his sight towards the stairs. Nights like this broke his heart. He hated to see her in pain; hated to watch her struggle.

"Is she ok?" asked Jethro quietly once he was sure Lori was out of earshot.

"Yeah," sighed Jake, running his hand through his hair. "Just not one of her better days."

"What happened?" asked the older man. "She's been really vague with me about it all."

"That's her story to tell, Jethro," replied Jake. "She still can't talk about it. Won't talk about it. Her leg was badly injured in the accident, then she had to have further surgery last January. She'll tell you in her own good time."

"Such a shame," sighed Jethro. "Such a beautiful girl to suffer so much."

"I won't argue with you there," agreed Jake. "She's quite something."

When she finally reached the bottom of the staircase, Lori paused for a moment. Every muscle in her thigh was screaming in protest at the ten floors she had climbed earlier, up and down. Adjusting her grip on her cane, she was ready to head down the hallway to the bedroom when she noticed Rich's door was open and that the light was still on. Slowly, she hobbled over, knocked the door, then stepped into the room.

"Hey, you ok?" she asked quietly, when she saw the guitarist lying on the bed, staring up at the ceiling.

Hearing her voice, Rich looked over and tried to force a smile. "I'll live."

"Can I get you anything?"

"Do you have anything stronger than Advil that won't kill my stomach?"

"I've got some Vicodin, but it might be too harsh for you," Lori replied. "I was just about to take two myself."

"I'll pass," said Rich, sitting up. "Doesn't agree with me. Are you ok?"

"Fine. Just very sore," she confessed. "Let me check the bathroom cabinet to see what else I have."

"It's ok. Advil will do," assured Rich, before adding quietly, "Some of this pain drugs can't reach."

"Do you need to talk?" asked Lori softly, moving to sit on the edge of the bed.

"I was lying here thinking back to recording the album. Right at the start of it. We had a lot of laughs at JJL and in your basement. All of us put everything into that record. It just doesn't feel right to celebrate launching it when Gary's not here to share in it all," began Rich, his voice thick with emotion. "Every time I look in the mirror, I'm reminded of that crash. Every time we play a song off the record, I'm reminded of him. It's tearing me apart that I was driving the car that killed him."

It was the first time Rich had opened up to her. His pain and guilt reminded her of how she had felt in the early days after her own accident. She understood only too well the torment he was going through. Taking a deep breath, Lori whispered, "I know how you feel. Probably know better than most folk, Rich. I've been in a similar place. Still there some days."

"You?"

Lori nodded, then swallowed, before continuing, "When I had my own accident, a little girl died. If I hadn't tried to save her, she might still be alive. If I'd done a better job. If I'd moved quicker. I reacted. I did what I could at the time, but it wasn't enough."

"I don't understand," said Rich, surprised to see her cheeks wet with tears.

"I was walking up Fifth Avenue on my way to the book store. A class of school kids were walking up the street in front of me. This one little girl was alone at the back of the group," began Lori, staring down at her hands. "At the crosswalk, she was lagging behind. I heard the roar of a motorbike coming towards us fast and the sirens of the police cars chasing it. She stepped off the sidewalk as the bike came round the corner. I jumped out to push her to safety. At least, that was my intention. The bike hit me instead of her. The police car chasing the bike hit the little girl. She was killed instantly."

"But if you hadn't tried to save her, the bike would've hit her anyway," said Rich slowly.

"And if you hadn't reacted as quickly as you did, that tanker could've killed all of you," countered Lori, wiping away her tears. "Neither of us can live our lives thinking "what if." Can we?"

The guitarist stared at her silently as she continued, "You look in the mirror and see a scar above your eye and Gary's shadow behind you. I look down at my leg and see scars. When I close my eyes, I see that little girl staring lifelessly at me from under the police car as I lay on the ground. The pain never completely goes away, Rich, but it gets easier to bear. No one blames either of us for what's happened. The only people blaming us are ourselves."

Understanding, Rich nodded, tears unshed in his own brown eyes.

"Do Gary proud and launch this record and this tour with everything you've got," said Lori with a smile. "Show the world that his memories live on in your music. Share in his passion for the success of it all."

Rich reached out and hugged her, his previously unshed tears gliding down his tender cheeks.

"I never knew, Lori," he said eventually, his voice husky.

"It's not an easy tale to tell," she whispered sadly. "Very few people know the truth. I'd like to keep it that way."

"I understand," agreed Rich, kissing her wet cheek. "Thank you for trusting me enough to tell me. It's helped."

"Then it was worth these tears," said Lori. Stiffly she got to her feet. "If you ever need to talk, you know where I am. And just so you know, Jake's a good listener too. Don't shut him out. Remember, he was there too and probably owes his life to you."

"Perhaps."

"Night, Rich," she said softly as she reached the doorway.

Gently, she closed the bedroom door behind her as she headed towards her own room.

It was almost midnight before Jake came into the bedroom. He was pleasantly surprised to find the light still on and Lori awake. Stripping off his T-shirt, he asked if she was ok.

"I'm fine, but I did resort to some strong pain meds," she replied as she slipped the marker into her book.

"That bad?"

Lori nodded. "That's the first time I've had to take them for months. Those stairs really took their toll on me earlier."

As he slipped into bed beside her, Jake noticed her eyes were red.

"Have you been crying, li'l lady?" he asked softly, bending over to kiss her.

"Yes," she confessed. "I was talking to Rich when I came down to bed. We had a bit of a heart to heart. I told him the truth about my accident. About the ghosts I live with. He's still in a really dark place about Gary. I just wanted him to realise I understand how he feels. We were both in tears."

"I wish he'd talk to me," sighed Jake, kissing her tenderly. "Thank you for reaching out to him. I know how tough that is on you. I wish I could take the pain away."

"You will," whispered Lori as she kissed him. "The wedding will do that."

"I hope so, li'l lady."

Fans were gathered outside the record company offices when

the minibus carrying Silver Lake pulled up at the kerb. As Jake stepped out, several young female fans started calling out his name. Painting on the smile, he went over to greet them, posing for photos and signing everything they thrust in front of him. Soon he was joined by his fellow band members, who were equally obliging to the fan requests. In the background, Maddy and Jethro kept an eye on things, allowing the fans their time with their heroes. Beside the management team, Lori and Linsey stood patiently waiting. After a few minutes, Maddy stepped forward and rounded up the band. With a final wave to their fans, Silver Lake entered the building.

The foyer was decorated with posters advertising the album launch. There was even a life-size cardboard cut-out of the Silver Lake imp. Life-size he looked even more tortured and tormented than ever. At Lori's suggestion, the band posed for photos with him while Maddy and Jethro looked on.

"Leave that poor creature alone," laughed Jethro. "Let's get upstairs before you're all late for your own launch party."

Silver Lake were joking about taking the imp out on stage with them as they rode up in the elevator. By the time they reached their floor, they were debating if they could get a mechanised model of him to appear on stage. When the elevator door opened, they were greeted by another life-size version of him guarding the door into the conference room. His presence triggered a fresh round of hilarity as they entered.

"Good afternoon, gentlemen!" called out Jason theatrically.

"Afternoon," called back Jake, reaching out to take Lori's hand. "Love the giant imps."

"Glad to hear it. He turned out rather well, don't you think?"

A couple of hours later, when the room was filled with their guests, record company personnel, potential promoters, media and even a few lucky fans, everyone seemed to be talking about the imp. Realising his creator was in their midst, Lori had been cornered by several journalists and interviewed about the inspiration behind the artwork. Discretely, the band slipped away from the party to prepare for the short set they were to play. Part of the room was screened off by a heavy, dark blue, velvet curtain and a small stage had been set up behind it.

With a glass of champagne in hand, Maddy came over to rescue Lori from yet another impromptu interview.

"How are you holding up?" asked the Goth, guiding her over to the side of the room. "You looked to be struggling a bit yesterday at lunch."

"I'm fine," assured Lori, lifting a glass of champagne from the tray of a passing waiter. "Glad to see you're looking healthier than you were at the last launch party."

"Lord, don't remind me," declared her friend, remembering how sick she had been. "It's been some year since then!"

"It sure has," agreed Lori, glancing round the room. "A far cry from the Surfside show I dragged you to!"

"It certainly is," Maddy acknowledged as Jethro came over to join them. "I'm just going to nip back and check that the boys are ready. I can see Jason giving me the evil eye."

"He sent me over," commented Jethro. "You've apparently got five minutes to get them on stage."

"Jesus," muttered Maddy. "He gets worse!"

While the band stood silently in position behind the curtain, Jason delivered a lengthy heartfelt speech to the assembled guests and media. He paused to toast Gary's memory, then formally welcomed Jethro to the "Silver Lake family." With a shake of his head and a brief salute, Jethro declined to join the flamboyant Englishman on stage.

"Ladies and gentlemen," declared Jason loudly. "After rising from their own Impossible Depths, let's welcome Silver Lake to the stage."

He stepped aside as the curtains drew back to reveal the band. Before the velvet drapes were fully in place, Rich and Grey had launched into the hard, heavy opening of Engine Room. The huge Silver Lake sound filled the conference room to the satisfaction of everyone present. Without pausing for breath, the band played Out Of The Shadows then Jake stepped forward. "You still with us? That came out louder than planned! Hope your ears aren't bleeding," he apologised with a mischievous grin. "This next one is called Depths. We've not played this live yet so I guess this is the premiere!"

The ghostly haunting intro spiralled through the room as Jake came in on vocals. He stood with his eyes closed, focussing on getting the mood and the lyrics right. With the haunting intro complete and the mood set, Grey's heavy bass riff set the tone for the remainder of the song. From her position at the side of the room, Lori listened to this heavy version of the song. Her mind wandered back to the air force base in Dover and she silently decided that she preferred the acoustic version Jake had performed there. In front of her, Silver Lake powered through the long, heavy epic song luring their audience into its tortured drowning theme. As Jake ended the song with a raspier version of the eerie intro, the room erupted with applause and cheers.

"Thank you," he said humbly. "If you like what you've heard, tell your friends. It's been a pleasure to play here today. We'll leave you in traditional Silver Lake fashion. Flyin' High, folks!"

Sitting alone in the departure lounge at Philadelphia Airport a few days later, Lori anxiously checked her watch. She had followed her usual pre-flight ritual – light meal at the sandwich bar, wander through the duty free and had then purchased a couple of magazines for the flight from Hudson News. As she had arrived at the airport, Jake had called her from Amsterdam, promising to meet her at the hotel in London mid-morning next day.

When she boarded the plane a short while later, Lori was surprised to find the first class section was full. She found herself seated next to a London lawyer. After exchanging a few pleasantries with him, she brought out her iPod and settled herself with her magazines. Spotting Silver Lake on the cover, she had picked up one of the music monthlies and smiled to herself as she read the interview with Jake and Grey, hearing their voices in her head. There was also an update on Weigh Station's 25th anniversary plans, confirming that the Wembley show on Oct 31st was the only event planned. Rehearsals for the show were set to begin Oct 28th according to the email Dan had sent to Jake before he left for the European promotional tour. The Weigh Station front man hadn't mentioned his health.

The overnight flight into Heathrow passed peacefully. To her right, the lawyer had fallen asleep after three double whiskeys and proceeded to snore his way across the Atlantic. Despite the sleeping noises coming from her travelling companion, Lori managed to snatch about four hours sleep and stepped off the plane feeling remarkably fresh. As she sat in the back of the taxi that was taking her to the hotel, she sent Jake a message. "Landed safely. On the way to the hotel. See you soon, L x"

A few seconds later, her phone chirped as his reply came through. "Just boarding. See you soon. Love you. J x"

Knowing that she would see him again in a few hours made her smile. Stuffing the phone back into her bag, Lori settled back to enjoy the drive across London. The cab driver chatted cheerfully to her, pointing out famous landmarks as he negotiated the traffic. At first she struggled with his strong South East London accent, but was soon tuned in to his quick way of speaking. It took them almost an hour to reach the smart, city centre hotel that she was booked into. The driver insisted on taking her suitcase right into the lobby for her, earning him a generous tip. With a wave, he left her standing at the reception desk.

"Good morning," greeted the smartly dressed receptionist.

"Morning," said Lori, stifling a yawn. "I have a reservation. It's in the name of Hyde and Power."

With the formalities of check in complete, Lori headed to the third floor room they had been allocated. When she opened the door, she found it was a large bright room with a separate sitting room and a small kitchen area, more akin to a studio apartment than a standard hotel room. Dropping her purse and coat on a chair, she fished out her phone to text Jake the room number then set about making herself a coffee.

An hour or so later, she was stretched out on the couch with a second cup of coffee and her magazine when there was a knock at the door. As quickly as she could, she limped over to the door and looked through the spy hole. A weary, slightly dishevelled Jake was standing in the corridor.

"Morning," she said with a smile as she opened the door.

"Morning, li'l lady," sighed Jake, wrapping his arms around her. "God, I've missed you."

"Missed you too, rock star," she purred, snuggling into his embrace.

Gently, he kissed her on the top of the head, breathing in the scent of her shampoo. Still smiling, Lori stepped aside to allow him to bring his bags and guitars into the room that they were to call home for the next week. As he looked around, Jake nodded his silent approval at their surroundings.

"What's the plans for the rest of the day?" asked Lori as she watched him remove his leather jacket and flop down onto the bed.

"We've got an interview at two downstairs, then that friend of Maddy's has us booked on her radio show between six and eight. After that, we're done for the day," he rhymed off. "I thought maybe you'd like to come out to the radio station with us then we can all head out for dinner."

"Fine by me," agreed Lori, as she lay down on the bed beside him. "Have you had lunch?"

"Not yet," Jake sighed, gazing up at her. After seven days apart, he was drinking in every inch of her, thinking for the millionth time how lucky he was.

"Why don't I order room service?" Lori suggested. "And we can grab a few minutes alone?"

"Sounds like a plan. You order for me while I jump in the shower. I slept in and never had time to freshen up before we left Amsterdam."

Jake had just emerged from the bathroom with a towel wrapped round his waist when their lunch was delivered. Not wanting to get caught in a state of undress, he stepped back into the bathroom while Lori tipped the boy who had delivered the tray of food. When he heard the bedroom door close again, Jake stepped back out into the room.

"That was close," giggled Lori, lifting the covers off the two bowls of soup she had ordered. "Come and eat before this gets cold."

As they ate, Jake filled her in on the highlights of the whirlwind week they had spent so far in Europe. It had been decided weeks before that only Rich and Jake would make the trip, accompanied by Jethro. So far things had gone smoothly and according to plan. Both musicians had been pleasantly surprised by the number of fans that had turned out to greet them. In Amsterdam, they had visited a radio station and had been met by an invited studio audience of fifty "Silver Lakers" as their

European fans were now calling themselves. Not wanting to disappoint any of them, both he and Rich has stayed on for almost two hours after the radio show finished, chatting to the fans, autographing CDs and T-shirts and posing for endless photographs. The love and warmth from this group of fans had really made an impression on both musicians and Jake confessed to having taken contact details from two of the girls, who wanted to set up a European fan page similar to the one Lucy ran for them back home.

"I don't know," teased Lori playfully. "I leave you alone for five minutes and you're asking strange women for their phone numbers."

Blushing, Jake protested, "It was her email address and she's a fellow school teacher. She's married with a teenage daughter!"

"So many personal details," she joked, with a giggle.

"There's only one girl for me and you know it, Mz Hyde," he declared emphatically.

"I'm playing with you, rock star," laughed Lori. "I think it's fabulous that you guys have so many dedicated fans over here already."

"It blows me away. It's incredible."

Their conversation was interrupted by a knock at the door. As Jake was still wearing only a towel, Lori went over to see who it was. Jethro and Rich were standing outside when she looked through the spy hole.

"You'd better get dressed, rock star," she suggested as she unlocked the door. "It's Jethro and Rich."

"Shit! What time is it?"

"Almost two," replied Lori as she opened the door.

"Shit. Shit. Shit," muttered Jake, leaping to his feet.

The sight of Jake rushing to try to find clean clothes in his suitcase had all of them in hysterics. Before he found clean underwear and socks, he had the contents of the bag scattered all over the bed. Eventually, he had pulled on a clean set of clothes, dragged a brush through his long hair and stuffed his feet back into his favourite boots.

"Fastest time yet, Mr Power," joked Jethro, tapping his watch. "You took forty- five seconds off it."

"Blame Lori," muttered Jake, stuffing his phone and his wallet into his jeans' pocket. "She distracted me!"

"And he's easily distracted," added Rich, slapping Jake on the back. "Come on. We're late."

"How long will you be?" asked Lori, giving him a quick hug.

"About an hour and a half, I think," said Jethro, ushering the two musicians out into the hallway. "I'll come up and fetch you before we head over to the radio station."

"Thanks, Jethro. I'll be ready," promised Lori with a wink. "Have fun, boys."

With the door closed again, she looked round the room. It looked like a clothes bomb had gone off! Jake's belongings were scattered from one end to the other. Shaking her head and giggling to herself, Lori checked the information file on the table and determined that the hotel offered a twenty-four hour laundry service.

"Just like home," she sighed to herself as she began to sort through Jake's clothes, trying to establish what was still clean and what needed laundered.

A few minutes later, she had a pile of neatly folded clean clothes and a bundle of dirty laundry. There was a canvas bag hanging in the wardrobe marked "Laundry Service" with their room number stamped on it. Quickly, she stuffed the dirty clothes inside, then called the number on the information sheet to arrange a pick up.

She had only just finished getting freshened up herself when Jethro returned to collect her. Lifting her jacket, cane, bag and key card, she followed the older man out into the corridor.

"How was your flight over?" asked the band's manager as they waited for the elevator.

"Fine. No hassles," replied Lori. "I even managed a few hours' sleep. How have things been this week for you?"

"Great. These guys are a dream to work with. No egos to get in the way," replied Jethro as the elevator doors opened. "They really come to life though when you're around. Nice to see Jake's smile back. He's been kind of quiet all week."

"How's Rich been?"

"A lot more upbeat," admitted Jethro as they stepped into the elevator. "I don't know what you said to him back in New York, but he's a different man. I think he's found his mojo again."

"Relieved to hear it," said Lori as the doors closed smoothly.

There was a small group of fans gathered outside the radio station when their taxi drew up outside. Politely as ever, the two musicians spared them a few minutes, then ran into the building out of the cold, October rain before they were soaked through. One of the production assistants was waiting inside and she showed them upstairs to the green room, walking them past the studio they would be visiting shortly. Debbie, the DJ, was already inside setting up for her show. When she saw the Silver Lake party outside the studio window, she waved and indicated that she would be with them in a few minutes. They were all seated in the lounge with coffees and chocolate biscuits when the DJ finally came through to join them.

"Welcome to London!" she called brightly.

Both Jake and Rich got up to give her a hug, pleased to see a familiar face.

"Glad to be here," said Jake, kissing her on the cheek. "Thanks for inviting us."

"Did you see the fans outside?" she asked as they retook their seats. "Apparently they've been out there since first thing this morning to see you guys."

"That's awesome," answered Rich. "We spoke to them before we came in."

"I'm just blown away by the fact that they care enough to wait out there for hours just to see us for a few minutes," sighed Jake. "We don't get that kind of attention back home too often.

"You've got a strong fan base here," Debbie acknowledged. "I get a lot of requests to play your music. I think you'll be pleasantly surprised by the reaction when you tour here in December. I hear a few of the shows are sold out already."

"Pleased to hear that," commented Jethro.

With a few minutes to spare before they needed to relocate to the studio, they chatted through the plan for the interview. Both musicians had brought their acoustic guitars with them and Jake apologised that he hadn't had time to do a proper vocal warm up. All too soon it was time for them to move next door.

"Are you guys ok through here?" Debbie asked Lori and Jethro.

"We'll be fine," replied Lori warmly. "Is the show broadcast through here?"

"I'll get one of the girls to switch it on for you," promised the DJ then turning to Jake and Rich, she said, "Ready, boys?"

Immediately after the six o'clock news bulletin, Debbie opened her show by playing Out Of The Shadows. Both Jake and Rich sat quietly, with their acoustic guitars resting up against the wall behind them, both feeling a little embarrassed at listening to their own single.

"Good evening, folks," began Debbie as she faded out the dying notes of the song. "Our show opener tonight was Out Of The Shadows by US rockers Silver Lake. My special guests in the studio this evening are Rich Santiago and the awesomely talented and handsome Jake Power from the band. We'll be talking to them shortly and taking some listener questions via phone and email."

Almost twenty minutes into the show, Debbie announced that she would be talking to Silver Lake after the next record. The three and a half minutes of the song were over in the blink of an eye and, before either of the boys realised it, Debbie was welcoming them to the show.

"When did you arrive in London?" she asked, easing them into the interview gently.

"This morning," replied Rich, leaning in towards the microphone. "We flew in from Amsterdam."

"Amsterdam?"

"We've been on a ten-day promotional tour of Europe for the new record," added Jake. "London's the final stop."

"Now the new album Impossible Depths came out ten days ago. It's already riding high in the UK rock charts. Where did the title come from?"

Both of them laughed, then Jake took up the tale, "We debated for days over that title! None of us could agree on it. We had narrowed it down to three or four possibilities, but just couldn't settle on one. When we finished the recording, we went out to dinner to celebrate still without the title agreed. Over dinner someone asked what the record was called and the debate started again. Eventually our manager wrote the possible titles down on three pieces of torn up paper napkin and put them in an empty glass. She asked Tom, one of our guests, to choose one. He pulled out Impossible Depths and that was it."

"Love it!" laughed Debbie. "It's quite different from your first album Dragon Song."

"It's not so different," disagreed Rich. "But I think we've grown into our sound on this one. We worked with the same producer, so he knew what we could do and used that to stretch us a bit further than we thought we could go. There were plenty of nights both Jake and I were sent away with our assignments for the night to re-write bits. Solos. Lyrics. Even the whole melody line on one track. All of us put our hearts and souls into every song on there and I think it shows in the end result."

"We're really proud of this record," added Jake.

"And so you should be. It's awesome," agreed Debbie. "Before we take some calls from our listeners, you are going to play one of tracks for us. Tell us what you are going to play and a bit about the background to the song."

"It's a song called Depths," began Jake, lifting his guitar. "The album version's a little heavier, but it's a song about drowning. In theory, about drowning in anything. Pity. Sorrow. Guilt. Water."

Out in the green room, Lori and Jethro sat on the couch listening intently to the show. When she heard the boys start to play the acoustic version of Depths, Lori said to Jethro to pay attention.

"This is fabulous as an acoustic track," she said with a proud smile. "I prefer it this way."

"I've not heard it before," commented the band's manager, setting his coffee cup down.

Together, they listened to Jake's haunting, eerie vocal creep out of the speakers and subtly work with the music to create the fear and panic of drowning before returning to a rougher, rasping vocal to finish. Nodding his appreciation, Jethro had to agree with Lori that the acoustic was the more powerfully dramatic version.

"It would be great if they'd play it live like that," he said. "I'll need to speak to them about trying it out."

"Don't tell Maddy but Jake already has. He played it at his solo show. The audience loved it," confided Lori quietly.

"Mm, he did, did he?" mused Jethro with a mischievous grin. "I'll need to have a word with young Mr Power."

"No," squealed Lori shrilly. "Don't! He'll know I told you."

Patting her knee, Jethro said, "I'm yanking your chain. I'll not say a word, princess."

"Thanks," said Lori, putting her hand on top of his. "You know, I'm glad you're here with them. I think these guys need you in their corner for a while."

"Exactly what Maddison said too."

As the two musicians laid their guitars gently against the wall. Debbie began asking them some of the listeners' questions that had come in via email. She fired three questions at each of them before saying that she was opening the phone lines.

"Hi, you're live on air," she said with a wink to the boys. "What's your question for Jake and Rich?"

A rather nervous sounding listener asked, "Jake, when did you first realise you could sing?"

"Oh, good question," sighed Jake. "I sang a bit in high school a long time ago for a couple of bands I put together, then did a vocal course as part of my college diploma. I never sang at all for a few years after graduation, but, when we were putting Silver Lake together, Grey asked both Rich and I if either of us could carry a tune. I gave it a trial and here we are."

"Did you seriously not realise what a talent you were hiding?" asked Debbie, somewhat taken aback by his answer.

"I never really took the singer bit seriously before," Jake confessed shyly. "I remember practising in my bedroom as a kid and my dad yelling at me to shut up. I think that put me off a bit for a long time. Dented the self-confidence."

"Our next caller is on the line," said Debbie. "And I believe your question is for Rich?"

"Hi. Yes," began the caller. "Rich, you taught my cousin in high school in Delaware. Do you miss teaching at all?"

"Hi. Yes, I do," admitted Rich openly. "I get a buzz out of teaching a class. Seeing them progress. Who is your cousin?"

"Kate Dirk."

"Ah, Kate!" he exclaimed, instantly recognising the name. "Fabulous vocalist. We're still in contact. Lovely girl. Really hope she does something with that voice."

"She's great," agreed the caller.

"Do you keep in touch with a lot of your former students?" interjected Debbie. "You both taught at the same high school for a while, didn't you?"

"Yes," began Jake. "And to echo Rich's comments, Kate has an awesome voice. I've had the pleasure of singing with her on a couple of occasions. We keep in touch with some students. We've also kept close to the school and do the occasional music workshop there when we have some free time."

The Q&A session lasted for a further twenty minutes before the DJ said it was time to play some more music before the next news bulletin. Another four or five songs followed the news ending with Engine Room.

"And that was Engine Room from the new Silver Lake record, Impossible Depths," announced Debbie. "Jake and Rich are still here in the studio with me and will be playing live again shortly. Now guys. I don't want to open up old wounds, but, as your fans know, there were a few rough months for the band over the summer. How hard has it been to move on from that?"

Running his hand nervously through his hair, Jake looked over at Rich, gave him a nod, then said, "It's been a tough journey for all of us. As I said to you back then, when we met up out at JJL, it's all too easy to torture yourself with "what ifs" but I'd be lying if I said we hadn't all done it to varying degrees."

"Physically have you both fully recovered from the injuries you sustained in the crash?"

"Apart from a few lingering sinus issues on my part," said Rich. "Yes, we're both back to full health."

"What keeps you both grounded? You are two of the most down to earth rock stars I've met. What keeps you there?"

"Family. Home," replied Jake immediately. "We all lead simple lives so it's the everyday stuff that keeps your feet on the ground."

"Like what?" asked the DJ, hoping for an insight into the Silver Lake life.

"Doing your own laundry in your hotel room and hanging your boxer shorts up to dry on the shower rail," confessed Rich, visualising his own hotel room.

"I had one of these surreal wake up moments last month," added Jake, trying hard not to laugh at his band mate's laundry dilemmas. "It was just after the MMR award ceremony in New York. Red carpet affair. Champagne. Glitz and glamour. Then a couple of days later, I'm in the food store doing grocery shopping then making grilled cheese sandwiches for lunch because my fiancée is working. Normal every day stuff that keeps our world turning smoothly."

"So what are you going to play for us now?" asked Debbie, keeping a watchful eye on the time.

"Ladies choice," offered Jake, with a flirtatious wink.

"So many to choose from," giggled Debbie, caught off guard momentarily. "How about Stronger Within?"

"If that's your choice, princess," teased Jake, lifting his guitar from its resting place on the floor.

"You've got the music from it tattooed on your arm, haven't you?"

"Part of it," acknowledged Jake.

"What's the story behind the song and the tattoo?"

"I wrote the song soon after I met a very special person in my life. The lyrics reflect them and their situation at that time. The tattoo followed on naturally in the grand scheme of things," explained Jake. "Every time I play it, I'm reminded of the first time I met them."

Sensing she was treading a fine line towards being too personal, Debbie said simply, "It's one of my favourites."

Back in the green room, Jethro was watching Lori's reaction to Jake's response to Debbie's line of questions about the song. Her cheeks reddened as she listened to her fiancé skirting round the truth behind the lyrics. Like Debbie, the song remained one of her favourites. As the first, it held a special place in her heart.

"What's the real story?" asked Jethro, curiosity getting the better of him.

"Not a million miles away from what was said," replied Lori softly. "It's the first song Jake ever played for me not long after we met. It reflects my situation at that time."

"You met on the beach, didn't you?"

Lori nodded. She looked at Jethro, noting the fatherly concern in his eyes, then continued, "I was a mess when I met Jake. Physically and mentally. I guess mentally I was stronger than I was physically. It was only a few months after my accident and things weren't healing the way I expected them to. The way I wanted them to. Without his friendship, love and encouragement, I don't think I'd have recovered half as well."

"And he saw you were "stronger within"?"

With a wistful smile, Lori nodded.

Not wanting to push her any harder, Jethro said, "There's no denying, it's a beautiful song."

Eventually time ran out and Debbie's show ended for the day as she handed over to a fellow DJ for a classic rock show. Having switched everything off and tidied up the desk while the boys stowed their guitars back in their cases, she asked what their plans were for the rest of the visit.

"More promo stuff tomorrow," replied Rich, opening the door for her. "And a photo shoot. It's all at the record company offices. Suspect it will be a long one."

"Then are you flying home?"

"No," said Jake. "I'm hanging on for a week or so. I've a guest slot with Weigh Station on the 31st."

"I'm going to hang on too," added Rich. "Keep him out of trouble."

"We tried to get Dan to come in before that show, but he's declined," commented Debbie as they arrived back in the green room. "Shame. I'd have loved to have them on the show for their anniversary."

"Pity," mused Jake, taking a mental note to call Dan. Spotting Lori getting to her feet, he said, "Mz Hyde, are you taking us to dinner?"

"I might," she teased. "Since you sang so beautifully for your supper."

"Debbie, do you want to join us?" invited Jake.

"Not this time, thanks. I've got plans. Maybe next time, if the offer's still open," she replied coyly. "Thanks for tonight. You guys were fabulous. Will you come back in when you're here in December?"

"If time allows. Did you get tickets for our show?"

"Yes," she replied. "I got a couple of standing tickets from your management."

"VIP?" checked Rich, glancing over at Jethro.

"No."

"Jethro," continued Jake, taking up on Rich's lead. "Can you sort a couple of passes out for Debbie, please? Full access."

"Sure. I'll get them to you. Before and after show?"

Both Jake and Rich nodded.

"Consider it done, boys," promised Jethro. "Now, can we go and eat before I die of hunger?"

♫

The following night, Friday, with the promo work completed, Jethro announced that he had organised a surprise for them. He had secured invites for them to a gig at a small venue in Islington.

"Who's playing?" asked Rich curiously.

"A new band Jason signed recently. He wants us to check them out as a possible support act for the shows he's trying to set up for the start of the year. They're called After Life," explained their manager.

"Ok, let's check them out," agreed Jake readily. "Always open to new musical experiences."

"Are we eating first?" Rich asked as they headed out of the record company offices in search of a taxi.

"Wasn't the plan," commented Jethro as he hailed a passing black cab. "We can get you something to tide you over if you're hungry."

"A burger would be good," Rich suggested as he climbed into the back of the cab.

Once they were settled in the taxi, Jake checked with Lori that she was alright about going to the concert. He had been a little concerned that his fiancée had been quiet all day and pale.

"Of course," she replied, taking his hand. "Actually, I spoke to Jason earlier. He's asked me to do their album artwork. They've just finished recording it."

"When does he want that done by?" asked Jake, knowing full well it would be another of Jason's rush jobs.

"End of November. Original artist let him down. Creative differences, I believe," explained Lori. "I've suggested he talk money with David though. I'm asking for at least double my usual fee for such a large rush job."

"Good for you, princess Don't let him push you around," stated Jethro, proud that she had stood up to the overbearing Jason.

"Not the first time we've had that discussion," laughed Lori, remembering the "rush job" that led to the creation of the Silver Lake imp. "David'll talk him round to a nice figure."

Fans were already queuing outside the small venue as their

taxi pulled up at the kerb. Leaving Jethro to pay the fare, Rich stepped out first, followed by Jake who then helped Lori out. He kept a protective hand on her waist as Jethro led them over to the doors. Fortunately, with their hoods up and dark glasses on, none of the After Life fans at the front of the line recognised the Silver Lake musicians. Once inside the venue, Jethro led them backstage to meet the band.

When Jethro entered the dressing room, After Life's manager called out a loud greeting.

"Nice to see you, Rocky," replied Jethro before introducing the two Silver Lake musicians and Lori.

"Delighted that you could come along, folks," said Rocky, reaching over to shake their hands. "Let me introduce the guys to you. Lying on the couch over there is Luke, our bass player. In the corner, on the phone, is Jack our drummer. Beside me, to my left is Taylor on guitar and to my right is Cal, the other guitarist. Our leading lady, Ellen, is still getting ready. She'll be through shortly."

It was almost an hour later before After Life's vocalist made an appearance. Both of the Silver Lake musicians were deep in conversation with After Life's guitarists while Lori was chatting with Rocky and Jethro about Jason's proposals. She was choosing her words carefully to avoid committing herself to the project and was silently relieved when Ellen's arrival interrupted the discussion.

"Darling," called out Rocky theatrically. "We have rock royalty in our humble midst."

When Jake looked up, at first glance Ellen's appearance caught him off guard. The singer was wearing skin tight black pants, spike heels that Maddy would covet, a purple corset with a black velvet cape draped over her slender shoulders. Over her right eye, she wore an eye patch with Egyptian hieroglyphics on it. It was the Eye of Horus, he realised after a few seconds. Her white blonde hair fell down below her waist. Striking didn't begin to cover her look, he thought.

"Ellen, let me introduce you to Jake Power and Rich Santiago from Silver Lake, their manager and my old mate, Jethro Steele, and the beautiful Mz Hyde," continued Rocky, guiding her over to join them.

Jake extended his hand to shake Ellen's as she approached and was a little surprised when she took it with her left.

"Nice to meet you. I was listening to your new album on the bus this morning," she said shyly. "Love the vocals on Depths and adore Mysteries."

"Thank you," replied Jake, feeling himself blush at her unexpected compliments. "You have me at a disadvantage, I'm afraid."

The strange singer turned her attention to Lori and commented that she hoped she would be able to do their artwork for them.

"I hope so too," Lori responded "If the numbers add up, we should have a deal. Are you playing anything from the new album tonight?"

"Three songs," revealed Ellen. "Pyramid, City Of Bones And Heartache then Cyclone near the end of the set."

"I'll listen out for them," promised Lori, noticing for the first time that girl's cloak rested unevenly down her right hand side.

"How'd you guys feel about jammin' with us on stage tonight?" asked Taylor, with a nod to Ellen. "We could jam one of your songs?"

"I'm up for it," agreed Rich, beer in hand. "But we'll need the loan of a couple of guitars."

"Not a problem," assured Rocky. "We can sort you both out with something."

"Will you duet Dragon Song with me?" Ellen asked Jake hopefully.

"Pick an easy one, why don't you?" joked Jake, flashing her one of his "Power" smiles. "It'd be my pleasure."

Shortly before nine, Rocky rounded up After Life and, accompanied by the Silver Lake party, moved them out of the dressing room towards the stage. The support act had just finished their set and squeezed past them in the narrow corridor. As they passed Ellen, someone's hand caught her cloak, drawing it back over her shoulder. Cursing loudly, she swiftly drew the velvet back round her, fully aware that Jake and Rich had seen the withered stump of her right arm, covered in its black satin sleeve. Neither of them said anything and they continued on their way to the side of the stage.

Safely positioned out of sight of the small audience, Jake stood with his arm around Lori's waist, watching closely as After Life took to the stage. Beside him, Rich was studying their potential support act intently and surveying the crowd, trying to determine what kind of fans they attracted. Neither of them were ready for the raw power of Ellen's voice. She had a surprisingly deep, husky voice, but it blended perfectly with the band and their image. With her long cloak on, she played the "black witch" persona to perfection. In front of the stage, the crowd were loving every minute of the set. Just beyond the midpoint of the main set, they watched as Ellen jumped nimbly down into the front of the crowd, staying on the stage side of the barrier, to woo the audience with a haunting ballad about the pits of hell.

At the end of the set, the band briefly left the small stage, stopping beside their special guests.

"You boys ready?" asked Taylor as their guitar tech handed the two Silver Lake musicians two guitars. "Watch for Ellen giving you the nod to come out."

Before the crowd grew too restless, Ellen led her band back out.

"There's a special blend of magic in this room tonight," she purred into the microphone. "Silvery, watery magic."

She paused, scanning the audience, before continuing, "Time to make it a little more rich and powerful."

The crowd cheered loudly, with a few fans down on the barrier, beginning to chant "Silver Lake, Silver Lake, Silver Lake Lake Lake."

"I'd like to welcome two new friends to the After Life," Ellen continued over the roar of the audience. "Rich Santiago and the heavenly Jake Power from Silver Lake, people!"

At the sight of the two members of Silver Lake, the crowd roared themselves into a frenzy as After Life began to play Silver Lake's Dragon Song. Despite having had no rehearsal, the two Silver Lake musicians slickly slotted in, with Jake allowing Ellen to lead the vocal. They shared the chorus and she graciously allowed him to take over for the second verse, but he brought her back in for the closing section and the final chorus. Their voices had complimented each other well.

"Ladies and gentlemen, give it up for Rich and Jake!" screamed Taylor loudly as the song ended. "Fucking awesome guys!"

In the centre of the stage, Ellen stepped into Jake's embrace and quickly asked if he would stay out for one more. He shook his head, kissed her on the cheek then left the stage behind Rich, to the raucous cheers of the small London audience.

They stood in the wings watching as After Life closed their show with a rendition of Deep Purple's Smoke On The Water.

A couple of hours later, as Rich and Jethro sat in Jake and Lori's hotel room enjoying some take away Chinese food that they had picked up on the way in, Jethro asked if they thought After Life would make a good support act for Silver Lake.

"That girl's got a fantastic voice," commented Jake, his mouth full of noodles. "What shows was Lord Jason thinking about?"

"He's trying to set up ten west coast shows for the end of January into February. Maybe a few in the Midwest too, if he can find a promoter. Nothing too big. Small sized venues. No more than two thousand seaters," explained Jethro calmly. "I think they'd be fantastic. She's quirky and, from experience, that goes down well out there."

"What's her story?" asked Lori quietly.

"Not sure the whole story. I asked Rocky but she came over and he never finished. She lost her eye and her arm in a night club accident in the Far East. Something about an explosion and a fire. That was five years ago, I think he said. She was only eighteen."

"Shit," muttered Rich, putting his empty food carton down on the table. "When I was talking to their guitarist. Taylor? He mentioned her arm. Said it was burn injuries. He said she's badly burned down her whole body on that side."

"Poor girl," whispered Lori sadly. "I loved her voice. I've a few ideas for their artwork too, having heard those new songs."

"And here I thought you were just enjoying the show," teased Jake in an effort to lighten the mood. "And all the while you were creating in that beautiful mind of yours, Mz Hyde."

Lori giggled.

"I think we should give them a shot," said Rich bluntly.

"Likewise," agreed Jake with a huge yawn.

"I'll make the call to Lord Jason in the morning," declared Jethro as he stood up. "Now, these old bones are tired. I'm calling it a night. What's everyone's plans for tomorrow?"

"Nothing planned," said Jake. "But I need to talk to the Weigh Station guys. How about we meet for lunch here around one and take it from there?"

"Count me out," said Jethro. "I could meet you for dinner, though."

"I'll skip both," declared Rich. "I called Alice earlier. I'm taking the train out to visit her and Tom. Meet Gary's parents. I'll be back on Monday."

"Give them our love," said Lori sleepily.

"Invite them to the wedding too," added Jake as he tried and failed to stifle another yawn.

Snuggled down in the large bed under the thick feather duvet, Jake watched Lori as she drifted off to sleep. Their lovemaking had been slow and gentle; neither of them in a rush to reach a climax; both of them comfortable to savour the intimacy of the other. No matter how often Jake made love to her, every time felt as special as the first. Watching his fiancée sink into a deep sleep in the crisp, white bed, he smiled. In a few short weeks he would be united forever with her. Tenderly he ran his fingers through the stray strands of her hair that were falling across her face. Her complexion was pale and he worried that their long day had taken its toll on her. No matter how many times she assured him that she was fine, Jake always worried about her. Gently he brushed a kiss across her forehead, then settled himself to sleep, curled protectively round her.

Next morning, he awoke to find Lori propped up on one elbow watching him sleep.

"Touché, li'l lady," he murmured sleepily.

"Pardon?"

"I watched you fall asleep last night. I like watching you sleep."

"Likewise," she purred as she leaned over to kiss him.

Before either of them could say or do anything else, Jake's phone began to ring. He reached out to grab it before his voicemail cut in.

"Hello," he said, his voice still husky with sleep.

"Jake, good morning," answered an unfamiliar English voice. "It's Mikey. Dan said to give you a call."

"Good morning," said Jake, sitting up in bed. "How is Dan? I was going to call tomorrow to see what the plan was."

"He's not great," admitted the Weigh Station guitarist. "But he's not giving in just yet. Plan's to meet up on Monday afternoon. How does that sit with your plans?"

"I'm fairly flexible," replied Jake. "We've finished all the promo work for the record so Lori and I were just playing it by ear for the next few days. Email me the address for rehearsals. What time do you need me on Monday?"

"The management will send a car to your hotel," said Mikey. "Does half two sound alright?"

"I'll be ready," promised Jake. "Looking forward to it."

"Appreciate you doing this for us. See you on Monday."

Placing the phone back on the bedside cabinet, he rolled over to face Lori, with a mischievous smile forming around his mouth.

"Now, where were we, Mz Hyde?" he teased as he pulled her roughly towards him.

With a squeal, she found herself lying on top of him in one swift movement.

"Playing games, are we?" she murmured as she licked each of his nipples in turn.

"Seems like it," he replied, then gasped as she bit his nipple hard. "Oh, that game!"

She laughed, filling the room with the beautiful, musical laugh that he adored, then rolled away from him, still giggling. He reached over and caught her, forcing her onto her back, then draped his long leg across her thighs, pinning her down.

Teasingly, he suckled at her breast, licked her nipple, then looked up into her eyes. As he watched her, he blew a cool breath across her breast, then bit the ripe, erect nipple.

"Ouch!" she squealed. "Guess I deserved that."

Circling with his tongue, Jake caressed her tender nipple, then sucked hard. Next he turned his attention to her other breast, suckling on it before allowing his tongue to trace its way down her ribcage, eliciting more giggles from her. When his tongue reached her hips, he switched sides and traced his way around the outline of her floral tattoo, before moving down her inner thigh. Beneath him, he could hear her breathing quicken, could detect the sweet aroma of her feminine moistness.

"Hungry again, li'l lady?" he commented as his hand moved to caress her between her thighs. His long, slender fingers found her moist and ready for him. Using his thumb, he rubbed the nub of her clitoris, causing her to arch her back and moan softly.

"Jake," she purred, reaching out to draw him towards her.

Swiftly he entered her and with a few long hard strokes had taken them both to the pinnacle of orgasm. Nuzzling into her neck and gently delivering kisses across her silky smooth throat, Jake thrust hard and fast. Her orgasm surged through her like a bolt of lightning. With a long, low howl of ecstasy, she lay back as Jake's own climax shuddered through him. Together they lay entwined in each other's arms, still intimately connected.

"I can't think of a better way to start the day," whispered Lori with a sleepy satiated smile. "That was heavenly, rock star."

"Why thank you, ma'am," he said, kissing her on the end of the nose.

He held her close for a few more minutes, then gently slid out of her and rolled over to his side of the huge bed. Staring up at the ceiling, Jake asked, "What did you want to do today?"

"I had no plans," replied Lori, glancing over at her phone to check the time. "We could go for a walk, explore a bit then grab some lunch."

"No museums?" he teased, knowing her love for the city's museums.

"Maybe," she suggested with a wink.

"I should really go for a run first," commented Jake. "I've not stretched my legs for a few days."

Sitting up, Lori suggested, "You go for a run while I get showered and dressed then we can go for brunch when you get back and we can take the day from there."

"Works for me," agreed Jake, swinging his long legs out of bed. "I'll not go far. Don't want to get lost. I'll be an hour at most."

Pounding the city streets felt good to Jake. It made a change from running along the sand at home, but he missed the ocean and the seabirds. Using the map application on his phone, he had run a ragged five mile circuit round the hotel. He was breathing hard, sweat pouring down his face, as he turned into the street just a few yards from the hotel entrance. As he approached the main door, he saw a small group of people gathered outside. When they saw him coming, a couple of them shouted his name. Silver Lakers! Forcing a smile and slowing to a gentle jog, Jake tried to catch his breath before he reached them.

"Morning," he acknowledged as he attempted to enter the building.

"Can we get a photo, Jake?" asked one girl boldly, clutching her phone.

"If you insist, but I'm a sweaty mess," replied Jake, feeling a little awkward.

"Just the way we like you," teased another fan.

Blushing, Jake humoured the fans for a few moments, then apologised that he would need to go before he got too cold. Fortunately, the girls were understanding and seemed more than happy to have had their moment or two of his time. With a final wave to them, Jake headed into the warmth of the foyer.

When Jake exited the building with Lori an hour later, the street was empty, much to his relief. While he had been out for his run, he had passed a small Italian restaurant near the British Museum. Ensuring they were walking at a pace Lori was comfortable with, they headed towards the restaurant. As they walked, she enthused about the architecture and heritage that surrounded them. Her enthusiasm and passion began to rub off on him and, as they reached the restaurant, he had to concede that London was a beautiful city.

"Table for two, sir?" asked the waiter as they entered.

"Please," answered Jake, relieved to be in out of the autumn chill.

"Follow me, please."

The waiter showed them to a table at the window, rhymed off the day's specials as he passed them the menus then took their drinks order. Several of the other tables were occupied, mainly with families and, much to Jake's relief, no one gave them a second glance. They had debated the choice for lunch before both of them opted for risotto. As they ate their meal, Lori asked Jake how he was feeling about the Weigh Station rehearsals.

"I'm not really sure," he admitted between mouthfuls of rice. "I still find it hard to believe that I'm playing with those guys, even after last year's tour."

"Do you think you could carry the full set if it came to that?"

"If I had to," said Jake quietly. "Hopefully, it won't come to that though. Now, what do you want to do with the rest of the day?"

With a mischievous giggle, Lori replied, "Well, I did see a sign down the street a bit for the British Museum."

Laughing, Jake declared, "I knew it! You're a museum junkie, li'l lady!"

It was drizzling when they left the restaurant to walk to the museum. Holding on tight to Lori's hand, Jake let her set the pace as they walked the few blocks to the main entrance of the museum on Great Russell Street. When he saw the imposing building with its pillared frontage, Jake had to agree it was impressive.

"Wait till you see inside," enthused Lori, leading him towards the front steps.

Once inside, they picked up a museum map, but before he could ask what she wanted to see first, Lori was leading the way towards the elevators.

"Ancient Egypt first," she stated, pressing the call button. "A little research for the After Life project."

"Have you decided to do it?" asked Jake as they stepped into the spacious elevator, closely followed by half a dozen fellow tourists.

"More or less, if the money adds up."

"So what are we looking for up here?"

"Shabtis," replied Lori with a wink.

"What?"

"You'll see in a minute," she promised.

A few moments later, they stood admiring a small, intricately carved wooden box from Thebes, dating back to 1290 BC. As Jake gazed at the small painted wooden figures, shabtis, Lori explained that these were placed in the tombs of the Ancient Egyptians to carry out hard physical labour to assist their owners in the afterlife. The wooden carved figurines acted as deputies for their wealthy deceased owners. A spell from the Book of the Dead was used to bring them back to life in the afterlife.

"Very clever, Mz Hyde," praised Jake, understanding where her train of thought was headed.

"Ellen gave the idea when she told me the song titles from the new album," explained Lori as they moved on from the exhibit case. "It reminded me of this and the idea's grown from there."

"And the spell fits in with her witch image," mused Jake with a smile. "I like the imagery. Slick."

Slowly, they meandered their way through the history of Europe and the Middle East, marvelling at the age of some of the exhibits. Knowing Jake's love of watches, Lori guided them towards a hall dedicated to watches and clocks, some of which dated back to the fifteenth century. As they made their way back towards the Great Court and the coffee shop, Jake had to admit that he was beginning to understand her love of the place.

While Lori sat finishing her coffee, Jake wandered over to explore the gift shop. She smiled at the childlike enthusiasm written all over his face as he explored. He disappeared out her line of sight. Seizing the chance, Lori swiftly fetched two painkillers from her bag, swallowing them with the last of her coffee before he returned.

In the busy museum gift store, Jake was searching swiftly for a surprise gift for Lori. He wanted to treat her to something special. There were so many things to choose from but he wanted something a little different. Just as he was about to opt for a book, he spotted a display cabinet of jewellery. Two silver bangles caught his eye. Both of them were a Mobius strip geometric design. One had a Buddhist prayer inscribed in it and the other a Shakespearean sonnet. There was also an Egyptian knot bracelet beside them.

"Can I help you, sir?" asked one of the gift shop assistants.

"I'm trying to choose between these three," replied Jake, still gazing down at the three pieces of jewellery. "The two twisted ones would make a lovely wedding gift for my fiancée but I love the Egyptian knot too."

"It's beautiful," commented the assistant. "It's based on an ancient belief that protective spells could be placed on the wearer through the knot."

"Neat idea," nodded Jake, reaching for his wallet. "What the hell! I'll take all three, but can you please wrap the knot one separately."

"Certainly, sir," she replied, reaching for her keys to unlock the cabinet. "Come over to the counter and I'll put these through for you."

With one small bag hidden in his inside jacket pocket and the other in his hand, Jake headed back towards the coffee shop. As an afterthought, he'd picked up a book on Ancient Egypt with the shabtis on the cover.

"What have you been buying?" asked Lori as he approached the table.

"A book," he replied with a wink. "Some inspiration for you. I'll show you later. Do you feel up to heading up to the Reading Room? I want to see that stone that's on the shirt you bought me last time you were here."

"Lead on," giggled Lori, getting to her feet, "Have I created a museum junkie here?"

"You might have," acknowledged Jake with a laugh. "This place is fabulous."

The museum was closing for the night when Lori finally led Jake back down the stone steps and out into the wet October evening. Rain was lashing down so Jake hailed a taxi to take them back to the hotel. As they sat huddled together in the back of the cab, Lori asked if she could see the book.

"Patience, li'l lady," he teased playfully. "Wait until we're back at the hotel."

She pretended to sulk, but couldn't keep the petted lip up without giggling.

"Are we having dinner with Jethro?"

Jake nodded. "That's the plan. I said I'd let him know when we were back. Not sure where he'll want to go."

"We could just stay in the hotel," suggested Lori, looking out the window at the rain. "It's too miserable to trail about looking for a restaurant tonight."

"Hotel's fine with me."

Once back in their room, Lori again asked Jake if she could see the book.

"In a second, li'l lady," he said as he took off his jacket. "Let me call Jethro first."

"Then can I see the book?" pleaded Lori.

"If you fetch us drink while I call the boss, then we can look at it together," promised Jake with a grin.

"Deal."

While Lori poured them both a drink from the mini bar, Jake called the band's manager.

The two men chatted for a few minutes, then agreed to meet in the hotel cocktail bar at seven for a pre-dinner drink. The older man promised to reserve them a table at the hotel's A La Carte restaurant.

Slipping his phone back into his pocket, Jake came over to sit beside his fiancée on the settee. She had her own phone in her hand and was busy scanning through her emails.

"You ready, li'l lady?" he asked, holding up the plastic bag from the gift shop.

Trying not to giggle, Lori nodded.

Jake handed her the bag, then watched as she slid the book out.

"Oh! There's something else in here!" she cried as she reached into the bag and brought out a square box.

Without saying a word, Jake watched as she opened the box and lifted out the Egyptian knot bangle.

"Jake, this is too much!"

"No, it's not, li'l lady," he replied, putting his arm around her shoulder. "The lady in the gift store told me that the Egyptians believed a protective spell could be placed on the person wearing the bangle. Or something like that. I thought you'd like it."

"It's gorgeous," declared Lori, sliding the bangle onto her slender wrist. "Thank you."

"Glad you like it," replied Jake, kissing her tenderly. "Now, tell me more about these shabti things."

♫

For once, Jake was ready and waiting in the hotel foyer when the car arrived to collect him for rehearsals on Monday afternoon. He had debated whether to take his guitar along or not and eventually decided to take two along with him, just in case he needed them. There were nerves fluttering in the pit of his stomach as he sat in the back of the car, looking out at the rain soaked London streets. He was driven across the city to an old warehouse building on an industrial estate.

"Is this the right place?" he asked the driver anxiously, as he climbed out of the car, suspicious of the remote location.

"Yes, sir," replied the chauffeur. "Weigh Station always rehearse here. It's out of the way. No distractions."

"I guess," conceded Jake as he followed him towards the entrance.

He was surprised when they stepped into the anonymous looking warehouse to find a fully kitted out rehearsal studio and offices. The door to the outside world opened into a small reception area that then led through to a large sumptuous lounge with a glass panelled back wall. Beyond the glass was a huge rehearsal space with a low stage set up, complete with lighting rig. Through the glass, he could see Mikey and Weigh Station's drummer already on stage. When they saw Jake, they waved for him to come on through.

"Afternoon, Mr Power," called Mikey as Jake wandered in. "You made it, then?"

"Hi," said Jake simply as he gazed round. "This is not what I was expecting."

"We've used this place for years," explained the guitarist. "We bought the original bit to store our stage gear, then bought the adjoining warehouse a few years later and converted it into this. It's far enough away from everything to afford us a little privacy."

"Beats Lori's basement," laughed Jake, setting down his two guitar cases. "So what's the plan?"

"We're still waiting for Steve and Dan to show," said Mikey. "The set list's been drawn up. We just need to see how it sounds as we run through it. Check what you can do. What you need to

383

learn. See what Dan can cope with."

Nodding, Jake said, "Sounds like a plan. Is there somewhere I can go to run through a vocal warm up?"

"Sure. There's three sound proof rooms through that door," explained Mikey, pointing to a blue painted door on the far side. "How long do you need?"

"About an hour?"

"Fine. Come back through when you're ready."

When Jake emerged from the small rehearsal room, Steve, the band's bass player, had arrived. There was still no sign of Dan. Several phone messages had been left for him and Jake could sense that the other three members of Weigh Station were growing anxious. While they waited, Mikey talked him through the proposed set list and handed him a soft covered, plastic folder, saying simply, "Lyrics."

"Thanks," said Jake, flicking through the pages. "Will we make a start?"

"Yeah," sighed Steve, glancing at his watch. "Let's start with Sunset After The Storm. He never could sing it live anyway!"

They had just completed a second run through of the song when the door opened and Dan marched in.

"I thought we said three!" yelled Steve. "Nice of you to finally join us!"

"Appointment over ran," muttered Dan hoarsely as he walked towards them. "Ah, Mr Power, you made it!"

"Said I'd be here," said Jake, jumping down from the low stage to greet his idol. "How are you doing?"

"We'll talk later," replied Dan evasively. "Where are we at with this rehearsal?"

"We just did Sunset," explained Mikey.

"Ok," nodded Dan, keeping his eyes on Jake. "Let's hear Jake sing the rest of the set from the top."

"The whole set?" Jake asked, a hint of concern in his voice.

"Yup. Need to know you can do it if you have to," stated Dan bluntly.

Over the next three hours, Jake worked his way through the set list with Weigh Station. There were numerous stops and starts. He messed up the lyrics on a few songs at the first attempt.

Standing centre stage, in front of an empty warehouse felt weird and it took him almost an hour to relax into the situation. Throughout the entire session, Dan sat silently watching from the side of the practice stage. Occasionally, he would stop them to suggest they change this or that. Once or twice, he stopped Jake and instructed him to relax, to make the song his own.

Eventually, it was Jake who called a halt.

"If you guys expect me to sing tomorrow, we need to call it a day," he said, sipping on a bottle of water. "I'm not wanting to push this too hard too fast."

"Sensible move," agreed Dan, walking out onto the stage. "Not your normal pace of vocals?"

"It's just different," acknowledged Jake, screwing the lid back onto the bottle. "What's the plan for tomorrow?"

"Same as today," stated Dan. "I'll maybe duet with you a bit. See what we can work out."

"Sounds like a plan."

"Alright. The car will pick you up at the same time," said Mikey, glancing at Dan as if to seek approval.

"Can we make it one thirty?" suggested Jake. "Then I can warm up fully beforehand. Buys us back a bit of time."

"Fine by us," stated Steve as he sat his bass down on a stand.

"I'll be here for one thirty," promised Dan, checking his phone. "I've no more appointments until Thursday morning."

When Jake walked into the rehearsal room the next day, Dan was sitting on the edge of the stage chatting on his phone. He looked up when he heard Jake's footsteps on the concrete floor and waved. With a smile, Jake waved back and gestured that he was going through to warm up.

A knock at the door half an hour later interrupted his well-practiced routine. The door opened and Dan came in to join him.

"You good to start, Jake?"

Seeing the Weigh Station front man under the bright lights in the small room, Jake noticed how pale the older man looked, noticed the blue tinge to his lips.

"Sure," he agreed, wishing silently that he could have finished his warm up routine. "You ok to sing today?"

"Need to try," sighed Dan. "Christ knows how this will sound.

My breathing's fucked, Jake. I've no idea how I'm going to do this in front of my boys never mind a sell-out fucking crowd."

"Want to try in here without an audience?" suggested Jake in an effort to be helpful.

"I probably should," admitted Dan. "But let's get out there. I need to be with the boys."

"Your call."

The remaining members of Weigh Station were all milling about the stage, sipping mugs of tea and coffee. When they saw Dan and Jake approach, they dispatched one of the young technicians to fetch two more mugs. After a brief debate, they decided to split the set into sections and to start the rehearsal with the opening three numbers.

"Dan, you take the opening number, then Jake can join you for Battle Scars," suggested Mikey as he plugged in his guitar.

Silently, Dan nodded.

"Mr Power," called out Mikey. "Want to play on this one? Would keep you on stage in case you need to step in on vocals."

"Sure," agreed Jake, setting his mug down on a nearby table. "Give me five to get set up. What's the tuning?"

"Open G."

All of them were silently holding their breath as Dan stepped up to the mic. His own worry was etched into his furrowed brow, but, ever the professional, he powered his way through the first vocal. Without pausing, they launched straight into Battle Scars but, before he had sung the first verse, Dan started to cough. Putting his hand up to his mouth, he turned his back on the rest of the band. When the coughing fit subsided, Dan paused for a few deep breaths before turning round. From his position on the stage, Jake could see fresh blood on his idol's lips.

"Ok," gasped Dan, trying to put a brave face on things. "Let's try that fucker again from the top, boys."

Once again Weigh Station began the song; as before Dan failed to make it through the first verse before another coughing fit seized control. He dropped to his knees on the stage. Mikey rushed over instantly. Unsure as to what to do, Jake fetched a bottle of water and passed it to the guitarist, not wanting to interfere. After a few minutes and a few mouthfuls of water, Mikey helped Dan to his feet.

"Mr Power," he said, his voice husky. "You take this one and make it your own."

"You sure?"

Dan nodded, gesticulating that they should all play on. He sat at the edge of the stage, listening and sipping on the water as Jake and Weigh Station ran through the song. When it was over, he said to Jake to sing the next one, which he accomplished flawlessly and then they were up to Sunset After The Storm on the set list. As the last notes of it faded out, Mikey asked, "Dan, you feeling up to trying Rock It Out On Fire?"

"Let's try something," suggested the ailing singer. "Jake, you take the verses and I'll come in on the chorus."

This time, they made it through the whole song with no interruptions. Jake fluffed one of the lines in the last verse, but the band played on; Dan's voice held out. Over the next hour, they worked their way through another six songs, sticking to the same formula. After a short break, they regrouped to play the second half of the set. Feeling more confident, Dan said he would take the lead on the next song. It was one of their biggest hits and, in his heart, Dan didn't want to let Jake sing this one. It was his song to own. Sensing he was surplus to requirements, Jake jumped off the stage and headed off to the men's room. He could hear Weigh Station start the song as he opened the door to the restroom. When he came out again into the narrow corridor, all he could hear echoing round was coughing and retching. His heart sank, knowing that failing to make it through that particular song would destroy Dan and shatter his fragile faith in himself. Taking a deep breath, Jake walked back through to the rehearsal hall.

Still coughing, Dan was on his hands and knees, struggling for breath, in the middle of the stage. In front of him was a pool of blood stained vomit.

"Jake!" yelled Mikey sharply. "Go and find Peter. The driver guy. We need to get Dan home."

"Sure. He's in the office," replied Jake, turning on his heel.

After Dan had left, Weigh Station called a halt to the rehearsal. From the anxious looks on their faces, Jake knew they all shared his concern about where this was heading. In two days' time the band were scheduled to play to a sell-out crowd at Wembley

Arena and, from where he was standing, things were suddenly looking pretty bleak.

"Jake," began Mikey calmly. "What's your thoughts here? Can you carry him through the set?"

For a fleeting moment, Jake was transported back to his bedroom as a teenager, when he would be singing along to his Weigh Station records, dreaming of one day seeing them live on stage. Now, twenty years down the line, he was being asked to carry the show. Running his hand nervously through his hair, Jake nodded, "If that's what you need me to do then that's what we do. I am going to need a few runs through this full set though. I don't want to fuck up here on your big night."

"And if Dan can't do any of it?" asked Phil, the drummer, his voice barely above a whisper, as he voiced what they all feared.

"Then you guys make the call as to whether to cancel or not," stated Jake bluntly. "It's your party, not mine."

"Hopefully that's a call we won't have to make," sighed Mikey as he checked the time on his watch. "It's just gone five. Let's run through the full set once, then call it a day."

It was after nine o'clock before Jake stepped out of the taxi in front of the hotel. He had had to borrow some English money from the band to cover the fare, promising to repay them in the morning. With a heavy heart, he made his way through the foyer and up to the room. He had called Lori while he was in the elevator and, as he walked along the corridor, he could see her standing in the doorway waiting for him. When he reached her and she saw the strained look on his face, she wrapped her arms around him. Burying his face in her hair, he held her tight, feeling the tension slide from his body as he breathed in her signature floral perfume.

"You look wiped out, rock star," she said as they stepped into the room together, closing the door on the rest of the world.

"I feel wiped out," sighed Jake as he slipped off his leather jacket, tossing it over the back of the chair. "It's been a tough day, li'l lady."

"Bad rehearsal?"

Silently, Jake nodded, then sank down onto the chair.

"Have you eaten yet?" asked Lori softly. "I didn't know what to do about dinner."

"No," answered Jake, trying to stifle a yawn. "Have you?"

"I had a snack about five, but I waited to have dinner with you," she confessed. "I'm starving. What do you fancy?"

"I can't face a restaurant tonight," admitted Jake wearily. "How about we order room service?"

"Suits me," she agreed. "But what do you want?"

"Pasta. Surprise me," stated Jake. "And I need a shower too."

"You jump in the shower and I'll order dinner."

The aroma of Bolognese filled Jake's nostrils as he came out of the bathroom, wearing one of the hotel's towelling robes. Smelling food, he suddenly realised he was ravenous. Lori was sitting on the couch with their meal laid out on the coffee table in front of her. An open bottle of wine sat beside two glasses.

"Perfect timing," she declared, pouring the wine. "I ordered Bolognese and carbonara. Which would you prefer?"

"Bolognese," said Jake, sitting beside her and reaching for the TV remote. Flicking channels, he added, "I'm in the mood for a movie too."

Soon they had found an action thriller to watch and were swiftly engrossed in the plot as they enjoyed their late supper. Gradually, the strained look disappeared from Jake's face and, when their meal was over, Lori finally risked asking, "How bad was rehearsal?"

"It wasn't so much bad as tragic," revealed her fiancé with a weary sigh. "I can't see any way that Dan can do this show. He was coughing his guts up as soon as he tried to sing. It was heart breaking to watch."

"Poor Dan. He lives for his boys. If he can't sing…."

"I know," interrupted Jake, running his hand nervously through his damp hair. "I've got a really bad feeling about all of this."

"What's the plan?" asked Lori, snuggling in closer to him. "Will they cancel?"

"I honestly don't know," he replied, putting his arm around her, pulling her closer to him. "Plan for tomorrow, as far as I know, is for me to run through the full set a few times. Make sure I know the lyrics. Refresh my playing on some of the guitar parts, then pray."

"Would it help if I came with you tomorrow?"

Shaking his head, Jake said, "I don't think so, li'l lady. Thanks for the offer. I appreciate the support, but I'll muddle through this somehow."

Next day Jake was the first to arrive at the rehearsal warehouse. Weigh Station's guitar and drum techs were working on the small stage when he walked in. They greeted him warmly, then Razor, Mikey's guitar tech called out, "Boss is running late. He called a few minutes ago. He'll be about an hour."

"Alright," acknowledged Jake with a glance at the time. "I'll go through the back and warm up while we're waiting."

Alone in the small soundproof room, Jake worked his way through his standard vocal warm up routine, wishing that he had allowed Lori to come with him.

Back at the hotel, Lori was trying to focus on completing her jewellery designs for the next LH collection. While Jake had been busy with the Weigh Station rehearsals, she had devoted her time to the designs. She was attempting to build on the success of the previous collections, but also to find a new influence to add to it. Several walks around London had provided some inspiration, but she was finding it a challenge to translate the ideas she had into the intricate designs that the collection demanded.

The page in front of her was covered with doodles of potential designs; the entire notebook was filled with doodles. Deciding to adopt a different approach, Lori tore all the pages out of the book and spread them out on the bed. There were twelve pages and they covered the duvet like graffiti. A glance at her watch told her that it was almost three – time for a break. Quickly she made herself a coffee, lifted one of the small packets of chocolate chip cookies from the basket beside the coffee maker then limped back over to the bed. As she sipped her drink and nibbled on the cookies, she studied the potential designs from all angles. Seeing them all spread out in front of her made it easier to spot trends and similarity of patterns emerge. With a flash of inspiration, Lori set the mug down on the nightstand and fetched her coloured pencils. Using a different colour for each theme, she circled the doodles that linked together. A few minutes later, with the coffee long forgotten, Lori had twelve sheets of potential designs covered in a rainbow of circles, but she also had the basics of her collection in front of her.

Taking a fresh sketchpad from the pocket at the back of her suitcase, Lori then gathered up the loose sheets and settled herself at the desk to work her way through each coloured "set", colour by colour. Engrossed in her work, she soon lost all track of time.

Rehearsals out at Weigh Station's warehouse studio ran smoothly once the band arrived. By the time Jake had finished his warm up, the three members of Weigh Station were gathered in front of the stage watching YouTube videos while they waited for him. Song by song, they ran through the entire set. Now that he was more familiar with the songs and less self-conscious among his idols, Jake allowed himself to relax. His usual stage confidence began to shine through. The three older musicians noticed the subtle change in their guest vocalist and they too began to relax a little more in his company.

By four o'clock there was still no sign of Dan.

While they took a short break, Mikey tried to call him, but the call went straight to voice mail. The ailing singer's non-appearance was bothering all of them.

"I'm calling Laughlan," stated Mikey. "I've got a bad feeling here."

Laughlan had been mysteriously absent all day too. Every other day, the band's burly Scottish manager had been in the office or had listened in on part of the rehearsal. No one had seen and or heard from him all day either.

"Fucking voice mail," muttered Mikey, ramming his phone back into his pocket. "Right, let's get back to work, boys."

At that moment, the door opened and Laughlan came striding in. One look at his sombre face alerted them all to the fact that all was not well.

"Boys, I need a word," he stated, his voice sounding strained and unnatural.

"What's up?" called Steve, the bass player.

"Sit down," suggested the manager solemnly.

All of them sat perched on the edge of the stage, staring at the large Scotsman.

"There's no easy way to say this," he began, his Glasgow accent echoing round the room. "Dan's been found dead at his flat. His cleaner found him a few hours ago."

The blood drained from the faces of all four musicians.

"Dead?" echoed Mikey disbelievingly.

Nodding, Laughlan continued, "I've been there all day. Been with the police. Looks like he took his own life. He was found in his music room. There's pills everywhere and a couple of empty whisky bottles. There's to be a post mortem, of course. It looked pretty obvious to me though."

"After the state he was in when he left here yesterday, I'm not surprised," commented Phil, the band's drummer, fighting back tears.

"But to end it all," began Steve, his voice thick with emotion. "To be on his own in that frame of mind."

"I should go," suggested Jake awkwardly. "You guys should be together just now. I'm intruding."

"Nonsense," snapped Mikey sharply. "He's left us all in this shit together. I can't fucking believe the selfish bastard's done this!"

The angry outburst hung in the air.

"His flat's been sealed off," restarted Laughlan quietly. "But the police let me take these."

He produced some envelopes from his inside jacket pocket and passed one to Mikey before handing another to Jake. The rest he returned to his pocket.

With trembling hands, Jake ripped open the pale cream envelope and removed a single folded sheet of paper. A small, folded up sheet fluttered down, landing at his feet. When he reached down, he saw the note was addressed to Lori. Without unfolding it, Jake slipped it into the back pocket of his jeans. Carefully, he unfolded the other sheet of paper, silently marvelling at the neatness of Dan's meticulous handwriting.

"*Jake, the reins are yours now. In my heart, I think I've always known I wouldn't make this show. There's no one else I'd rather see out on a stage belting out my songs. Make them your own. Stick with my boys. The anniversary show has to happen. The boys need it to. Don't*

mourn me. Celebrate the life I've lived. It's been a hell of a party. Dan
 P.S. If you fuck up my lyrics, I'll come back to haunt you! D"

Jake re-read the note and smiled.

Beside him, Mikey had opened his letter and was now attempting to read it through a curtain of tears.

"Here, Jake," said the grief stricken guitarist, choking back a sob. "Read this out."

"You sure?"

The Weigh Station guitarist nodded.

"Mikey, I can hear you yelling about what a selfish bastard I'm being but I can't take this pain anymore. Today showed me that all that I live for is gone. If I can't stand on that stage beside you boys and sing for the fans then I don't have a life left that's worth living. My time was going to be short anyway. Now is the right time to bring down the final curtain.

The anniversary show has to go on as planned. I'm leaving you in very capable, younger, Power-ful hands. Use and abuse that kid! He's your future. Rock that joint to the rafters on Thursday night, then party till dawn. If you can't do it for yourselves, do it for the fans. Do it for me.

I love you like family. All of you. Look out for my girls. Dan," read Jake, his voice remarkably calm, but with trembling hands.

Silence echoed round the rehearsal room as they all sat lost in their own thoughts and grief. Weigh Station's manager was the first to speak, "We need to cancel, of course."

"No!" growled Mikey, Steve and Phil in harmony. Glaring at Laughlan, Mikey added, "We go ahead as planned."

"You don't seriously want to go out there tomorrow night, do you?"

"We owe it to him," stated Mikey flatly. "It's all we know how to do. Assuming, that is, that Jake here's up for it."

"If it's what you want. What Dan wanted, then we play," agreed Jake, feeling his stomach lurch at the commitment he had just voiced.

"Well, if you're all sure," began Laughlan hesitantly. "I'll prepare a press statement. The media are sure to pick up on the news tonight."

"Can you do a video release?" suggested Jake, remembering the video message he had recorded after Gary's death. "Make it more personal for your fans rather than a paper statement?"

"Not a bad idea, Mr Power," approved Mikey, wiping a stray tear from his rugged cheek.

"What? An amateur recording on your social media pages?" scoffed Laughlan brusquely.

"Exactly that," stated Jake, staring coldly at the Scotsman. "It shows the boys reaching out in a personal way, just when it matters most."

"Let's do it," agreed Mikey. "Get one of the girls in here that deals with the fan stuff."

It took a while for the remaining members of Weigh Station to agree on a suitably worded announcement, but eventually they came up with a short, heartfelt message. Nursing a cold cup of coffee, Jake stood back out of the way and watched as they recorded the short video then re-joined them to listen to the playback. It was perfect. Within minutes of it being recorded, the message announcing Dan's sudden death to the Weigh Station fans was online. The band promised to honour and celebrate their front man's life at the anniversary show, confirming that the show would still go ahead as planned.

The hotel foyer was empty as Jake walked wearily through towards the elevator. He had just pressed the call button when he became aware of his name being called from the cocktail bar to his left. Turning towards the voice, he saw Jethro and Rich waving at him. From the number of empty glasses and coffee cups in front of them, he guessed they'd been there all evening. With a sad smile, Jake headed over to break the news to them.

"Long day?" asked Rich, noting the drawn look on his friend's face.

"Something like that," sighed Jake as he sank down into the seat across from them. "Dan was found dead earlier today."

"Dead?" echoed Jethro in disbelief. "How? When?"

Jake nodded, then added quietly so no one around them could overhear, "Yesterday broke him. He took his own life last night or early this morning."

"Shit. Poor guy," sympathised Rich shaking his head slowly. "He must've been in a hell of a bad way to resort to that."

"He was. He was dying from lung cancer," confessed Jake sadly. "However, he's left written instructions that the show's to go ahead. Tomorrow night is still on."

"They're not cancelling?" Jethro commented. "Can those boys hold it together to play?"

"Christ, I hope so," prayed Jake, sub-consciously running his hands through his hair. "I hope I can hold it together!"

"Big ask of you, Mr Power," agreed the Silver Lake manager. "Huge ask."

"I owe it to him to give it my best shot," Jake declared, getting to his feet. "I need to go and break the news to Lori. He's left a note for her too. I'll see you in the morning."

"What time are you getting picked up at?" asked Rich as he reached out for his glass.

"Eleven. Are you both coming with us?"

"Yes," said his band mate before Jethro could object. "We'll meet you in the foyer just before eleven."

"Fine," agreed Jake. "Night, guys. Raise a glass for Dan."

When he entered the hotel room, Lori was sitting at the desk, totally absorbed in her work. At the sound of the door closing, she looked up and laid her pencil down. One look at Jake was enough to tell her that something was wrong. Instinctively, she knew what it was.

"Dan?" she asked softly as Jake came over to put his arms around her.

He nodded, his eyes filled with unshed tears.

"Oh, Jake, I'm sorry," she whispered, reaching out to hug him.

"He just couldn't do it. Couldn't go on." Jake's voice was husky and choked with his emotions. "He left you this. I haven't read it."

He brought the creased note out of the back pocket of his jeans and handed it to her. Slowly, Lori unfolded it and read it over to herself, a single tear gliding down her cheek.

"I got one too," said Jake softly.

With tears almost blinding her, Lori began to read aloud, "Mz

Hyde, Lori, thank you. You knew when we met at your home in New York that my end was coming sooner than the doctors were telling me. I saw it in your eyes, princess. Thank you for not saying anything. Thank you for all that you've done for me and the boys over the years. From the scrawny college kid begging me to be allowed to design for us to the stunning young star you became. We owe you a lot. Thank you for bringing the future to Weigh Station. I'm guessing that without you, we'd never have had the honour of meeting Mr Power that first time in the studio in New York. If Weigh Station still has a future, he is it. Look after him, princess. Wipe those tears away and celebrate life. Love and lingering lust, Dan."

"Sense of humour to the end," smiled Jake. "I always suspected he had a soft spot for you, li'l lady."

Wiping away her tears, Lori smiled and revealed, "I knew he did." She paused, then added, "So now what?"

"Now I've a show to front tomorrow night in front of twelve thousand Weigh Station fans mourning their idol."

"He wouldn't have offered it to you if he didn't know you could do it for him."

♪

As their car drew up outside the arena next day, Jake was consumed with self-doubt. He'd spent a restless night tossing and turning. When he did finally get to sleep, it was filled with nightmares of stage fright and forgotten lyrics. At five thirty, he had crept out of the hotel for a long, early morning run. The cool October morning air had cleared his head, but had done little to settle his growing nerves.

"Show time," whispered Lori quietly as the driver opened the car door for them.

Their way into the arena was lined with sombre Weigh Station fans. Around a hundred fans were standing along the pavement, all either in black or with a black armband on. One group of girls were holding up homemade signs saying "R.I.P. Dan". Keeping his head bowed, Jake walked towards the entrance. Behind him, the remaining members of Weigh Station were pausing to speak to their fans, taking the time to talk to each and every one of them, politely accepting all their condolences.

Before Jake and Lori reached the door, Jethro stopped them and indicated that Jake should go back to be with Weigh Station.

"No," he said calmly. "I'm the outsider here today. I'm just the hired voice. Those guys need this moment alone with those kids."

"I agree," added Rich solemnly as he looked around at the shrine of flowers and T-shirts that was spreading along the wall behind him.

In her hand, Lori had a small drawing, hastily completed over breakfast, but her own silent tribute to her old friend. Squeezing Jake's hand, she said she'd be back in a moment and headed over to the shrine, leaning heavily on her cane. The cold, damp weather was disagreeing with the lingering pain in her leg. With tears stinging at her eyes, she read the messages of sympathy and sorrow; smiled at the fan photos that had been left among the flowers. There was a space beside a faded Weigh Station T-shirt that looked like the perfect spot for her own small tribute. The design on the shirt was the first album cover she had created for Dan and his boys.

"Rest easy," she whispered as she propped her drawing up

beside the T-shirt. "Dan, if you're listening, guide the boys and Jake through this."

Tears were gliding down her cheeks as she felt a hand on her shoulder. It was Jethro.

"Time to go in, princess," he said warmly. "Jake's already inside."

Silently, she nodded and allowed the Silver Lake manager to put a supporting arm around her waist and guide her into the building.

Once inside the venue, everything felt like the normal pre-show energy. The mood of the crew and the venue staff was possibly a little more subdued than usual, but everyone seemed to be putting a brave face on their grief. In the back stage communal lounge, the itinerary was posted on the door – lunch, press, sound check, VIP Meet and Greet, dinner, show. Someone had scored out "after show" but when he saw this, Mikey wrote it back on with a pen he borrowed from Lori.

It had been arranged for the band plus Jake to meet with the press inside the arena itself, using the stage as the backdrop. At Jake's insistence, both Rich and Lori had followed the band through, then discretely took a seat in the stand.

"Glad it's not me standing down there," confessed Rich as they watched the barrage of photography flashes. "I've no idea how he's doing this."

"He has to," stated Lori simply. "No choice. Show must go on and all that."

Standing beside Mikey during the press event, Jake struggled to keep his nerves and emotions in check. Seeing the vast concert hall again, empty, reminded him of his last appearance here with Weigh Station- his famous shirtless appearances.

"Jake, you've stepped up tonight to lead these guys out. Tell us how that came about?" asked one journalist, bringing his attention back to the moment.

"About a month ago Dan asked if I'd come along and sing a few songs with him. It was as simple as that," explained Jake, forcing a smile. "Originally, we planned just a couple of numbers, but that wasn't to be."

"We've already heard that tonight's going ahead at Dan's personal request. Was it also his personal request that you take his place?" enquired another journalist. "Or was it always the plan to have you on standby?"

Before Jake could formulate an answer, Mikey butted in sharply, "Dan knew he was sick when he first spoke to Jake. My guess is that he knew there was a chance he'd be too sick to do the whole set. The deal with Jake was always that he'd sing what he had to. We never quantified how few or how many songs that would be."

"And have you shortened the set for tonight?"

"On the contrary," said Jake with a nod to Mikey. "We've actually added in two songs. I'm not trying to fill Dan's shoes here. No one can do that. I'm here to lend my voice to support Weigh Station celebrate Dan's life as he wanted them to."

"Do you know all the lyrics?" asked one female reporter with a wink at him. "You've not had long to learn the whole set."

"Most of them," laughed Jake, fidgeting nervously. "I've been a huge fan of these guys for a long time. I've got all their records. We've had a couple of days of rehearsal. All I can promise everyone, Dan included if he's listening, is that I'll give it my best shot."

Laughlan, closely followed by Jethro, chose that moment to call a halt to the interview, much to Weigh Station and Jake's relief. There was just time for a few more photos then they were ushered back stage to prepare for sound check.

Sensing they would be in the way if they returned back stage, Rich and Lori remained seated in the stand, chatting quietly as they watched the Weigh Station crew finish off setting up the stage. They were treated to a run through of some of the lighting, as the rig was tested. Before the band were due out on stage, the arena doors opened and the two hundred VIP fans entered the hall. Like everyone else, they too seemed more subdued than usual as a member of the arena's staff shepherded them towards the stage.

In the dressing room, Jake was pacing restlessly as he waited on the three members of Weigh Station joining him. Their manager had spirited them away for a "band meeting", leaving him to do a short warm up ahead of the sound check. There were a few invited media personnel and photographers milling about and he got caught up in a conversation about NASCAR with a young American photographer. While they debated the pros and cons of the sport animatedly, Weigh Station re-entered the room. The three older musicians looked strained, but were putting on a brave face that mirrored his own.

"Mr Power," called out Mikey abruptly. "You ready?"

"Always," called back Jake, sounding calmer than he felt.

As they walked through the maze of corridors to the side of the stage, the four of them discussed their approach for the sound check. Jake requested a full run through of a couple of the songs on the set list plus one of the numbers that they had slotted in. The others nodded in agreement as Mikey added that he had a few solos he wanted to try. His guitar technician had been rebuilding one of his original guitars and he wanted the chance to try it out. With their plan of attack agreed, they stepped out onto the stage to a polite cheer from the VIP fans.

"Afternoon," shouted Mikey with a forced smile. "We'll be with you shortly, folks. Bear with us while we work a few things out up here."

Behind him, Jake was flicking through the book of lyric sheets, his hands trembling as he sought out the first song they were to run through. Eventually he found the right page, laid the book on the stage at his feet and adjusted the mic stand to his preferred level. A few moments later, after a nod from Mikey, Weigh Station started to play. They made it through the first couple of songs with no issues, much to everyone's relief. While the drummer ran through part of his solo, Mikey and Steve huddled together with Jake. Once the drummer was happy with his set up, it was Jake's turn to test his guitar skills. There were a few tweaks needed to the amp he had been allocated but he was soon satisfied with the sound and stood casually playing the riff from Weigh Station's most famous anthem, Battle Scars. He was aware of the eyes of the Weigh Station fans boring into him.

"Want to run through that one?" asked Steve. "We don't want to balls it up later."

Jake nodded his agreement, then stepped forward to address the small group of fans.

"Thanks for your patience, folks," he said warmly. "It would be a huge help to me if you sang along on this one. You all know the words to Battle Scars, right?"

"Yes, but do you?" called back one fan with a wink up at him.

"Most of them," joked Jake with a smile. "It's been a lot to learn in a short space of time. Be gentle with me, please."

Without further ado, Mikey and Steve launched straight into their famous rock anthem and were quickly joined by Phil's thunderous drum beat. Clutching the mic in his sweating hands, Jake began the vocal, praying that he would remember the words. If it all fell apart at this point, he was terrified that his nerves would seize control.

From their seats in the stand, Rich and Lori recognised the anxious look on Jake's face. As soon as he had reached the end of the first verse, they saw his shoulders drop a little as he began to relax. With Battle Scars safely under his belt, they watched Jake and Weigh Station work their way through the sound check. There was little engagement with their fans, but, under the circumstances, no one seemed to mind. After a while, they took a short break and the fans were herded back out of the arena, towards the conference room that was set up for the meet and greet session. This left the fragile musicians in peace to finish up. Just as they were about done, Mikey stepped over to Jake's microphone and called out across the void, "Mr Santiago, care to join us?"

Looking surprised, Rich got to his feet and made his way down from the tiered seating. Not wanting to be left behind, Lori carefully followed him down the steps to the arena floor.

As Rich reached the stage, Mikey asked, "Feel up to a guest slot up here tonight?"

"Sure, if you think it'll work," agreed Rich, clambering up onto the stage. "What did you have in mind?"

"How about guesting on Sunset After The Storm?"

"Fine by me."

Quietly, Lori slipped out of the arena and headed backstage to find Jethro and a cup of coffee. She was sitting reading her book when Jake and the others returned to the lounge area an hour or so later. They were all talking animatedly about the meet and greet session. All of them touched by how understanding the fans had been. Spotting his fiancée sitting on her own, Jake came over to join her.

"Hey, li'l lady," he said with a relaxed smile. "You ok over here?"

"I'm fine, rock star," she replied softly. "More to the point, though, are you?"

"More or less," replied Jake as he sat beside her. Stretching his long legs out in front of him and his arms up over his head, he added, "It all feels a bit surreal. I keep expecting to wake up in bed beside you and realise this was all a nightmare. I can't quite get my head round the fact I'm fronting Weigh Station in a few hours' time in front of a sell-out London crowd. Or round the fact that Dan's gone."

"You're not dreaming," assured Lori, putting her hand on his thigh. "And you'll be incredible out there tonight. Dan placed his faith in you."

"I just don't want to let these guys down," sighed Jake, looking over at the three Weigh Station guys, who were huddled together again in the far corner with their manager.

"How are they holding up?"

"Better than I thought they would," he replied, keeping his voice quiet. "Laughlan's keeping a close eye on them. There's been a few pep talks. I don't honestly think it's hit home yet."

"Perhaps," agreed Lori sadly. "It can't be easy for them, or for you, in the circumstances."

"All I can do is give it my best shot," conceded Jake, running his hands through his hair.

A few short hours later, Jake was alone in a small dressing room, finishing his vocal warm up routine. Both Rich and Lori had gone up to the side of the stage to watch the two support acts over an hour earlier. Left on his own, he had taken time to warm up properly and to focus his mind on the set. The lyrics folder lay open on a chair in front of him. As he reached down to close it over, he said quietly, "Dan, I hope you knew what you were doing when you set this up."

A knock at the door brought him back to reality with a start.

"Jake," called Mikey, poking his head into the small room.

"You ready?"

"As I'll ever be," declared Jake, picking up the folder.

"Laughlan wants us all together before we head out there."

When the two musicians entered the backstage lounge, the other members of Weigh Station and assorted personnel were all gathered, each holding a shot glass. A young female assistant handed Mikey and Jake a glass. One sniff informed Jake it was tequila.

"Thanks, everyone," began Laughlan, glancing round the room. "I've been given a short note to read out tonight. Before he left us, Dan wrote to a few folk. You know who you are. He left me a note with this one sealed inside it and instructions to only open it now. He said you all had to have a shot of tequila in your hand when I read it."

Passing his glass to Jethro, the burly Scotsman tore open the small white envelope in front of them. He accepted his glass back, then slowly began to read out loud, "Boys and girls, raise your glasses to welcome the start of a new Weigh Station generation. I ask that you welcome Jake as your new front man. Keep him right out there tonight. Now get your sorry asses out there and rock the fucking roof off this joint."

Folding the note over, Laughlan raised his glass, "To Dan."

Breaking his own pre-show "no alcohol rule", Jake downed the shot of tequila in one gulp. The late singer's last request had stunned him. Judging by the silence in the room, it had stunned them all.

"Let's fucking do this!" yelled Mikey, slamming his glass down.

Standing at the side of the stage a few minutes later, listening to the crowd cheering and chanting for Weigh Station, Jake was visibly trembling with nerves. A few feet away, Lori and Rich stood in the shadows watching the fans. He glanced over at them, managing to catch Lori's eye. Playfully, she blew him a kiss and mouthed, "I love you, rock star." With an anxious smile, he pretended to catch the kiss and blew one back.

Weigh Station's intro tape began to play. The capacity crowd went wild, their cheers echoing up to the rafters. As agreed earlier, Jake allowed the three members of the band to run out on stage first. Centre stage, a single spotlight shone on the empty mic stand, forever Dan's mic stand.

"Toss me another mic," said Jake to the roadie beside him. "Change of plan."

Holding the radio mic in his clammy hand, Jake loped out on stage to a thunderous welcome from the audience. As soon as he was in position, Phil began the snare drum intro to the set opener. Steve slid in on bass, then Mikey joined them on guitar. With a quick glance at the Weigh Station guitarist for reassurance, Jake launched into Wreckless. Deliberately, he stood to one side of the microphone stand that stood centre stage. A fan in the front row threw a single red rose onto the stage. Another fan tossed up a Weigh Station scarf. While Mikey took the spotlight for his first solo of the night, Jake used the scarf to tie the rose onto the mic stand.

With the first number in the bag, Weigh Station charged straight into their second song, Midnight Raiders, a fast paced, hard and heavy Weigh Station classic. Once the second song was successfully executed, Jake felt his nerves begin to settle as he sang his way through the third number. At the end of the song, he stepped forward to address the crowd for the first time, "Good evening, Wembley!"

A roar from the fans came straight back at him.

"I said, good evening, Wembley!" bellowed Jake with a grin.

This time the audience's response was deafening.

"Much better," he acknowledged, gazing out at the endless sea of upturned faces. "Thank you for coming out tonight. And thank you for such a warm welcome."

Another cheer went up.

"It was Dan's wish that tonight went ahead as planned so, in honour of the great man, I'd like you all to join in with us on the next one. This is Battle Scars!"

In the wings, Jethro had come out to stand between Rich and Lori, all three of them focussed on the stage, following Jake's every move. He was playing the "guest" vocalist role to perfection and had easily won over the grieving Weigh Station fans. At the odd moment where he faltered slightly on the lyrics, the crowd came to his rescue.

"Leaving that mic stand empty was an inspired move," said Jethro, whispering loudly into Lori's ear.

"A nice show of respect," she agreed, keeping her eyes fixed on her fiancé.

"Time I went to get ready," stated Rich, moving round behind them. "Hope I don't screw this up."

"You'll be fine, son," assured Jethro, clapping him on the back.

Out on stage, Jake had finally relaxed into his role as Weigh Station front man. There was one more number on the set list before Rich was due to join them for Sunset After The Storm.

"Ok, folks?" he called out loudly. "Still with us?"

Looking across to Mikey and then to Steve on his other side, he was relieved to see the older musicians smiling at him. With a deep sigh, Jake began, "I think you all know this next one. This was one of Weigh Station's first hit singles. I remember standing in my bedroom, trying to master this one on my guitar a long time ago. It's a huge honour to be up here singing it with these guys, especially tonight."

A huge unexpected cheer went up.

"Folks, this is Download!"

Word perfect, the fans sang along, supporting Jake through the Weigh Station anthem. Hearing the Wembley choir accompanying him made Jake dig deeper and sing stronger. He was aware of Mikey and Steve moving into position behind him, just as they would've done if it had been Dan holding the microphone. It felt good; it felt like he was being given the seal of approval. It felt appropriate.

When the song ended, Mikey nudged him and said simply, "Shirt off."

Remembering his half-dressed state the last time he had performed on that same stage with Dan and the boys, Jake nodded then carefully peeled off his sweat soaked shirt.

Clutching it in one hand, he yelled, "Ladies and gentlemen, give a huge London welcome to our special guest for the next song. Let's hear it for my good friend from Silver Lake, Mr Rich Santiago!"

Obligingly, the Weigh Station fans cheered loudly as Rich stepped out on stage to join the band. Tucking his T-shirt into his belt, Jake accepted his own guitar from the guitar tech. While he got himself settled and plugged in, he announced, "Sunset After The Storm."

Spotting a group of young female fans pointing to the shirt tucked into his belt, Jake laughed, then tossed it down into the crowd.

Focussing all his energies on the fast paced song, Jake powered his way through Sunset After The Storm. Having Rich out on stage with him restored a feeling of normality for a few short minutes. All too soon the song reached its final chorus and Rich was waving farewell to the London audience. He stepped forward to hug his friend. "You're doing an amazing job out here."

"Thanks, buddy," said Jake, breathing heavily after the exertion of the song. "Home strait now."

Turning to face the fans, Jake cried out, "London, let's hear it for Rich Santiago!"

He let the cheers and whistles die down before he said simply, "Broken Bottle Empty Glass."

Singing the gentle, husky lyrics without Dan by his side felt surreal. As he sang his way through the first verse, Jake could feel his control over his emotions sliding out of his grasp. It struck him hard that Dan had written this ballad about an alcoholic's battle with his demons before finally succumbing. In the circumstances, it felt inappropriate. Realising that Dan had died in a mirror image of the song chilled him to the core. Somehow, he found an inner resolve and made it through to the last verse. As he sang the final lines, his emotions seized control, forcing Jake to allow the audience to carry the song through the final chorus. Turning his back on the arena, Jake signalled to Mikey that he needed a moment to compose himself. Seeing the younger man's emotional distress, Mikey walked over and clapped him on the shoulder, then stepped to the front of the huge stage.

"Ladies and gentlemen, we couldn't have stood up here tonight without the help of Jake here. He's been incredible all week. A real tower of strength. Let's hear a huge Wembley cheer for the awesomely talented Jake Power!"

Having wiped himself down with a towel and swallowed a

few mouthfuls of water, Jake gathered himself to resume his duties as front man.

"Thank you," he said humbly. As Mikey and Steve began the intro to the final number of the set, Jake raised his arms in the air to conduct the crowd to clap along in time to another Weigh Station classic anthem, Long Travelled Roads.

"Let me see those fucking hands in the air!"

The immediate and passionate response from the fans filled him with pride. A few minutes later as the last notes faded away, he heard himself yell out, "Thank you, London. You've been fucking awesome tonight. You've all done Dan proud."

With a wave to the crowd, the band left the stage to deafening cheers. As they stood, out of sight, at the side of the stage, drying themselves off and grabbing bottles of water, behind them the crowd began to sing a Weigh Station song that had been left out of the set – Miles From Home."

"Do you know that one?" demanded Mikey sharply.

Jake nodded, "It's been a while, but, yes, sir, I do."

"Change of encore, boys," ordered the guitarist. "If that's the one those fans want, then that's what we play next then the encore as planned."

When the band walked back out onto the stage, the crowd went wild. Raising his hand for quiet, Jake said, "We've got the message, guys. Unrehearsed, here's Miles From Home. Especially for each and every one of you. Help me out here if you can. It's been a while."

Despite the lack of pre-show rehearsal, Jake's years of practice in his bedroom as a teenager stood him in good stead. He roared his way word perfect through the hard, fast classic rock track.

Gasping a bit for breath, he thanked the crowd. "I'd like to thank you folks for making tonight special. For helping the boys and I celebrate Dan's career and his all too short life. I'd ask you to indulge me for a few minutes. Dan was my idol when I first began to sing. It was an incredible honour to share a stage with him. I'd like to honour his memory now by singing the last song he sang with me and Silver Lake a few months back. This is Simple Man."

Behind him, Mikey had swapped his electric guitar for a twelve string acoustic. With a nod to Jake, he began the delicately picked intro to the southern rock classic.

"Well mama told me," sang Jake, his voice warm and slightly husky.

In front of him, the arena lit up in a sea of cell phone lights, flickering like candles as far back as he could see. The crowd swayed gently in time to the classic song and sang along beautifully with the chorus. As he gazed out across the room, Jake hoped that somewhere Dan was out there looking down on the beautifully poignant tribute to him.

"Let's end this party in true Weigh Station style!" screamed out Mikey. "We'll bid you farewell as we Rock It Out On Fire!"

Stepping off stage for the night, Jake stepped straight into Lori's arms. Her cheeks were wet with tears and, disregarding his half naked sweaty state, she held him tight. Around them, Weigh Station finally let their grief show as the enormity of what they had just achieved out on stage hit them. Brusquely, Laughlan was chasing the lingering media personnel and photographers down the hallway to give the band some privacy. Out in the arena, the fans were trooping out, while the PA system played "Always Look On The Bright Side Of Life."

"You ok?" asked Lori softly as Jake bent to kiss her.

"Yeah," he replied hoarsely, kissing her slowly and deeply.

"Hey, Romeo," teased Jethro, putting his arms round them both. "Grab a beer, hit the shower then we're expected to party till dawn."

"I hear you," answered Jake. "Give me half an hour."

A private function suite in a nearby hotel had been booked for the after show party. When Jake walked into the room with his arm protectively round Lori's waist, he was greeted with a round of applause from the Weigh Station crew. Theatrically, he bowed, then accepted a shot glass from a passing waitress. Again, in Dan's honour, the tequila was flowing like water. In the centre of the room, Laughlan was holding court with two young girls, both of whom looked too young to be there. Spotting Jake and Lori, the burly Scot waved them over to join him.

"Jake," he began, putting his arm around the two girls. "Have you met Melissa and Jenny?"

"I don't think so," replied Jake, sounding surprisingly shy. His voice was still hoarse after the show and he cleared his throat before adding. "Pleasure to meet you both."

There was something familiar about the girls, but he couldn't quite put his finger on it. As usual, it was Lori, who stepped in to his rescue.

"Long time no see," she said, hugging them both warmly. "I'm so sorry about your dad."

Instantly, the penny dropped, and before he could help himself, Jake blurted out, "You're Dan's daughters!"

Giggling, Melissa nodded before wrapping her arms around him. "Thank you for tonight. Dad would've loved that show."

"It was an honour," replied Jake, brushing her cheek with a kiss. "And I'm sorry he wasn't here to see me suffering out there."

"You did an incredible job," enthused Jenny, the younger of the two sisters. "And you played my favourite song."

"What one?" asked Jake, flashing her a "Power" smile.

"Miles From Home," she revealed with a hint of her grief creeping into her voice.

"I'm glad that one worked out," confessed Jake, downing his shot of tequila. "We hadn't rehearsed it and when the fans started singing it, we knew we had to play it. I've not sung that since I was about seventeen."

Beside him, he could feel Lori trying to stifle a giggle.

"What's so funny, li'l lady?" he enquired, raising one eyebrow at her.

Giggling uncontrollably, Lori said, "I just got a mental picture of you singing into a hairbrush microphone in front of the mirror in your bedroom. Tennis racquet guitar in hand."

"It was a real guitar," laughed Jake, remembering the scene vividly. "But it was a deodorant can not a hairbrush, if you must know."

A voice from behind them interrupted their laughter.

"What's so funny?" asked Mikey, handing Jake another shot glass. "Pray tell?

"Sorry, Uncle Mike," teased Melissa, kissing the older musician on the cheek. "You had to be here."

"Hmph," he snorted as he downed his shot. "How're you girls holding up?"

Putting her hand on Jake's arm, Lori silently indicated that they should circulate the room.

Arm in arm, they slowly worked their way round the guests, pausing to talk to several members of the Weigh Station entourage. At one table, Lori met several fellow artist friends that she hadn't seen for some time. While she caught up with them, Jake moved on in search of Rich and Jethro. Hostesses glided round the room with trays of tequila shots, but Jake resisted temptation. As he passed the bar, he asked for a large glass of water and a beer. His throat was tight after singing the unfamiliar set and he still felt more than a little dehydrated. Standing at the bar, he gazed round the room, scarcely able to believe it was all real. The cold water helped to chill the fire in his throat and he prayed silently that he hadn't strained it again. Watching Lori chat animatedly at the far side of the room made him smile. She was positively glowing.

"You're a lucky man," commented Jethro, interrupting his thoughts. "She's a beautiful creature."

Nodding, Jake added, "Lady Butterfly herself."

"Whereas you are more like a moth," mused the Silver Lake manager cryptically.

"Pardon?"

"A moth to the flame of rock stardom," Jethro explained. "Front man of two major rock bands. Not a bad flame to choose."

"Well, I don't know about fronting two bands," said Jake, chugging on his ice cold beer.

"Laughlan assures me the guys are up for it," Jethro continued seriously. "Even before he read out that letter earlier on, Mikey had suggested they make you an offer. That was what all the huddling in corners was about. The job's all yours, Mr Power."

"Me? Front Weigh Station?"

"You already have," observed the older man wisely. "And you were incredible out there tonight. I had my reservations, but you pulled off a miracle. Think seriously about this, Jake."

"I will," he agreed, before downing the rest of his beer.

Above him, the fasten seatbelt sign was still lit; beside him, Lori had dozed off, worn out after two late nights. The night after the show, they had been invited to a private dinner with the members of Weigh Station and their families at Mikey's house in

North London. It had been late when the taxi had dropped them off at the hotel and their six o'clock alarm call to get them up in time for their flight home had been most unwelcome. Now, two hours into the flight back to Philadelphia, Lori was sound asleep with her head resting on his shoulder. In slumber, she looked pale, but peaceful. Gently fingering her hair, Jake smiled to himself. In a few short weeks, they would be married. There was just the small matter of Silver Lake's European tour to complete and then they would be joined together as husband and wife; moth to butterfly, as Jethro had phrased it. Behind him, he could hear the band's manager and Rich discussing technical details of the planned stage equipment set up for the UK shows. Both of them passionately debating pedals, amps and voltage. With a yawn, Jake lifted the plastic champagne glass from the tray table in front of him. Silently, he toasted the future – friends, family, health, happiness and rock and fucking roll.

The story of Jake and Lori will continue in Book 3 in the Silver Lake series

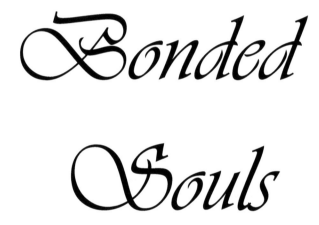

Excerpt from **Bonded Souls – Book 3 in the Silver Lake series** due to be published in 2017

Warmth and the buzz of conversation welcomed Jake and Lori as they entered Amarone a few minutes after seven. Spotting them almost instantly, Marco, the maître d', was at their side showing them to a discrete, candlelit corner table and offering to take their coats. He helped Lori to slip her wool jacket from her shoulders, then turned to take Jake's leather jacket. Politely, Jake declined the offer, hanging his jacket over the back of the chair instead. Beside the table, as requested, sat an ice bucket with a bottle of Lori's favourite champagne chilling inside. Both of them were relieved to note that none of the other diners had given them a second glance.

Having hung Lori's jacket up, Marco returned with the menus and offered to open the champagne. Suppressing a giggle, Lori watched as he struggled with the cork before it finally came loose with a resounding POP.

"Can we keep that one, please?" asked Jake, his question surprising both the maître d' and his fiancée.

"But of course, Mr Power," replied Marco, handing the cork to him.

Lori was looking at him quizzically.

"Call me old fashioned," began Jake, after they had been left alone with their champagne. "My mom always used to keep the cork from any special bottles. She said it brought luck if you put a silver coin in the cork."

Rummaging in his pocket, Jake produced a dime and rammed it hard into the swollen damp cork base.

"A gift from me to you, to wish you luck for tomorrow," he said warmly, passing the cork to Lori.

Giggling, she accepted it graciously, turning it over in her hand a few times before putting it carefully into her small purse.

"Thank you," she whispered, suddenly feeling very emotional.

Raising his glass, Jake smiled at her, "Here's to us, li'l lady."

"To us," echoed Lori, mirroring his smile before taking a small sip from the glass.

Amidst more nervous laughter, they both opted for their favourite dishes from the menu, realising that they both almost always chose the same thing when they dined there. As ever, the meal was delicious, both of them relishing in the company of the other. Completely relaxed, they chatted animatedly about their hopes and fears about the wedding, both of them confessing to being more than a little nervous about being the centre of attention for the day.

"That's rich coming from you," laughed Lori. "You can stand on that stage and sing to thousands of fans, but you're scared of facing our closest friends and family in the lounge room!"

Blushing, Jake nodded silently.

"I love you, rock star," she said, reaching across the table to take his hand.

"I love you too, Mz Hyde," he declared formally. "And to show it, I have a gift, well two actually, for you."

Jake reached round into the inside pocket of his leather jacket and brought out two small silver cloth bags with a blue cord fastening each of them.

"I wasn't sure when was the right moment to give you these," he said, feeling like a tongue tied teenager on a first date.

Accepting the two small bags, Lori carefully untied the bows and lifted out two silver bangles. The two silver bangles Jake had purchased in London when they visited the British Museum. Looking puzzled, Lori turned them over in her hand.

"They're perfect, Jake," she breathed. "Thank you."

Both bangles were an identical Mobius strip design; both had a different verse engraved into them. Silently she read the first one, "May all beings be peaceful. May all beings be happy. May all beings be safe. May all beings awaken to the light of their true nature. May all beings be true."

"It's a Metta prayer," explained Jake shyly. "A Buddhist meditation."

"And the other one?" asked Lori, admiring it.

"It's an extract of a Shakespearean sonnet. Sonnet 116 to be exact," he replied. Clearing his throat, Jake began to recite the verse,

"Let me not to the marriage of true minds
Admit impediments. Love is not love
Which alters when it alteration finds,
Or bends with the remover to remove:
O no; it is an ever-fixed mark,
That looks on tempests, and is never shaken;
It is the star to every wandering bark,
Whose worth's unknown, although his height be taken.
Love's not Time's fool, though rosy lips and cheeks
Within his bending sickle's compass come;
Love alters not with his brief hours and weeks,
But bears it out even to the edge of doom.
If this be error and upon me proved,
I never writ, nor no man ever loved."

"Beautiful," sighed Lori, feeling her emotions threatening to overcome her again. "Thank you. I feel guilty now. I didn't bring you a gift."

"No need," assured her fiancé with a smile. "Will you wear these tomorrow?"

"Of course," she promised, slipping them back into their little bags. "They are absolutely perfect."

"That's what I thought when I saw them in London."

"London?" she echoed.

"I've had these since our trip to the British Museum back in October," confessed Jake. "I couldn't choose between them so thought "what the hell" and bought them both."

"And here I thought you only had your mind on the ancient Egyptians when you were in the gift store," giggled Lori, remembering their afternoon in museum fondly.

Coral McCallum lives in Gourock, a small town on the West coast of Scotland with her husband, two teenage children and her beloved cats.

https://coralmccallum.wordpress.com

https://www.facebook.com/pages/Coral-McCallum

https://twitter.com/CoralMcCallum

12593313R00243

Printed in Great Britain
by Amazon